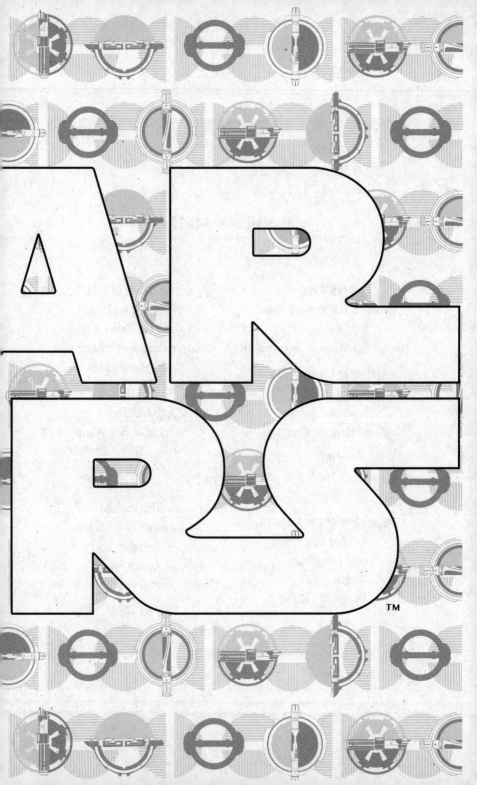

RISE OF THE RED BLADE

RANDOM HOUSE

WORLDS
NEW YORK

STAR WARS

INQUISITOR

RISE
OF THE
RED
BLADE

DELILAH S. DAWSON

2024 Random House Worlds Trade Paperback Edition

Copyright © 2023 by Lucasfilm Ltd. & ® or ™
where indicated. All rights reserved.
Excerpt from *Star Wars: Shadow of the Sith* by
Adam Christopher copyright © 2022 by Lucasfilm Ltd. & ® or ™
where indicated. All rights reserved.

Published in the United States by Random House Worlds,
an imprint of Random House, a division of
Penguin Random House LLC, New York.

RANDOM HOUSE is a registered trademark, and
RANDOM HOUSE WORLDS and colophon are
trademarks of Penguin Random House LLC.

Originally published in hardcover in the United States
by Random House Worlds, an imprint of Random House,
a division of Penguin Random House LLC, in 2023.

ISBN 978-0-593-59862-7
Ebook ISBN 978-0-593-59859-7

Printed in the United States of America on acid-free paper

randomhousebooks.com

2 4 6 8 9 7 5 3 1

Book design by Elizabeth A. D. Eno

For those who never quite fit in.
For those who were bullied for what they love.
For those who have never felt normal.
Luminous beings are we.
Don't let anyone tell you differently.

AUTHOR'S NOTE

Like Iskat, I'm going to be blunt. A character in this book takes their own life, something we don't often see in *Star Wars*.

When I was much younger, I had a suicide attempt.

It was terrifying. It was painful. It was a mistake.

Thankfully, I failed.

The next day I started a notebook of little things that made me happy—the sun on my face, the wind at the beach, walking barefoot in soft grass, rubbing my cat's belly. I made a list of reasons to keep going. Even though I have struggled with—and still struggle with—mental health, I have never again thought of returning to that dark place. I am thankful every day that I'm alive.

But I have lost family members to suicide. I have watched them fall into addiction. I see them struggle. I know that every day is a fight.

As a suicide survivor, as a mother, and as a neurodivergent person who has always felt different, I have a great deal of love and sympathy for this character. They had support, they had a loving family, they had intelligence, they had talent, and still they couldn't see a way out of their pain. Their choice had ripples that spread out among their community and those they held most dear—their choice had tragic consequences.

If you struggle with mental health, please know that it gets better. That there is always hope. That there is always a reason to go on, even if it seems like a terribly small reason. That you are loved. That the galaxy needs you in it, and that your absence would be a tragedy. You have your own story to tell. There are resources out there and people who will listen.

May the Force be with you,
Delilah

THE STAR WARS NOVELS TIMELINE

THE HIGH REPUBLIC

Convergence
The Battle of Jedha
Cataclysm

Light of the Jedi
The Rising Storm
Tempest Runner
The Fallen Star
The Eye of Darkness
Temptation of the Force
Trials of the Jedi

Dooku: Jedi Lost
Master and Apprentice
The Living Force

I THE PHANTOM MENACE

II ATTACK OF THE CLONES

Brotherhood
The Thrawn Ascendancy Trilogy
Dark Disciple: A Clone Wars Novel

III REVENGE OF THE SITH

Inquisitor: Rise of the Red Blade
Catalyst: A Rogue One Novel
Lords of the Sith
Tarkin
Jedi: Battle Scars

SOLO

Thrawn
A New Dawn: A Rebels Novel
Thrawn: Alliances
Thrawn: Treason

ROGUE ONE

IV A NEW HOPE

Battlefront II: Inferno Squad
Heir to the Jedi
Doctor Aphra
Battlefront: Twilight Company

V THE EMPIRE STRIKES BACK

VI RETURN OF THE JEDI

The Princess and the Scoundrel
The Alphabet Squadron Trilogy
The Aftermath Trilogy
Last Shot

Shadow of the Sith
Bloodline
Phasma
Canto Bight

VII THE FORCE AWAKENS

VIII THE LAST JEDI

Resistance Reborn
Galaxy's Edge: Black Spire

IX THE RISE OF SKYWALKER

A long time ago in a galaxy far, far away. . . .

PART
ONE

/ 1.

JEDI PADAWAN ISKAT AKARIS WANTED nothing more than to please her master.

That, unfortunately, was a rare occurrence.

"Come look closer, Iskat. What do you feel?"

Jedi Master Sember Vey moved aside so that Iskat had a better view of the ancient text she'd just unwrapped from an old, soft eopie hide. On the other side of the counter, the Togruta shopkeeper fidgeted with long strands of beads around his neck; he couldn't stop nervously glancing at Sember's lightsaber where it hung on her belt.

Iskat's long, red fingers reached for the—well, it wasn't exactly a book. More like many old, brittle skins barely held together by gut string—but before she could touch it, Sember clicked her tongue. Iskat's hands flew behind her back. Sember had never been an active and involved teacher, rarely utilizing lectures or lessons like the Jedi instructors back at the Temple. Instead of offering clear instruction, she expected Iskat to watch and learn. She often waited silently, hopeful that Iskat would figure out the next step herself; it was what she was doing now, her dark eyes focused and patient. The human woman was in her early forties, with golden skin and bluish-black hair that she kept immaculately braided, and she was waiting for Iskat to . . . what? Say something? Do something? Iskat had no idea.

Since Sember had chosen Iskat as a Padawan after the Jedi Tournament, they constantly traveled together like this, landing on backwater planets and busy trading moons to visit shopkeepers and collectors and archaeologists galore, negotiating the purchase of curiosities to be added to the Jedi Archives. Iskat had seen texts like this one, elaborate scrolls, ancient lightsabers crusted with barnacles or sand, even a rancor tooth covered in intricate carvings from a long-forgotten language. Sember was a sharp and stone-faced negotiator, and Iskat understood that her duty was to observe her master and gain the skills to recognize and acquire lost artifacts of Jedi history so that they might help further educate the next generation of scholars of the Force.

But, as usual, Iskat could not decipher her master's silence. "Without touching it, what can you tell us, my Padawan?" Sember prodded, finally.

Iskat put her long, braided brown hair over her shoulder, focused on the object before her, and took a deep breath, opening her senses. "The text appears to be ancient, Master. I'm not familiar with the language. The pages are some kind of animal skin, almost translucent. The ink is dark red." She leaned close, careful not to touch the skins, and inhaled. "The tang of iron. Blood? Mixed with some sort of mineral powder."

"That is what you can *see*. Reach out through the Force. What do you *feel*?"

Iskat closed her eyes. "Darkness. Yearning," she said wonderingly. "It . . . it wants to be read, touched. It wants to be known."

She opened her eyes, bright blue against her crimson skin, and looked questioningly toward her master. They'd retrieved dozens of artifacts over the years, and Iskat had never felt anything like this.

Sember nodded once, the closest thing to praise she ever offered her apprentice.

"This is no Jedi artifact," Sember said. "It is a Sith text."

"Do you not want it, then?" the shopkeeper said, reaching to take it back.

"I didn't say that." With a gloved hand, Sember flipped the tanned hide back over the text, hiding it from view. "We will take it at the promised price. Rest assured it will be stored safely, so that it won't fall into the wrong hands."

Iskat was supposed to observe carefully as Sember haggled with the shopkeeper, but her attention was drawn to the text, now just a squarish lump under the hide. She'd never seen a Sith artifact before. No wonder Sember hadn't let her touch it. She could still feel it, though, like a small child with arms reaching out, begging to be held.

"Your assistant. What is she?" the shopkeeper asked as they turned to leave.

Sember considered him. "She is a Jedi."

"But what species? Never seen one like her. Red skin, but not a Zeltron or Devaronian . . ."

"I'm a Jedi," Iskat said firmly.

"Okay, okay," he wheedled. "Just curious."

Despite the firmness of her response, Iskat was curious, too. No one in the Temple knew anything about her species, and according to Sember, her records didn't indicate a birth planet. She had two hearts, long fingers, and unusually keen senses, but in all their travels and studies, she had never found any further information about her biology or history. This was not the first time someone had asked the awkward question she could not answer.

On the way back to their ship, Sember carried the text by its hide wrapping, dangling it from two fingers as if trying to minimize contact. They walked up the ramp of their T-6 shuttle, which Iskat had decided to call the *Lyre* after reading somewhere that ships needed names; Sember just called it T6-315. As Iskat fired up the engines, her master immediately stowed the bundle in the safe they used when transporting their valuable finds back to the Temple.

"Can you read it?" Iskat asked.

Sember was horrified by the thought. "I wouldn't dare try. Do your best to forget this thing; close yourself away from it. The dark side is cloying, like yista bugs burrowing under your skin and slowly sickening you. The Jedi Council will decide what to do with it, but our duty is to keep it away from anyone who might seek to use it for harm. In your travels, if you find anything similar, you must obtain it with the same skill as any Jedi artifact and contain it as soon as possible. Don't touch it, don't read it. Acknowledge your curiosity, but let it pass. I wanted you to feel it in the Force so that you would be able to recognize something similar later, but any such contact should be brief. Some knowledge is not worth the cost."

Iskat tucked that away for later and went about securing the rest of the cargo as Sember took the pilot's seat. Even locked in the safe, she could feel the text reaching out with the blind probing of a plant mindlessly sending vines out to seek sunlight. Sember was entirely dedicated to hunting down artifacts and cataloging Jedi knowledge, and this was the first time she'd stood on the side of ignorance in all their time together.

They had acquired many treasures on this trip, and Iskat could tell her master was eager to begin the laborious job of analyzing and categorizing their finds, a task she relished and always undertook privately, leaving her Padawan to fend for herself. As Iskat understood it, some masters and their Padawans had lively relationships filled with laughter and kind words, but Sember Vey was an aloof and often neglectful master, alternating between an otherworldly serenity and an obsession with her work that made her forget anything else existed. Although Iskat would've liked a warmer connection, she understood that Sember had been given important duties beyond teaching her Padawan. It was up to Iskat to learn what she could by observing her master's unique skills and taking advantage of any instruction offered. She was determined to become the best Jedi she could be, despite her master's . . .

Well, her failings.

Iskat wasn't even sure why Sember had chosen her. She felt no special connection between them and often worried that Sember didn't seem to like her very much. "Why are you just standing there, Iskat? Buckle in and prepare for your meditations," Sember said, as if just noticing that Iskat was there at all.

"Yes, Master."

Iskat tried to calm her mind as the ship took off smoothly. Once they were in hyperspace, she sought her cushion and got comfortable, closing her eyes and centering herself. Her hand wrapped around an amulet Sember had given her, a small cabochon of blue stone that was supposed to help her focus. It was like wading into a stream of moving water, and time fell away as Iskat floated along. Meditation had been so difficult for her, at first, but Sember and the other Jedi Masters had agreed that her main goal as a Padawan should be learning to calm and control herself. After the incident with the column . . .

No.

She wouldn't dwell on that.

She was supposed to do the opposite.

There is no emotion, there is peace, she told herself.

There is no ignorance, there is knowledge.

There is no passion, there is serenity.

There is no chaos, there is harmony.

When she'd begun meditating as a youngling, she'd felt anxious and bored and fidgety, desperate to do literally anything other than nothing. Her energy was so chaotic that for once Sember's patience had worn thin, and she'd accused Iskat of being actively disobedient. But Master Klefan Opus, once Sember's own master, had taken a personal interest in her progress and had spent many a morning in the Temple sitting by Iskat's side, allowing her to immerse herself in the calm that he had reached over many decades and, bit by bit, teaching her to access that same tranquillity.

Masters Sember and Klefan had indeed been right. The deeper Iskat's connection with the Force became through meditation, the better control she maintained over her emotions. She hadn't lost her temper at all, recently, and she was proud of how far she'd come. Sember never commented on her progress, but Klefan had, and that was enough.

The days fell into a companionable silence as they traveled through hyperspace toward Bar'leth, a Core world where one of their favorite traders had promised a unique find. Sember spent most of her time with the artifacts behind the closed door of her chamber, but she kept Iskat busy with a schedule that changed daily and included lightsaber training with a remote, calisthenics, readings on flora and fauna, and, of course, more meditation. Iskat had always loved lightsaber training the most and wished for more one-on-one time sparring with her master instead of constantly being assigned to battle the unsophisticated remote she'd surpassed long ago, but she knew better than to ask.

From time to time, Iskat's concentration was broken by the Sith text in the safe, almost like it was bored and clamoring for attention, but she ignored it. She thought about mentioning it to Sember, but she didn't want to give her master any reason to doubt her or chide her. Things were best, really, when she remained silent and did as Sember suggested without questions or arguments. And besides, perhaps this was yet another test. Her master had urged her to resist the call of the Sith artifact, and failure to do so would only reveal another weakness.

When they finally dropped out of hyperspace, the ship's comm signaled a message.

"Sember Vey, we know that your current mission is not complete, but we need you to return to the Jedi Temple on Coruscant immediately," Jedi Master Mace Windu said, his deep, commanding voice sharp with an unusual sense of urgency. "All nonessential missions are temporarily suspended as we deal with a developing situation. We need you here."

The comm went silent, and Sember sighed and began plotting a new course back to the Temple.

"Do you know what's happening?" Iskat asked her master.

"I have all the same information you do," Sember answered calmly, as if this message didn't signal anything new or exciting. "I was really looking forward to visiting with Gamodar. He said he had a truly special find."

They were not far from Coruscant, and so Iskat had even less time than usual to prepare herself to leave the busy silence and strict order of her days traveling with Sember and immerse herself in the culture of the Jedi Temple. Like all Padawans, she'd been raised there since she was very young, and she had many fond memories of lightsaber training with Master Yoda or outings to other planets with energetic young Jedi Knights. But then, when she was thirteen, the column incident had happened, and since then she and Sember were almost always on a mission, and . . . now she always felt strange when they returned to the Temple. No one was unkind, because Jedi were Jedi, but Iskat always felt like some of the other Padawans were nervous around her, especially Charlin and Onielle who'd suffered small, easily healed injuries from the column incident. Iskat dreaded seeing them, even though they were all five years older now and traveling the galaxy with their own masters and, hopefully, becoming more mature.

As Coruscant loomed large in the viewport and Sember piloted the ship toward the Temple, Iskat couldn't help noticing that there was a lot more traffic than usual around the home of the Jedi Order. They had to wait for an open landing pad, and when the ramp lowered, Sember hurried away, pushing the safe along on its hoverlift. Iskat followed her master, but Sember glanced back as if surprised to find her there.

"Oh. Iskat. I must report to the Council. You should get in some lightsaber training, if you can."

Iskat continued to follow, now curious. Lightsaber training was Sember's least favorite subject to teach, and although she made sure Iskat spent plenty of time with a training remote, Sember had never encouraged her student's intrinsic interest in dueling. When Iskat asked her, early on, about her aversion to what seemed an integral part of the Jedi life, Sember reminded her that proficiency did not equal interest and left it at that.

"Why lightsaber training?" Iskat asked. "Why now? Are they sending us on a new mission?"

Sember continued on at her measured pace and didn't turn around as she spoke. "Look around, Padawan. Everyone has been called back. Don't you feel the urgency? The thrum of anticipation? Something big is happening. Now go and practice. Just remember to center yourself and maintain control. Trust in the Force."

"Yes, Master."

Iskat clutched her blue stone amulet as she turned toward the lightsaber training room favored by the Padawans of her age group, leaving Sember to deliver their many finds to the Jedi High Council. As the safe moved away, Iskat could sense the ancient text within, its call growing fainter and fainter. She hoped the Council kept such things in a very safe place, or maybe even destroyed them. It felt dangerous, that such a thing should be here, in the Temple, surrounded by Jedi and curious children. Iskat herself was curious, but she knew that the dark side was seductive and must be actively repelled. Sember had always made that very clear. It wasn't the Jedi way, to give in to such things, much less seek them out.

They hadn't been to the Temple in a long time, but very little had changed. Sember was right—the halls were busier than usual, brown-robed Jedi hurrying along instead of walking side by side in stately calm. Servants and droids scurried among them carrying cargo. As Iskat neared her destination, she heard the familiar sound of training sabers buzzing and clashing and the shuffle of boots on stone.

She paused before the door. She was older now, a good bit taller, her brown hair grown almost to her waist and perfectly braided. Her robes were a little too short but well kept, her boots worn with use. She hadn't seen many of her childhood companions in years, as they'd all been spread out over the galaxy with their own masters. Well, except one who'd chosen to leave, because of Iskat's folly, which didn't bear thinking about.

Iskat straightened the collar of her cloak, clutched her amulet, and urged her hearts to quiet. Unwelcome emotions rose up—excitement, worry, even fear. Things Jedi weren't supposed to feel, or at least things they were supposed to move past. What if her dueling skills were subpar? What if she lost control? What if something terrible happened again?

She closed her eyes and sought her center.

There is no emotion, there is peace.

There is no ignorance, there is knowledge.

There is no passion, there is serenity.

There is no chaos, there is harmony.

Serenity did not come naturally to her; just as her senses were keener than those of the other Padawans, so, too, were her emotions more intense and explosive. She often wondered if it was this difficult for every Jedi to maintain their trademark calm or if perhaps Sember had neglected to teach her something important that everyone else just naturally understood. She had always felt very different from her master, who was so unflappable that sometimes it seemed as if she were made of stone, whereas Iskat felt like a storm of emotion, changeable as the sea.

No matter. She was a Jedi. Her job was to find peace, even if she had to wrestle it to the ground and hold it there.

Her master had urged her to train, so she would train.

/ 2.

WHEN ISKAT WALKED INTO THE training room, she felt like she was making some grand entrance, but no one even looked up. The others were too busy sparring or watching duels and calling out helpful suggestions. They ranged in age from thirteen to perhaps twenty, all Padawans who hadn't yet become Jedi Knights. Iskat knew everyone by name and wasn't surprised to see several members of her own youngling clan. These beings had grown up alongside her and faced the Jedi Tournament with her, and it was strange to see how many of them had grown into near adults in the time that they'd all been away.

Her gaze immediately searched for her favorite among the other Padawans, a black-skinned Twi'lek named Tualon, who had two long head-tails framing his face. Like Iskat, he'd been away on missions with his young and energetic master, a Nautolan named Bavoc Ansho, ever since the tournament. Tualon had grown significantly, his once chubby cheeks now angular but his smile just as friendly and mischievous as ever. Unlike some of the other Padawans, he'd never shown any fear or apprehension around Iskat and had even joined her by her favorite fish-filled pool in the meditation garden on many a morning. Iskat went to stand beside him where he squatted, lanky elbows on his knees as he avidly watched Charlin, the pink-skinned Twi'lek girl, fight with Fvorn, a quiet Duros who had nearly doubled in size since Iskat had last seen him.

"Charlin doesn't have a chance," Iskat began.

Tualon looked up at her, his orange eyes burning like embers. He grinned, and her hearts stuttered. "Maybe not when it comes to mass, but she's always been quick. Did you just return?"

"Just now, yes. We were on Ringo Vinda most recently. Do you know why everyone was called back?"

The rest of the room hissed as Fvorn landed a solid hit, but Tualon kept his attention on Iskat, and frowned. "Master Ansho said it was something unprecedented in our lifetimes, that we need all the Jedi we can gather. There's some sort of Separatist threat I'm sure we'll find out soon."

For a long moment, they watched the fight, but then Charlin did a somersault over Fvorn and landed what would've been a killing stroke, had they been using real blades instead of training sabers. Fvorn groaned and bowed, before returning to the crowd, where his Rodian friend Zeeth clapped him on the shoulder and murmured, "You'll get her next time."

As for Charlin, she preened a little more than Jedi were supposed to, tossing her striped pink lekku and grinning.

Something flared in Iskat's chest, annoyance and maybe a pang of jealousy.

"She really has improved her form," Tualon said, impressed. "I heard she got to train in zama-shiwo martial arts with some of Jedha's best fighters on her last mission."

Before she could stop herself, Iskat stepped forward. "Has anyone called the next round?"

Charlin looked up, and Iskat was oddly gratified to see her green eyes widen in alarm. That brief accident of honesty was swiftly snuffed out as Charlin smiled at her like they were friends. "No, but it's the training room. All are welcome to take part."

Iskat ached to unhook her lightsaber. Its hilt was short and a good bit wider than most to accommodate her longer fingers, crafted of polished burgundy wood with the polished tooth of a Firaxan shark at the end. Compared with Charlin's elegant and gleaming chrome hilt, it seemed brutish and strange, but Iskat was proud of it. Of course, training with real lightsabers was discouraged for the Padawans. She held out her hand, and Fvorn tossed her the training saber he'd been using. She fought better with her own weapon, but she'd long ago learned how to wield the smaller hilts that most Jedi preferred.

Charlin lit her training saber and Iskat lit hers. The room went quiet; the other duels had stopped. All the other Padawans ringed the space, silent and watchful. Iskat's hearts sped up as she realized that she was suddenly part of a spectacle, but she took control of that burst of emotion, cooling it with the calm she'd worked so hard to master. Her senses went on high alert, the world around her coalescing with intricate detail. She could see every bump on the floor, every handhold on the wall, every weapon that might be used to her advantage if she were disarmed. When someone else was experiencing a strong emotion, especially anticipation, she could sense it in the Force—not that she'd ever revealed this information to others, even her master, who already kept her at arm's length. No one here was taking care to hide their excitement just now. The others were hoping for a show, their feelings amplified by their youthful high spirits after so much time apart with somber masters. Charlin was prideful and confident, but she was also a little scared.

Iskat could use that.

She recalled from their earlier training that Charlin never aggressed; she generally waited patiently for her opponent to make the first move. Iskat had always taken advantage of this knowledge to rush in suddenly and set the other student off guard, but this time, she waited, circling warily and mirroring Charlin's movements. She couldn't help grinning as she watched Charlin falter, so certain that Iskat would use the same old strategy. Master Vey hadn't sparred with Iskat in months, and Iskat realized she had missed this feeling, had missed sharpening herself against a competitor like a blade against a whetstone. The longer she neglected to attack, the more uncertain Charlin became.

"Aren't you going to do anything?" Charlin asked, frustrated.

"I am doing something. Aren't you?"

"I haven't decided yet."

Unable to contain herself, Charlin burst forward in a classic attack, which Iskat parried easily. Charlin broadcast her moves, and although she had clearly been training and improving, she simply wasn't a natural fighter. All her strikes followed the rigid forms they'd practiced over and over, and her creativity with a blade was limited to what had been drilled into her instincts. Iskat met her every slash and jab calmly, expending as little energy as necessary.

It was obvious that Charlin was growing annoyed, her form slipping, as the Twi'lek tired. Iskat was playing with her—and Charlin knew it, and it made her sloppy. The next time Charlin attempted to get under her guard, Iskat leapt over the blade, slashing down mid-flip to smack Charlin on the head with her training blade, barely and politely missing her sensitive lekku.

"You're out," Iskat said after landing neatly.

"It was just a tap," Charlin argued, gritting her teeth against what had to be a painful bruise. Iskat could see it, a brighter pink welt on the top of Charlin's head.

"If we were using real lightsabers, you'd either be grievously injured or dead."

Charlin glared, her cheeks nearly magenta; she wasn't accustomed to losing. "I'm not done."

"According to the rules, you are."

Onielle stepped up beside her closest friend and lit her own training saber. The human girl had orange hair and freckles, and Iskat could feel her trying to corral her own eagerness, her cheeks as pink as Charlin's. "Then I'll take the next round."

Iskat inclined her head and held up her weapon. "Like Charlin said, all are welcome to take part."

Onielle wasn't quite as graceful as Charlin, but her master had trained her well, and her attacks had improved and intensified since Iskat had seen her last. Her arms were longer, giving her excellent reach. Onielle immediately aggressed, and it took Iskat a moment of furious, surprised parrying to catch up and find her own flow in the fight.

Oh, how she'd missed this part of training. When she had a weapon in her hand and an opponent in her sights, she felt truly alive, focused and tapped into the Force instantly, in a way that often took hours of meditation to reach. It was almost as if she could see what would happen next, like she knew Onielle was going for a specific combination they'd studied with Master Yoda, and her saber just naturally met each hit with exactly the right amount of impact.

"She's good," she heard someone whisper.

They kept their voices low, but of course no one in the room knew quite how acute Iskat's senses were. Sember knew, which was one of the many reasons she always brought her Padawan along to haggle, so that she could use her sharp eyesight, keen nose, and sensitive ears to evaluate the artifacts on offer. But the other Padawans had no idea.

"She was always good with a lightsaber. I just hope she doesn't lose her temper again . . ."

"Jedi aren't even supposed to have tempers. Is that why Master Vey always keeps her away on long missions?"

"That would make sense. Were you there when the column—"

"Yeah, I was right next to it when it happened. Barely dodged it—"

"To think they used to be friends. Poor Tika."

Hearing that name shattered Iskat's calm. It was as if she'd been contentedly swimming in the Force, and then suddenly it became a deluge, a brash flood, battering her as the memories surged back. She clutched her amulet, fighting one-handed, seeking the cool, blue connection that promised peace, but that lifeline wasn't strong enough to hold back the old feelings she'd worked so hard to overcome, or at least push down.

Apparently despite all her hard work, they were just as strong as ever.

Completely ignorant of the tumult in Iskat's mind and body, Onielle attempted a two-handed slash, and Iskat caught it on her blade, kicked Onielle backward with a boot in her gut, and then followed with a downstroke that made the other girl cry out in shock, slashing across the chest of her robes as she lay on the ground, hands up and training saber dropped.

Iskat stood over her, training blade at Onielle's throat, close enough to make her gasp.

Strong hands grabbed Iskat's shoulders, pulling her away.

"Iskat, that's enough," Tualon said.

Hearing his voice so near, she froze and dropped the training saber, realizing what she'd done. It wasn't that winning a duel was frowned upon among the Jedi, but her attack had been unnecessarily brutal, which went very much against their code, the code Iskat had lived under and believed in all her life. Shame flooded her, that she'd had so many witnesses to yet another mistake.

Ever since Tika and the column, her sole goal had been to learn to master her emotions and control her connection with the Force. She needed to be a gentle, steady river, not a gushing waterfall, and yet in her first visit back to the training room in years, it had nearly happened all over again. She'd almost lost her temper.

"I'm sorry," she muttered. "Thank you, Tualon."

At least she didn't let herself run away. She stepped away from Tualon and, with as much dignity as she could muster, strode calmly from the room, holding back tears.

Jedi were not supposed to dwell on anger. They were not supposed to do things that provoked shame. They were not supposed to cry from embarrassment. Iskat wanted nothing more than to be a good Jedi, and she had dedicated her life to seeking the control and peace that were required. She followed her master's schedules with happy hearts, meditated often, maintained a good attitude, strove to replace her heavy, clinging emotions with good works and intense studies.

And now, back home, among her cohort, she had spectacularly failed.

She went immediately to her master's chamber and knocked on the door. She heard furtive noises within, and after a long moment, Sember answered, a little breathless.

"Come in."

Iskat stepped into the small, tidy room. Sember stood before her wardrobe, the doors closed.

"Master, something happened in the training room. I . . . I felt it again." Iskat hung her head.

Sember took a deep breath and sighed a long sigh out her nose. Iskat looked up and saw the pain in her eyes, the disappointment. "What happened?"

The story Iskat told her master was mostly true, but she neglected to mention many of the emotions that she knew she wasn't supposed to feel deeply, that she tried so hard to suppress. She focused on the heat of the battle while leaving out the part where she chose the duel on purpose and then gleefully provoked her opponent.

"I was doing fine, until someone mentioned Tika . . ." She trailed off and again looked up into the older woman's dark eyes.

Sember had never been the kindly, loving sort of master, nor the playful, friendly sort of master. She was disconnected, distracted, so cool that she was almost cold, as if she lived on another, far more serene, plane and her Padawan was simply a distraction. Iskat often felt little ripples from her, emotions the older woman tried to hide—annoyance at interruptions, sure, but also regret and a sad sort of yearning. She knew that Sember wasn't about to comfort her or encourage her or joke with her, but she also knew that her master was honest and that she wanted her Padawan to succeed.

"Duels often bring out emotions that can otherwise be kept at bay," Sember finally said. "A fight, even if a playful fight, is still a fight. It is a dance between life and death. We are all given unique gifts and challenges, and it just so happens that yours are one and the same. Your connection with the Force is both powerful and hard to control, but it is not insurmountable. Mastering yourself is the work of a lifetime. You have grown so much, but you are still in many ways a child."

"Master, I try so hard—"

"As Master Yoda once told me when I was much younger, do or do not, there is no try." Sember gave a small and almost fond smile.

"How do I do, then? More meditation? Another amulet? I want so badly to be better, but it's like there is something *broken* inside me."

Master Sember put a hand on her shoulder, the touch a rare kindness. "You are not broken. We are all imperfect beings, striving for enlightenment. You just have to strive a little more than most."

Iskat nodded. "I will try. I mean, I will. I'll work harder."

"I'm sure you will." Another sigh, and Sember's spine straightened.

"But now is not the time to meditate. There is unrest in the Temple. It's no wonder the training room is charged—you young ones can sense the undercurrent of change." Sember's hand rested briefly on her lightsaber. "Iskat, we've been recalled here because we are needed. We're being sent to Geonosis to rescue Obi-Wan Kenobi. He was attacked—."

"By the Separatists," Iskat said, remembering Tualon's words from earlier.

Sember nodded. "The Separatists have joined with the Trade Federation and Count Dooku. They've amassed a droid army. We'll be leaving shortly. Can you exhibit adequate control on a rescue mission that may involve real danger?"

"Yes, Master."

Iskat felt a little lift in her hearts. Sure, she'd been on dozens of missions with Sember over the past few years, but they'd all been peaceful, basically just glorified shopping. What they did served a great purpose to the Jedi, but it wasn't particularly interesting to Iskat. This, on the other hand, sounded exciting. Surely it wasn't wrong, to be excited at the prospect of doing good in the galaxy?

And what a strange mission—calling in all the available Jedi just to rescue one person. Obi-Wan had always been kind to her, when he'd taken his turn teaching the younglings, but he'd been kind to everyone. He was exactly the kind of Jedi Master she would've chosen—knowledgeable and skilled, but with a friendly nature and quick with a positive word, when it was deserved. She would be proud to be part of the mission that ensured his safety.

"Now go, my Padawan. Prepare yourself for the journey to come. We leave at dusk."

Iskat bowed her head and did exactly as Sember had bade her. She didn't encounter any of the other Padawans, and she suspected that was because they were still in the training room, talking about her. She could only hope this mission would be brief and successful, and that the might of the Jedi would swiftly rout the Separatist army threatening the Republic. Soon she and Sember would be back on their own ship, where she could recommit herself to finding her peace with the Force, elusive as it seemed.

/ 3.

AS THE SHUTTLE THUNDERED THROUGH the atmosphere of the arid planet Geonosis, Iskat struggled to shut out the staggering cacophony of sensory input and focus on finding her center amid the chaos. This wasn't just a rescue mission—it was a military operation. The Jedi were soldiers now, but they weren't fighting alone. Thousands of clone troopers had appeared, seemingly overnight, to join them in supporting the Republic; there was even a clone flying their ship. After years of relative peace throughout the galaxy, the Jedi had swiftly mobilized to do their part as protectors of democracy, justice, and freedom.

Iskat was thrilled . . . and also overwhelmed.

She steadied her breathing and closed her eyes, one hand wrapped around her amulet, and the rest of the Jedi around her faded away to stillness.

There is no emotion, there is peace.
There is no ignorance, there is knowledge.
There is no passion, there is serenity.
There is no chaos, there is harmony.

Master Klefan had urged her to turn to this mantra in the early days after the accident, and Master Sember had repeated it with her many times. The words were stamped on her brain, on her hearts. They transported her to the quiet within, made her feel as if she were the Jedi she was meant to be: calm, cool, collected, peaceful.

Reflecting on the Jedi Code almost made her forget Tika, but did she want to forget—?

No. She couldn't think about that now.

That was years ago.

It hadn't happened again.

Her teachers had seen to that, as had Iskat.

She'd studied. She'd practiced. She'd gained the control demanded of her. And now she was on a rescue mission, surrounded by Jedi Masters, Knights, and Padawans. She'd never drawn her lightsaber in real combat before, but it wasn't her courage or proficiency that worried her, that made her two hearts beat so loud she was certain Tualon could hear them from beside her. She risked a glance at her fellow Padawan, with his glossy black lekku and look of determination.

"You ready?" he asked with an encouraging smile.

"As ready as anyone," she answered.

Which wasn't entirely honest. She felt more than ready. But Jedi were supposed to be humble and modest, and she knew that Tualon was a stickler for that sort of thing and didn't want to appear too cocky. She admired him for his humility—as well as for his outgoing nature and genuine altruism. Tualon was the sort of Jedi she wished to be, the sort of Jedi she admired.

If she was truly honest with herself, Iskat had to admit that while she had no doubts about her dexterity, skill, or bravery, after yesterday's duels with Charlin and Onielle, she had new doubts about her ability to handle herself when the stakes were high and a weapon was in her hand. She'd expected better of herself. And although no one had mentioned the incident with Onielle, she could feel the stares of her fellow Padawans as they sat beside their masters, buckled into place while they hurtled toward the desert sands of Geonosis. She could feel their eyes on her, sense their uncertainty.

Seated across the ship, Master Klefan Opus caught her eye and offered a nod and an encouraging smile. Iskat returned it, grateful to know that one master, at least, had faith in her.

She hoped that faith would not prove misplaced.

"Have you seen combat before?" she asked Tualon quietly. "On missions, I mean?"

He turned toward her to whisper. "A little. Master Ansho usually handles that sort of thing himself, but I helped fight off some bandits when we were escorting a senator on a diplomatic mission. Thankfully all our training—it just falls into place. I didn't want to hurt anyone, but we had to protect the senator. How about you?"

"We've never even drawn our lightsabers," she admitted. "Usually, we either stand over a counter to haggle like normal customers, or some old adventurer invites us into his tent for tea. It's all been very peaceful."

She looked around the ship, which juddered and shook as it plummeted toward the planet's surface. The air was thick and still, reeking of fuel and sweat. There were nearly twenty Jedi altogether. She wondered what sorts of adventures the other Padawans had experienced, if it was unusual for a Jedi of her age to be this inexperienced with actual combat.

"Do you think—" she began.

"That's enough chatter," Master Vey murmured from her other side. "It's almost time. Remember your mantra. Concentrate on your breathing exercises, my Padawan. Don't let the chaos in again."

Iskat's skin didn't show a blush, but she felt the heat of shame at being reprimanded in front of Tualon and the others. Considering what they were about to face on the planet below, a rousing speech would've been more appropriate than public censure, or even some whispered reassurance. Tualon went silent and looked politely away so as not to entice her with further conversation.

Iskat's long, red fingers wrapped around the cold metal bench as she closed her eyes and silently recited the Jedi Code again.

There is no emotion, there is peace . . .

The words became a comforting rhythm in counterpoint to the ship's engines, a focal point that brought her consciousness into a state of calm where she was beyond shame, beyond worry, beyond fear.

"Landing in T minus three minutes," the clone pilot announced.

Although she knew there were thousands of clones just like him headed to Geonosis, the pilot was the first of the Republic's new troopers that Iskat had encountered. She had no idea what he looked like under his armor. How old he was, what color his eyes were, if he was more prone to smiling or frowning. All she knew was that his voice was sharp, his skills as a pilot were immaculate, and they would soon fight side by side.

The Jedi had surprisingly little intel regarding the mission; they only knew that Obi-Wan Kenobi had been ambushed by the massing Separatist army. Every available Jedi in fighting form was on a ship right now, just like Iskat. Unlike her missions with Master Vey, she had no way to know what role she would play, but she was excited to be among her fellow Jedi and pleased that the masters had deemed her skilled enough to take part in such an important undertaking.

She would prove worthy of their trust. She would follow their orders and embody their teachings. She would be part of the team that saved the day.

And yet, there was this persistent thought that kept breaking past her barriers, a pesky unwanted whisper wondering what might happen if instead of calming herself and quelling her emotions, Iskat relinquished the control for which she'd fought so hard and allowed the Force to fully flow through her. What strength might she find in that surrender? What power might she find beneath layers of repression? What might she accomplish now that she was facing actual adversaries instead of other children on a training field?

She clutched her amulet and banished the thought with the same energy she'd used to silence the cloying voice of the Sith artifact. This was a dangerous way of thinking. The Jedi Code existed for a reason, and history taught that those who stepped off the path often found tragedy. True greatness came from peace. From knowledge, serenity, and harmony. Iskat wanted to be great, and she wanted to do honor to the Jedi. In addition to Sember, other masters would be watching her closely during this mission. Her performance here might influence her future within the Order.

The shuttle whined and shook as it slowed, gravity pulling at Iskat's bones. The metal under her boots trembled, and as if she could already feel the hot sun outside, sweat beaded on her lip. They were close to the surface now, and she imagined that if she could see through the viewport, she would look upon a world of sand and spires, bright orange striped with harsh black shadows.

It was almost time.

They were almost there.

It felt as if she were about to cross some important line, like this rescue—now seeming very much like it would become a battle—would change things forever, both for the Jedi and for Iskat herself.

She could not forget how close she'd come to washing out in the Jedi Tournament, how horrible she'd felt waiting for a master to claim her as a Padawan until Sember had, to Iskat's great surprise, stepped up in what felt like the last possible moment. She sometimes worried that between the distracted teachings of her master and the mistakes she made in the past that she required more observation and guidance than other Padawans, that everyone was all too aware that Iskat was lacking as a Jedi and might ultimately wash out for good.

There was no way she would let that happen.

The shuttle's thrusters went to work as they landed, and Iskat's stomach swooped with excitement. If only she could see out the shuttle's viewports and begin to take stock of the battle to come. They'd been briefed on Geonosis, on how the hive mind worked, but they wouldn't know what they would face here until they were on the ground and received more specific orders.

After a bouncing thump, the ship went still. The door slid open, harsh light burning into a space packed with nervous bodies clad in brown robes. Iskat struggled to release her chest harness but managed it before Sember had to unbuckle her. Her feet were numb as they hit the metal floor, but her fingers were already wrapped around her lightsaber.

As the Jedi all stood, Master Klefan Opus blocked the open door. He was an Askajian, and he usually kept himself overhydrated so that his epidermal sacs would swell, making him seem jolly and giving his eyes kind wrinkles in the corners. Today he had chosen a more slender and agile form, and Iskat was fascinated by the change in his demeanor. Usually a mild-mannered center of calm, he now clasped his lightsaber at his side and gave off a determined air. He held out a holoprojector, and an image of Mace Windu appeared, lightsaber ready in his other hand.

"Klefan Opus here," the master said. "We're on the ground, to the northwest."

"Welcome to Geonosis. We need your detachment to help secure the arena where Count Dooku is preparing to execute Obi-Wan, along with Anakin Skywalker and Senator Padmé Amidala."

There were gasps and whispers around the shuttle. Why was Skywalker here? And how had a senator become involved?

"Head for the nearest spire and make your way upward to the stands," Master Windu continued. "Find any cannons or long-range weapons and take them out. We'll do the rest. Be on your guard and may the Force be with you." The figure disappeared, and Klefan stowed the projector in a pocket.

He looked over the array of Jedi, from a sixteen-year-old Rodian Padawan to the white-haired but still energetic Arkanian Master Theca who was rumored to be well past two hundred, and nodded in approval. "You all heard our orders. Padawans, stay with your masters. Defend yourselves as you must, but do not act rashly. Remember: This is a rescue mission. We're looking for long-range weapons." He looked around the shuttle, taking stock. When he paused on Iskat, she imagined that his eyes narrowed, just the smallest bit. "And may the Force be with you."

Turning, he hurried down the ramp, and the Jedi fell in behind him.

"Focus on your control," Master Sember whispered as they waited their turn to disembark. "The peace you seek is within you. Trust yourself, but you must not give in to your emotions, my Padawan."

Iskat's blood pounded in her ears as she ran down the ramp, following Sember's swinging robes. They were in a desert of reddish sand and stark sunlight. Tall spires pierced the sky like melting candles, and somewhere nearby, a crowd buzzed and hummed and screamed. The air felt as if it were charging up with lightning, for all that the sky was clear.

"But where are the Geonosians?" she asked Sember as they ran side by side.

"Did you think they would just be out in the open waiting for us?" her master asked in return. "Klefan will lead us where we need to go."

Sure enough, Master Klefan was directing the Jedi into a hole in the base of one of the towers. Iskat noticed that each Jedi ignited their lightsaber before entering the dark tunnel. Beams of blue and green disappeared into the shadows as Iskat ran across the hot sands, the heat penetrating the soles of her boots as she followed her master. She'd been on desert planets before, and although she couldn't remember her home, she had always known there was no way she could be from such a place. She was already sweating, the back of her neck itching where her long hair was tightly braided back.

It didn't matter. She had to concentrate.

There is no emotion, there is peace.

Master Sember stopped at the tower door, ignited her blue blade, and nodded to Iskat, who obediently thumbed the switch on her green lightsaber and edged inside. They were headed down a narrow set of spiraling stairs, the darkness lit only by the glow of their weapons. The Geonosians, Iskat knew, were an insectile people, and they probably used senses other than sight to navigate. Her ears told her this staircase was long and went deep underground, judging by the sounds echoing back to her. Master Ansho was behind her, then Tualon, and she was grateful to be surrounded by such powerful Jedi in this strange and unfamiliar place.

The stairs finally emptied out into a tall hallway with intricate architectural details, almost like a temple. The floor was a metal grate, and the Jedi made not a sound as they spread out, following Master Klefan. Iskat was between Sember and Ansho still, the masters having naturally spaced themselves between the less experienced Padawans. Fvorn was nearby, along with his friend Zeeth and their masters. Charlin and Onielle were also part of their party, but they were fortunately out of Iskat's immediate area. Jedi were not supposed to hold grudges, but Iskat supposed that if she could, so could they, and she was glad to have some distance from the Padawans who most likely still wore the bruises she'd recently inflicted.

"Iskat," Sember hissed, and Iskat hurried to catch up as they entered a vast factory that had gone cold and still. Molten metal still glowed cherry red amid the enormous machinery, but there were no workers, not even droids. The effect was eerie, as if the Geonosians had recently walked away, leaving their work behind. Master Klefan led the Jedi toward a smaller door that opened into a tunnel. The space was about three meters tall and equally wide, with carved murals of Geonosian scenes covering every surface. Iskat could sense a faraway crowd on the other end of the long hallway, cheering and stomping and buzzing. Her senses were dizzy with new input, her hearts beating faster as the Jedi neared their goal. One by one, they entered the tunnel, their blades casting colorful light over the sculpted stone.

Up ahead, a dark shadow detached from the wall, and Fvorn screeched as a pike slammed into his back. The entire hallway lit up with electricity as he shook and screamed, and the acrid scent of oily, burning Duros flesh filled the air. Master Klefan spun and struck down the Geonosian with his lightsaber, but it was too late. Fvorn wasn't moving, and Iskat went entirely still as she felt him die, a startling, tearing, wrenching pain in the Force unlike anything she'd ever experienced. Zeeth's scream of rage and loss filled the air as he deactivated his lightsaber and knelt by his friend.

Iskat had never felt someone die so violently before, and it was like she died a little herself. Fvorn had always been there, a constant in her life, at first a quiet and easygoing playmate and then a respected Padawan, and then he was just . . . gone. It happened so quickly, so easily, and Fvorn was a good Jedi, a good fighter. He didn't deserve to die like that, so far away from the Temple, where he'd hoped to work as a diplomat one day.

Fvorn had died in pain, surprised and scared, and that brutal suddenness echoed in Iskat's bones.

A tiny scrape made the hairs in her ears twitch.

She went tense and looked to the wall.

What they'd taken to be a sculpted mural was actually a clever contingent of Geonosians with weapons waiting to strike.

Iskat spun just in time to raise her lightsaber. The clever contingent of Geonosians leapt off the wall, and the nearest one flew directly at her, pike aimed for her chest.

/ 4.

THE GEONOSIAN CHITTERED MADLY AS it flew toward Iskat, its wings beating so fast that they were a blur. Her entire body froze and went tense, her mind running calculations, her hearts stammering out of sync with absolute terror. She'd never been attacked before—not like this.

Not for real.

But her body knew exactly what to do.

It didn't need her brain or her hearts.

With a swift flash, her arm shot out as if of its own volition.

As her blade met the Geonosian's chest, she was intricately aware of the strange sensation of flesh parting, the sharp click of chitin and the softer thickness within. She had barely realized she was being attacked, and now the flying Geonosian fell at her feet, nearly split in two. The being was strange, unlike anything she'd seen before, almost more an insect than a person. But they wore a sort of uniform, and they carried a weapon, and they were indeed a person, and she had killed them, just as one of them had killed Fvorn.

A Geonosian, a person, someone's child, maybe someone's parent.

Alive, and now dead. Because of her.

She'd been trained to reach into the pulse of the Force, to feel the unique signature of every plant and person around her, to tap into that harmony. They had prepared her to defend. To protect.

But they had also trained her to hit targets and aim for vital organs and parry and slash and stab and kill, and it had happened so quickly, so easily. Her body had responded like it knew exactly what to do, like the instinct had been bred into her.

She was a killer now.

For a good cause, of course. To help save her fellow Jedi.

If she hadn't killed the Geonosian, they would've killed her, and probably given it a hell of a lot less thought.

It had to be done, and she had done it, and now there was a strange, hollow emptiness in her chest. She'd felt the Geonosian leave the Force, had felt their body gasp in surprise and pain. Had been intricately aware of the razor-blade difference between there and gone, someone and no one, alive and empty.

There was no time to think about that now.

More and more Geonosians appeared. They peeled off the wall, skittered across the ceiling. The darkness hid endless hiding places, and the Geonosians buzzed angrily, a choir of rage. The Jedi Masters and Knights immediately sprang into action, hurrying their Padawans down the hall and toward what had to be the arena beyond, fighting only as necessary for self-defense. Onielle cried out as she was struck by a sonic beam from a blaster, and Charlin helped her to stand and supported her as they limped away.

"Hurry," Sember told Iskat, and she turned to run down the hall.

But Zeeth was still on the ground by his friend Fvorn as Master Klefan tried and failed to get him to move toward safety. In the chaos, they were in danger of being left behind. Or worse—killed.

Iskat watched Sember's robes disappear down the hall. Her master was so certain that she would follow orders, but she couldn't leave Zeeth behind. Fvorn and Zeeth had always been kind to her, never shown any apprehension, even after the accident.

As she watched, an attacking Geonosian went for Zeeth with a pike, and Master Klefan stood to fight back. As more Geonosians moved toward the isolated Jedi, Iskat knew she couldn't just follow the others. She ran back down the hall toward Zeeth, and when a Geonosian warrior peeled off the wall to attack, she ducked under the jab and sliced the creature in half with her lightsaber. Before she could process it, before she could blink away the image of the top half sliding off the bottom half, another warrior appeared.

And then a beautiful thing happened.

Iskat's thoughts and worries fell away, and she became . . .

A song, a poem, a dance.

A being of pure focus, intent on a singular goal.

Kill.

Geonosians swarmed, and she sliced, ducked, leapt, parried, punched, hacked, elbowed, kneed, threw and caught, kicked and flipped and cartwheeled and stabbed. She didn't hold back, didn't worry that she was doing something wrong. She forgot Charlin and Onielle and their constant suspicion, she forgot the stern eyes of her master, she forgot her promise to seek her inner peace. There was only Iskat, her blade, her body, and the enemies who would kill her if she gave them the slightest advantage. Time lost all meaning, her senses in perfect harmony. For the first time in her life, she wasn't struggling to hold herself in check and do what had been asked of her.

She simply was, perfectly, herself.

And then she spun, blade up, to find that there was no one left to fight. Zeeth still clung to his friend's body, but Master Klefan was staring at Iskat as if seeing her for the first time.

"Enough, Iskat," Master Klefan said, voice barely rising above a whisper. "They're all dead."

The world spun around and refocused, and Iskat gazed around her. Geonosians were strewn everywhere like broken dolls, their weapons scattered and their yellow blood slicking the stones. She looked down to find her knuckles bruised, that same yellow blood on her hands and on the elbows of her robes. Her lightsaber had instantly cauterized the wounds it caused, but her flesh still carried the marks of her brutality.

"What an unusual fighting style," Master Klefan said. But the way he said it suggested this was not a good thing.

Iskat said nothing. There was no answer to that. She merely nodded and flicked off her weapon, noting to herself that one of the many benefits of a lightsaber, a benefit she had never considered before, was that one never had to clean blood off the blade.

Together, she and Master Klefan dragged Zeeth to standing and led him down the hall, sidestepping the corpses of a dozen Geonosians. The Rodian was in shock, clumsy and heavy with grief.

"Rejoice, for he is one with the Force," Master Klefan said softly. "Now is a time of action, Zeeth. We will grieve together when it is safe to do so. For now, the galaxy needs you."

"But we can't leave him behind . . ." Zeeth began, stopping in place.

Master Klefan put a gentle hand on the Padawan's shoulder. "He would not want others to die when his spirit has already moved on." His hand moved to Zeeth's chest. "In the Force, your friend is with you always. Feel him here, like a light that will never go out."

He removed his hand, and Zeeth placed his long fingers over his heart and closed his eyes. "It's like I can feel him," he said wonderingly, then opened his eyes. "He would want me to go on."

Master Klefan nodded sagely and turned, and Zeeth followed him down the hall. Iskat was glad Klefan's words had helped and could feel Zeeth's newfound comfort radiating through the Force, but something about the exchange left her feeling off balance. She glanced over her shoulder, back to where the shadowy lump of Fvorn's body was lost amid the dead Geonosians. They were all equally dead, and she briefly shivered before turning around and hurrying to rejoin the Jedi.

When they reached the rest of the group waiting in a quiet antechamber, they found yet more dead Geonosians, and Iskat sensed the trepidation of the other Padawans, many of whom likely felt that same empty sickness she'd experienced with her first kill. Several of them were wide-eyed and trembling, possibly in shock. The masters around them stayed on high alert as they whispered encouragement to their charges. Zeeth's master, Gobi, put an arm around her Padawan, and Master Klefan moved to lead the group up a grand set of carved stone steps. Sember detached from the larger group and joined Iskat, who sensed a strange disquiet in her master's manner.

"Calm," Sember intoned, giving Iskat a significant look. "Find your center."

I did, Iskat almost said. But instead, she just nodded. This spiral staircase was wider and more formal than the last one, and the cheers of the crowd outside were nearly earsplitting. Iskat was glad for Master Sember's calisthenics program as she walked up and up and up, her lightsaber at the ready. The stairs led to a great, arched doorway with a huge window to the bright daylight beyond, and as Master Klefan spoke to Mace Windu through his holoprojector and waited for all the Jedi to converge, it was as if Iskat saw the world with new eyes. The colors were brighter, the sounds sharper. The fight had given her a confidence she'd never before experienced. She'd exhibited strength and skill before, but never true excellence. Not merely passable, as Master Sember so often said, but genuinely brilliant.

And yet . . . to be good . . . at killing? Was that a laudable thing?

Was it a good thing for a Jedi to be?

And to take pride in it?

The masters would not approve. They would remind her to revisit the Jedi Code.

What she'd done was self-defense. She'd saved Zeeth. That was her duty.

Now was not the time for feelings, for excuses. She knew what she had to do.

Iskat closed her eyes, clutched her amulet, and began to silently recite her mantra.

There is no—

"Why is there blood all over her hands?" Onielle whispered to Zeeth, low enough that anyone without Iskat's heightened hearing might miss it—but that Iskat definitely had no choice but to hear. Such was her curse: No one knew anything about her species, so no one knew she heard every word they whispered about her. "Did you see what happened?"

"She killed them all," Zeeth murmured. "A dozen. They went for me and Master Klefan, and she slaughtered them."

Charlin sucked in a breath. "I struck one, although it didn't die, and it was awful. I can't imagine killing so many."

"And when she came up the stairs, she was *smiling*," Onielle added.

Iskat took care to school her face as she looked out the window and down into the immense arena below where the prisoners were chained to columns.

"She was the only one of us who stayed behind. She did well," Tualon said from beside Onielle. Iskat felt a surge of gratitude for Tualon, who genuinely strove to follow the Code, and not just because the masters were watching.

Iskat felt Charlin's cold stare. "She didn't have to stay behind. The masters told us what to do, and she did . . . something else. Something brutal. First Tika, and now this. I'm not comfortable being around someone so dangerous."

"Then stay away from Mace Windu," Master Ansho said, breaking up the circle with his presence. His large black eyes glistened, and his blue head tresses twitched as the powerful Nautolan let each Padawan feel the weight of his gaze. "And even Master Yoda. Jedi do what they must. We're on a mission. This isn't training anymore; sometimes out in the greater galaxy it's kill or be killed. I'm sure Iskat regrets what must be done, as do we all."

And—she did regret it. At least the first one, she regretted. She was fairly certain the look in the Geonosian's insectile eyes as he died would haunt her forever.

After that first one, she simply stopped looking in their eyes.

That made it a lot easier.

She wondered if Master Vey was familiar with this feeling, if she had killed any of the Geonosians herself, farther up the tunnel. Her master had taught her many things, but very little about death and violence. Iskat suspected the life Sember had planned for her was meant to be a peaceful one, a life where she would not be provoked.

If today's mission was any indication, such peace was no longer an option.

Up ahead, Master Klefan paused in the shadows by the arched door that led to the arena and slipped his holoprojector back into his pocket. The sound of cheers and hisses and clicks erupted so loudly, Iskat immediately understood that the twenty or so Geonosians they'd encountered were but grains of sand on a beach. There were many thousands of them in the stands, and whatever was happening in the arena, it wasn't good.

"Obi-Wan Kenobi, Anakin Skywalker, and Senator Amidala are fighting for their lives," Master Klefan said solemnly. "The spectators in the stands may not be armed, but they may still attack, as will the sentries and guards. Our scouts have spotted several cannons on this level. We're also looking for sonic blasters and carbines. We don't want anyone from the audience to take aim at our people on the ground. Padawans, follow your masters." He inclined his head toward the door.

"Remember your training," Master Sember told Iskat, a dark and measuring look in her eyes. When she ran through the door, Iskat followed.

The sun briefly blinded her, and then Iskat looked down on a scene of absolute chaos. The arena was an enormous bowl of burning orange, carved and built from the sand itself, with rows and rows of seats surrounded by the towers she'd seen from the sky. Far below, three human figures fought an impossible battle as beasts and guards harried and chased them around the arena. The Geonosians in the crowd screeched and gibbered, their wings buzzing in excitement as the three captives in the arena took control of a rampaging reek and seemed as if they might actually escape. That must've been what upset the crowd so much, earlier . . .

The prisoners were fighting back.

"Iskat, hurry!" Sember called.

Squinting, Iskat ran after her master, silently moving behind the stands as the Geonosians leapt and howled in their seats. Each time they ran past an aisle, ducking low, Iskat dared a look at what was happening on the ground.

The crowd made a new noise, frantic and predatory, as droids rolled into the arena to surround the two Jedi and the senator. Iskat could only catch glimpses as she followed Sember toward a cannon operated by two Geonosian sentries who were likewise screeching their rage at the scene below.

A flash of purple caught Iskat's eye, and she saw Mace Windu himself appear on a dais on the other side of the fighting grounds, his lightsaber an unmistakable beacon. All around the lower levels of the arena, a rainbow of flashing lightsabers lit one after the other, a sea of green and blue that filled Iskat's hearts with hope. In response, a jolt of unease rippled through the thousands of Geonosians in the crowd. Half of them took to the air, a great, brown cloud of buzzing wings, and the other half leapt from their seats and ran for the archways on clicking feet. Master Sember grabbed the back of Iskat's robes and yanked her into the shadows of a round portico as a stampede of frantic spectators ran past, a strange chemical scent like cut grass rising from their bodies. Iskat couldn't see what was happening on the ground, but her hand was on her lightsaber, aching for the next fight.

Most of the Geonosians had disappeared into the factory by the time the sound of blasterfire cut through the odd silence.

"Now!" Master Sember said, finally releasing Iskat's robes, and together they ran out into the stands and toward the nearest cannon.

Iskat glanced down at the arena as she ran. Dozens, maybe hundreds of Jedi cut swaths through an army of droids as an acklay and a reek ran riot through the battle. Geonosian guards patrolled with pikes on orrays and in chariots, trying in vain to corral their escaped prey.

"Iskat! Pay attention!" Master Sember called.

The Geonosian soldier firing the sonic cannon must've heard her. He tried to spin the weapon around to aim it at the approaching Jedi, but Iskat threw her lightsaber, taking down the enemy before calling it back to her hand. Master Sember didn't even pause; she seized the cannon's barrel, then jammed her lightsaber into its belly, which melted around her blade and began leaking oil and smoke.

"Stay hidden," Sember hissed. "Wait for the all-clear." She wedged herself behind the cannon, but there was no room there for her Padawan.

Iskat ducked behind the empty stands. All the spectators had fled, and the next cannon in view was already being destroyed by Tualon and Ansho. The real battle was happening on the sand below as Jedi leapt and somersaulted, cutting down droids and Geonosians alike. The number of droids somehow seemed to be increasing as they marched and rolled in from every direction, and they already outnumbered the

Jedi. Blaster bolts flew everywhere, and the Jedi were in danger of being overwhelmed, which hadn't seemed possible. Iskat's gaze was drawn to the stone columns in the center of the arena, the ones meant to hold the prisoners during execution.

She had to do something. She had to help.

She reached out a hand toward one of the columns as droids marched past . . .

Then curled those fingers around her amulet instead.

A thrum of rage plucked at Iskat's hearts as she thought about the accident she'd caused all those years ago with a very similar piece of architecture. Her assignment had been to use the Force to pull her lightsaber off a shelf, high up on a heavy stone column, so high that she couldn't see it, but something had gone wrong. Instead of bringing her lightsaber gently floating to her hand, as the other Padawans had, she'd pulled down the entire column—on top of her closest friend, a sweet Iktotchi Initiate named Tika. The column had broken Tika's back in several places, damaging her spinal cord. Iskat would never forget the way her usually quiet friend had screamed as they'd carried her to the infirmary. Charlin and Onielle had taken their own wounds, suffering broken bones and contusions, their blood staining the stones and their trust in Iskat shattered forever. After that, Tika had been taken elsewhere for more intensive care than the Jedi healers could offer. According to Master Vey, Tika had made great strides but had ultimately decided not to return to the Temple.

"She has chosen her own future," Master Vey said gently after Iskat repeatedly asked to visit her friend. "As the Force wills it."

Iskat never saw the girl again.

Losing Tika—knowing she was responsible for her friend's pain—weighed heavily on Iskat. When she was in the Temple, it was as if she were always waiting to see Tika appear around each corner, smiling her cheerful grin, before remembering the truth and reliving that day over and over in her head, feeling the same shame and fear and guilt. She preferred to be on her missions with Sember, even if they were boring, if it meant the other Padawans wouldn't stare at her as if wishing to see Tika still there instead and Iskat gone from the Order.

After the accident, her teachers watched her more closely. The other Initiates didn't trust her. No one wanted to be her training partner. Once she was chosen to be Master Vey's Padawan, Iskat was instructed to wake up early each morning to practice relaxation and breathing and meditation. She had to learn to focus, she was told; her powers had to be kept in check. She'd been sloppy and careless, and it had caused permanent damage. The next time she faced the column, she was alone with her master, and she was so gentle that her lightsaber barely twitched off the shelf to float down like a feather.

Iskat had heard the other Padawans whisper about her; after the column, they didn't exactly fear her, but they certainly didn't trust her. She gave them space, hoping that with time and hard work, she could prove to them that she was the same girl they'd grown up with, laughed with, played games with. Life in the Temple continued as it always had, just with a lot more meditations with Master Klefan or Master Uumay, the ancient Bimm who spent so much time communing with the Force that most people assumed he was napping. Iskat didn't form any more close friendships, didn't try to push her way into conversations. Sometimes she almost felt excluded, but she found comfort in the Force, in her meditations. She accepted that life among the Jedi wasn't meant to be fun and frivolous—it was a life of service and responsibility. Iskat was determined to hold herself carefully in check, making sure she would never make such a mistake again. Once she began traveling with Master Vey, her loneliness was easier to bear.

Still, she never forgot the power within her, the power she struggled so hard to contain.

Fighting, here and now, on Geonosis, she had felt it again, for the first time in years.

As she looked down at those columns, at all the structures of the arena, she was flooded with a sense of urgency. If the masters would've allowed it, she could've taken out all the droids down there on the sand. She was certain of it; she could feel the Force flowing through her, the pressure building like it wanted to explode. With one swipe of a hand, she could throw dozens of droids to the ground, maybe even cause them to short out. She could topple the columns onto the Geonosian guards. She could do so much good, if she were down there in the midst of the real battle instead of up here, hiding in the empty stands as the murderous Geonosians flew away to safety.

She could save the captives. She could save everyone.

Instead, she was doing nothing.

Following their orders, all the Jedi from her shuttle had destroyed their cannons, and any Geonosian soldiers who'd held plasma rifles were no longer an issue. From the youngest Padawan to the most capable of the masters, they were hiding in place, waiting patiently for further instruction. Too far from the battle to effect any change, they could only watch as their fellow Jedi were either struck down or herded into the center of the arena by heavily armed droids. From up here, it looked like they were losing.

"Retreat!" Master Klefan called from an arched doorway under the nearest portico.

Iskat didn't immediately run; what was happening below was riveting, the Jedi in the arena slowly forced into a glittering group of flashing lightsabers as the battle droids pulled the noose of their defense tighter. She squeezed her amulet so she wouldn't be tempted to—

"Iskat!" Master Vey shouted. She'd left her hiding place behind the cannon and was running toward Master Klefan and the portico. "Hurry!"

Iskat stood and ran to join her.

A flash of movement caught her eye—

"Master, behind you!" she shouted as she ignited her lightsaber.

But it was too late.

A Geonosian soldier had flown up from the lower levels, taking aim with a sonic blaster. His shot caught Sember in the chest, knocked her off her feet, and sent her flying over the portico wall and down into the stands, her brown robes fluttering like the wings of a dying bird.

/ 5.

ISKAT FOCUSED ON THE SOURCE of the blaster bolt and growled as the Geonosian rotated in midair, weapon in hand, hunting for his next target. As if it had a mind of its own, her hand threw her lightsaber, beheading the guard before spinning back neatly to her grasp. She didn't watch the guard fall, didn't feel the pulse of another life lost in the Force; she was too busy leaping over the portico wall to land in the upper level of the stands, where she knelt by her master. Maybe Sember wasn't dead; surely she was tough enough to live through one hit, no matter how direct.

"Master?" Iskat asked, rolling Sember onto her back.

Sember's hand reached out toward Iskat's face, but her eyes looked beyond her Padawan, wet and pleading. "I'm sorry, Feyra. I tried," she whispered before coughing wetly, splattering Iskat with blood.

Iskat grabbed her master's hand, held it to her chest. "Master, who is Feyra? It's me. Iskat. I'm right here. Can't you see me?"

Sember's head rocked back and forth drunkenly as if she'd heard nothing. "Feyra, I couldn't stop it. She's so much like you. You made me promise to help her, and I did, but there was only so much I could do—"

"Master Sember?"

Sember reached for Iskat's robes with her other hand, clutching the plain brown cloth in her blood-slick fist. "I kept my promise. She's a good Padawan. You would be proud. She tries so hard, Feyra, but maybe I was never enough . . ."

Nearby, blaster bolts whipped through the air, but Iskat could only focus on her master. "Sember, Master, I don't understand. Who is Feyra? What promise?"

Sember's eyes went wide and she gave a little gasp as she fell back.

Iskat felt it in the Force—the moment her master was gone.

"Master Sember! Please! I need you!"

Strong hands grabbed her shoulders and pulled her roughly upright. "Iskat. Hurry!" Master Klefan barked.

"I have to carry Master Sember—"

"There's no time. Leave her. It's too late. The ship is waiting."

"But—"

The older man pulled her to standing and shoved her toward the stairs that led up to the portico, where Iskat could see Tualon standing with Ansho.

A master and an apprentice together, as it should be.

"I can carry her," Iskat told Master Klefan, and for the first time, she didn't make herself smaller or pitch her voice soft.

"We can't risk it," he said. "Like Fvorn, she wouldn't want to be the cause of yet more death. Many Jedi lost their lives today, and she wouldn't want you to be one of them. We will mourn properly when we're safely back at the Temple. Now go."

Iskat threw one last look at Master Vey, now just a still, brown lump in the empty stands. She felt a sudden softness for her mentor, now that she was gone. In her last moments, had Sember been talking about her—saying she was good, that she would make someone proud? That was the highest praise Iskat had ever heard from her master. Maybe, deep down, somewhere past the aloof serenity that had always stood between them, her master truly had cared for her. Without Sember, Iskat didn't know what her future would hold. She wasn't ready to take on the dogged task of artifact acquisition on her own, hadn't yet developed the relationships and knack for haggling Sember's missions required. None of the traders took her seriously.

Perhaps another Jedi would now step up to take her on as Padawan. And yet—no one had seemed so inclined after the tournament.

Padawans needed masters. How else could she possibly find her way?

Wrapping her fingers around her amulet, Iskat reached out in the Force, hoping Sember might be with her, as Zeeth said he could feel Fvorn with him.

She felt nothing.

Nothing but emptiness and coldness and despair.

She could tell Master Klefan was about to touch her shoulder again, as he had with Zeeth to communicate sympathy, and she knew she couldn't stand it, so she released her amulet and ran to join the others.

Along with Tualon and Ansho, Iskat and Klefan ran through the shadows of the arena's sunless interior, dodging droids and Geonosians as they returned to where the ship waited. They emerged from the base of the tower, and Iskat shielded her eyes against the reflection of the midday sun off the hot sand. The clear reddish-orange sky was dark with hundreds of incoming shuttles, each ship landing in a cloud of sand to disgorge dozens of clone troopers. What had been a landing area was now a war zone filled with blaster bolts and shouts. Iskat and Klefan were the last ones on board, and Iskat noted that there were unoccupied seats, but she was in no shape to name the Jedi who were missing.

The shuttle was oddly quiet, but her senses were still on high alert. She smelled tired bodies and sweat and blood, sand and metal and the strange, grasslike reek of Geonosian death. She heard sighs and sniffles and sobs, boots shuffling and murmurs of comfort. It was odd, she realized, how she'd felt so calm during the fight, and yet now her hearts were thundering, her breath coming in pants, her mind running too fast to make sense of anything.

She was all too aware of the empty seat beside her . . . until Master Klefan sat there.

"Your first battle," he said contemplatively, facing forward, as if it was easier to speak with her when he wasn't looking directly at her.

"Yes, Master," she said, because it hadn't actually been a question.

"You performed well. Sember's training has made you formidable. I know you will miss her, but we must always remember that death is a part of life, and that she will live on within our hearts. Rejoice, for she is one with the Force."

A sick feeling roiled in Iskat's stomach.

How did it do anyone any good to pretend death was something to be celebrated?

Was it supposed to make the living fear death less? Help them forget the loss of those who were no longer among them?

"How?" she asked, voice ragged.

"How what?" Master Klefan asked with genuine curiosity.

"How can I rejoice when my master is dead?"

Klefan heaved a gentle sigh. "There is no death, there is only the Force. The Force includes both life and death equally, and everything that lives must die. When a fellow Jedi falls, you have a choice to mourn or to celebrate, and who would choose grieving over joy, to know that your kind master is now one with the Force to which she dedicated her life? There is no use in mourning. The Jedi must serve all, not a select few. This is why we do not form attachments. To mourn goes directly against our tenets."

Perhaps Master Klefan was trying to be helpful; his tone was certainly kindly. But all Iskat heard were the same creeds and quotes she'd been taught all her life stitched together into a ragged facsimile of wisdom. She didn't believe that Master Klefan understood death any better than she did, for all that he'd been alive much, much longer. He was just regurgitating the same old teachings.

"Do you understand, Padawan Iskat?"

"Yes, Master."

But what she understood wasn't how to rejoice in death.

It was that Master Klefan wasn't telling her the truth. His smile didn't reach his eyes. He seemed tired and old and hopeless. He'd probably already forgotten which of the Padawans had died. He called both Fvorn and Zeeth "lad," most of the time, anyway. Sember had once been his Padawan, and from what Iskat could see, he was just as upset, body and soul, as she was, and yet he was pretending that he was at peace.

He said these things to comfort her, but he didn't seem to believe them himself. Perhaps it was easier to say a bunch of platitudes than it was to confront the horrifying trauma she'd just faced—and that he'd witnessed.

The Jedi had taught her so much, and yet they couldn't help her deal with this pain.

It was like they didn't even know how.

Today, Iskat had lost a friend. She'd lost her master. She'd taken her first life. She'd taken many lives, had lost herself in a dance of death and just kept on going as if her entire world hadn't been rocked to its core. As the battle raged in the arena, she'd seen firsthand that the greatest fighters in the galaxy, knowledgeable and strong in the Force, had barely been able to beat some droids. And she'd left the bodies of fellow Jedi behind, where they would never undergo the proper Jedi funerals.

All her training had not prepared her for . . . any of this.

Her mind and hearts and soul felt as if they were fractured. Too much had happened too quickly. As she looked around the ship, she saw life going on as usual. Two masters were tending to Onielle's leg. Master Ansho was telling Tualon about a new attack he wanted him to practice when they returned to the Temple. Sure, some Jedi were clearly upset, but for the most part, it was as if Fvorn and Master Sember and the other missing Jedi had never existed. The shuttle was full of beings who had been through the same life-altering event, but no one else seemed to be experiencing the same desolation. Iskat felt entirely alone. Her head was too full of her own emotions, emotions she had dedicated years of her life to controlling. They were supposed to wash away like waves on a beach, but instead they threatened to drown her. She longed to be free of so much intensity of feeling.

But how? How could someone not feel things when there were so many things to feel?

There is no emotion, there is peace were easy words to reflect on when emotions weren't battering at her hearts like a storm.

"You are uneasy," Master Klefan noted.

"Today has been . . . a lot."

He nodded sagely. "When we've returned to the Jedi Temple, you should meditate by the pool. Practice what your master has taught you, carry on her teachings—that is how to do her honor. You are her legacy.

Remember: There is no chaos, there is harmony. Find your harmony, Iskat Akaris, and you will again know peace."

It took everything Iskat had not to scream in his face.

Nothing about today had been peaceful.

The Jedi had been training her since she was an infant, but they had not trained her for this.

Meditation could not make these feelings go away.

She felt the Force swelling in her chest, but not the calm, peaceful stream she'd learned to tap into. No, today, it was like a dark maelstrom trying to drag her down. Before, Sember had centered her. Now there was no one to anchor her. The amulet was not enough.

And what had her master's last words meant?

Who was Feyra, and why were they owed an apology? What was it that couldn't be stopped?

She thought about asking Master Klefan, but her patience with his proverbs was wearing thin. She looked around the shuttle at the other masters, but most of them were leading their Padawans in meditation or helping to bandage up wounds. Beside her, Master Klefan let out a rumbling snore. A few seats over, Tualon's eyes were closed as he, too, sought peace in the calming mantras they'd been taught.

There was no one here she could ask, no one to whom she could speak with any honesty. Iskat hadn't revealed much of her inner workings to Master Vey, but she was fairly certain her master had seen through to the truth of her, had known that despite all her hard work, Iskat remained flawed.

The shuttle returned to the much larger cruiser orbiting Geonosis, and Iskat went to her assigned bunk, curling up with her back to the room. Sember should've been on the bunk underneath her, a calming presence, but now it was empty. Master Klefan brought her food and more platitudes, but she couldn't digest either. She tried to meditate, but she was numb, as if the still waters of her center had frozen.

Time passed, but then again, time meant nothing.

As the shuttle rumbled down into the courtyard of the Jedi Temple on Coruscant, Iskat surfaced from her strange limbo to find the Jedi discussing what would happen next. With the success of their rescue mission on Geonosis, it seemed the Separatists and the Republic were now truly at war. No one knew what was to come, but surely the Jedi would be expected to be part of the ongoing effort to preserve and defend the Republic. They were peacekeepers, and so they would defend peace, no matter the cost.

She looked around the ship and was overcome with the realization that she had no idea what to do with herself. Things rarely changed in the Jedi Temple, but now her master was gone, and the Jedi were at war. Iskat had lost her foundation, her compass. Was this growing up, she thought, finding your place when there was no one to instruct you? She had taken many lives and lost a mentor, all in the span of one day, but that didn't make her any wiser or more knowledgeable.

The clone pilot ordered everyone to buckle in for landing, and Iskat took her seat beside Master Klefan. "Master Klefan, what do I do now?" she asked her dead master's master.

He blinked at her and smiled his soft smile. "Carry on as you always have. Keep the schedule Sember prescribed until a new Jedi Master is assigned to guide you. Continue your studies. Train with the other Padawans and find serenity in their presence. New orders will come as the situation develops, so be ready to leave at any time. And as always, when in doubt, meditate."

The ship landed, and everyone unbuckled and stood. They seemed so calm, Iskat thought—just like Master Vey had always been. Iskat felt like she was missing something; her body still wanted to run, to fight, to move. Master Klefan put a heavy hand on her shoulder before departing, but Iskat found no comfort there.

His answers continued to plague her with their vagueness. Yes, she would go through the motions as if Sember were still instructing her, but that didn't tell her how to move on. That didn't tell her how to prepare for an uncertain future.

It was odd, finding her place in the mass of Jedi stepping off the shuttle. Normally, she followed Sember, doing her best to represent her master well. Now there was no one to tell her where to go, and she was just expected to figure it out herself.

With no direction, Iskat's feet led her to her favorite meditation garden, with its soothing pools filled with flickering orange fish and wide green leaves. She was the only one there, and the silence was disquieting. No matter how hard she tried, no matter how many times she recited her mantra, no matter how closely she held her amulet, she could not access the calm she sought. When her stomach's growling overshadowed the gentle drip of water, she visited the cafeteria and ate like she'd been starving, like she was trying to fill a bottomless pit. She wandered the halls of the Temple, but she didn't feel like dueling or reading or running. It was as if she were haunting her own home, as if she were the one who had died, a little ghost no one else recognized.

As night fell, she returned to her small sleep chamber. It was spare, as all Jedi chambers were. She performed her ablutions, surprised to find red splatters of blood on her face, a gory handprint crusted into her robes.

From Sember—when she'd coughed.

When she'd grabbed Iskat to pull her close, in those final moments.

This was her master's blood.

Why had no one told her she'd been wandering around like that all this time, covered in gore?

Did anyone even really look at her, really see her?

Were they all too overcome with the fallout of Geonosis to see what was right in front of them, or was it just her?

As she watched the red-tinged water swirl away, she wondered what had become of her master's body, the bodies of all the Jedi they'd left behind, Jedi who would never receive their proper funerary rites. Perhaps the dead didn't care, but Iskat did. Not that it mattered. Not that it changed anything.

Lying in her bed, staring up into the darkness, Iskat couldn't quiet her mind. As she tossed and turned, Geonosis played through her head like watching a holo. Fvorn, Sember, the Geonosians, the flash of Jedi lightsabers bright against the sand. Something important had happened in the Petranaki arena—something in her hearts had forever changed— and there was no ritual to mark it, no one to discuss it with. Now that Sember was gone, she would never have that sort of guidance again.

And yet . . . perhaps that might be a blessing. Without the heavy weight of Sember's expectations, who might Iskat Akaris become?

/ 6.

THE NEXT MORNING, ISKAT RECEIVED word that as the Padawan of Sember Vey, it was her duty to clean out her master's chamber and organize her things. She was unfamiliar with this tradition, and it felt very strange indeed to enter Sember's room without knocking and find it empty and silent. Because they'd spent the majority of their time as master and Padawan traveling, Iskat could count on one hand the number of times she'd stepped through this door, where she'd never felt welcome.

There wasn't much within, as Sember was an ascetic sort of Jedi who avoided all attachment and ornamentation. A simple rug to warm the stone floors. A humble bed neatly made. A plain wardrobe in which clean tunics, leggings, and cloaks hung at perfect angles. Iskat folded each item and placed it in the storage chest she'd been given. Once the hangers were empty, she pulled out the bottom drawer and realized she was staring at her dead master's underclothes. Sember had been a very private person, so the thought of handling such private items made Iskat deeply uncomfortable.

Not that it mattered. Iskat was nothing if not dutiful, and she began to think of this as a gift to Sember, as a token of her appreciation for all that her master had done for her. Perhaps their bond had not been perfect, but if Sember hadn't chosen her as Padawan, Iskat knew she would have had no place in the Jedi Order, and she was grateful to be there.

Thankfully, that task was soon accomplished, and Iskat moved on to the bottom drawer, which held the warm clothing they needed when traveling to colder climates. She sorted through hats and gloves and scarves, remembering how Sember had enjoyed finding locally produced yarns on their travels to incorporate in her crochet work. Part of her wanted to keep something to remember her master by, but this exercise was about letting Sember go.

Much to her surprise, there was something in the very back of Sember's drawer, an oblong object wrapped in a crocheted scarf of simple undyed wool. Iskat was instantly curious. What would the austere and modest Jedi Master Sember Vey possess that she might wish to keep hidden and secret?

Iskat unwrapped the object, stunned to find a lightsaber she'd never seen before.

The moment her fingers wrapped around the hilt, a jolt of recognition made her shudder.

This was not simply any saber, but one with a hilt just like hers: extra wide, made for longer fingers than most species possessed.

A perfect fit.

Holding it felt right.

She ignited the blade and was amazed to see that it was yellow.

She'd never seen a saber that color before, outside of the Jedi Temple Guards.

This lightsaber—it was special. It was meant to be hers.

It called to her.

But why did Master Vey have a second lightsaber, and one with a hilt so wide that human fingers would've struggled to wield it? Why would someone who disliked dueling and delegated all lightsaber training to a remote have a second saber at all?

Possessions were not forbidden among the Jedi, but attachment was frowned upon. To keep such an object suggested a definite attachment, and the fact that it had been hidden confirmed that this was no ordinary artifact. There were no other items of interest in the room or on the ship they'd shared. Iskat had seen dozens of treasures pass through Sember's hands over the years, objects of great value and beauty, including lightsabers far more intricate and grand than this one. They had walked through bazaars together, visited jewelers and museums, and Sember had never shown any preference for one object over another. Why this lightsaber?

The mystery called to her almost as much as the weapon.

Iskat tucked it into her robe, feeling the rightness of its weight. As she looked around the empty room, all its contents fitting in one unmarked storage chest, she couldn't help but wonder how many chambers in the Temple were empty now, how many Padawans were filling trunks with clothes that would never be worn again. So many lives lost, their passing tidied away so quickly. Would new Jedi called home from their missions take these rooms, or would the looming conflict claim more and more from their ranks, leaving such chambers empty? She'd heard the whispers in the halls, knew they'd lost nearly two hundred Jedi at Geonosis, two hundred they couldn't spare.

At least the Republic had taken control of Geonosis after the conflict, Iskat had heard. At least the bodies of the fallen Jedi would be claimed and returned to the Temple for their proper rites. It soothed something in Iskat's soul, to know that Master Vey had not been abandoned to rot on that faraway desert planet, left behind by the Order to which she had dedicated her life. As she left her master's old chamber for the last time, Iskat felt a brief swell of guilt over taking the lightsaber. Maybe she should've left it in the trunk with Sember's things, or perhaps she should've delivered it to Master Klefan. And yet something about it called to her, as it must've called to her master.

She would keep it, then, in honor of Sember Vey.

That was what she told herself, at least.

/ 1.

IN THE DAYS THAT FOLLOWED, Iskat tried to go about her life as if everything was normal, and yet everything had changed. There was no Sember waiting at her door with a list of contacts and artifacts scattered around the galaxy, no ritualistic packing of the T-6 as her aloof master lost herself in the hunt for some moldering text. She ate alone, meditated in the garden, read about communing with and riding the native fauna of various worlds until the words blurred together, ran through halls and gardens that seemed to echo more than they once had. She was constantly aware of how many Jedi were missing, how empty the Temple seemed.

Tan, Lumas, Galdos . . . she hadn't seen any of them since the battle. She'd heard that the youngest Padawan who'd fallen had been just fourteen.

It was one thing to know a catastrophe had happened, even to witness it and live through it. It was another thing entirely to start counting how many people were missing from everyday life.

There was a funeral soon after Geonosis, and when she heard the bell tolling, Iskat brushed out her hair and put on her formal robes and took her place in the ritual chamber. It was a relief to know that most of the fallen Jedi had been recovered from Geonosis and would receive the honor they deserved. She stood alone, and as she stared down at the six cloth-covered biers laid out on the floor, she was struck by the equalizing power of death. Sember was here, somewhere, her body indistinguishable from the other warriors, just another lump under the same embroidered cloth. Closing her eyes, Iskat reached out in the Force, searching for Sember's spirit, but again, as ever, she found nothing save emptiness.

Poor Sember. All the woman had ever wanted was to retrieve her precious artifacts and bring them home to the Temple, where they might help to enrich knowledge of the Force. She'd worn her lightsaber like any Jedi, but she had rarely used it. If only she hadn't stopped her retreat to tell Iskat to hurry. If only Iskat had already been following orders.

Iskat could've carried Sember. She was strong enough, fast enough.

But Master Klefan had stopped her.

He didn't have faith in her.

He would've left Sember, once his own Padawan, to rot under the unforgiving sun.

Iskat's hands tightened to fists at her sides, and it took effort to find her center and refocus on the ceremony. Mace Windu spoke, his voice filling the chamber, but his solemn words whispered like the wind, meaningless. The bodies were lowered beneath the floor, and Iskat understood that this was only a token ceremony, that the biers she watched disappear with grave decorum represented only a small fraction of the Jedi who'd fallen. It was a farce, a symbol. They didn't even know the names of those six they'd watched sink below the surface. Over two hundred Jedi were dead.

The funeral brought her no comfort. The supposedly solemn ritual held a level of artifice that only served to make her feel more alone. As she left the chamber, she felt as if she walked in slow motion. She felt numb.

Days passed, and she waited, and yet no new master approached her. No one summoned her. She had been forgotten.

With no mentor to set her schedule and command her attention, Iskat's thoughts were consumed by the mysteries of Sember's last words and her hidden lightsaber. She began in the Jedi Archives, where she attempted to search for the name Feyra.

She was disappointed to find an oddly incomplete file. There was no age, no species, no clan, no other details. It simply said, "left the Jedi Order."

While she was there, Iskat typed in her own name, something she'd never tried before. She was again disappointed.

Species: unknown.

Home planet: unknown.

Just like Feyra.

Iskat knew Sember had always looked up to Chief Librarian Jocasta Nu, so she searched the stacks until she found the prim, gray-haired Jedi Master helping a youngling access a holotape he was too short to reach.

"Master Jocasta, you knew my Master, Sember Vey, didn't you?" Iskat began, once the youngling had returned to his table.

Jocasta paused, holotape in hand, a brief look of pain flitting across her eyes.

"Oh, yes. Sember always loved the archives, and her dedication brought many rare and useful volumes to our shelves. Do you share her love of knowledge?"

Iskat kept her face bland; she had never felt such a calling, but no one else needed to know that. "I always hope to serve the Jedi Order in the best way that I'm able."

"Well, hopefully, you've learned her methods. Sember was a great gift to the Order." Jocasta looked off into the seemingly endless repository of knowledge, wistful, before smiling placidly. "But she is one with the Force now and at peace. Did you have a question?"

There it was again—a Jedi ignoring the real pain in their own heart to proclaim that death wasn't really so bad. Iskat brushed away her own flare of annoyance. She needed answers.

"Sember said something while she was . . ." Iskat's voice broke. "While she was dying. A name. She called out to someone named Feyra. I looked her up in the archives, but the file seems incomplete."

That had Jocasta's attention. Holotape still in hand, she marched to the databank and said, "Show me."

Iskat performed the same search and received the same answer. Jocasta motioned her away from the keyboard and typed in several commands before pulling away, puzzled.

"Strange," she murmured. "Someone has purposefully deleted information that was previously in the file, and I'm unable to retrieve it."

"Did Sember have that kind of access?"

Jocasta looked at her sharply. "Long ago, she did. She worked here when she was younger, but I can't imagine why she would need to change a file."

"This person—Feyra. With her dying words, Sember apologized to her. She was very emotional. It seemed important."

Jocasta looked up at the ceiling as if scrolling back through time. "A friend of hers once, I seem to recall. But then gone. The file says she left the Order, and so left she must, but that's all I can tell you. Is there anything else I can help you with?"

If there was information that Jocasta Nu couldn't find, that meant Iskat was at a dead end.

"You don't remember anything more about Feyra? What she looked like, maybe?"

And there it was—the look Jocasta gave younglings who overstayed their welcome or tracked mud into the archives.

"If Sember wanted you to know, then I suppose you would know. Your master had her reasons, I'm sure."

"It seems like perhaps you knew her better than I did," Iskat said. "One last thing, do you know if she ever fought with two lightsabers?"

Jocasta cocked her head. "Sember Vey? Oh, no. She could barely tolerate one. She was skilled, of course, always an alert and talented student, but she preferred texts to fighting, as I'm sure you know. You might ask Master Pong Krell about dueling with multiple sabers and see if perhaps he can recommend someone to work with you, if you're interested in learning."

"So Sember never trained with two lightsabers?"

Jocasta's eyes shone with an old fondness. "Not that I know of. She didn't want to go out on missions, at first. She loved the archives, you know. She would've lived in the stacks and slept under a desk, if she'd had her way."

This was news to Iskat. She'd known of her master's interest in texts and scrolls, but only as a function of their missions. Sember had never mentioned the library unless she was sending Iskat there to study. "So why didn't she? Work here, I mean."

Jocasta put a hand on Iskat's shoulder, gave it a gentle squeeze. This gesture was beginning to grate on her.

"When the Force brings a master and Padawan together," Jocasta told her, "that bond is more important than a fondness for texts. She was called to train you. I suspect, once you passed your Jedi trials, she would've settled here and eventually taken my place."

Iskat thanked Jocasta for her help and said she'd speak with Master Krell about lightsaber training, although she had no intention of doing so. If she showed anyone the lightsaber she'd found in Sember's wardrobe, they might take it away, and then she would never know the truth of it. No, she would have to find her answers another way. About the lightsaber that Sember had clearly not used for her own training, and about the mysterious Feyra. Iskat was no closer to knowing who she might be, but at least now she knew that Feyra had been a Jedi—once.

Before bed that night, Iskat put the lightsaber under her pillow.

This was her first real secret.

/ 8.

THE DAYS TURNED INTO WEEKS, and Iskat settled into her schedule and tried to quiet her mind by keeping her body busy. She continued her meditations, pushed her stamina like never before, and practiced her lightsaber forms at odd hours. After the training duels and then Geonosis, she didn't want to feel trepidation and doubt bloom among the other Jedi when she ignited her training saber. She didn't want to give herself any chance of losing control again.

Although it was noticeably less populated, the Temple remained a busy place, the hallways filled with Jedi embarking on missions or returning from them. There were funerals every now and then, but thankfully no one else Iskat knew. What had begun as a rescue mission had become an all-out war. News arrived daily detailing how the Jedi and the Republic, along with their new clone troopers, battled the Separatists and their droid army. Iskat had never paid much attention to politics before, as her journeys with Master Vey had rarely required it. But now her duty was to be ready when called upon, and so she constantly waited to be called upon.

Much to her annoyance, that call didn't come.

No masters sought her out for further training, and she wasn't included in any missions.

She was frustrated, but then again, she wasn't actively seeking more responsibility, was she? Perhaps she needed to show more initiative. When she crossed paths with Master Klefan one day, she turned to follow him and fell in step beside him. His epidermal sacs were again swollen with water, giving him a weight and gravitas that belied his agility and strength.

"Ah, Iskat. Have you continued your meditations?"

"Yes, Master." She paused, considering the right words. "I've kept the schedule Master Vey set, but I was wondering what my next steps might be. Are there any masters who might take me on so that I could better continue my training? I keep hoping I'll be assigned a mission so that I might help in the war . . ." She trailed off and looked up at him hopefully.

Klefan didn't slow, but his brows drew down. "We've a shortage of both masters and time, my dear. Formal training has fallen by the wayside." Iskat noticed a bit of frustration, or perhaps just weariness, creep into Klefan's voice as he spoke.

She cleared her throat. "I know Sember was once your Padawan—"

He interrupted her so swiftly that it felt like a slight. "I'm sorry to disappoint you, Iskat, and under other circumstances, I would certainly be honored to train you. But my current schedule does not allow me the time to take on a Padawan. Perhaps you might consider consulting Jocasta and Noxi in the archives? I know Sember hoped your future would lead you there."

Iskat tried to hide her revulsion, but her smile felt like a lie. "An interesting possibility. Do you know any other Jedi Masters who might currently be without a Padawan?"

Klefan sighed. "Let the Force guide you. I'm on my way to the Council Chamber just now, and I'll be sure to let them know that you're anxious to contribute, but you must remember: All things in their time."

He sped up, but she kept up with him. "One more question, if I may. When Master Sember was . . . dying . . . she said something. A name. Feyra. Do you know who that is?"

He was silent for a moment as she jogged by his side. "I'm afraid I can't help you. Probably best to let the past stay in the past. Good day, and may the Force be with you."

They'd reached the turbolifts that led up to the Council Chamber, and with flawless timing, Master Klefan stepped through the open doors right before they slid shut, leaving Iskat alone again. She felt a little flare of . . . not quite rage. Jedi did not feel rage.

Annoyance.

Master Klefan, she knew, had plenty of time. She'd seen him napping in the garden recently, and he often wandered the Temple halls enjoying cups of tea with Master Uumay. That meant that he had other reasons for not taking Iskat on as a Padawan. Did he not think that she was worth training? Had Master Sember complained too often of her difficult charge? Iskat thought herself a dutiful and hardworking student, and it was disappointing to be rejected by the Jedi Master with whom she'd felt the strongest bond, outside of Sember.

And what was that about Feyra—about letting the past stay in the past? Klefan knew something—something he didn't want Iskat to know. If Sember had tampered with the file and Klefan was avoiding the subject, there was something about Feyra that was purposefully being kept hidden.

So frustrating, to know an answer was so close and yet so out of reach.

So maddening, that Master Klefan was so slippery with the truth on multiple topics.

Well, fine.

If Master Klefan didn't want to work with her, then she didn't want to work with him, and she definitely didn't want to consign herself to the strict silence and enforced stillness of the archives. Iskat wasn't a scholar or a trader or an archivist; she wanted to be out in the war, on real missions, making a real difference. She just needed a real leader, someone to help her find her way. There were plenty of other masters, even if they weren't all available. Perhaps this time she would choose one she actually liked and not simply the one that seemed the most convenient.

Iskat was done with feeling adrift. She was done feeling rejected. It was time to go after what she wanted. With a newfound determination, she set out to find Tualon's master, Ansho, who was briefly home between missions. She found her old friend and his Nautolan mentor playfully sparring in one of the smaller training rooms, teasing each other with an air of camaraderie that made Iskat's hearts ache. When they saw her standing in the doorway, they deactivated their lightsabers. Tualon gave her a small wave, which she returned.

"Good morning, Iskat. Did you need something?" Ansho asked her, his huge black eyes blinking in a friendly manner.

She bowed her head. "With my master gone, I'm not quite sure what to do. I could really use some guidance."

"Have you asked Master Klefan? I know you've studied with him before."

She had to step carefully here.

"I did, but his schedule unfortunately doesn't allow time for individual instruction. He suggested I seek out new mentors, and I remembered you've been teaching Tualon some new lightsaber forms. Would you mind if I watch as you practice?"

Ansho shook out his bluish-gray head tresses and chuckled. "I think we've practiced enough for one morning, but you're welcome to join us as we change focus. Does your lightsaber need maintenance? I've been telling Tualon that after any big battle, it's always good to take your weapon apart and put it back together so you know exactly what's going on inside. That Geonosian sand can be very irritating. It gets everywhere!"

Iskat smiled and held up her weapon. She'd already done exactly as he prescribed, but if joining them would allow her to feel a little less alone, she would gladly take her lightsaber apart twenty times in a row. Ansho and Tualon moved toward a workbench, and she took her place beside Tualon as Master Ansho unrolled a leather tool kit.

Before Iskat could select a spanner, however, a solemn bell began to toll—the one that announced an issue of grave importance. This bell had rung right before the mission to the Petranaki arena on Geonosis, and it had also called the Jedi to the funeral chamber for the ceremony to honor those lost there. It had tolled often lately, to signal more funerals, but each time, only once. Now it rang continuously.

"What is it, Master?" Tualon asked.

Ansho's head tresses twitched uneasily. "I don't know. Let's go find out."

Iskat followed Tualon, who followed Ansho. The halls were filled with Jedi of all ages, from the tiniest younglings to the most elderly masters. Even Yoda hobbled along with his cane, a line of Initiates behind him, still wearing their huge helmets from practicing with training sabers. When they arrived in the courtyard under the shadow of the Great Tree, Iskat reflexively scanned the crowd for Sember before remembering she wouldn't be there.

So this is loss, she thought. *Always looking for someone who is never there.*

As the murmuring Jedi filled the courtyard, several members of the Jedi High Council watched from the center, their faces somber and their hands clasped. The rest of the Jedi stood in loose clusters: Jedi Masters with their Padawans, gaggles of Initiates and younglings with their instructors, battle-worn Knights who seemed no better informed about why they'd been assembled. Obi-Wan Kenobi was there, along with his Padawan, Anakin Skywalker. They looked well, considering they'd barely escaped execution back on Geonosis.

A few weeks ago, Iskat had seen many of these Jedi fighting for their lives in that first battle, lightsabers glittering as battle droids and Geonosians overran them and their friends fell in droves. Now, they were in crisp, clean robes, their weapons hidden away, and their hands clasped peacefully. Mace Windu stepped forward, and his voice filled every crevice of the round space.

"My fellow Jedi, the Battle of Geonosis marked a great tragedy for the Jedi Order. We sent hundreds of Jedi into the Petranaki arena." Mace's eyes were hard as he looked around the courtyard. "We brought back only twenty-nine."

He paused for a moment, his head bowed, before continuing.

"Many of you were there. Even more of you lost a master, a Padawan, or a friend. We must remind ourselves they are one with the Force. They died as they lived, valiantly and with true dedication." Mace's hands flexed into fists briefly. "We almost captured Count Dooku. But that's a problem for another day."

"A first battle it was for many Padawans, yes. And admirably you all performed." Master Yoda leaned on his walking stick and nodded earnestly. "You must learn from that day. The best teacher, our experience often is."

"Such is the journey of all Jedi," Mace continued. "First you are trained by the Temple as a whole, nurtured in your clans. Then you are selected to study with a master uniquely called to you by the Force. But the next step . . ." He chuckled darkly. "Usually you would undergo your trials and become a Jedi Knight in the proper time. But we are entering a new era. My fellow Jedi, we are at war. The time for pomp and patience has passed. After an emergency meeting of the Jedi High Council, we have decided that we need Jedi Knights more than we need another ritual. We have conferred with those who know you best, and we will now read out the names of the Padawans who will henceforth serve as Jedi Knights."

Iskat turned, still half expecting Sember to be there, but instead she found Tualon.

"No trials?" he asked, his orange eyes wide.

"You've already faced the greatest trial of them all," Ansho said from beside him, one hand on his Padawan's shoulder. "Geonosis was a demanding teacher, and you both performed well."

Iskat was momentarily stunned to hear a master speak so freely; Sember had not been eager with praise. Iskat's master had friends, the Jedi she'd spent time with, but Iskat honestly knew very little about her as an individual. Now that she'd found the lightsaber hidden among Sember's belongings, and had spoken to Jocasta Nu, she was realizing that Sember had indeed had a life outside of her, whereas Iskat's master had basically been her life. No wonder she felt so lost.

"Iskat Akaris," Mace Windu called, and Iskat looked to the dais.

"Me?"

Master Ansho gave her back a gentle push and smiled his encouragement. "Master Windu doesn't make mistakes. Go on up, Jedi Knight."

The crowd edged away to give her room to walk to the center of the courtyard. Most of the Padawans and younglings were clustered together, whispering their surprise. Iskat drew back her shoulders, held her chin up, and did her best to appear strong, confident, and unshakable. She was glad she'd put on fresh robes this morning and brushed out her hair.

Iskat finally stood before Master Windu and the present members of the Council, each of whom gave her a warm smile. She kept her fists in her sleeves so that no one would see them trembling. She'd waited her whole life for the Knighting ceremony, and Sember had suggested it was a holy and personal journey that required constant preparation and humility. And yet here she stood before the assembled Jedi, already selected to make that transition to a wider world. Her hearts thundered with pride, and it took everything she had to keep her face tranquil instead of letting her joy and excitement shine out. She wanted to jump up and down and screech with happiness, but she held fast to her control. Jedi were supposed to be modest.

Iskat was the first new Knight, but she was not the only one. As each name was read out, many of the Padawans Iskat had grown up with—including Onielle, Zeeth, Charlin, and Tualon—joined her to stand in a line through the center of the courtyard. When Anakin Skywalker was called, a little ripple of surprise went through the crowd. Iskat didn't know him terribly well, but she could always feel disquiet radiating from Skywalker whenever she was in his proximity, as if a dark cloud forever floated over his head, threatening rain. Still, she'd seen him fight at Geonosis, and if she was ready for Knighthood, then so was he. He'd more than proven his skills as a Jedi in the arena battle.

Iskat considered each person as they joined the line, understanding why the Jedi Council might find each of them worthy. As Padawans still in the crowd waited for their names to be called and were skipped over, she saw shoulders slump, eyes go wet with sorrow, the tiniest hints that some Jedi still struggled with their emotions, even if briefly. That was when it struck her—why was she here?

Iskat was not considered an outstanding Padawan. She wasn't a natural leader like Tualon, not blessed with an unusually strong affinity for animals like Onielle, not supposedly the Chosen One who would bring balance to the Force, like Anakin. Up until Geonosis, Iskat had been very aware that she had no great strength that made her stand out among her fellow Jedi. She had barely been able to become a Padawan. She knew that humility was an important part of being a Jedi and had long ago accepted that despite her own personal interests, she was more likely to continue Sember's work securing artifacts and researching Jedi knowledge than she was to rise in rank to one day serve on the High Council.

Yet here she was, among the greatest Padawans in the Temple, standing before much of the assembled Jedi Order. Before Geonosis, the courtyard would've been uncomfortably full, but today there was far too much room, far too many empty spots. Iskat longed to see Sember looking back at her from the crowd, would've died to see pride in her master's eyes.

But Sember was gone, and she had never seemed proud of Iskat, and now she never would be.

The hum of a lightsaber pulled Iskat's attention back to the moment. Master Windu had ignited his violet blade. Yoda ignited his green one, and then all the masters held their glowing lightsabers aloft.

"By the right of the Council, by the will of the Force, I dub thee Knights of the Order," Mace said solemnly, his voice echoing.

He moved to stand before Iskat. Her hearts pounded in time. She'd never been this close to Master Windu before, never looked into his fathomless eyes, as hard as stone. She didn't know if she should kneel, or bow, or close her eyes, or if there was something she was supposed to say that Sember had never taught her because she'd never thought this day would come.

But then Mace's lightsaber blade came down with a gentle scritch, and Iskat's Padawan braid fluttered to the ground. Mace inclined his head and stepped to Onielle, cutting her braid as well.

A mad thought entered into Iskat's mind: What if he accidentally chopped off one of Charlin's lekku instead of severing the chain of beads she wore in lieu of a Padawan braid?

She stopped herself before she could snort a laugh.

A lekku was a sensitive body part, nothing like a Padawan braid at all, and it was a strange, sick idea.

What was happening to her?

Iskat had spent so much time controlling her mind and her wandering thoughts that she wasn't sure how such an awful image had slipped in. She had to be more vigilant. She had to remember her mantras.

Iskat had complained to Sember about Charlin once. Just once. Sember had told her that there was no bullying among the Jedi, and that Charlin simply took things quite literally and was very focused on the rules, and that Iskat should give her the benefit of the doubt. "You would do well to emulate Charlin," Sember told her. "She is a well-behaved, talented Padawan with a great future among the Jedi. There is no chaos, there is harmony. Do not cause chaos, Iskat, even if it comes naturally for you."

After that, Iskat didn't change her attitude around Charlin—she simply tried to avoid her. And now they were standing in the same line, becoming Jedi Knights.

When Tualon had been Knighted and Mace had removed the chain he wore among his lekku, the Jedi High Council held their lightsabers aloft.

"You are Jedi Knights," Master Windu boomed. "Responsibility. Peace. Discipline. You are the examples the galaxy looks to. Your successes will carry through the Republic and beyond. As will your mistakes. Your choices will matter, helping the Jedi maintain peace in a time of discord." He paused, lips pursed in thought. "The younglings look up to you. Your choices matter to them. And some of you will receive Padawans of your own. Your choices will matter to them as well."

Iskat scanned the crowd of younglings. Might one of these children be assigned to her? Would she have the chance to nurture a young mind, to provide some future Jedi with the attention and connection she herself had always craved?

That hope died quickly.

It was unlikely the masters would trust her with such a duty, considering her past.

"We are at war," Mace continued. "This is unprecedented within our lifetimes. And you are among the first to reach Knighthood during this time. Remember that war is like a fire across the galaxy. It spreads and it consumes. We must never waver in the face of that fire. We are keepers of the peace. We are Jedi. The Republic needs us more than ever, which means our faith in the Force, our connection to the Force must never waver."

Master Windu looked at Iskat, their eyes locking for just a moment. Iskat felt the strangest quiver in the Force then, as if the great Mace Windu was . . . worried. About more than the war. About something deeper. Something darker. And then, like any ripple, it disappeared.

"It's your time to serve the galaxy and the Republic," he said with finality. "May the Force be with you."

Everyone in the courtyard bowed as Mace joined Yoda and the other Council members. The Padawans—no, Jedi Knights—around Iskat whispered excitedly and congratulated one another as the masters congregated for their own discussion.

An electronic chirp interrupted the excited atmosphere, and a hologram of Chancellor Palpatine appeared in the center of the courtyard. The collected Jedi went silent.

"Master Yoda, Master Windu. We have urgent news that is sure to impact the war effort. Cato Neimoidia has been bombed."

Iskat watched Yoda turn to the rest of the assembly. "Padawans and younglings, this discussion they do not need. To further study they should go." He then turned back to Mace, exchanging a serious glance.

Left out of their machinations, Obi-Wan Kenobi gamely went to gather the younglings. "You there," he said to Iskat, who stood nearest them. "Can I trust you to get these little ones back to their studies with Master Beq in the crèche?"

Iskat looked to either side, certain he wasn't talking to her. "Me?"

His smile was gentle, his eyes twinkling. "You're a Jedi Knight now. It looks like your first duty will be to calm frightened children—quite the challenge indeed." She nodded, and he added, "I'm sorry to hear about your master, by the way. Sember always spoke of your potential with great enthusiasm."

Caught off guard, Iskat nearly spluttered. "My master? Sember Vey?"

He nodded. "She would've been very proud of you today."

Iskat could only nod and murmur her thanks. She couldn't imagine Sember speaking of her potential with great enthusiasm. Outside of collecting artifacts, Sember hadn't done anything with great enthusiasm. And yet Sember must've said something positive to Obi-Wan, because Iskat could tell he wasn't lying.

Obi-Wan gave her a wave and left to rejoin the other masters, leaving her with a collection of younglings looking up at her. "What's your name?" the closest little boy asked her.

"Iskat Akaris."

"Ithkat, when can I be a Jedi Knight, too?" he asked with a lisp, eyes shining as he looked at the cluster of new Jedi Knights standing nervously among the masters.

"When the Force wills it, I suppose," she answered. She still wasn't sure why she'd been chosen, but at least she had a job now. "Come along. Tell me, what were you studying when the bell rang?"

Iskat walked the younglings back to the crèche, and when Master Kelleran Beq was nowhere to be found there, she gave them some pointers on facing the training remotes. The children seemed to be in awe of her, and it was pleasant to be among beings who didn't have preconceived notions about her abilities. She was surprised at how comfortable she felt teaching them and kindly, gently correcting their errors. Once Master Beq returned to finish their lesson, Iskat wandered back to the training room where she'd found Tualon and Ansho earlier, but they were gone. On her way to her own chamber, the hairs in her ears twitched, and she slipped into a side hall as Charlin and Onielle passed by.

"Why her, though?" Charlin whispered.

"Probably because of Geonosis. She saved Zeeth and Master Klefan," Onielle whispered back.

"It still doesn't seem right, killing so many people."

"It wasn't right when they killed so many Jedi," Iskat said, stepping out to face them. The look of embarrassed surprise on both of their faces was a triumph. "And it wasn't right when they were going to execute a senator and two of our Jedi. Or would you prefer to have been among those missing today?"

"I could've held my own," Charlin shot back.

Iskat's lips twitched. "How many Geonosians did you kill?"

Charlin tossed her lekku. "I helped neutralize a cannon, which was our actual mission. I didn't need to kill anyone. I prefer to save people."

"Then I suppose the High Council finds both accomplishments equally valuable, since we're both Jedi Knights now." Iskat gave her an insolent grin and went the other way down the hall.

Perhaps she hadn't been courteous, but she had no master now to disapprove of her behavior. She would never have a Jedi Master again. Iskat was a Jedi Knight, and she was above Charlin's judgment. Maybe there were other privileges that would come with her Knighthood, maybe even ways she could research Feyra and the lightsaber—

"Iskat Akaris?" a voice called, interrupting her train of thought. Iskat turned to find Noxi Kell, the young assistant librarian with an eager smile, standing there. "Master Jocasta would like to speak with you."

/ 9.

ISKAT FOLLOWED NOXI TO THE archives with a growing sense of dread.

"Do you know why I've been summoned?" she asked.

"Master Jocasta will explain things herself. She's like that—very hands on." Noxi smiled encouragingly—she'd always been bright and friendly in contrast to the chief librarian's more austere mien.

The archives were quiet after the unusual excitement of the Knighting. Jocasta Nu was waiting near the door, hands clasped and . . . smiling? At Iskat? Something very strange was happening.

"You wanted to see me, Master Nu?" Iskat said, once again drawing upon her ability to appear calm even when she was uncertain.

"Congratulations on your promotion. I know Sember would've been pleased." Jocasta bowed her head briefly. "Master Klefan recently mentioned that you were looking for guidance, now that your master has become one with the Force."

Iskat struggled to keep the smile on her face. She didn't like where this was going.

"Yes, Master. After the battle on Geonosis, I think I would be a valuable asset in the field, and I've been anxious to do my part for the war effort."

Jocasta's smile faltered, and she cocked her head. "I was given to understand Sember was training you to take her place. We had high hopes that you would join us here in the archives when time allowed and, eventually, return to the task of securing artifacts on behalf of the Jedi Order. Sember did say you were almost ready, the last time we spoke."

While Iskat was grateful to hear that Sember had faith in her, her hearts sank. She felt no calling toward the archives, nor even toward taking up the torch Sember's absence had left behind. Iskat had never felt more alive than she did fighting on Geonosis, and the thought of abandoning that calling, of returning to a life of haggling over a hot cup of Deychin tea to secure dusty old datacrons . . . it felt like her life would become a tunnel with a dead end.

"Master Jocasta, I am grateful that you think me worthy of such a role," she said earnestly. "But I feel that the Force compels me to a different kind of service. After what I saw on Geonosis, I think I would have difficulty . . ."

Not killing, she thought but did not say.

Not fighting was still too harsh.

Doing nothing would sound like an insult.

"Settling in here when I feel called elsewhere," she finished.

Jocasta's brow furrowed, and beside her, Noxi fidgeted nervously.

"It is unusual, for a Jedi to reject an offered role," the elderly librarian said, looking troubled. "Sember seemed certain that this would be your path, and I had already spoken to Master Klefan about the possibility. You are aware that taking this post would still give you the opportunity to serve in the war effort, but that when you were in the Temple, your time would be spent here, doing valuable work for which you've been uniquely trained?"

Iskat couldn't look in Jocasta's eyes. It felt as if she were making a horrible mistake, and yet if she agreed to this post, she knew she would regret it every day of her life. "I think perhaps Master Sember confused her hopes for me with my own preferences and strengths. I am grateful for her faith, and for yours, but the Force does not call me here."

Master Jocasta Nu looked at her for some time as if trying to figure out a puzzle and then shook her head. "We can only do as the Force wills. Know that if you should change your mind, the archives will always be here for you." With a bow of her head, she disappeared into the bowels of the archives, leaving Iskat standing there with Noxi.

"Well, you've succeeded in surprising Jocasta Nu," Noxi said, her smile returning. "I don't think anyone saw that coming."

"I truly regret that I can't accept such a generous appointment," Iskat started, so filled with guilt that she could barely breathe.

Noxi waved a hand, cutting her off. "As Master Nu said, we must all trust in the Force and allow it to guide us. That's the only honest and true way to move forward as Jedi. It's good that you have the confidence to follow your path." She looked around the archives, up at its soaring ceilings. "For me, I've always known my home was the library."

With Jocasta out of the picture and the archives otherwise empty, Iskat realized that she had a new route to solving her mystery. What was done was done; she would live with her choice. Now she was free to pursue her own interests again.

"Noxi, you've been working here a long time, haven't you?"

Noxi nodded eagerly. "Not as long as Jocasta, of course, but I feel as if I've always been here."

"Do you know anything about my species or home planet?"

That caught the human woman by surprise. She seemed to focus on Iskat as if paying close attention to her for the first time, studying her. "No, but xenoanthropology is not my specialty. I'm sure it's somewhere in the archives—everything is, essentially. We just have to find it."

"But have you ever met anyone who looked like me? Was there perhaps another Jedi in the past of my same species? It's just . . . I'm the only one. I'd like to know more about myself."

Before Noxi could answer, Jocasta Nu reappeared as if materializing from the shadows. Her earlier openness had fled, leaving her the same somber librarian Iskat had feared for much of her childhood. "You are not the only Jedi from a species uncommonly seen on Coruscant. I know it must be difficult, wanting answers, but sometimes the answers would only bring more questions. You are a Jedi, Iskat Akaris. A Jedi Knight now. What more do you need to know about yourself?"

The answer only frustrated Iskat more. "I want to know why I have two hearts. I want to know why my senses seem to work differently than other people's. I want to know the name of my planet so that when people ask me where I'm from, I can tell them and not look ignorant."

"Tell them you're a Jedi. That's what's important. Nothing else matters. Attachment is forbidden, and that includes attachment to a name, a people, a place. The Force chose you, Iskat. Your future is more important than your past. Make it count."

Iskat could tell it was a dismissal. For all that Jedi were supposed to focus on peace and serenity, she was fairly certain her refusal of a life in the archives had insulted Jocasta Nu. This place did not seem so welcoming just now. She was unlikely to find the answers she sought, especially if the head librarian was unwilling to help.

"Thank you, Master. I'll do my best to take your advice."

Jocasta inclined her head and glided off to her work, with Noxi following in her wake, and Iskat ground her teeth in frustration.

As she looked around the towering space, at the many shelves holding what was said to be the total of all galactic knowledge, she knew that the information she sought had to be here somewhere. Even Noxi had said so. Iskat knew there were secret parts of the library, but she didn't know where they were or how to get to them. Hoping to escape Jocasta's sharp glare, she delved deeper into the shelves than she ever had before, into parts of the library so old and out-of-date that she had no idea why anyone needed them, willing the Force to guide her to the information she sought, but she felt only emptiness and this strange, annoying sense that something was being kept from her.

What was the point of such a place if anyone could just erase information from a file? Why bother haggling for texts and datatapes if it was impossible to find what she was looking for among them? Her fingers twitched with the urge to rebelliously pull thousands of texts and holobooks down from their shelves. She longed to hear that thunder, to feel the release of all the tension held deep inside her. Something had changed in the hallway back on Geonosis. When she'd opened herself to battle and let the violence flow through her, it was as if all the barriers she'd worked so hard to build had come down, and now they refused to go back up. Without Master Vey to guide her and keep her mind occupied, she was having a harder time controlling her emotions and watching her tongue. She tired of niceties and tenets and control. She was sick of ignoring her curiosity. She wanted to know who Feyra was, and she wanted to know more about the lightsaber now hidden in the drawer of her own wardrobe, and she was beginning to suspect that both mysteries were deeply entwined with her own past.

A name spoken with her master's dying breath, a promise Sember had kept to a presence long gone about helping someone. Considering that Sember had taken her on as a Padawan when they'd had no prior closeness and committed her life to guiding her, that someone had to be Iskat. And a lightsaber specifically crafted to fit a hand the same size as Iskat's, when she was the only one of her kind? The lightsaber had belonged to someone like her.

Could Feyra be . . . Iskat's mother? Or some other relation?

The same species, at least, and once friends with Sember Vey. If so, it was no wonder no one would answer Iskat's questions, no wonder the librarian wouldn't help her in the archives. If Iskat's guess was right, Masters Klefan and Jocasta were withholding information about someone very close to her, someone who shared the same blood. Someone who was no longer in the Jedi Temple. They wouldn't freely offer that information. Attachments were forbidden, after all, and most Jedi had no interest in their home planets.

Then again, most Jedi *knew* their home planets. They had sufficient information on the history and biology of their species and had even met others who looked as they did. Iskat's training had focused on finding her center and understanding her connection with the Force, but sometimes it was as if she didn't even understand who she was as a person, only who she was supposed to become to better serve the Jedi. Deep down, she felt like until she knew these seemingly foundational aspects of herself, she would always be looking for answers. Perhaps it went against the Jedi way, but Iskat's curiosity was dominating her thinking.

She had to find out how she was related to Feyra, and she had to learn why Feyra was no longer among the Jedi. She had to learn how Master Vey had come to possess that lightsaber, and why she had decided to keep it hidden—even though that, too, was against the Code.

Before she lost control of her barely held frustrations, Iskat spotted a door she'd never seen before hidden in a corner and hurried along the shelf. She didn't know if the door would open, or if perhaps it was one of the restricted sections she'd heard about, but she needed an escape, and she needed it now.

/ 10.

THE DOOR PUSHED OPEN EASILY onto a small walled garden. Iskat had never had a real affinity for plants, but there was a pleasant, forgotten, overgrown energy here. Vines looped down from the walls, dripping with bright-purple berries, while spreading trees filled the air with the soft scent of balooma blooms. Raised beds contained carefully labeled rows of flowering plants, and a bench sat invitingly in the plentiful shade beside a burbling fountain. Iskat sat and breathed out, trying to access the center she'd worked so hard to find—and had recently lost.

But meditation didn't work as well as it once had; perhaps Sember's presence and will had contributed to Iskat's apparently artificial calm. She felt every bump on the stone bench and could hear the sound of younglings somewhere nearby, raucous in their play. She stood to inspect the beds of flowers, realizing that several of them had names she vaguely remembered from Sember's assigned readings. There were helpful plants like bota and bachani, but then some of the species had deleterious effects, as well. Iskat was stunned to see Nakkis leaf, coma-bloom, and mosterna innocently flourishing in a Jedi space.

A door in the wall she hadn't noticed opened, and a mouse droid wobbled uneasily into the courtyard, followed by a Selonian she'd never seen before wearing dark goggles and the uniform of a Temple staff technician. He was over two meters tall, with a languid, lanky look to him and a knit cap pulled down over chestnut-brown fur with soft beige stripes. The long sleeves of his tunic were rolled up to his elbows, and a thick, sleek tail with a white tip waved behind his bare feet. Or were they paws?

"Your balance is definitely off, my friend," he said to the mouse droid before looking up in surprise at Iskat. His eyes traveled up and down her tall form, and he jerked his chin at the flower beds. "I wouldn't touch that, if I were you. Mosterna root will make you itch for days."

She withdrew her hand. "I wasn't going to touch the roots."

He chuckled. "Yeah, well, stand around long enough for it to sense your heat signature, and the roots will touch you."

Sure enough, the long, gray-green roots were subtly seeking her hand. She stepped back. "I take your point."

"Wise, but I learned the hard way." He nodded at the little droid. "Am I interrupting you? This courtyard is usually empty. I work better in the open air."

"Not at all." Iskat returned to the bench, and the technician sat cross-legged in the shadiest corner and took off his goggles and hat, shaking out his fur and blinking. Iskat was trying not to stare, but it was hard. She'd never seen a Selonian before.

With a sigh of contentment, he pulled a tool kit from a soft leather bag on his back and unrolled his tools. Iskat watched him turn the mouse droid over, muttering to it softly in a language of clicks and whistles. He looked up at her and smiled with pointy teeth. "Sorry. I talk to droids in Mandaba. Wouldn't want to seem rude, but I'm guessing you're not that interested in balance sensors."

"Droids aren't my forte. But it doesn't bother me. It's an interesting language." She leaned back and stared up at the sky. "Is your homeworld far away?"

"Not far at all. Corellian sector. But I haven't been back since I left."

There was a prickly shift to his fur that suggested she shouldn't continue this line of questioning, for all that she desperately wanted to. She couldn't read his emotions as easily as she could most people's— probably something biological or pheromonal—but his ruffled fur spoke volumes. So she changed tactics.

"I take it you know your way around the Temple . . ." she began.

A shrug as he fiddled with the droid.

"Do you know anything about hidden parts of the library?"

He glanced at her, one whiskered eyebrow up. "In my experience, hidden things are generally hidden for a reason, especially among the Jedi. Why do you ask?"

"In my experience, people looking for hidden things also have their reasons."

He winked, showing sharp teeth, and popped the droid's frame open.

It was odd—Iskat usually felt uncomfortable around new people.

In truth, she felt uncomfortable around *most* people.

Even among a vast panoply of Jedi of all ages and worlds, being the only one of a species no one had ever seen or heard of before was lonely. Her time away with Sember had only served to make her feel more other. But the technician had a calm, gentle energy, and he didn't stare. If anything, his fingers and claws were longer than hers, and he wasn't afraid to use his own language in front of her as he talked to an inanimate object. He wasn't a Padawan who quietly feared her or felt superior to her or a master intent on teaching and passing judgment. He was just a person doing a job that was none of her business, and it was pleasant to share space with someone who had no expectations of her.

There had always been Temple staff around, but it was often as if they were invisible to the Jedi and the Jedi were invisible to them, as if they led parallel lives in the same space. Temple staff had their own hallways, their own doors, their own little world. She didn't want to destroy the peace he'd found in this place, but she didn't want to leave, either.

Iskat turned to lie down on her back on the bench, letting her eyes go unfocused as she stared through the dappled leaves and up at a sky full of space lanes and glittering lights. The technician murmured to his droid, coaxing it like a reticent child, and Iskat focused on her breathing. It was harder than it had been in years, but something about the courtyard and the breezy shade and the drip of the fountain helped her connect with the Force and find that cool, blue place of peace. Her eyes fluttered closed, and for a while she slipped in and out of sleep, her amulet clutched in one hand.

When she woke, the technician and his droid were gone. The only evidence that he had been there at all were a few bits of snipped wire gleaming dully on the stone. Iskat felt an odd sense of tranquillity, as if she had gone without sleep for days and had finally found true rest.

The next morning, she reported to Outfitting with her fellow recently promoted Jedi Knights. There was a solemnity about them now, as if the responsibility of their newfound status weighed heavily; Iskat was grateful that her fellows were too busy worrying about their own new rank to whisper about her. She was given several new sets of robes, some nicer boots, a utility belt, a comlink, and even some credit chips. She enjoyed the clanking reality of the metal in her fingertips and wondered where they planned to send her, that she might need the food capsules, tools, and breather stored in the belt.

Back in her chamber, she changed into her new robes, noting the finer, softer weave of the thick fabric, the crisp folds. Everything about her promotion felt so . . . significant. Heavy, weighty, serious. And yet . . . oddly rushed? Knighthood usually involved meditating, fasting, specific tests meant to delve fully into the Jedi's hearts, mind, and connection to the Force. Instead, it felt like they were simply large children who'd fumbled through a poorly planned battle, lived thanks to their masters, and had their braids sheared off, throwing them into a new life with little preparation. Unlike many of the other newly promoted Jedi Knights, Iskat still hadn't found anyone to step in as her mentor, and no one had offered. On the one hand, she felt forgotten, but on the other she was enjoying her newfound freedom.

If she was truly honest with herself, she felt like she still needed a Jedi Master. So far, she'd made one huge decision, and she still wasn't certain that it was the right one. She was confident in her skills but not necessarily in her ability to select a path and take her first steps toward what felt like her destiny. Perhaps if she'd accepted Jocasta's offer, she would've found comfort in having someone to guide her, but that would've felt like making the easy choice instead of the right one. At least now she was free to pursue her own interests, in regard to training.

New boots creaking, she returned to the bench in the little courtyard. The plants glistened with water; someone had been here, caring for them. Iskat wondered who it was, whether it was a Jedi or one of the Temple staff. She was curious what would happen, now that she was a Jedi Knight and had turned down a place with Jocasta Nu, whether she would be assigned a different job here at the Temple, or if the High Council understood she was ready to be sent on missions. Could they still command her to work in the archives—was that their plan for her all along?

No. Surely not. The Jedi had told her to trust in the Force, and the Force was leading her down a different path.

As she mulled over the battle at Petranaki arena, Iskat felt as if perhaps she'd finally found her true talent—and it wasn't haggling with shopkeepers over statues or replacing holobooks on shelves. When the Geonosians had attacked, she hadn't hesitated or run, like the other Padawans. She'd thrown herself into the fight and hadn't taken a single wound. Her body had moved like a finely tuned instrument, working on instinct and in perfect harmony with the Force. That feeling of flow, of rightness, as she'd slashed her way through the enemy . . . was that how the other Padawans felt when they did what they loved, what they excelled at? Had Iskat had a natural gift all this time and simply never known because she'd never had to use it?

The side door opened, breaking her train of thought. It was the Selonian droid technician again, but she didn't mind the interruption. He nodded to her with a toothy grin and sat down in the shade, gesturing at a round-bellied LEP droid that had followed him in to stop and hold still. It beeped softly, its earlike antennas going down as if dreading what was to come. After a few moments of silent tinkering, he glanced up.

"New robes?"

"I'm a Jedi Knight now."

A nod. "Congratulations! Big promotion."

"So they say."

He cocked his head. "I understand most of your folk are excited about such things."

Iskat adjusted her collar, which rubbed at the back of her neck. "I should be excited, but so much has changed so quickly that I'm still finding my bearings. My master is dead, and I just feel . . . lost."

"From what I'm hearing, that battle on Geonosis did some damage. The Temple does feel a bit empty." He looked around the courtyard and lowered his voice. "I hear we're at war."

"That's what they say. Now I'm just waiting to learn where they'll send me. Or maybe I'll be assigned a Padawan to train. Or stuck here, in the archives, where they want me to be. That's part of the problem. We don't know anything, and I've been told I need to be patient. But I need a job, a focus. I feel like I'm the only one here who doesn't know what to do."

With a sigh, the Selonian stood and cracked his back. "Where I come from, it's all about family. Protect the den, protect the queen. Everyone puts the community first." He took off his hat and shook out his fur. "I'm the odd one. I believe in individual freedom, in curiosity, in exploring the galaxy. So here I am. Haven't seen a fellow Selonian in decades. I didn't know what to do at first, either. Then I decided to follow my heart."

"I feel different, too." Iskat looked down, rolled a fallen berry around on the bench with one long finger. "No one even knows what my species is. Some of the other Padawans—and now Jedi Knights—are scared of me." It felt a little exciting, a little forbidden to say it out loud. "I've spent all my life trying to understand the Force and grow as a Jedi so that I could reach Knighthood, and now that I'm here, I feel more different than ever. I don't know what my hearts say."

"Maybe you've never listened. If you've been trying so hard to be what you're not, maybe you've never asked yourself what your heart wants."

"I have two hearts, actually."

A chuckle. "So that's twice the desire, then."

"And I think . . ." She wasn't sure how much to tell this stranger. She felt a certain freedom with him as a non-Jedi, but she was still a Jedi herself, and she'd been taught not to speak of certain truths. "There are so many things I want to know, so many answers that I can't find anywhere. That's why I asked you about other parts of the library, the last time I was here. I know the staff have alternative routes throughout the Temple. There's a certain person I'm trying to learn more about. I thought maybe something happened to her that they wanted to hide." She stood, long fingers curling into fists. "But no one will tell me the truth."

The Selonian's whiskers twitched. "I don't know about records in the library, but there are hidden parts of the Temple," he said quietly. "All I know is that they have something to do with . . ." His eyes met hers, bright black like beetles in the sun.

"The dark side."

/ 11.

THE DARK SIDE.

Those words were rarely spoken in the Temple, and when they were uttered, it was quietly and solemnly by Jedi Masters warning their charges of the most dangerous thing they might ever face. Iskat had last heard the term when Sember had urged her to ignore the call of the Sith text they'd retrieved on their final mission.

"My master mentioned such a place to me once—a place where dark side objects were kept for safekeeping. Do you know where it might be?"

The Selonian raised a shoulder in a shrug as he refocused on the LEP droid. "Not my business to know. I've just heard the cleaning staff talk, is all."

A shiver rippled over Iskat's skin, raising the tiny hairs on her arms.

She looked up at the Tranquillity Spire soaring over the Temple. "There's so much they don't tell us," she said softly, thinking about her experience on Geonosis, on what it felt like when the killing took over. "We spend so much time studying and meditating and keeping our bodies fit, but when we ask questions, we get quotes and platitudes instead of honesty."

"That's what the people in charge always do. If you knew too much, you might . . ."

He trailed off.

"Might what?"

A grunt as he dug around in the droid. "Let's just say that in my experience, if somebody doesn't want you to know something, it benefits them more than it benefits you."

"I just wonder if I might have . . . untapped potential. If I've been told to ignore aspects of myself that I might've nurtured instead."

"It's never too late to learn and grow. The time will pass either way."

Iskat smiled. She'd never thought about it like that before, but it was comforting. On Geonosis, she'd learned something new about herself, and now she could explore it.

Especially since Sember was no longer here to call her to task.

No.

That was a tempting, but forbidden, line of thought.

Her duty was to deepen her center of control in the Force.

She refocused on the moment. Sember was gone, but Iskat felt a connection with this droid technician. She felt more open with him than anyone she'd ever known—than with any of the Jedi. He listened without judgment, without apprehension, without rushing to remind her of tenets she'd long ago memorized. And he spoke honestly of his own feelings, which was not something she'd experienced among the Jedi, who were not encouraged to explore their inner passions and fears.

"Can I ask your name?"

The Selonian looked up with a grin. "Heezo."

"And I'm Iskat. Nice to meet you."

Heezo twirled his spanner and hummed. "Iskat. I think I've heard them talk about you."

Her head hung, just a little. "I'm sure they talk about me a lot. I've got quite a reputation."

"It wasn't bad, what I heard. If only I could remember. My memory isn't what it once was. I'm not as young as I look." He tapped the grayish streaks near his small ears.

"Well—"

The new comlink on her belt beeped. "Iskat Akaris, report to the Jellani Garden," a crisp voice said.

Iskat broke out in a hopeful grin.

"Is that good?" Heezo asked. "When I'm told to report to someone, it's usually because I'm in trouble, but you seem pleased."

"I was just issued my comlink, and this is my first summons. I keep waiting for something to happen, and maybe it finally has." She stood and smoothed out the sleeves on her robe. *At least they didn't call me to the archives,* she thought.

Heezo squinted up at the endless lines of ships slicing across the sky. "Probably shouldn't be telling you this, but you're not the only person summoned to Jellani Garden today. Haven't you noticed all the shuttles taking off? There's something brewing."

That was promising. Iskat had definitely noticed the shuttles, but considering the traffic on Coruscant, she hadn't found their presence unusual.

"If you use the other door, you can save some time. It leads into a hallway near Outfitting," Heezo told her. "I don't think there are any rules about Jedi using the staff halls, and you seem awfully eager."

Iskat changed direction, glad for the chance to avoid Jocasta's stern stare in the library. She stopped at the door out of the garden, the one Heezo tended to use.

"Thank you," she told him.

He looked up, surprised. "For what?"

"For letting me talk and listening without judging. I don't get to do that very often."

"Wasn't your master there for you? I know how it is, among the Jedi."

Iskat reflexively reached for her amulet. "She did her best to help me, but I don't think she liked me very much. She certainly didn't understand me."

"Everyone deserves to be understood," Heezo said. "Especially if they feel different."

"Again, not something said very often in the Jedi Temple, so thank you."

With a nod of appreciation, she pushed out the door and found herself in a narrow, unadorned hallway. The passage led to a door that emerged near Outfitting, and Iskat took the lift to the Temple rooftop where the various meditation gardens unfurled underneath the soaring spires. She'd thought such a summons might come from one of the Jedi councils, but now she had no idea who had called her and why. Since things rarely changed in the Temple, Iskat's curiosity only grew at this new development.

At the entrance of the garden, she slowed and tucked her hair back, arranging her sleeves and making sure her shoulders were down. She wanted to convey the confidence of a Jedi Knight, calm and composed and centered, even if she was excited and a little worried on the inside . . . and even if she still, if she was honest, felt like a Padawan.

Jellani Garden was a verdant space boasting blooms from all over the galaxy, and the fragrance of the flowers washed over Iskat as pink blossoms rained down in the breeze. Yoda and the Tholothian Master Adi Gallia sat on two stone benches, a crate between them. A Jedi Knight named Josk Nivar stood before them, watching Iskat approach with a carefully bland smile.

"Iskat Akaris," Yoda said. "One more we await."

Iskat nodded to both masters, with a smaller nod of recognition for Josk. She knew of his reputation but had never studied with him. He was a light-skinned, light-haired human man who was generally well liked and who had spent the last several years on a diplomatic mission to Chandrila. Iskat was briefly surprised to see him without his energetic young Sullustan Padawan until she remembered that the poor girl had been among those lost at Geonosis.

When Tualon hurried into the garden, Iskat's hearts fluttered, and her curiosity about the meeting deepened. Yoda gestured the three Jedi Knights forward, and Iskat took her place between Josk and Tualon, noting that Tualon seemed to stand a little taller, now that he was a Jedi Knight. And he was tall to begin with.

"Begun in earnest the war has," Yoda began, sounding tired, even for someone hundreds of years old. "But even with new duties, the Jedi must protect the Republic. Master Gallia?"

Adi Gallia lifted three datapads from the crate and held them out.

"We need you on Thule. We've received word from Republic Intelligence that the Separatist Army is finalizing construction on a new factory to build more battle droids. It is imperative that the factory be shut down immediately, before it can begin production. You'll be supported by a company of clone troopers. Your goal will be to get past any defenses protecting the factory and ensure they can't make any weapons."

The three Jedi Knights each took one of the datapads, and Iskat began scanning through hers.

Josk's hand shot up, and Gallia inclined her head. Iskat found his need to raise a hand ridiculous.

"Master, why doesn't the Republic just bomb it from the air?"

"It's heavily armored. And we can't get into the habit of destroying planets," Gallia said firmly. "We also need the factory intact because we have reason to believe that if we can slice into their system, we'll have intel on other such factories, including their locations and production schedules. We have to be subtle here, which is why you'll be on your own. We can't have any signals traced back to Coruscant."

Tualon's hand went up next.

"Master, why are we worried about a factory on Thule when the Separatists are strip-mining Praadost II and decimating the population? The air there is unbreathable now. According to—"

Master Gallia waved a hand. "The Jedi High Council is working closely with the Senate and the Supreme Chancellor to plan the strategies that will do the most to stop the Separatists once and for all. The Jedi are called to serve, and this is how we need you to serve."

Iskat's nose wrinkled up in the way Master Sember had tried and apparently failed to excise from her expressions. Although Iskat didn't keep up with the holonet like Tualon did, he made an excellent point. Stopping droids from making droids didn't seem as important as stopping strip-mining from destroying a planet's ecosystem, breathable air, and population.

"Know the Supreme Chancellor's mind you do not," Yoda reminded him. "But an important part to play, you have."

"These datapads include maps, schematics, and the various tactical strategies recommended by our leaders. Josk will be in charge, with

Iskat and Tualon serving under him. You've been assigned a company of clone troopers with whom you will be working closely for the forseeable future, so it's a good idea to get to know them and how they work. Captain CT-1123 got his company in and out of Geonosis with no loss of life. You can count on him and his troops.

"Time is against us. Leave immediately you must." Yoda sighed heavily, as if he'd given this same speech too many times today. "May the Force be with you."

Iskat looked to Josk and Tualon. Josk seemed determined, but Tualon looked as lost as she felt. This would be his first mission without Master Ansho, and although the Twi'lek was usually self-assured, Iskat wondered if perhaps part of his confidence came from always having a talented and supportive mentor by his side. Up until Geonosis, they'd both been closely watched Padawans, and today they were being sent to a faraway planet to lead an army.

That was when it truly sank in: the scope of the war that now controlled their lives. That was when she truly understood how much damage the Jedi Order had taken at the arena.

How many lives had been lost.

There were barely any masters left.

There were Padawans without masters, younglings without teachers, empty seats on every council. And instead of focusing on the next generation, the High Council was forced to send children out to war.

Now the Jedi Knights had to step up and shoulder a weight they weren't prepared to bear.

All the freedom Iskat had felt after the Knighting ceremony dissolved into foreboding.

She'd wanted a job, and now she had one.

And she wasn't sure she was capable of performing it.

Just because someone said she had a new rank didn't mean she deserved it or would be able to live up to it.

Without a battle-hardened master in charge, with the young and unproven Josk Nivar calling the shots, Iskat worried that they were sending her out to die.

She briefly thought of taking Jocasta Nu up on her offer to stay in the archives, but . . . well, then she'd be a coward, the kind of person who neglected their duty out of fear. She'd wanted this—she'd wanted a mission. And now she had one, and she would prove herself, no matter what. Her determination solidified, the Force flowing through her as she committed herself completely to this new reality.

"Let's go, then," Josk said, gesturing at the garden gate before walking through it first.

Josk was trying a little too hard to appear competent and upbeat, but Iskat could feel the apprehension radiating off him, and it didn't inspire her trust. His last Padawan had died, and even if that wasn't his fault, it didn't mean Iskat was ready to put her life in his hands.

But she had no choice. Even if Master Vey had been alive, Iskat was a Jedi Knight now and beyond a master's protection. She existed to do the bidding of the High Council and serve the galaxy. They had decided that she was to follow the orders of Josk Nivar, and so that was what she had to do. Tualon politely let her go first, and Iskat followed Josk out of the garden and into the hall to the lift, where he walked with an annoyingly slow sort of swagger. He was showing off to hide his trepidation, Iskat realized.

"We need to hurry to the landing pad," he said a little too loudly. "I wouldn't want our team to disappoint the Council."

She looked at Tualon. She'd always had trouble reading him; his emotional control had become a battlement. It was one of the things she liked about him—he was mysterious, plus she'd never picked up on any apprehension toward her. She often wondered what would've happened if the other Jedi had been able to read her mind, especially Master Vey. Would they have questioned whether she should be a Jedi at all? There were so many parts of herself that she'd carefully tamped down, so many forbidden feelings that were not in keeping with the Jedi tenets. She wanted so badly to be a good Jedi and longed to live this life with more natural ease. Sember had assured her that with time, Iskat would master these feelings or they would diminish. Iskat had believed her and doubled down on her studies and meditations.

And yet the emotions had not lessened.

If anything, they had only grown in scope, especially recently.

As she passed the hallway that led back to the courtyard where she'd recently talked to Heezo, Iskat thought about what he'd told her—that there were hidden places in the Jedi Temple. Were those spaces shielded somehow so that the objects within couldn't send out their siren call, as the Sith text had? Why weren't such things outright destroyed? The Sith text remained in her mind, no matter how badly she wanted to forget it. She could still recall the feel of the strange energy around it, its plaintive song, and she wondered just how close it really was.

"Are you ready?" Tualon asked her, voice low, breaking the flow of her thoughts.

She always composed herself so carefully when she spoke to him, always tried so hard not to say anything offensive or strange that might urge him to keep his distance. She had to try even harder now. He was not the sort of person who would give in to questions about the dark side, of that much she was certain.

"Part of being a Jedi is serving even if you're not ready," she said evenly. "Learning by doing and trusting in the Force. The Council needs us, and it's our job to rise to the occasion."

Tualon grinned, teeth gleaming against his black skin. "Our job is to rise to the occasion. I like that. I didn't feel ready when we were in the shuttle to Geonosis, but then, once we were there, it felt like our training clicked into place, don't you think?"

Iskat's lips quirked as she thought about fighting the Geonosians, almost dancing with her lightsaber. "It's good to know that our masters taught us well."

Tualon stopped a moment, frowning. "Oh, no. I didn't tell Ansho goodbye."

Iskat didn't get to tell Sember goodbye, either. There was always an emptiness in her chest now, as if she'd lost something she hadn't really known she'd possessed.

"I'm sure Master Yoda will tell him," Iskat assured him. "Master Ansho knows what it's like to be sent on a mission, I'm sure."

"Of course." Tualon chuckled sadly. "Of course he knows. Still, it feels strange, not saying goodbye."

"Get used to it," Josk said from just ahead. "You're not a Padawan anymore, Tualon. You can't go running to your old master every time you have a runny nose."

Iskat felt it then—a little flare of anger from Tualon. It made her like him all the more. Perhaps she wasn't the only one who had trouble keeping anger in check, now that the stakes were real.

Josk led them out toward the landing pad, where Iskat was surprised to see multiple gunships waiting in neat rows. A clone with a geometric design that resembled a spider on his red-finned helmet waited for them, his posture stiff and his air alert and testing.

"Captain CT-1123?" Josk said, and it wasn't really a question.

"General Nivar," the clone responded with a nod of respect. "You can call me Captain Spider. Are you ready to depart?"

Josk's chin rose a little higher as he clasped his hands in the sleeves of his robe.

"Take us to Thule. Let's shut down this little droid factory."

12

THE NU-CLASS ATTACK SHUTTLE BARRELED through hyperspace toward Thule. Iskat fought a cascade of worry as she sat at a table with Tualon, surrounded by eerily silent clones in identical armor. But this time, there was no Master Vey calling her to task, no Master Klefan watching her with deceptively sleepy eyes as they arced toward the Petranaki arena. It was just Josk, two newly minted Jedi Knights, and a company of troopers armed to the teeth and ready to support their Jedi leaders in a war.

Tualon was zipping through his datapad for the hundredth time, so Iskat pulled out her own tablet and went over what little direction they'd been given. Thule wasn't a planet she'd ever heard of before, and there wasn't much information on it available. Thurra system, Esstran sector, Outer Rim. No listing of nearby planets or known hyperspace routes. It had a Type I atmosphere and normal gravity, but the landscape was listed only as arid, the geography as mountainous. There was no history described and nothing about its inhabitants, if it even had any. They had far more information on the factory, which was being built in a canyon and extended deep underground.

The plan was to set up a hidden base in the canyon, infiltrate the factory to gain Separatist intel on where other factories were to be built, and then render the factory unusable by sabotaging the nearby power grid's control system.

Iskat was surprised that they'd been entrusted with such an important task. She'd seen multiple Jedi Masters and Jedi Knights looking serious and heading off in different directions with datapads over the past few weeks, and as Heezo had mentioned, trooper shuttles coming and going had become an hourly occurrence. She hadn't heard anyone talking about their assignments, but then again, her datapad had informed her that this was a top-secret mission, so maybe everyone had received that same admonition. With many of the masters lost in the Battle of Geonosis, the Council had to be desperate to send three unseasoned Jedi Knights so far away to do something so important without an experienced leader.

Tualon looked up from his datapad to Josk. "Well, General, we have the mission brief, but is there anything else we need to know?"

Josk finished typing something and looked up. "Judging by the maps, we're going to want to land far away from the factory and hike in. The intel suggests it's controlled entirely by droids, but we don't want to be seen by any scouts. Everything depends on surprise. Captain Spider, anything to add?"

Captain Spider sat on a crate nearby, helmet at his feet. This was Iskat's first time seeing a clone's face, and there was a stern, serious, competent look about him. His hair was slightly longer on top, shaved beneath, a dark brown that matched his eyes. "My troops will offer some protection, but it's up to you three to sneak in and do the dirty work. I have twenty-seven in my company. We've seen multiple battles thus far and shut down a smelting operation recently. You can count on us to back you up."

Josk looked to Tualon. "They tell me you're our best slicer. Can you get inside the factory and tap into their system?"

Tualon nodded. "That shouldn't be a problem. I brought my kit."

"Good. We'll send some clones along to provide cover. Iskat, you'll be with me. We'll be in place at the power grid, and once Tualon is clear of the factory, we'll overload the control circuits to shut down the entire system. The ship picks us up at the rendezvous point, and we disappear into hyperspace. If everything goes according to plan, I don't expect any issues."

Captain Spider snorted. "General, if you don't mind my saying so, there are always issues."

Iskat's fingers curled nervously around her seat. She hadn't realized it until Captain Spider said it, but if anything went wrong, Josk would be calling the shots. She definitely wasn't comfortable knowing that his decisions would determine if she lived through her first mission without an experienced master at the helm.

Then again, the experienced masters had planned the Geonosis rescue, and look how that had turned out.

Iskat read through her datapad again and again until they dropped out of hyperspace and a planet appeared, hanging against the black like a swirled gray marble. A little tremor of excitement skittered up her back, as it always did when she saw a place for the first time. Thule was where everything would change for her, she decided—a new beginning. She was part of a mission, a Jedi Knight, a general, and even if Josk was slightly senior, there were no masters here to watch and judge her. She would only be judged by the success of their mission, and Iskat intended to succeed. Perhaps she hadn't been an ideal Initiate or Padawan, and maybe she would've been a terrible librarian, but she could still be a commendable Jedi Knight.

Josk and Captain Spider conferred with the pilot and navigator to confirm the best approach, and soon they exploded through thick, smoky clouds into a sky of burning orange. Iskat couldn't see much of the planet below through the viewport, but everything seemed to be in shadowy shades of gray with blackened spires that reminded her all too much of the towers on Geonosis. The ship landed in a canyon so deep and wide it defied comprehension, and Iskat stood and accepted the pack one of Spider's men handed her. It was heavy, and around her, each of the clones was outfitted with something similar. She followed Josk and Tualon out onto the gravel-strewn ground as the troopers outfitted two speeder bikes with the cargo crates they'd been using as seats.

Thule was like nothing Iskat had ever seen, a dark and barren place of jagged stone with a sky headed from a fiery sunset to what seemed almost a perpetual twilight, dotted with swooping black bats, or perhaps they were birds. As she looked up past the high canyon walls to the stars overhead, a brilliant bolt of lightning lit the sky, starting pink and ending light green. Other than a strange, glowing moss, there were no plants that she could see, no cheerful cities or fluffy beasts peacefully grazing. There was nothing to graze upon. The planet seemed, to the naked eye, entirely dead.

And yet . . . there was something about it.

Something beautiful and strange in the starkness.

The moment her boots landed on the ground, she felt an instant connection to it, an affinity for Thule. This planet wasn't pastoral or welcoming, and yet she found it utterly bewitching.

It was rough, sharp, shadowy, unapologetic in its desolation. It seemed to quietly exude a certain power, a certain dignity. Iskat didn't know which planet she had come from, but she felt a certain comfort here and wondered if her homeworld was perhaps quite similar. It was almost as if there were a gentle, purring hum just outside her hearing. She knelt and put a palm to the ground as if stroking a sleeping beast. There was nothing living nearby, and yet it felt . . . alive.

"This place is grim," Josk said. "Perfect place for the Separatists to get cozy, actually."

"I can't believe we don't have more information on this system or sector." Tualon swiped through his datapad. "I wish we'd known more about the planet before we arrived. Inhabitants? Natural predators? Dangerous plants?"

"Maybe there are no predators. The Separatists likely chose it because there was nothing and no one here." Iskat spoke softly, respectfully. To shout here, at night, in the midst of the stark, black canyon . . . somehow seemed like a bad idea.

"Keep your weapons ready," Josk said, one hand brushing his lightsaber hilt. "We don't know what we might encounter."

With one of the clones taking the lead to navigate, they set out through the canyon, headed toward the factory. Iskat had visited many planets, from Ilum, where she found her kyber crystal, to the various stops for Sember's artifact acquisition, to Geonosis. In the past years, she'd seen beautiful waterworlds, verdant jungle moons, even planets that represented every biome imaginable, and yet she found she preferred this challenging, unfriendly environment. She wasn't worried about the Separatists and the droids programmed to kill her on sight; she wanted more time to explore this place and uncover its secrets.

As they marched, Iskat wrapped her fingers around her amulet and sought her center. Even on the ship, she had kept up with her meditations, ever hopeful that she would find the tranquillity Sember had urged her to cultivate. It was so easy this time, dropping into the cool, blue flow of the Force, and she felt buoyed and supported and strengthened. She wasn't sure why, but it seemed easier for her to connect with the Force here. Maybe there was something about being somewhere new, on her own with a mission instead of in the Temple under constant scrutiny. Or maybe something really had changed in her when she'd become a Jedi Knight. She felt different, freer and more naturally relaxed, and it was a welcome distinction.

After several hours of hiking along the bottom of the canyon, Captain Spider stopped and pointed at a wide opening in the stone wall, the shadows within blacker than black. "This cavern would be an ideal place to set up camp, General. The overhang will keep us hidden from any scouts, and the factory is about two klicks away. There's enough room for everything inside."

"Excellent," Josk said with a nod. "Tualon, Iskat—let's make sure it's safe first. Lightsabers at the ready."

He ignited his blue lightsaber and stalked toward the cave, but Tualon gave Iskat a pointed look and took off his heavy rucksack first. She followed suit, grateful for the lightness in her shoulders.

Three glowing blades blazed in the lightless cavern. Nothing moved, and as Iskat threw out her senses in the Force, she found only a distinct lack of the life she would've expected. Not even the tiniest of mammals scurried along the ground or rustled in the corners of the ceiling. The moss seemed to only coat the rocks outside, as they were barren within. A flash of movement and the softest crunching sound alerted her to big, bumpy slugs clinging to the walls, blending in perfectly against the charcoal-black stone as they ever-so-gently chewed the walls into sand that feathered down to the ground. They barely made any impression in the Force at all.

The cavern was large and seemed perfectly constructed for their needs. The ground was flat and devoid of debris, the walls solid dark gray stone. A single opening in the back of the rock wall, a deep and velvety void, drew Iskat's eye; it was clearly not a natural structure.

"What's that?" she asked, walking cautiously toward it.

She put a hand to the stone, stunned to find a narrow hallway with perfectly straight sides and a ceiling that met at a point, almost like some of the halls in the Jedi Temple.

"I'll go first," Josk said, turning sideways to squeeze past her.

Iskat followed him, but far enough back that she wouldn't be in danger if he spun around with his lightsaber. It was a tight fit for him, but Iskat moved more freely. Tualon was behind her, and she realized with a little gasp that they hadn't really thought this out.

"Perhaps all three of us shouldn't be in the tunnel?" she said, less firmly than she would've preferred. "If it should collapse—"

"It won't," Josk said, not slowing down. "It's solid stone. But you and Tualon can turn around if you're worried."

In that moment Iskat committed to following him to the center of the planet, if necessary, just so he wouldn't mistake her concern for cowardice again. She didn't particularly enjoy being in a narrow space underground, trapped between two lightsabers, but then again she was confident she could face anything other than a cave-in. And she didn't sense anything sinister in the area. This place—it seemed almost welcoming.

Finally the hallway opened up into a wider space, and Iskat stepped within and to the side to make room for Tualon. The chamber was perhaps five meters square with a high, domed ceiling. Every line was immaculate, with no visible masonry marks.

"What's this?" Josk said.

Iskat stepped over to the far wall, where Josk held out his lightsaber. There was a sculpture—no. A crystal, carefully set on a base carved from the rock itself. As Iskat gazed into the violet depths, she couldn't help reaching out a hand to touch it.

"Stop!" Josk barked.

She stepped back and withdrew her hand, barely hiding a snarl.

"We don't know what it is, Iskat."

"It's an altar," she said. "This temple must've been made by the planet's original inhabitants. I suppose it must've been nice here, once, with forests and creatures. I wish we knew more about it."

She knelt down to inspect the altar's base and caught herself before she could gasp and betray her discovery. The repeating motif carved into the ebony stone was something she'd seen only once before— a circle surrounded by four flames.

She recognized it from the Sith text Sember had asked her to inspect, which meant . . .

This, too, must be a Sith artifact.

"See anything interesting?" Josk asked from over in the corner, where he was looking for more evidence of past use or present dangers.

Slowly, fingers shaking, she reached out to touch the carved symbol.

"Nothing."

13

ISKAT WASN'T EXACTLY SURE WHY she'd lied to Josk. Maybe it was because the cavern was perfect for their needs and she didn't want him to decide that it wasn't suitable and send them on another long hike into enemy territory. Or maybe it was because she didn't want him to focus less on the mission and more on the presence of what might be a dark side artifact. Sember had told Iskat that it was a Jedi's duty to return Sith antiquities to the High Council so that such dangerous objects could be contained somewhere safe instead of falling into the wrong hands. The thought of Josk and the clones hacking the beautiful and ancient altar out of the living rock made Iskat feel . . . conflicted.

But if she was truly honest with herself, the main reason she'd lied was because she was curious, and she was fairly certain she was the only one who was.

She definitely wasn't sure why she'd touched it. It was almost as if her fingers had reached out before her brain could catch up. Did she imagine the stone had wanted—maybe even demanded—to be touched?

She'd read the many warnings against the dark side back in the Jedi Temple, and Master Vey had warned her that giving in to emotion and ignoring the Jedi tenets might lead her down that much-maligned path. Iskat knew that hate led to the dark side. She knew that even great Jedi had fallen to the dark side, and that she wasn't supposed to touch Sith artifacts, and that the dark side was cloying and seductive.

And yet something about the dark side felt like a tale told to scare children, like something that happened to other people long ago. She wouldn't be so foolish as to fall for it herself, but perhaps it was better to know more than less, to be fully informed regarding such dangers. Here, on Thule, after years of identifying ancient Force objects with her master, Iskat was filled with questions and had no one to answer them. If only there were some way to find out more about who had carved the altar from the rock and why the crystal was important.

"We'll camp here," Josk said, his voice grating on Iskat's nerves.

"Not in this chamber, though?" Tualon checked.

"Of course not. In the big room." Josk looked around, frowning. "Wouldn't want to get cornered back here if something attacked."

He returned to the hallway, and Tualon followed him as they headed back toward the cave entrance where Captain Spider and the rest of the clones were waiting. Iskat, still by the altar, put a hand on the crystal. It was warm and flared with light at her touch, a low, brief glow like a greeting from an old friend. Fearing one of the other Jedi would return and notice, she pulled her hand away and hurried down the hallway in their wake.

The clone troopers were eager to set up camp in the larger cavern. As soon as Josk gave Captain Spider the word, they began unpacking crates from their speeders. One side of the cavern was for bedrolls, the other for supplies and rations, with a string of lanterns placed around the perimeter for light. As they took off their helmets, she tried not to stare at the repeated faces with only the slightest variations in hair configuration. A clone handed Iskat a meal kit, and she thanked him and watched the others to see how to eat it.

All around her, the troopers and Jedi dug into their self-heating meal packets. She considered how many rations it took for one meal, looked at the crates, and wondered where all these supplies had come from. The clones, their uniforms and weapons, the ships, the food and water.

Who was supplying the credits? How had they obtained the supplies so quickly and in such gargantuan amounts? She was beginning to see that this war was more than just Jedi being sent out on missions; it was an enormous undertaking requiring planning, money, and vast amounts of intel. She was struck by how quickly the Jedi had pivoted from peace-keeping to a war machine.

When it was time to sleep, Iskat had reason to miss her spare chamber and simple bunk in the Temple. For all that the floor looked flat, she felt every bump. The clones were laid out in neat rows, and it seemed they all knew exactly how to fall asleep the moment their heads hit their small, flat pillows. On one side of her, Josk snored and spluttered and murmured in his sleep. On her other side, Tualon was doing the same thing she was—pretending to sleep while actually being on high alert. She was desperately aware of him. For all that it had been drilled into her that romance was forbidden among the Jedi, she had never been able to dull her admiration for him, never learned how to stop her hearts from fluttering when he was nearby.

But they weren't in the Temple now—they were on an uninhabited planet, and they were Jedi Knights, and there was no harm in talking.

Iskat rolled over to face his back. "Tualon?"

He rolled over to face her, half a meter between them. His skin was so dark she could only see the glimmer of his orange eyes and white teeth. "Did you need something?"

"No. Just having trouble getting to sleep."

A sigh of relief, like he was glad he wasn't the only one. "It's been a surprising day. We woke up in our chambers, just like any other day of our lives, and now we're fighting a war. Master Ansho told me his first mission as a Jedi Knight was to take a group of Padawans foraging on Naboo, and even then, there was a master along, just in case."

"It was different, when all the masters were still with us. There are so few left."

"I'm sorry about Sember, by the way." Tualon reached out like he was going to touch her arm, then pulled back. "It's one thing going to funerals for elders you never knew, but to lose your closest friend . . ." He trailed off.

Something about the darkness, the privacy, the fact that they were probably the only sentient beings awake on the entire planet, made her bold. "Sember wasn't really my friend," she said softly. "My master . . . she never really liked me. She wasn't affable like Ansho. I sometimes wonder why she even selected me as her Padawan. If it was only because she took pity on me when no one else stepped forward."

"Surely you don't believe that," he said, genuinely surprised. "Masters only take on Padawans if they feel a genuine call in the Force, a real connection. I heard her once tell Master Ansho that you were coming along well. Some masters are sterner than others. I guess they hope it will serve their Padawans better than coddling."

Her hand went to her amulet; it felt cold now. "There was definitely no coddling. I did exactly as she asked, did everything she ever asked of me, but I still feel out of balance. All these efforts to seek my center, and it's never become any easier. I just don't know what I'm doing wrong. I want to be great, to live up to the Jedi's expectations, but I just feel . . . mediocre."

Iskat was shocked by her own honesty, but what was the use in lying or pretending? Sember was gone, and she and Tualon were Jedi Knights now, equals. With no one else to confide in, why not him? He would never betray her trust; she knew that much.

"Mediocre? Iskat, come on. I was there, on Geonosis. I've known you all my life, and I've never seen you move like that. The Force was strong in you that day. It's strong in you now. That's why they chose you to be a Jedi Knight. We all saw it. You saved Zeeth and and Master Klefan."

She looked down at her long fingers, nervously playing with her amulet. "But . . . it wasn't honorable, was it? That wasn't peace or harmony or serenity. I took lives. I felt them leave the Force, like little flames, all snuffed out."

This time Tualon did reach over and place his hand over hers, calming her twitching fingers. "Perhaps in a time of peace, the Jedi would require you to be peaceful. But this is a time of war, and maybe what we need is someone like you. A *defender* of peace."

Little flutters started up in Iskat's stomach, and something about the strange beauty of Thule and the intimacy of the darkness in the cave made her feel open and perhaps a little wild. She was about to say something she might regret when Josk rolled over with a grunt on her other side, muttering, "Stop whispering and go to sleep. That's an order."

Tualon gave her hand a gentle squeeze before withdrawing. He rolled over, and Iskat turned her back to him and settled down on her side, playing with the shiny black pebbles that littered the hard ground. His words had given her hope—hope that she really did have a newfound value, and that despite Sember's concerns and criticism, Iskat now had a chance at making the Jedi Order proud in her own unique way. Sleep still eluded her, but she felt much better, almost effervescent. What Tualon had said about the Jedi Order needing her—it was the best compliment she'd ever received. Jedi were not supposed to crave praise, but there was no one around to see her indulge in a little well-deserved satisfaction. For perhaps the first time in her life, she went to sleep truly happy and filled with hope.

In the darkest part of the night, Iskat dreamed of a girl with a face like hers, the same red skin and long, brown hair in braids. Tears streamed down the girl's cheeks, and she held a familiar, yellow-bladed lightsaber in her long-fingered hands. Her blue eyes squeezed shut, her face twisting with anger and pain, the girl threw the lightsaber away and ran off into the darkness. Iskat sat up, shivering, to find tears on her cheeks.

"Feyra?" she whispered, touching her own face.

That girl—

Looking into her eyes, Iskat had felt more compassion and empathy, more understanding, more connection, than she'd ever felt for another being in her entire life.

She plumbed her memory of the dream, hoping for context, but that one stark image was all that remained.

But why had the dream come to her? Was it a message? A memory in the Force? Or perhaps nothing more than a dream, her sleeping mind making connections and telling stories, giving her the answer she'd been desperate to find?

And if it was real, what had caused Feyra to feel such intense pain? Why had she thrown down her lightsaber and run?

The databanks said only that Feyra had left the Jedi. They said nothing about *why*.

Troubled, Iskat fell into a restless sleep. When she woke again just before dawn, she was inexplicably in the chamber beyond the hallway, curled up before the crystal altar. She dusted the gritty black sand from her cheek and hurried back into the larger cave, hearts beating fast at the thought of being discovered there. Even if Josk and Tualon didn't recognize the Sith altar, even if they couldn't *feel* it, they would have questions she wasn't ready to answer.

/ 14.

THE MORNING WAS A BLEAK affair. When the entire cave and everything in it was a dull black that seemed to absorb all light, it was apparently quite hard to feel cheerful. Iskat liked the place for some reason, but that didn't make her body ache any less after a night of tossing and turning on the ground. She accepted a cup of very rough caf and joined Josk, Tualon, and Captain Spider where they stood at the mouth of the cavern, the sky outside lit in shades of bruised lavender and peach and the moss glowing an acidic chartreuse where it dotted the black stone.

"Captain Spider, have your scouts found anything?" Josk asked.

"Cannons," Spider confirmed, holding out a datapad showing a map. "Four total—two on either side of the canyon, up at the rim overlooking the factory. They appear to be operational. We'll need to disarm them before we continue with the rest of the mission, as they can take out individuals on the ground as well as ships in the air."

Josk sipped his caf and looked up at the rim of the canyon far, far overhead. "Then that's our first objective. We can't fly up, as they'd see us. So we'll have to climb. Luckily, we have climbing gear on hand. Iskat, Tualon, are you ready?"

A grin played at Iskat's lips. She was good at climbing. It wasn't a skill that they practiced frequently at the Temple, but she had no fear of heights and found that her long fingers and sharp nails helped her cling tightly as she skittered upward.

"Definitely," she said, and Tualon nodded his agreement.

"Iskat, you'll climb with me on this side. Tualon, you'll go it alone on the far side. Captain Spider and his troops will be on the ground with blasters ready on the off chance that there's any interference. Any questions so far?"

Iskat and Tualon both shook their heads.

"Good. Just to make sure we're all on the same vector, once the cannons are down, Tualon will infiltrate the factory with three troopers and copy plans from the nearest data console, and Iskat and I will take fourteen troopers to the power grid. Captain Spider, we'll need the rest of your men packing up camp and backing us up. Once Tualon is out of the factory with the intel, that's when we overload the power grid and render the factory inoperable. The ship will pick us up at the rendezvous point. We get out before any Separatists show up to investigate. Tualon, have you memorized the factory schematics?"

Tualon nodded. He was an excellent slicer and a good climber, too. Iskat wished she was paired with him instead of Josk, but she wasn't about to question the plan. Part of being a Jedi was knowing when to trust your superior. And maybe she didn't have great faith in Josk, but the Jedi Council did, and she had to abide their judgment.

They finished their breakfast and suited up to climb. Bulky brown robes would only slow them down and stand out against the darkness of the rock, so they borrowed some of the black body gloves the troopers wore under their armor. Josk gave Iskat a set of climbing spikes, and she hooked her lightsaber on her utility belt and tightly braided her long brown hair as Sember had taught her and tucked it under the tightly fitting black fabric. Sitting on a crate, she scrolled through her datapad, going over the power grid plans one more time. Sure, Josk would be with her, but she wanted to be completely prepared and give him no reason to question her competence.

"Ready?" he asked, tightening the climbing spikes on his boots.

Josk and Iskat took the near side of the canyon while Tualon jogged toward the far side. Iskat tore her attention away from him and watched Josk select the best route to the top, which was the same one Iskat would've chosen: a natural curve with shadows that would hide them from any droid scouts outside the factory proper. The clones took their places on the ground, blasters out as one trooper used binocs to watch the rim of the canyon. Josk hooked into the wall and began to climb, and Iskat waited a few moments, giving him plenty of space.

She lodged a spike into the wall and reached for the first handhold. The stone was pleasantly dry and jagged, with plenty of nooks to grab or wedge in a foot. She didn't even need the spikes on her boots, really. As she powered upward, careful not to zip past Josk and leave him behind, she was filled with a sense of exhilaration.

This was what she was meant to do—not meditate in the Temple, not barter for scraps of a decomposing text, not file datatapes under the watchful eye of Jocasta Nu. She was meant to be out in the galaxy doing things—challenging physical things. Much like the fight on Geonosis, she found that when she was out of the Temple and it was her against the galaxy, she had an inborn confidence and competence that shone through.

All her life, she'd thought maybe she was a bad Jedi, but more and more she was learning that maybe she was just a bad student. She was meant to do, not to be judged. Act, not prepare. Fight, not meditate. Perhaps in times of peace, the galaxy needed ascetics and archivists, but Tualon was right—this was a time of war.

"Do you know why I kept you with me?" Josk asked.

Iskat paused, nails digging into the wall. "No."

"I wasn't there that day, when Tika was injured." He grunted as he swung over to the next handhold. "But I saw the column afterward, fallen and nearly shattered. There's no way a Padawan should've been able to do that, and there were many that questioned your future. You've done an excellent job gaining more control over the years, but I heard about what happened on Geonosis. It was brave but foolish, what you did, and some still debate your abilities. I asked the Council if I might take you under my wing, especially considering your own master has become one with the Force."

Iskat couldn't think of a single response that wasn't impudent or a lie, so she remained silent and continued climbing. Inside, she was fuming. She'd wanted a mentor, yes, but someone mature and talented who was worthy of her time. There was nothing Josk Nivar could teach her, no skill he possessed where she didn't already excel. He'd already lost one Padawan; Iskat would never be able to trust him. Plus, she had a feeling nothing she did would ever be good enough, that Josk was the kind of person who would always have some helpful little comment that felt like criticism. She wanted what Tualon had with Master Ansho, a leader who would lift her spirits and inspire her instead of dragging her down.

"The Jedi Code emphasizes compassion and harmony, and I feel a particular calling to help you in the wake of your sudden promotion and the loss of Sember," he went on, oblivious to her disdain. "I know how hard she worked to keep you on the right path, and I want you to know that I'm here to help guide you through the next stage of your training."

Iskat drew a steadying breath. Her chest was tight, her face hot.

She'd spent a long time tamping down her emotions, her rage, but it never got any easier. She knew the key was to let the emotion pass and move on once she'd achieved a state of balance and control, but this feeling, this anger, had settled in behind her hearts like a sarlacc, immense and burrowed deep.

Josk was waiting for her to say something. He was entirely earnest and genuinely wanted to help her; she could feel his sincerity radiating in the Force. She gritted her teeth.

There was only one thing she could say.

"Thank you, General."

She couldn't dwell on her anger, couldn't let it run riot while she had to concentrate on her mission, hundreds of meters up a flat stone wall. She hadn't chosen her first mentor, and now she didn't get to choose her second one—not even a master yet, just a Jedi Knight who wanted to help her overcome her lifelong struggle. As if she weren't constantly trying. As if it were easy and natural. Her fingers curled into the dark stone, and she climbed faster, now just a little higher up than Josk.

The sky glowed cerulean blue overhead in what passed for daytime on Thule but seemed like twilight on another planet. They were halfway up the wall now, and Iskat could see the barrel of the first cannon overhead, constantly rotating to scan the sky. Although she knew better than to look down, she did anyway. The troopers on the ground were scanning the skies, the cannons, the canyon, ready with their blasters for any enemy movement. She dared a glance across the canyon and saw Tualon just a little bit lower down, almost completely camouflaged against the shadows of the wall and so far away that he was just a smudge. She wondered if he felt at home here, too.

Something closer by caught her eye, some little flutter of movement, and she noticed a gnarled slug as long as her forearm, perfectly camouflaged against the cliff face. She'd seen the smaller version of these creatures in the cave last night, and they were even more interesting outside with better light. With long, questioning eye stalks and bumpy backs dappled with a hundred shades of black and gray, they seemed like a species uniquely suited to this place. As the slug moved, its sides rippled, showing a flash of crimson that suggested its belly provided the only color on the entire planet. In a silence punctuated only by Josk's grunts and the solid crunch of his spikes into the wall, Iskat could hear the slug's jaws quietly grinding away at the rock.

Now that she'd seen one, she realized there were more and more the higher they climbed, hundreds of them grazing like sheep on a vertical hill. They nestled among the patches of moss and contorted their bodies around a series of perfectly round holes carved into the stone.

"Watch out for the slugs," she told Josk, thinking he was exactly the kind of person who would focus so hard on his handholds that he might accidentally pierce one with a climbing spike.

"What slugs?" he asked, and when he planted his next spike, it did indeed go right through one of the creatures.

The big, heavy slug thrashed madly, and Josk's spike pulled free from the stone. Panicking, he grabbed for one of the holes, digging his fingers in to keep from falling as the slug slipped off his spike and fell. Iskat gasped as a cloud of small black birds burst from the hole in the cliff, rising up in an angry, fluttering cloud, shrieking, beating their thick, dusty wings around Josk's head and pecking at his cheeks with their bright red beaks. He screamed, and Iskat watched bloody wounds open on his face. With her fingers jammed into crevices in the rock and her boot spikes sunk into the wall, surrounded by huge slugs and furious birds, she could only cling to the canyon as Josk let go of his handholds to protect his head.

There was a moment, perhaps, when Iskat could've reached out with the Force to hold him in place, to help him keep his balance. But instead, she froze and could only watch as he slowly fell backward and plummeted to the hard ground below.

/ 15.

IN THE SILENCE OF THE canyon, Iskat heard Josk's body land with a sick thump far below. He should've been able to right himself, should've twisted his body to land on his feet in the crouch Jedi naturally assumed while leaping and sparring. He should've been able to tap into the Force and slow himself, just enough to save his bones from the impact. And yet, when she looked down, he was in a heap of crooked limbs and didn't seem to be moving.

The troopers ran over, and she saw one open a medkit. Iskat had to focus on her current predicament; she held very, very still. She didn't know if the birds would sense her as a threat and attack her. As she waited, they took turns diving into the holes in the rock until they had all but disappeared. She could hear them, deep within the cliff, screeching to one another as they settled down. A bird's face appeared in the nearest hole, its bright black eyes regarding her as it wiped its sharply pointed, red-stained beak on the stone. Silent, still, she considered her next move.

She could hurry down to help, but applying first aid had never been her best skill, and it looked like Josk was beyond her meager attempts at calming pain. She wanted to use her comlink to ask if Josk had survived the fall, but she was clinging to a wall, hundreds of meters overhead, and didn't want to disturb the birds or the slugs or risk losing her own balance. She looked over to Tualon, who was so focused on his climb that he hadn't noticed the accident. He was higher up than she was now and would soon be at the top of the canyon and working on dismantling his cannon.

If Iskat didn't do the same, it was only a matter of time before someone—or, more likely, something—noticed the interlopers and the barrels of those fully functional cannons swiveled downward toward their troops. If Josk was dead, there was nothing she could personally do for him, nothing anyone could do. If he was mortally wounded, she might be able to temporarily alleviate some pain, but it would soon come roaring back. In that case, the troopers would have medicines that would do far more for Josk than Iskat could.

No, returning to the ground wouldn't do anyone any good, and someone would still have to climb back up and render the cannons on this side useless. She was so close; it wouldn't take her long at all to accomplish her part of this mission. With a deep breath, she looked up and made her decision.

She had to keep climbing.

She would use her comlink once she and Tualon were both safely on the canyon's rim. She would tell him to watch out not only for the slugs, but also for the birds. Or perhaps, unlike Josk, he had already recognized the threat.

She was careful, this time, not to touch the slugs and to avoid the easy handholds that the birds' nesting holes might have provided. The way they'd attacked Josk—it was almost predatory, or at least more strategic and defensive than she would've anticipated from a smallish bird. The rasp of the much larger slugs chewing on the stone dominated her hearing, and a thought settled soft as ash:

Had they . . . helped make this canyon?

Had they chewed away the stone for millennia, creating the sand below?

Iskat knew nothing of Thule, but it was a place of constant fascination for her.

Hand over hand, boot spikes carefully placed, she was soon at the top of the canyon, dragging herself up to standing. She edged away from the rim and pressed her comlink.

"How is he?" she asked.

"Not good," Captain Spider answered.

"How is who?" Tualon asked, a little breathless.

A long moment of silence.

"Worry about the cannons first, and then we'll talk," Spider said grimly.

That was all the answer Iskat needed. She hurried to the first cannon, being sure to stay behind its barrel. Remembering how Master Vey had disarmed the cannons on Geonosis, Iskat ignited her lightsaber and severed the visible wires, then sliced the narrowest juncture of the weapon. When the barrel of the cannon thunked to the ground, Iskat grinned and looked up.

Across the canyon, Tualon was but a tiny speck, waving at her. His cannon was likewise a broken hunk of metal.

"What happened?" he asked on his comlink.

"Josk fell. The troopers are tending to him. On the way back down, watch out for the slugs, and don't trust the nesting holes. They're full of killer birds."

"I saw the slugs and heard the birds," Tualon said. "But—"

"Let's stay on mission. We still have two more cannons."

"Okay . . ."

Tualon peeked over the canyon rim. Iskat didn't want to look down again, so she hurried to the other cannon and repeated the process, destroying it. Across the canyon, Tualon did the same. Now the cannons couldn't target them as they approached the factory; nor could they shoot down their ship as they left the planet. Part one of the mission was accomplished.

From high up on the cliff, Iskat was now able to comfortably look down at the factory they were here to deactivate. It was built into the widest part of the canyon, only its roof open to the elements. Huge metal hatches suggested this was where deliveries were made. The shiny corrugated metal looked unnatural against the dull, dark stone, unwelcome as a knife blade sunk in to the hilt.

Iskat followed her boot prints in the sand back to the edge of the canyon. As she eased over the rim and sank her spikes into the wall, she had a giddy moment of . . . not fear. Not anxiety. A wild sort of excitement, maybe?

What she was doing—when did normal people get to do this? What would it be like, to be born with no Force affinity and grow up with a simple family focused on grinding a life out of the dust? To never know the ability to reach out with the Force, to sense other creatures and moods and the shifts in the weather? She reveled in the ease with which she was able to navigate the steep climb, straight down, while avoiding the bigger patches of slugs, and areas concentrated with bird nests. She felt the strength in the ancient stone, raised millennia ago when plates crashed violently together and were then slowly ground away by water and wind and the seeking mouths of slugs. Most people who were born on Coruscant never saw another planet, but Iskat was only beginning her adventures. She would help people, help the galaxy, by pushing herself to her limits. By doing things other people could never even dream of doing.

Now that she had left the confines of the Jedi Temple, she was beginning to see the possibilities of life as a Jedi Knight, and of the gifts she'd been born with. Maybe it wasn't that she was the worst of the Padawans—maybe she had simply been in the wrong environment, doomed to fail. Maybe her place to shine was anywhere but the Jedi Temple, out among the galaxy. And not just hunting artifacts—climbing and fighting, actively changing the course of a war.

All the way down the sheer cliff face, she was careful to edge around the slugs. Now that she knew what to look for, a subtle change in texture from the rock, she noticed that they seemed to congregate in patches, almost like lichen growing on trees. If she stuck to the smoother areas, she could easily avoid them. At the very least, she knew to use her climbing spikes and avoid what seemed like perfect handholds. Being ready for that sort of thing was the difference between making it down alive and following Josk in a swift and disastrous fall.

She . . . she couldn't think too hard about that.

She had to shove it down and focus on the job at hand. She loved climbing, but she was well aware that there were a hundred ways to die up here. That knowledge only sharpened her senses.

When she was about five meters from the ground, she pushed away from the wall in a controlled fall and dropped into a crouch, hurrying to where the troopers had carried Josk just under a small overhang. He was laid out on his back, his arms limp at his sides and his legs flailed out. The skin on his cheeks and forehead was tinged grayish blue around tiny, swollen, leaking wounds. As she got close enough to see the slack look on his face, the dry emptiness of his eyes, it finally hit her:

Josk Nivar was dead.

Unlike with Sember's death, Iskat wasn't running for her life, wasn't being urged away by a master's admonitions. She had nothing else to do but stand there and stare at what was left of her fellow Jedi Knight. She'd been so shocked, so busy staying alive, that she hadn't felt him become one with the Force. She'd never really focused on a dead body before, and for all that she understood that death was natural, it was soul-shaking to suddenly come face-to-face with it on a faraway planet.

Iskat knelt at Josk's side and put her hands over his chest, but she couldn't sense even the tiniest spark there. It was too late for splints, too late for bacta. The clone with the unopened medkit at his side looked up at her.

"There was nothing we could do," he said. "The impact was too much."

Tualon ran up beside her and knelt close enough that he jostled her.

"What happened?" he asked, his fingers hovering over Josk's body as he, too, searched for some sign of life.

"The birds. He put a hand into one of their nesting holes. They rose up in a cloud and attacked him."

"And he just let go? Didn't even try to arrest his fall?"

The clone medic held up one of Josk's hands, which was unusually puffy and the same bluish gray as the skin near his facial wounds. "We think the birds have some kind of venom. It's likely he experienced paralysis, or even a shock to his heart. By the time we reached him, he wasn't breathing."

Tualon looked to Iskat; for all that he usually took care to conceal his emotions, she could feel him in the Force, sense his anguish. His head hung, his lekku falling forward. He closed Josk's eyes. "May the Force be with you, Josk Nivar."

"May the Force be with you," Iskat repeated.

With a determined exhale, Tualon stood, and Iskat followed suit.

He turned to her, all business now. "We still have to take down that factory. Shall we share command equally?"

Iskat nodded, feeling a sense of satisfaction. "His datapad might have more intel on the plans. If you want to get your kit, I'll check to see if there's anything else we need to know."

Tualon went under the overhang to change into his robes and get his kit, and Iskat took a shuddering breath and knelt, carefully removing Josk's datapad from his pack. The most recent entry was a message in draft form, queued to send to Mace Windu titled "Strategies," which she opened. As she scanned the message, she was shocked to see that it wasn't about how to destroy the factory.

It was about managing her.

> Iskat continues to display potential, but I detect a certain willfulness and perhaps some secrecy in her manner. She doesn't demonstrate the control and maturity expected of most Jedi Knights, and I can sense her irritation and impatience, but I'm endeavoring to use her strengths on this mission and will try to take her under my wing, although I sense that she chafes at any hint of guidance. Tualon remains a solid second in command and I appreciate his ability to maintain a calm environment in which she will thrive. She shows a marked preference for him, which I expect to—

Iskat deleted the message and scrolled to one titled "Schematics," quickly paging through until she reached a map of the power grid.

"Find anything?" Tualon called.

"Just the same schematics I have on my own datapad." She scanned the rest of the messages but didn't see anything else that looked like it might be about her. "Do you have what you need?"

"My part seems fairly simple," Tualon said. "Do you have what you need?"

Iskat glanced toward the overhang where Josk still lay, surrounded by troopers who didn't really seem to know what to do when a battle wasn't immediately raging. "The faster we finish here, the faster we get back to Coruscant and give him the funeral he deserves."

Tualon's eyes met hers, and Iskat felt a flash of connection, of understanding. Josk was gone, but she and Tualon were confident, competent Jedi Knights, and they would see this through to the end—together.

"Captain Spider?" Tualon called.

When the clone captain joined them, Tualon confirmed the plans with him one more time while Iskat listened. He had suggested they would approach command equally, but she was glad to let him speak on her behalf, just now. She would be leading the troopers to the power station instead of Josk, after all, and that would be her first real test of leadership. No matter what Josk had told Mace, no matter that Mace was basically having her watched, she was ready. She wasn't that same scared little youngling who'd pulled down a column and run away crying.

She had hard-won control. She had talents. And now she had confidence and the opportunity to show those talents.

Soon she was marching toward the power field with fifteen clone troopers as Tualon and his three clones took the two speeder bikes to the factory and the rest of the clones waited in reserve or returned to the shuttle to prepare for pickup. Her troopers in their white armor stood out against the black stone of the planet, but it wasn't like anyone was there to see it. According to their intel, this operation was run by a skeleton crew of droids.

The power grid was in an offshoot of the canyon. At each of the corners of its fenced rectangular perimeter, a small building housed one of the four command stations that controlled and monitored the system. If this factory was set up like other Separatist installations, as their intel suggested, each command station would be operated by two droids, which were not outfitted for battle and should be easily dispatched. All Iskat and her troopers had to do was get to each command station, destroy the droids, and turn several specific dials into the red. With all four stations overheating, the power grid would overload, and its components would melt, permanently destroying it and making it impossible to get the factory online.

Iskat stalked along with her troopers in two neat lines behind her. Leading them, she felt a glow of pride. It was a tragedy that they'd lost Josk, but she could do this herself. She was a Jedi general. All she had to do was get to her assigned station, dispatch a few confused droids, follow a procedure she'd memorized perfectly, and get to the rendezvous point. She knew she could count on her troopers to do the same.

The first power station came into view, and Iskat turned to the clones and nodded. They nodded back. Three clones joined her, while the other twelve separated into three groups of four. Each of the four teams headed to a different command station. They were all synced to the same timer and would turn their dials at the same moment. Iskat's team would take the closest station; that way, she'd be available as backup if the other teams had any issues, plus she could tell them what to expect via comlink, should anything differ from the schematics they'd been provided.

Buoyed by the crisp response of the troopers, Iskat had her lightsaber in hand as she approached the first control station, a spare and simple building of dull gray metal. Rickety stairs wound up to a second floor, where the two droids within would be focused on their screens. The most dangerous moment would come on the stairs, when the sounds of their boots would ring out against the metal steps, the only noise in the entire canyon, other than the whispering wind.

But as Iskat and her troopers neared the stairs, a klaxon rang out, screaming through the canyon. Red lights flashed, and even over the screeching alarm, Iskat could hear the heavy thumps of droid feet—too many droid feet—coming down the stairs. Iskat counted at least a dozen B1 battle droids armed with blaster rifles, followed by one of the larger B2 droids she'd seen on the ground at Geonosis—the big, heavily armored kind with wrist blasters that had corralled the Jedi in the arena.

"Open fire!" a B1 commander bleated.

Blaster bolts filled the air, and Iskat's clones returned fire. Her hearts thrumming and her lightsaber twirling, Iskat deflected several bolts with her blade, taking down two of the B1 droids, but they didn't stop marching. One by one, her clones fell, their armor no match for the onslaught.

The intel she'd been given said this factory was still under construction, that the power grid was just starting to come online. The intel said they would have no problem catching the unarmed droids within the command stations unaware.

But the intel was wrong.

The power grid was active, and judging by the shriek of blaster bolts echoing across the canyon along with the klaxon, more droids were on the way.

/ 16.

ISKAT HAD TO HELP HER troopers. The ones who'd fallen were beyond help, but she had three more teams—twelve men—who might still have a chance. But first, she had to take down the droids in front of her. Opening herself to the Force, Iskat sought that same dancing flow she'd felt on Geonosis. Time seemed to slow as she focused on the battle at hand, whirling and slashing, deflecting blaster bolts back at the B1 droids. She focused her fire on the command droid, knowing that once it was out of commission, the rest of the droids would be rudderless. It may have been more intelligent, but it was just as vulnerable. Soon all the B1 droids were on the ground, struggling to stand, but the big B2 droid simply absorbed the shots and kept coming. Iskat's comlink pinged.

"General Akaris, the other control stations are—there are battle droids—!"

The shouts and screams of her troopers at the other stations were overlaid with the sound of the blasterfire that had erupted all around the canyon, the klaxon continually screaming in counterpoint.

She couldn't answer her comlink; she was too busy fending off the B2 droid. What would she tell them, anyway? It was too late. If they couldn't defend themselves, she couldn't get there in time. Her comm quickly went silent.

She turned to face the B2 droid. Deflecting its own shots did little good; she'd have to get in close with her lightsaber and cut off some vital machinery. But before she had chosen her moment to attack, a grenade exploded against the B2, knocking it over in a plume of smoke. She didn't hesitate. She ran and leapt, her blade swinging down to cut off both its arms before severing it at the waist.

"What do we do, sir?" One of the clones—CT-0528—appeared, his white armor wearing the black scars of blaster bolts.

"Is anyone from your team still standing?" she asked him.

He shook his head. "It doesn't look good."

"We've got to get inside the command station. Cover me."

"Yes, sir."

She had to silence the alarm and ensure that the droids inside the station could no longer communicate with the factory. Tualon and his troopers were still inside, and they needed every chance they could get to succeed, even if Iskat's mission was a loss.

She put on a burst of speed and vaulted upward to the landing, trusting that CT-0528 would follow on the stairs. Throwing open the station door, she leapt between the two droids monitoring the wide bank of instruments, beheading them both before they could even turn around. One droid still had a hand on the alarm, which she turned off, grateful for the silence.

Finally, she took a breath and picked up her comlink. "Captain Spider, come in. We were ambushed by droids. We need reinforcements at the power grid."

Spider answered immediately. "Yes, sir. Six troopers are on their way to your position."

Iskat calculated how long it might take them to reach her—too long, even if they didn't encounter any more droids. She changed channels.

"Tualon, you done in there?"

His voice was hushed and hurried. "Almost."

"Might want to hurry. Our intel was wrong. The power grid is crawling with battle droids. We've lost most of our team. Has your team seen any security?"

"No security. I managed to slice into a control panel just inside the door, so we're not that far in. Will you be able to take down the power grid?"

She stared at the control panel, hundreds of buttons and switches and blinking lights. She knew what to do—as long as she had three other people doing the same thing in the other control stations. "I'll find a way."

"Then I guess we'll see you at the rendezvous point."

She breathed a sigh of relief. No matter what happened here, as long as that intel reached the Council, at least they'd gained something for the Republic. "Good. Be ready for us."

She switched channels. "Squad One, come in. Squad Two, Squad Three? Anybody?"

Her blood ran cold as the only response was silence.

Of her fifteen clones, only one was alive.

Her last trooper appeared in the doorway. "I think it's just us, sir."

Iskat looked out the viewport at the power grid. The machinery filled the space between the canyon walls, a rectangle far longer than it was wide. With six clones gone, there was no way for Iskat and CT-0528 to overload the system. Even if she turned the correct dial in this station, it would self-correct before she could run to the far stations. They all had to be synced up, overloading at the same time, or the system would self-regulate thanks to built-in safety protocols. Maybe if she and her remaining trooper each took a short side—

But there was a chance that wouldn't work.

There was a chance the blasterfire had alerted the factory droids to a problem.

There was a chance someone had already found Tualon and his men.

And there was a certainty that there were battle droids at the other stations on the lookout for more trouble. She'd survived this squad with no damage, and her clone had escaped his own skirmish, but that didn't mean they could face three more B2 droids and live. Captain Spider had sent six more troopers, but even if they arrived in time, they still had to get past those droids.

Iskat's job was to shut down this factory, and she'd been given—Josk had been given—very explicit directions that would simply melt the guts of the power grid and render it useless. That didn't mean a new power grid wouldn't be built. That didn't mean they wouldn't find a new way to power the factory.

No, she had to shut this operation down for good. The whole thing.

An idea began to form.

"Tualon, are you out of the factory yet?"

"Yes, we're headed back to the rendezvous point on the speeders. The shuttle is already in place."

"Let me know when you're there."

A long pause.

"Iskat, what are you doing?"

Another long pause.

"What I have to do."

"And what is that?"

Her fingers played over the big dial that controlled the power grid output. It was set to low, perhaps because the factory wasn't fully on board yet.

She clicked off her comlink.

She'd run the numbers in her head, and there was no way Tualon and his troopers could get here on time, even on the speeders. And even if they could, they'd have six people spread out over four command stations facing multiple droid battalions. Even with Captain Spider's additional troopers, the numbers wouldn't add up.

She would just have to get creative.

"Stay here," she told her trooper. "I'll comm you when I get to the next station. You're going to turn this dial as far as it'll go."

His helmet tilted in question.

"But don't we need to overload all four systems at once, sir?"

She thought of the schematics she'd studied, the manual on running each station. She whipped out her datapad, swiped through the diagrams, read the bright-red type under the word WARNING.

What she was doing—it should work. She just didn't know how *fast* it would work.

The manual didn't say how quickly things would happen when disaster struck.

But what was the real disaster—going back a failure, or dying here?

No.

She wasn't going to die. Not today.

Not like the clone troopers outside.

Not like Josk.

She would accomplish her mission. And she was going to shut down this factory completely.

"We can do it with two," she told her trooper, only a little bit of a lie. "As soon as you've turned the knob all the way up, run for the rendezvous point and let me know when you're there. The shuttle is waiting."

Iskat could feel his eyes on her even through the helmet. "Yes, sir," he said doubtfully, and she took off running.

Once she was on the landing, she leapt over the railing and down to the ground, bypassing the stairs entirely. Turning on her comlink, she asked "Tualon, where are you?"

When he came in, he was breathing hard. "We're at the shuttle. It's fully packed. Josk is . . . they have him on board. I know that's important to you. Will you be able to shut down the power grid or not? Do you have a plan? Even if—"

She took a deep breath and switched her comm to the trooper's channel, cutting Tualon off. In the silence, the sound of marching droids echoed through the canyon. She waded into the toppled mess of destroyed battle droids, aiming for one she'd noticed in particular and snatching what she needed from his pack.

"General Akaris?" CT-0528 asked through the comm.

"I'm almost there," she told him.

With a deep, centering breath, she ran for the next nearest control station. A squad of droids spotted her, and blaster bolts zinged toward her as they approached. She didn't stop running; she reached within and, as if unlocking a door long kept bolted, unleashed all the control she'd been holding tightly for so long. With one swipe of her hand, a dozen droids slammed into the canyon wall and fell to the ground, broken and dented and useless and sparking—even the bigger B2.

It felt so good, so freeing, so utterly delicious not to hold back. Her stride opened up as she grinned, and she leapt, hurtling onto the landing of the next command station. She felt weightless, filled to the brim with energy. She beheaded the two droids within and went to the dial.

"I'm here," she told her trooper. "Turn it all the way, on three. One, two . . . three."

Her long, red fingers twisted her own dial up and up and up, past the red.

A warning siren immediately went off, and a dozen lights began blinking frantically. She ignited her lightsaber and ran outside. The moment she saw more droids marching toward her, she reached out in the Force and swept them out of her path like a flood tossing trees. It felt so good, so right, so *easy* without holding back, without fear that she might accidentally hurt someone. When these droids hit the canyon wall, they fell down in one big mass of metal, as if they'd been smelted together.

She ran until she was past the power grid with a straight shot to the ship waiting at the rendezvous point.

"Five-Two-Eight, are you at the rendezvous point?"

"Almost, sir." He was out of breath. "I just met the reinforcements. Do you want us to come back and cover you?"

She looked around the canyon, listening carefully for more droids. She didn't hear anything, but then again, the alarm was going off. This one had a different sort of urgency from the defense klaxon, which gave her hope.

This alarm sounded desperate. It sounded scared.

"No. Get everyone on the shuttle. I'll join you shortly. Make sure the ship is ready to leave the second I hit the ramp."

"Yes, sir."

She couldn't tell if her plan was working yet, or if perhaps there was some fail-safe built into the power grid. Maybe someone really did have to turn the dial at all four stations simultaneously, or maybe the droids at the other two control stations were able to override the dials she and her trooper had turned. There was no way to know except to wait and see, and they weren't going to do that. They didn't have time.

She needed some way to be sure.

Which was why she'd stopped to pull a thermal detonator from the pack of the grenade droid.

She'd never actually held one before, but she knew how it worked—in theory. She also knew that she was far too close to the power field to use it. She adjusted the timer, took off running toward the ship, and right before the bend in the canyon, she paused, thumbed the detonator, and used the Force to throw it as far as she could. It barely took any effort to guide it over the wall and far into the center of the power grid.

For a moment, she stood there, watching it soar. And then a blaster bolt nearly took off her left ear as droids poured out of the canyon.

She ran faster than she'd ever run in her life, boots pounding against the black sand as the droids marched behind her, sending blaster bolts hurtling past. She tapped into the Force, ducking and weaving and leaping, occasionally turning around to send a bolt into their ranks, knocking one down and hopefully tripping his fellows.

Only as the shuttle came into view did she remember that she'd left behind six troopers—without checking to see if they were alive and capable of being saved. Just because they hadn't answered their comms didn't mean they were dead. A flush of shame shimmied through her, but she shook it off.

They were soldiers who'd fallen in battle. Like Sember, the Jedi couldn't risk the entire operation to do their corpses justice. She told herself there was no way the troopers could've lived through that droid onslaught—if they had, they would've answered her comms. They were gone, and that was war, and she had to accept it.

As if in punctuation, a line of fire burned the top of her arm, a blaster bolt finding home as she spent too much time thinking and too little time reacting. The pain galvanized her, infuriated her, and she stopped and spun, screaming her rage as she used the Force to throw the droids backward in a spray of sand and smoke.

With the threat neutralized, she kept running. The shuttle was ready for liftoff, and the moment Iskat hit the ramp, it rose into the sky, kicking up a fierce and glittering wind of black sand with a few chaotically twirling black birds caught in the storm. Tualon met her on the ramp, helping her into the shuttle proper even though they both knew she didn't need any help. She glanced around and saw CT-0528 sitting nearby, almost indistinguishable from the other clones save for the black streaks of blaster fire on his armor and the fact that he was bent over, trying to catch his breath. Nearly half the ship was empty. The remaining troopers were silent.

Captain Spider strode back from the cockpit as Iskat and Tualon found their seats.

"General Akaris, can you tell me what happened to my men?" he asked tiredly.

"Our intel said the power grid wasn't defended, that there were two unarmed droids at each control station. But there were dozens of battle droids with blasters. B1s, B2s, commanders, grenadiers. They surprised us. We'd already split up when they appeared. I took down as many as I could, but it was too late. I'm so sorry—"

Captain Spider put up a hand. "Just a little advice, sir. Generals don't apologize. Not for decisions made in the heat of battle. Otherwise you'd do nothing else."

Iskat bristled a bit; that felt like an insult added on to patronizing advice, but then again, he'd just lost fifteen of his men. He was allowed to be upset with the situation.

"How did you shut down the grid with only two people?" Tualon asked.

"I had to improvise. But I don't think the factory will be operational for much longer."

He cocked his head. "I don't like the sound of that. Did you not follow orders?"

"Our objective was to stop the factory from producing droids. They gave us bad intel, and then things went wrong. We're Jedi. We have to be able to think on our feet. So if the factory gets shut down, then does it really matter how?"

"Of course it matters," he argued. "Because Jedi don't—"

Iskat didn't get to hear more on Tualon's ideas regarding what Jedi didn't do, because the power grid exploded in a giant fireball burning bright against the twilight sky.

/ 17.

THE SHUTTLE ROCKED SIDEWAYS WITH the power of the explosion, and Iskat lurched against Tualon, who moved away more quickly than she would've preferred.

"Did you blow up the entire grid?" he asked, incredulous.

"I told you I had to improvise."

"But—"

A second explosion made the ship shake even harder, and Iskat stood and hurried to the cockpit, steadying herself as the shuttle climbed ever higher. Outside, there were two gigantic fireballs, two huge plumes of smoke.

"Looks like the factory went up, too," the pilot said.

She could just see it, the flat metal roof torn open and billowing foul black smoke. As she watched, a third, smaller explosion erupted from the canyon, leaving behind a jagged scar.

"Mission accomplished!" she said. "That factory won't be making any droids."

Tualon joined her at the viewport, looking down at the carnage. "We weren't supposed to blow it up. Master Gallia said it was supposed to be subtle. Something that could be blamed on malfunctioning equipment."

"I think the moment armed battle droids arrived, our cover was blown," she argued.

Tualon scrolled through his datapad. "Three explosions. I don't know how the Council is going to take this."

She shook her head. "It was either this, or utter failure." She looked into Tualon's eyes, the liquid orange of a sunset on water. "Would you want to return to the Temple, just you and I and half our troopers and Josk's body, and tell Master Windu and the others that we had failed, that it was all for nothing?"

He held up a datacard. "Not for nothing. I got the plans they wanted."

"Then we both accomplished our missions."

How she hated the look he gave her then, disappointed and almost pitying.

For the entire journey back to Coruscant, Iskat and Tualon kept their distance from each other. Iskat's triumph had been dampened by Tualon's criticism, and the troopers were somber after the loss of their fellows. Iskat couldn't forget that the long, wrapped shape nestled near the ramp was once the earnest but arrogant Jedi Knight Josk Nivar, especially when a familiar voice began emitting from that particular spot in the ship as they neared Coruscant.

"General Nivar, report. We see you entering Coruscant airspace. Report." Master Adi Gallia's voice was muffled by the fabric wrappings.

Tualon pulled out his own comlink. "We're here, Master Gallia."

"Where is Josk?"

Tualon sighed. "That's a longer story."

A pause. "We await your full account. We've heard some troubling reports out of Thule."

Tualon gave Iskat a pained look and said, "It's a tale better told in full, Master."

As they descended through the atmosphere and neared the glittering heights of Coruscant and the five towers atop the Jedi Temple came into view, a familiar and unwelcome feeling settled over Iskat like a suffocating blanket.

Worry. And shame.

Like she'd done something wrong and would soon have to explain it to someone who'd already formed an opinion and was unlikely to change it no matter how well she argued her point of view.

When they deboarded at the landing pad, Master Yoda and Master Gallia were waiting. Master Gallia looked disappointed, but Yoda looked contemplative.

"Three Jedi traveled to Thule, but only two return," he said.

"We lost Josk Nivar during the mission," Tualon began.

"But we succeeded—" Iskat interrupted.

Master Yoda held up a hand.

"Speak of it here we will not. To the chamber we will go." He began walking, and Master Gallia fell in beside him. Iskat and Tualon shared a look and followed.

Iskat had grown up in the Temple, but since Geonosis she had begun to see her home with new eyes. These halls she'd walked for so long now seemed somehow smaller, the haughty spires and soaring ceilings like a farce. What did such careful control and cold beauty matter when the galaxy's peacekeepers were failing to keep peace? The halls were more empty than usual, with almost no Jedi Masters or Knights in view. The Initiates who passed by were quiet and in a perfect line, and a few of them stole worried glances at her. They were so young, so soft and tiny that it made her hearts ache. What would happen when they ran out of Jedi to fight this war? Who would train these younglings when there were no Jedi left? And what sort of galaxy would they inherit?

Instead of returning to Jellani Garden, they went directly to the Council Chamber, and Iskat's shame returned in full force. She had not seen the interior of the chamber before, and she regretted that it was under such inauspicious circumstances. Master Gallia motioned for Iskat and Tualon to sit, and Iskat settled into the indicated chair but found everything uncomfortable. The fine black grit of Thule had worked its way into her clothing and hair, the blaster burns on her ear and upper arm ached, and her hands were sore from climbing. So much had happened so quickly. Everything had changed in just a couple of days.

She had no idea what to expect.

Maybe they would tell Iskat she was a hero.

Or maybe she would be punished.

"We haven't had any communication in a worrisome amount of time, and we've received word of massive amounts of damage," Master Gallia began; she looked tired and sounded like this wasn't the first bad news she'd received today. "When and how did we lose General Nivar?"

Iskat opened her mouth to speak, but Tualon beat her to it. "There were four cannons guarding the factory. We were climbing the canyon walls to disable them, and he fell."

"Fell and died a Jedi Knight did?" Yoda asked. "Very unusual that seems."

"There were birds," Iskat hurried to say. "Creatures native to Thule. Josk disturbed a nest, and they attacked him. We think their bites are venomous, based on Josk's behavior and the color of his skin after he was bitten. There were large slugs as well, and I think perhaps that's how the birds came to have poison on their beaks. He appeared to have been unconscious even before he hit the ground, or paralyzed, or perhaps his heart was affected."

Yoda nodded, but remained silent.

Master Gallia leaned forward. "And what happened after Josk was lost?"

"We decided to share command," Tualon said, his face hard.

He looked at Iskat, and she began. "Tualon and I were able to destroy the cannons with no issues. After that, we climbed back down and Tualon prepared to infiltrate the factory as planned." She nodded at Tualon to continue.

"I led my troopers to the factory, where I was able to download everything you requested." He handed over the datacard. "Then we headed back to the rendezvous point."

A pause as Iskat chose her words carefully. "With Josk gone, I focused on overloading the power grid. Our intel suggested the facility was still under construction and wouldn't be defended, but as soon as we approached, dozens of battle droids arrived. We lost all but one of my clones. With the element of surprise gone and too few people to perform the correct inputs at all four stations, I decided we would have to settle for overloading only two control stations. I wasn't sure if that would be enough to shut the system down, so I threw a thermal detonator into the grid. And then we left."

"Which caused three explosions on Thule," Master Gallia continued, shaking her head. "We made it clear this mission was to be subtle—"

A flare of anger made Iskat interrupt her. "Our stated goal was to make sure that factory couldn't produce any more droids for the Separatists, and we accomplished that goal."

"You also sent shock waves through an occupied planet that will not look kindly upon our intrusion," Gallia said sharply. "In addition to the power grid and the factory, the effects of your thermal detonator took out a small underground settlement of engineers and laborers. We had hoped the information Tualon gained from the factory databanks would give us a secret advantage over the Separatists, that we would know more about their production plans and how better to interrupt them. But now they'll be increasing the security at every factory from here on out. A historical site was damaged as well."

"The altar," Iskat said quietly.

"Altar?" Gallia pressed.

"We found an ancient stone altar in the cavern where we set up camp. It had a carved base with a large crystal. The motif in the carvings was . . . interesting."

Master Yoda's ears drooped as if he felt every one of his years. "A Sith world Thule was long ago." He and Master Gallia shared a look.

But Iskat's mind was reeling. A Sith world? Did that mean the planet was steeped in the dark side? She'd felt so at home there, which made her uneasy. Perhaps it wasn't the way the planet and its bones sat in the Force—maybe her planet of birth had merely looked similar or shared the same mix of gases and gravity. She remembered the call of the Sith text Sember had found, and she couldn't help wondering if, in its own way, the planet had called to her, too. She remembered how her hand had moved to touch the Sith emblem, the brief flare of the crystal under her fingertips. And then there was the dream, and the way she'd woken up beside the altar . . .

No, she couldn't tell anyone about that. Couldn't give anyone further reason to doubt her.

"Masters . . ." Tualon had his head in his hands, his lekku hanging dejectedly. "I feel as if I've let you down. After Josk fell, I should've—"

"Your fault it is, hmm?" Yoda jabbed his cane at Tualon. "No! Messy, war is. Confusing. Even the Force cannot see where it might lead."

"We'll arrange for Josk's funeral," Master Gallia said, her tone far softer than it had been the rest of the conversation. "Remember: You're Jedi Knights now, but you're not alone. Even if you're beyond a master's sole attention, there are always those willing to teach you or train with you. You'll also take turns instructing the younglings. With so few masters available, they will need your guidance more than ever."

She gestured, and Tualon and Iskat stood and walked toward the door.

"Iskat, one more thing," Master Gallia said.

Tualon gave Iskat a significant look and left the garden, the door closing softly behind him.

Alone with the two masters, Iskat had a sinking feeling in her chest. Before, she'd felt as if maybe she'd made a small error in judgment, but it had been acceptable and reasonable. Now, with Tualon gone, she knew nothing good could happen behind that closed door.

"We know you're having a hard time," Master Gallia began, "with the loss of your master, with your first real mission without her guidance."

"Everyone is having a hard time," Iskat said stiffly, clutching her amulet.

"Losing a master is a pivotal moment for a Jedi, one Tualon can't yet comprehend. But it is a natural and inevitable part of our journey in the Force. It can set your internal compass spinning. The Knighting Ceremony is meant to be a ritual timed appropriately to allow reflection and to celebrate your outgrowth from mentorship, but we realize that you were hurried through this process and that you might need some time to find your path."

Iskat struggled not to raise her voice, to keep it careful and even. She had to center herself, had to show Masters Yoda and Gallia that she was worthy of their trust and confident in her actions. She released her amulet and stood straighter.

"I don't need time. My actions on Thule are not related to the passing of my master. I would've made the same decision at the power grid whether Sember was alive or not. It was the right choice. We had to accomplish our goal. We didn't want to let you down."

"Civilian casualties there were," Yoda said softly.

"We were told the area was occupied only by droids," Iskat argued. "There was no mention of civilians. We didn't see any evidence of living beings from the air or the ground. How were we to know?"

"Josk knew. This information was among his schematics." Master Gallia scrolled through her datapad and shook her head again. "His file contained additional details of every aspect of the factory. Perhaps he decided that information wasn't relevant to your plans. It's true that there were fewer than a dozen casualties, mostly builders and administrators. But, again, it was meant to be a stealth mission with no loss of life, and here we are."

Yoda put both his hands on his cane, and leaned forward. "More careful you must be in the future, yes?"

More careful?

More careful?

In war?

Her hands were in fists now.

"But weren't they Separatists? Weren't they the enemy? Like the Geonosians we fought on the way to the arena?"

"The Geonosians were armed and attacking. The people below the factory were just working to feed their families. Someone hired to build a factory would be considered largely innocent at this juncture." Master Gallia's eyes were tired. "Many of your fellow Jedi are learning how to be leaders during a war after a lifetime of peace, and you are likewise learning to be a Jedi Knight and a general. Mistakes will be made. Your job is to meditate on your reasoning and impulsiveness and learn to do better. Your current disrespect and aggression are unbecoming in a Jedi."

The word *unbecoming* hit Iskat like a punch to the gut, and the words came out before she could stop them. "Is that why Josk was reporting on me to Mace Windu?"

Master Gallia quickly hid her brief flash of surprise. "Master Windu has expressed concerns about your fitness to lead—"

"Then why did he make me a Jedi Knight? Many Padawans were left out of that ceremony."

"Valuable strength and power you have," Yoda said firmly. "Control and maturity?" He shook his head. "Uncertain are we at this time."

"Am I in trouble?" Iskat asked, breathless.

"Trouble, no," Yoda said. "But careful you must be, Iskat Akaris. Anger. Fear." He shook his head, white hairs wagging. "In times of war, easier it is to move down a dark path. Devote yourself to finding peace in the Force you should."

"Master Klefan and Master Uumay will be in the Temple and available to you. Let them help you process what happened on Geonosis and Thule. Continue to focus on your control and discipline. Your team did accomplish the overall goal, but there is always room for improvement." Master Gallia gave a weary smile, as if even this conversation was not the worst one she'd had that day. "Why don't you go wash off the travel dust and get a meal?"

Iskat knew a dismissal when she heard one, and she was more than happy to be out from under their scrutiny. How quickly she'd gone from pride and triumph to shame and . . .

Well, not anger.

Not *just* anger.

Resentment.

She simply didn't agree with Yoda and Gallia—and Mace Windu. She was barely allowed to defend her actions, and the way they'd patronized her, rebuking her like a child after she'd managed to turn a loss into a win—who could accept that without argument? And now they were foisting her off onto Masters Klefan and Uumay, ensuring there would continue to be eyes always upon her. Jedi Knights were supposed to be beyond such overbearing management.

Hiding her resentment—a practice she had long since perfected—she bathed, dressed in her robes, ate, and went to meditate beside her favorite pool, where the flickering of orange fish always soothed her. Tualon was there, sitting cross-legged on a smooth stone. The moment she entered, he looked up. His forehead wrinkled with worry, and he stood.

"You don't have to leave because of me," Iskat said.

He wouldn't quite meet her eyes. "I guess I just wanted to be alone."

"The masters said we should seek solace in our fellow Jedi during difficult times . . ." She smiled softly up at him.

He stepped back. "Iskat, I don't understand you. You argued with Master Yoda and Master Gallia in there. You questioned their wisdom. You still can't see that what you did on Thule was wrong."

"Maybe I don't think it was wrong. And how can we learn if we never question anything?"

"You question too much. You're impudent. You think you're hiding your anger, but the masters can sense it. We all can. You've been here all your life, just like the rest of us, and it's like you just don't get it. You're so close, but then you do something that the rest of us can see is foolish. I just . . . I don't want to be around that kind of energy. We're Jedi Knights now, generals." His eyes pled with her. "We have to act like it."

He left quickly, and Iskat looked down into the crystal-blue water. She'd never felt so far from centered. Tualon had practically run away from her.

She hadn't done anything wrong on Thule—she was certain of it. She'd made the right choice in the moment with the information and resources she had been given. Josk could've told her about the civilians, and that choice had had consequences. This was a war, and if she was to be a soldier, then she would do her part. And yet the masters had reprimanded her, Mace was watching her, and now Tualon didn't want to be near her.

Iskat wanted to be a good Jedi. She wanted to be the best. She wanted the Council to be pleased with her, and her fellow Jedi Knights to welcome her company. She wanted to be an asset, an example. She wanted the Padawans to look up to her. She wanted to make a difference in the galaxy.

And she had. The droid factory on Thule would never be operational, and after what had happened to the power grid, it was unlikely they would attempt to rebuild there.

She'd succeeded.

It would've been so much worse, to come home with Josk's body and a failed mission.

They'd called her conduct unbecoming. Tualon had implied she was impudent and smug.

How did none of them see her potential?

What Iskat wanted more than anything was to be back out in the galaxy, away from the Temple and putting her skills to good use. She wanted to fight and climb and let the Force flow fiercely through her as it had when she'd thrown the battle droids and slaughtered the Geonosians. That meant that she had to convince Masters Yoda and Gallia and Windu that she was trying—that she could be trusted, and that they should send her back out into the field. Her only choice going forward was to become exactly what they wanted her to be. Calm, pliant, unfeeling, willing to follow orders perfectly without question, and without getting too creative or ambitious.

Maybe in another life, she would've told Josk about the slugs earlier, or caught him before he fell, and the whole mission's failure would've been on his shoulders. He would've made the call at the power grid, and Iskat would've done her best not to die. Maybe in another life, she would've just been a good Jedi who followed orders and returned to the Temple with a datacard full of factory intel and tales of barely escaping unexpected battle droids.

Maybe in another life, things would've been different, but in this one, Iskat Akaris had been the one to make the call, and despite the discomfort of her recent dressing-down by Yoda and Gallia, if she was honest with herself, she did not regret it.

The consequence of her success was that she now had to swallow down her true thoughts and feelings and shove herself into a mold if she wanted to continue to advance as a Jedi. And if she couldn't find that balance, if she couldn't be who they wanted her to be . . .

Then maybe, like Feyra, she'd throw down her lightsaber and walk away.

/ **18.**

THE NEXT MORNING, ISKAT RECEIVED a summons to teach the younglings, guiding them in memorizing the Jedi Code that would steer their lives. The crèche felt confining, and it was a beautiful day, so she brought her twelve little students out into the garden and arranged them to sit in a circle.

It was easy enough, leading their breathing until they were all in tune, at least those with lungs that worked that way. The younglings were well behaved and didn't so much as dare to open an eye. Iskat, however, had a wandering mind. Certain memories kept bubbling up as she sat among them, little moments from her own time in the crèche that she'd tried to forget. Reprimands for not focusing, for asking too many questions, for pushing Charlin in anger after she said that Iskat was distracting her by fidgeting too much. She could see in hindsight that even if Jedi younglings were supposed to be peaceful and have self-control from a young age, they were still children who made mistakes, and Iskat had made more than most. It was as if the other children had known some secret she didn't, and Iskat had worked twice as hard just to keep up.

And then she'd accidentally pulled the column down on Tika, and she'd lost her closest friend and the trust of her clan, all in one fell swoop.

"Master Akaris, you're not breathing with us," the youngling nearest her whispered, a shy little Sullustan girl.

"You're right," Iskat whispered back, enjoying the sound of *Master* before her name even if it was an honorific instead of a title. Then she raised her voice slightly so all the younglings could hear her. "This is an important lesson for all of us. No matter how old you are, there will always be moments when you need to stop and look inside to find your center. There will always be opportunities to improve ourselves, to strengthen our focus and connection to the world around us, and thus to the Force." She paused, then turned back to the Sullustan and whispered again, "I should do better to focus, shouldn't I?" The girl giggled politely and nodded.

Iskat closed her eyes and joined the younglings, lengthening her breaths and doing her best to clear her mind. Despite the fact that she'd practiced this exercise every day that she could remember, her internal landscape remained stubbornly busy. It was harder than ever to prevent her emotions from dominating her thoughts. The anger and resentment over Thule was not lessening, as it should've been.

It was growing.

The dream from Thule replayed in her mind, over and over again: the pain and rage visible on a face so like her own, then the arc of a lightsaber tossed away. In the dream, she didn't see the girl's face after she turned to run, but did she imagine a wave of . . . relief?

It didn't matter. She shoved the thought aside. She was doing the opposite of what she'd instructed the younglings to do.

She'd lost her center. Together, breathing with the little ones, she would find it.

"There is no emotion, there is peace," she said softly.

"There is no emotion, there is peace," the children repeated.

"There is no ignorance, there is knowledge."

"There is no ignorance, there is knowledge."

"There is no serenity, there is passion."

The children did not repeat after her, and she opened her eyes to find them all staring at her.

"What's wrong?" she asked.

"You said it backward," the Sullustan told her.

Iskat suddenly felt as if she'd committed some horrible transgression she couldn't remember. Her fingers tingled where they rested on her knees, her feet gone numb. She felt as if everyone in the Temple could see her now, could feel her wrongness.

"You said, there is no serenity, there is passion, but it's the other way around," a human boy added.

Her throat gone dry, Iskat forced on a bland smile and nodded. "Very good. That was a test to see if you know your Jedi Code. And you all passed. Let's keep going." She took a deep breath, centering herself again, grasping for the familiar words she'd long ago committed to memory. "There is no passion, there is serenity."

With a barely perceptible sigh of relief, the children intoned, "There is no passion, there is serenity."

"There is no chaos, there is harmony."

"There is no chaos, there is harmony."

"There is no death, there is the Force."

"There is no death, there is the Force."

In the silence after the last line, Iskat tasted bile rising in her throat.

It wasn't true, was it?

There was death. There was lots of death.

Master Vey had died, and the Geonosians had died, and Josk had died, and the clone troopers had died, and whoever had been near the factory had died. As the war went on, more and more beings would die, Jedi and clone troopers and Separatists and civilians. Thousands, maybe millions of beings.

Maybe even children like these innocent younglings.

The thought made her shiver.

"Master, are you cold?"

The little Sullustan was annoyingly astute and empathetic.

"A little. My biology is different, I suppose," she said.

The girl cocked her head. "What species are you?"

A familiar sadness tugged at Iskat's hearts. "I don't know. No one I've ever met knows the name of my species or my planet."

"Maybe you're the only one left," the human boy said in awe. "In the whole galaxy. The only person like you!"

It took everything Iskat had for her to raise her head with a kind smile. "I'm not the only person like me. I'm a Jedi, like you. The Jedi are my family, and now I get to serve the galaxy and help people. Who could ask for anything more?"

Iskat could.

Iskat could ask for a lot more.

Understanding. Acceptance. Respect. Praise.

Real empathy from her masters and fellow Jedi Knights. A master who would truly try to understand her, to meet her where she was, and to see her powers as gifts instead of problems. A clean slate in which Charlin and Onielle and the others didn't seem always on edge around her, in which Tika hadn't chosen to leave the Jedi Order because of her, in which Tualon didn't see her as a bad influence, in which Josk was still alive because her instinct had been to save him instead of watch, fascinated, as he fell.

Yes, there were a lot of things Iskat Akaris wanted with all her hearts, but she would never tell another living soul that. The only thing worse than feeling those horrible, forbidden feelings and not being able to banish them was imagining what it would be like if anyone else knew her secrets.

Once her time with the younglings was over, Iskat made a beeline for a certain courtyard outside the archives that provided a solace she'd never found anywhere else in the Jedi Temple. She'd been eager to sojourn there since returning from Thule. Other than some weeding among the herb beds, nothing had changed since her last visit, and yet . . . everything had. She felt a heaviness now, a responsibility. Before, failing her master meant disappointing an older woman who didn't really like her. Now failure meant people were dead and the remaining masters trusted her even less.

She was happy to see Heezo there, sleeping under the tree with his cap pulled down over his eyes and another mouse droid in his lap. The moment she settled on the bench, he startled awake guiltily and then grinned at her, showing his pointy little teeth.

"How'd the mission go?" he asked.

"Other than the fact that we accomplished our goal, it was a total failure." She leaned back and tipped her face up to the sky. "I was supposed to zap a power grid, but instead I blew it up. And a factory, too. And a Jedi, our leader, died. All because of me."

Heezo gave the soft growl that she'd come to recognize as a tired sigh. "Hey, that's not the worst thing I've heard. Another recent mission got two Jedi Knights and a Padawan killed chasing a bounty hunter, and they didn't even meet their objective. Another mission lost a master and a couple of dozen clone troopers during a shoot-out in a busy market that left the locals wailing in the streets." He shrugged and opened up the mouse droid. "War is messy."

"But they're trying to pretend that it's not. As if our affinity for the Force means we can accomplish any mission without collateral damage. We have special skills, sure, but blasters can still kill us, falls can still kill us. We're not invincible." Iskat watched the traffic lanes, thinking about how each set of lights represented someone living an entirely different life, going from one place to another—by choice. "It's almost like I spent so much time meditating that I didn't really live life, and now it's caught up to me. So many of my skills are useless now. There's so much I don't know. I can haggle with a shopkeeper for a cracked old kyber crystal, but I don't know how to forage in the wilderness and can barely tend to a wound. I can kill, but they frown on that."

"Killing seems like a valuable skill, during a war."

Iskat sat up suddenly. "You'd think so, but I was trained for peace, not strategy. They call me a general, but I didn't even earn that title. They just . . . gave it to me."

Heezo blew some dust out of the mouse droid and sneezed. "Just because you're born into a society doesn't mean you're fit for it. I came here to escape my fate. But being here is your fate, or so you've been told. And now suddenly they're saying your fate might be to die on some lonely planet, trying to protect people who resent you so that the senators can give each other standing ovations. I'd be mad, too."

"I'm not mad," she said, too quickly; no Jedi was ever supposed to be mad, or at least they weren't supposed to be mad for long or admit to it. "I just feel like my abilities are wasted."

She looked around. Even though they were alone in the courtyard, protected by high walls and the constant drone of traffic overhead, she was still a little paranoid about speaking so freely. If Mace Windu had asked one Jedi to report on her, he might ask another, and the gardens were open to all.

"You don't report to Mace Windu, do you?" she asked him.

Heezo's eyes met hers, his nose wrinkled up. "No. I report to Jopar Tandil in Tech Management. Mace Windu is a little bit terrifying. Like he sees right through you, you know?"

He wasn't lying, at least—she could feel it in the Force.

"It's just, Mace Windu and the other masters—they're making me hold myself back. I have talents that could save lives, if they sent me to the right place. I could've helped in the arena on Geonosis, and then maybe we wouldn't have lost so many of our most well-trained Jedi."

"Well, did you tell them that?"

Iskat snorted. "Of course not! They treat me like a blaster without a safety. I can't be my true self—they won't teach me how to tap into the part of the Force that could really help the war effort. I'm just supposed to squash my abilities down and hide them. There are probably more Jedi like me, afraid to show their true talents. Why does the Council get to decide which abilities are good and bad? Shouldn't we use everything we have to end this war before more people die?"

Heezo carefully put down the mouse droid and looked up at her, light flashing in his eyes. "I've been in this Temple for forty years. Most people assume I don't speak Basic, so I hear a lot of things. I've heard tales that in the past, other Force-users had unusual abilities, too, skills the masters didn't approve of, or urged them to ignore."

Iskat's breath caught in her throat. "What happened to them?"

"They argued with the Council and were urged to seek balance in the Force. But a few refused and sought greater power, and so they had to . . ." His lips pulled back, showing his teeth. "Leave the Jedi."

It felt like there were black slugs crawling up and down Iskat's arms, soft and cloying but deadly, making goosebumps rise. "But . . . what would someone even do, if they left the Jedi?"

A shrug. "What does anyone do? Pursue a different life, I suppose. Maybe explore those abilities that the Jedi reject. It's all whispers and rumors, really. Anything that has to do with leaving, anything that has to do with the dark side, they don't talk about it. They bury it so deep no one can ever find it. They consider that sort of knowledge to be dangerous. But it's out there, somewhere. The Jedi don't like destroying knowledge, even if it has to be locked away."

"Why have knowledge that people can't use? Why keep us in the dark about our own abilities?"

A chuckle. "You're asking the wrong guy. I just fix droids, and sometimes, when I'm near the right pipes, I hear people talk. All I can tell you is that the Jedi have lots of secrets, and that people who want to know more about that sort of thing never get the answers they want here. They just quietly choose to disappear."

A sudden thought sprang to Iskat's mind. "Wait. You said you've been here for forty years. I had a vision of a girl who looked a lot like me dropping her lightsaber and running away. Do you know anything about that? Maybe her name was Feyra?"

At that, Heezo picked up the droid again and gave her a sad smile. "There was a girl who looked like you, maybe twenty years ago. Red skin stands out, even among the Jedi. Never saw anyone else that looked like that, until you showed up."

"I've been wondering if maybe she was related to me?" Her hearts sped up as she spoke the words aloud for the first time. "Possibly even my mother."

A long, significant pause. Iskat could barely breathe as he considered it.

"Jedi don't have mothers, is what I've always heard," Heezo said breezily.

Iskat looked at the door, feeling guilty. She wasn't supposed to care about her mother, it was true. But why would Master Vey keep Feyra's lightsaber when attachment was forbidden? And why were her final words an apology to Feyra—what did Sember think she'd done wrong?

And why had Iskat had that dream on Thule, so exact in its detail, so significant?

"I don't know why I need to know so badly, but I do. I need to know how we're related, and I need to know why she left. Did she have abilities like mine? Did she have unanswered questions? Was she one of the ones who left to . . . pursue the dark side?"

Heezo shook his head.

"I can't tell you that. All I know is that she looked like you, and one day, she was gone. I never saw her again."

/ 19.

A FEW DAYS LATER, ISKAT was again called to the Council Chambers. All
the way up the lift she was smiling, wondering where she might be sent
next. She was well aware that she would be reporting to a more senior
Jedi, an experienced Jedi Knight or master, or possibly even Tualon,
which she wouldn't mind at all, really. She'd been rebuked, but every
Jedi was needed for the war effort. Maybe she wouldn't be in charge, but
at least she would be out in the galaxy, on the front lines, seeing exciting
new planets and using her skills instead of merely practicing them.

In the stately chambers high in a spire, she found Master Gallia joined
by not Yoda, but Mace Windu. His sharp eyes fell heavily on Iskat, and
she met his gaze bravely, chin up.

"Iskat Akaris," Master Windu said, fingers steepled. "Have you given
thought to what happened on Thule?"

"I have, Master Windu."

"And what are your conclusions?"

She slipped her hands into the sleeves of her robes to hide their shaking. "At the time, I thought I was making the right call, but I realize now
that there were other options. I could've retreated and worked out a

new solution with Tualon after reviewing the intel he downloaded in the factory. I could've asked Captain Spider his thoughts and decided on a new strategy or waited for reinforcements. I took a risk, and although it paid off, it also caused harm. In the future, I will seek input from my mission partners and won't act rashly alone."

Mace blinked once, slowly. "A well-spoken answer, and the right one, but is it what you feel in your hearts?"

Iskat faltered for a moment, wondering exactly how well she was hiding her thoughts from the canny master. "I know that it's the right answer, and that is more important than what I feel. The Jedi Order and its service to the Republic are more important than the individual."

"I'm glad to hear you say that." Mace sat back. "We have your next assignment."

Iskat stood taller. "Yes, Master?"

Mace gestured to Master Gallia, who sat up with a pleased sort of energy. "You've done an excellent job working with the younglings, and it has not gone unnoticed. Since Geonosis, they've had rotating instructors, which has made it difficult for them to truly find healing and move forward with their studies. We feel that having one fully committed instructor would benefit them most." She leaned forward and held out a hand. "And we think you're the ideal choice for this position."

For a long moment, Iskat said nothing. She'd come here excited about her next mission offplanet, but they were effectively grounding her. All of Mace's careful compliments didn't change the fact that this wasn't just a disappointment—it was a demotion.

It was a punishment.

"Master, this is a great honor—"

"But?" Mace's eyebrows rose.

"But I feel that the Force calls me to serve the Jedi and the Republic through service in the field. I know you think I've suffered a lapse in judgment, or that I'm not ready to lead, but I'm ready to follow." Iskat's hearts were thumping, and she struggled to maintain her composure. She had to convince Mace that this was the wrong decision.

But Mace didn't even appear to consider it. "Iskat, the Council is in agreement. For now, this is how you can best serve the Jedi Order. It is a post of the utmost importance. These children represent our future, and there is no greater calling than to provide the routine and support they require to thrive."

Master Gallia added, "We feel that this arrangement will be mutually beneficial."

"But I'm a Jedi Knight—" Iskat began.

"And this is a post generally occupied by a Jedi Master, so perhaps that will bring you some comfort," Mace finished.

Iskat looked down and unclasped her hands, which tightened into fists. "Master Windu, I know that you asked Josk to keep an eye on me on Thule. I know that you don't trust me. But I'll do anything to prove to you that I'm fit for duty and that I have truly learned from my errors."

"If you truly want to prove that you're fit for duty," Mace said, "then you'll take this assignment with grace and humility and dedicate yourself to teaching the younglings and further developing your control within the Force. I'll be watching you here, too, along with Masters Klefan and Uumay. We will determine when you're ready for a different post. Until then, you have some work to do. Understood?"

Iskat actively fought her body's desire to slump over in defeat. "Yes, Master. I'll do my best."

"I trust that you will." Mace's datapad beeped, and he frowned at it. "But first, would you please meet Chancellor Palpatine at landing pad seven and escort him here?" He looked to Master Gallia. "He's early."

That, at least, gave Iskat a jolt of excitement. She had seen holos of the Chancellor, of course, but she'd never been in his presence. He was the most powerful politician in the Republic, and even if Mace didn't trust her on the battlefield, at least he trusted her enough to extend the hospitality of the Jedi Temple to someone so important.

"Of course, Master."

She inclined her head, then forced herself to exit the chamber calmly. In the lift, she shook out her body and took a few deep, cleansing breaths. She smoothed back the little hairs that always escaped from her long braid and arranged her sleeves. Once the lift opened, she swiftly walked out to the landing pad, slowing her pace and smiling warmly as she approached the sleek chrome yacht. Much to her surprise, instead of traveling with a retinue or even a secretary, the Chancellor was alone. He was an older man with gray hair brushed back, and he wore long, formal burgundy robes with puffed sleeves. He gave off an air of benevolent kindness, and Iskat immediately liked him.

"Chancellor Palpatine, welcome. I'm Iskat Akaris. Master Mace Windu has asked me to conduct you to the Council Chambers for your meeting."

Palpatine's answering smile was warm and genuine, and he inclined his head. "It is a pleasure to meet you, Iskat. Your name seems familiar. Do I remember correctly that you were among those recently promoted to Jedi Knight?"

Iskat's hearts stuttered, to think he might know anything about her. As she led him to the lift, she said, "You're correct, Chancellor. It's only been a few weeks."

"And what have you done since then? I know we depend on our Jedi Knights as part of the war effort, and the people of the galaxy are grateful for your service."

The slow, formal speech was like a dance, and Iskat felt alive, speaking to someone so important as if they were equals. "I was sent to Thule, where we disarmed a Separatist droid factory."

The lift opened, and Iskat gestured for Palpatine to proceed inside and then followed, standing by his side at a respectful distance.

"Ah, Thule." Palpatine gave a small sigh and clasped his hands. "The Jedi Council was disappointed in the outcome there, but after some thought, I personally take a somewhat more optimistic view. That's one less factory, and perhaps it will give pause to the Separatists and those who would serve them. This is a war, after all, and I for one am pleased to know that another manufactory of weapons against our Republic will never be brought online."

Relief spread through Iskat's chest, to hear that he wasn't disappointed. "I'm afraid the Council disagrees with that opinion, Chancellor, but it's just . . . the Jedi could do so much more . . ." She trailed off.

"Go on," Palpatine urged. "I am not your Council, and I am curious what you would do differently. New perspectives are always welcome."

Iskat realized she only had a few brief moments to speak candidly before the lift doors opened on the High Council and the sharp ears of her masters. "We are peacekeepers, but peace cannot be earned solely through defense. The Jedi—some of the Jedi—have untapped abilities that could be honed to serve the Republic. We could take a more assertive role. Diplomacy is well and good, but the High Council insists that we remain passive when we can do more."

When I can do more, she wanted to say.

The lift doors opened, and Palpatine stepped out. "I enjoyed our talk, Iskat Akaris, and I will take your thoughts into consideration. I feel certain you have a bright future ahead of you."

"I've been told I'm to teach the children now, rather than go on another mission," she said, unable to hide her frustration.

He put a hand to the lift door, holding it open. "How fortunate for the children. They are our future, after all, and they can only benefit from your knowledge. I'm sure we'll see you in the field again soon. The Republic needs more Jedi like you." His eyes twinkled as he inclined his head in farewell and allowed the lift doors to close, leaving her alone.

As the lift descended, Iskat felt a glimmer of hope. Maybe Mace Windu didn't have faith in her, but in one brief meeting, Chancellor Palpatine had suggested he did. She'd felt it in the Force, felt the chancellor's goodwill and approval. He'd said they needed more Jedi like her.

It felt good, and she hoped she would encounter him again soon.

For now, however, she had her orders. Whether or not she liked them, she would follow them. Until something changed, it was her duty to attend to the younglings, and if she toed the line, then perhaps Master Windu would see her dedication and tenacity and consider sending her back into the field. Judging by the rate at which they were losing Jedi with their current strategies, there would come a day when Iskat might be their best option.

Days became weeks became months. Iskat's time with the younglings fell into a comfortable pattern, and as much as she hated to admit it, Mace had been correct: Working patiently with the children helped

Iskat find her own center. Helping them understand death better helped her process her own losses. There was a peace among the small, bright souls in the crèche, and although Iskat felt a stab of jealousy every time she watched a shuttle depart for some faraway place, she told herself again and again that her work was valuable, too. She was starting to believe it.

She visited with Heezo in the little courtyard from time to time, but her days were busy and uncomplicated, so she didn't have much to talk about. He often brought her news of the war, which made her feel both informed and, well, jealous. No matter how hard she worked, how tenaciously she sought serenity, the anger and resentment were still there, simmering deep down in her hearts. She'd just gotten better at ignoring them, better at rationalizing why her current path was as the Force willed it. She told herself that it was foolish to argue with reality; her duty was with the children, and railing against that truth wouldn't get her anywhere. The quickest path to her true goals was following her orders with a serene attitude.

Outside of the children, her life became a little lonely. She'd grown accustomed to Sember's ways, to the simple comfort of living in someone else's firm orbit and always being on the move to some interesting new place. The Temple was nearly empty, and there were days when the training rooms were silent and there was no one with whom to spar. The oldest of the Jedi were still around, of course, including Jocasta Nu, who gave Iskat an inscrutable look every time she set foot in the archives, something between disappointment and suspicion. The search for Feyra had gone cold, and no new dreams troubled her sleep. Iskat often took the mysterious lightsaber out of her drawer and held it, marveling at its yellow blade, so strange and beautiful, and wishing she knew more about the hands that had crafted it.

The few familiar Jedi she did see were constantly busy, dedicated to the war effort. Most of her fellow Jedi Knights were either on missions or recovering from the wounds they'd incurred. As it turned out, the Jedi she spent the most time with was Master Uumay Hawlatha, an ancient Bimm with soft black fur speckled with gray and long, floppy ears. It seemed as if the diminutive Jedi hadn't really noticed that he'd been left behind and that almost all his fellows were elsewhere. Iskat spent an hour with him at dawn every morning by her favorite pool, practicing the same meditations Sember had spent years teaching her. The only difference now was that while Sember had stressed pure uninterrupted silence, Master Uumay sang a soft, sweet song in Bimmini that reminded her of birds in trees, and he never offered any sort of criticism.

One morning, however, Iskat woke up peevish from poor sleep and bad dreams she couldn't remember, and on the way to meditate she ran into Tualon. He was in high spirits and told her that he, Ansho, and Charlin were being sent on an important mission to Kamino.

"Are you joining us?" he asked, friendlier than she'd seen him in months.

"Unfortunately, no. I'll be teaching the younglings, just like every other day."

She was too tired to hide her annoyance, and Tualon faltered for a moment. "It's important work," he finally said. "You must be doing a really good job."

"Don't patronize me, Tualon. We both know why I'm here. Now go. Hurry, before the masters find a reason to be displeased with you, too."

The pity in his orange eyes made her feel even worse.

"If you could just see it from a different perspective—" he started.

"It doesn't matter. This is my life. Good luck on your mission." She crossed her arms and waited, and he took another confused look at her before turning tail and heading off to the landing pads.

She was sick with herself for allowing her frustration to surface so clearly. Even to her own ears, it had been petulant, and Jedi were never petulant. Every time she thought she'd reached a place of calm, every time she felt pleased with her progress, something seemingly insignificant happened and she lost her composure. It was as if she couldn't make any real gains; everything was washed away again like waves destroying castles made of sand.

After she'd sat on her stone by the pool, meditating for some time, she looked to the old Bimm on his favorite cushion; he always seemed perfectly happy and at ease with exactly where he was and exactly what he was doing. Their time together was mostly silent, but Iskat needed more than a song to help guide her through her current troubles.

"Master Uumay, how can I reach serenity, as you have?"

He opened one sleepy eye and closed it again, shaking out his ears. "Live in the now," he intoned. "The past and the future are illusions. There is only the current moment. If you can find peace here, you will always know peace."

Iskat held in an annoyed sigh; cryptic, circular answers did her no good. "But what if . . . what if I want something different than what's happening in the now? What if the Force wants me to do something different? I feel like it wants me out in the galaxy, helping people. I felt it so keenly when I was on Thule. I want to serve the Jedi and the Republic."

Uumay opened both his bright eyes and looked more closely at her, as if seeing her for the first time. "We serve as we are needed. The Force gives us a path to become our best selves and do the most good, and we must walk that path without looking for other, brighter paths. Do you not find value in developing young minds and shepherding forth the next generation of Jedi? After we are gone, these younglings will carry our teachings in their hearts and minds. We are part of a long chain of knowledge and compassion stretching back through the eons. We are all connected. It is a gift, to mold young souls."

"But perhaps it isn't my gift," she argued. "When I was fighting on Geonosis and climbing on Thule, I felt the most peace I've ever felt within the Force. I finally felt the serenity everyone expects me to find by meditating. The Force calls me to action. My hearts tell me this is right."

Uumay cocked his head. "It can be hard to tell the difference between the Force's will and your own will, especially for the young. That's why you must be patient. Now release these feelings into the Force, and let them flow away like blossoms on the breeze."

He closed his eyes and went back to his song, but Iskat was unable to get her head in the right space to meditate. All she could think about was Tualon and Charlin on a ship together, hurtling through hyperspace toward the kind of mission Iskat dreamed of every night as she tried to fall asleep.

"Settle, settle," Master Uumay sang. "Settle down on your branch, little tang tang bird. The sun will go on shining, with or without you."

But Iskat couldn't settle.

No matter what the masters said, she knew that she was meant for more.

She left the garden, holding in her annoyance until she reached the courtyard, where Heezo was working on an LEP droid.

"You seem upset," the Selonian observed.

Iskat paced the small garden, barely noting the rich fragrance of a recently bloomed patch of flowers among the herbs. Her thoughts ran riot, and she didn't know where to begin. "Everything inside me tells me I'm meant to be out there, doing something great—I feel it in the Force—but they're keeping me here on purpose. They're holding me back."

"Why?"

She sat on the bench, her head in her hands. "For Thule. For being unpredictable. For being defiant." A shuttle took off, and she watched it disappear against the lavender sky. "If you had a weapon, wouldn't you use it? Instead of using me, the Jedi send me to meditate, to recite the tenets again and again with the younglings, as if that will make me finally, truly believe them." Her fingers clenched around the stone bench so hard she felt a nail snap. "They don't trust me. They've always been scared of what I could do, and their only answer is to tighten their hold on me."

Heezo looked up from the droid, one lip lifted in something like a snarl. "So what will you do?"

"I don't know!"

The words burst out of her, nearly a shout, and a bird exploded out of a nearby tree.

Iskat had to get herself under control. Jedi did not shout like that in the Temple. Even the youngest younglings didn't raise their voices in anger.

She stood and paced, flexing her fingers into fists and back. "Master Uumay told me I had to be patient."

"So be patient."

She leaned back against the wall and crossed her arms as she stared at him. "What?"

Heezo cocked his head and looked up into the skylanes like he might find answers there. "So do as they ask. Be patient. Play their game. Wait until they trust you again."

Her head fell. "Do you know how hard it is to pretend to be something you're not, day in and day out? To smile and nod and contort your soul into a tight little knot?"

A soft growl. "I know something about that, yes. But you didn't let me finish. Play their game and regain their trust. But while you do that, maybe you can find ways to secretly nurture what's inside of you. That's what I'd do. Hone your skills. Find new ways to use them. Explore what they tell you to repress. Didn't you say you'd found another lightsaber?"

"I think—I know it belonged to my mother."

He grinned. "So learn how to fight with two lightsabers. Plenty of Jedi do that. I've seen Jedi Skywalker's new Padawan in the training rooms. Leave the Temple and go out into Coruscant and practice whatever it is they won't let you do here. You still have freedom, don't you? Use it."

It was as if a door opened in that moment. Iskat had felt so small, so trapped, so stuck. And yet . . . Heezo was right. There were other places to practice, other skills to learn. Why hadn't she thought of it sooner? She'd been so wrapped up in what she'd been told to do that she'd forgotten she could do other things, too.

She would meditate and teach the younglings . . . and then she would follow her hearts. She didn't have to be on a mission to do that.

She could do whatever she wanted to—just not here, in the Temple.

PART
TWO

/ 20.

ISKAT IMMERSED HERSELF IN A new kind of training. She sought texts in the library about unusual lightsaber techniques, mastering telekinesis, and using unconventional ways to channel the Force in battle. She read up on strange species of animals, as well as the plants in the little courtyard. She continued to meditate with Master Uumay at dawn and teach the younglings until the evening, but her nights were her own, and she took full advantage of that time.

Thanks to her busy daytime schedule, she didn't see Heezo very often, but she was glad for the way their time together felt . . . easy. With everyone else in her life, she was always on edge, watching every word and controlling her facial expressions, but with Heezo, she could simply relax and be herself. He had no expectation of her, nor she of him. Sometimes they spoke, and sometimes he muttered to his droids in his language of clicks and whistles and she dozed, staring up at the leaves of the hesafia tree as they changed from green to yellow to brown and back again as time truly began to pass.

And then, at night . . . it was as if the real Iskat Akaris came alive. Finally, she'd found something that calmed her mind: training according to her own interests, honing the weapon of her body while everyone else was asleep. She ran and climbed all over Coruscant, getting to know more of the planet she'd lived on most of her life but had only seen from behind the windows of the Jedi Temple. On one of her nightly runs, she discovered an abandoned construction site in the planet's lowest levels, far away from any homes or businesses, even farther away from the glamour of the highest spires. There, alone, unseen, she began practicing her telekinesis without worrying that anyone might be harmed. After she pulled the column down on top of Tika, she'd grown reticent and delicate whenever using the Force to move things, but Geonosis and Thule had allowed her to really unleash her full strength. Throwing the droids had filled her with satisfaction. Now she could revel in her full power, learning the limits of how she could manipulate the Force and gaining the subtlety Sember had hoped she'd learn through less direct means.

In the Temple, she sparred with every training droid she could find—and even had Heezo add some additional programming to further challenge her skills fighting with two blades. Anakin's Padawan, Ahsoka Tano, gave her a few pointers and suggested some texts to read on the art of dual lightsabers, but she was generally too busy to spar. Iskat sought to train with Master Pong Krell, who was extremely skilled, but he was rarely in the Temple and suggested she speak with Master Kelleran Beq. Kelleran was a thoughtful and detailed instructor, but he was committed to training the younglings with a dedication and energy that Iskat herself had never felt, so he rarely had time to spare. Instead, Master Klefan would occasionally take up two training blades and lead Iskat through new forms that she could later practice on her own, and she would seek out Kelleran if she had specific questions.

She built a second green lightsaber to fit her hand, a simple thing that she could use when sparring or working with Klefan. The mysterious yellow blade she'd found in Sember's chest had to remain a secret. Whether it had belonged to Feyra, who might've been Iskat's mother or some other relation, or whether it had been built by some random stranger who just so happened to need a wide hilt, it felt right in Iskat's hand, as if it had been made to fit her. Whoever had built it, now it was hers, and she worried that if anyone else found out about it, she'd be admonished for cleaving to a possession. Or worse, they'd whisk it away like all the other relics Sember had collected. Only at the forgotten construction site in the lower levels of Coruscant could she practice her newfound skills with one yellow blade and one green flashing in the shadows, unafraid of discovery.

As for the mystery of Feyra, that trail remained cold. There were no more dreams, no more databank searches, no more trusted people she felt safe asking. Perhaps one day she would learn the truth, but until then, she had the lightsaber, and it would have to be enough.

If anyone noticed her new focus, they didn't mention it. At their morning meditations, Master Uumay remained his same sleepy and enigmatic self; the children continued to be children, and the remaining masters were too busy to worry about the strange habits of a single Jedi Knight. No one noticed her slip away after dark, and if anyone saw her when she returned at dawn, they assumed she'd just awakened. She learned to live on less sleep—learned to thrive on it. The nights were her only taste of freedom, and she guarded them jealously, even from oblivion.

The war kept the Jedi busy, and people came and went—mostly went. It seemed like Iskat heard about some faraway death every day, names she'd never even heard before on planets she hadn't known existed as well as people she'd grown up with on planets she'd heard far too much about. When bodies were returned to the Temple, there were funerals, but as time went on it seemed there were fewer Jedi left to observe the remembrances.

Iskat attended every funeral.

And at every ceremony, she heard the same calls to rejoice as another Jedi became one with the Force. But it felt like the same speech repeated again and again, the same mourners with heads held low who would swiftly return to business after the bodies were lowered beneath the floor. Every Jedi was a hero of the Republic. Every fallen soldier was a vibrant light in the galaxy, a luminous being whose body was only a temporary vessel. But their funerals were all the same. To Iskat, it began to feel uncaring.

She was told, again and again, that the fallen Jedi would live on forever through her and in the Force, but all she saw were corpses.

She thought about what it must be like, being sent out into a galaxy at war, as untrained and unprepared as she'd been, and dying there, far from the only place that felt like home, the only home a Jedi would ever know. As they lay on the ground, staring up at an unfamiliar sky, did her fellow Jedi think about the Force and the peace they might find once they joined it, or did they think of happy moments in the crèche, when their lives had spread out before them, full of promise? Did they leave this life filled with fury and regret at what they might've otherwise become? Did they die, as she suspected, frightened and alone?

Iskat had watched death happen, had witnessed the moment a soul crossed over in the Force, and she had not seen the peace and serenity Master Uumay and all of her studies had promised. She'd sensed pain and confusion and fear in Sember, her usually placid master. Perhaps Jedi were special, connected to the Force, but that didn't mean they faced dying with any more dignity than any other creature. In that final moment, a Jedi could be just as lost and abandoned as anyone else.

Iskat certainly understood loneliness. As fulfilling as it was to follow her own passions while learning and training, she still felt adrift as she moved through the quiet halls of the Temple. It especially stung that Tualon seemed determined to continue avoiding her, even after so much time had passed. That brief flare of friendliness—she'd killed it with her candor. His eyes looked straight through her, and he walked with a hurried purpose that suggested he was always on his way somewhere important. When she approached him at Master Ansho's funeral to offer her condolences, Tualon just stared straight ahead and mumbled his thanks before disappearing.

Feeling disconnected, Iskat kept up with the war, any way she could. The news feeds told one story, but people told another. She heard details from Heezo that never made the news. Masters whispered at the funerals. Vendors complained in the streets in the lower levels. No one really felt safe anymore. The few times she was again asked to escort Chancellor Palpatine to the Council chambers, she could feel an uncertainty in him, a growing tension, and although he was polite and always remembered her, he seemed more and more distracted. The Republic was in trouble.

There were so many battles she couldn't keep track of them all, but every time she heard about some daring rescue by the Jedi or a dastardly political plot by the Separatists that had almost succeeded, she secretly fumed.

Maybe if she'd been there, the tides would've turned.

Maybe if the Jedi used her like the weapon she'd become, she could actually do some good.

The war, it seemed, would go on for a long, long time. Although she had done everything the Council had asked of her, Iskat began to lose faith that she would ever be allowed to take part in it again. The training schedule she'd created for herself was so physically grueling that she fell into bed exhausted on the nights when she made it to bed at all. She'd planned it that way, because it was the only way to keep from staring at the ceiling in the dark and seething that she was playing games with children instead of making a difference.

And then one day, she was summoned . . . to the chambers of the Jedi High Council.

There were only two members of the Council present: Yoda and Mace Windu. Masters Klefan and Uumay stood off to their side, and she couldn't tell from their expressions why she'd been called here.

Iskat had been building up her confidence through her self-led training, but standing before two of the most powerful Jedi in the galaxy was daunting to say the least. She set her shoulders back and her chin up, her braided hair sweeping down her back, and was glad that she always kept her robes neat even if there was no one in the Temple who would notice.

"Jedi Knight Iskat Akaris," Master Windu said, leaning forward. "It's been over two years since Thule. What have you learned since then?"

Iskat's fingers twitched but did not make fists.

She'd thought about this.

A lot.

She clasped her hands. "Masters, I have dedicated my days to teaching the younglings at the Council's request, and that has taught me patience and enabled me to find my center. Explaining the Jedi Code to the children has deepened my own understanding of our tenets, and helping the children process the uncertainty and loss the war has brought to the galaxy has helped me process my own. I've spent my personal time seeking to better myself through my studies and training. I meditate with Master Uumay every morning and have greatly improved my lightsaber skills with Master Klefan."

Mace nodded slowly but silently, his intense eyes boring into her. "Jocasta Nu tells us you're a frequent visitor to the library."

A small smile hid her flash of concern. "Yes, I'm sure she's sick of me pestering her for new texts, but there's so much Master Vey never got to teach me. I never took full advantage of our archives before, and now, even if it's not my calling to work there, I'm anxious to catch up."

Jocasta had not extended the offer to work in the archives again, and Iskat now worried that she might be sent from teaching in the crèche directly back to the library. Neither future appealed, but she understood that she was at the mercy of the Force—and these Jedi Masters.

"Master Uumay, has Iskat made good progress with you?" Mace asked.

The old Bimm blinked sleepily and nodded. "Yes, yes, she is an exemplary student. The little tang tang bird has finally learned to settle. If only all the young Jedi Knights would spend as much time meditating."

"Crowded the meditation gardens would be," Yoda said with a chuckle that Uumay shared.

Mace turned to Klefan Opus. "Master Klefan, you were Sember's master, and you were with Iskat on Geonosis. Some would say you know her best. What's your opinion?"

Master Klefan turned his attention to Iskat. His epidermal sacs were full of water, lending him an air of thoughtful gravity. "You could hardly find a Jedi more proficient with two lightsabers, and she proved on Geonosis that she was quite skilled with one. I was there when she saved another Padawan's life under great duress, as well as my own. Of course, Sember came to me occasionally to share her concerns, but I have witnessed Iskat humbly applying herself to her studies in the Force, and I am satisfied with her work. She can be impertinent and a little too curious, but that is hardly unique among the Jedi, is it not? I feel she will do honor to the Order when representing us and the Republic on the battlefield."

Iskat nearly shivered with joy to hear him praise her skills and suggest she finally be released from her duties at the Temple. She didn't like learning that Sember had gone to Klefan with concerns, but when she thought about Sember's final words, it was clear her Master felt that she had somehow failed her Padawan, that she hadn't done enough. Perhaps, then, Iskat hadn't been the problem. Perhaps the problem had been her master.

Mace and Yoda shared a look, and Mace stood.

"Iskat, do you feel that you're ready to be back in the field? Physically and emotionally?"

Her hearts jacked up as hope bloomed. "I do, Master."

"As Klefan said, Sember used to call you hotheaded and rebellious. She had concerns that you might not thrive in situations of intense stress. She even expressed doubts that you would ever rise to the rank of Jedi Knight. How would you respond to that?"

Iskat swallowed down her anger at Sember. "My master was determined, I think, to see the worst in me so that she might help me better succeed. A child's job is to make mistakes and learn from them. I made plenty of mistakes, perhaps more than many of my fellow Jedi, but that means I learned more from those missteps. Sember was dedicated to her work and often left me to practice on my own when I would've preferred personal instruction, but I appreciate the energy and time she put into shaping me and hope to make her memory proud."

For a long moment, Mace and Yoda stared at her as if the truth might be written on her face. She made her breathing even and calm, hid her emotions, locked her mouth in a close-lipped smile, and kept her hands clasped in the sleeves of her robes so the masters would not see their nervous twitching.

"Great faith in you these masters have," Yoda finally said. "Ready they believe you are. Chancellor Palpatine, too. Uncertain am I, but . . ." He sighed. "Great, our need is."

"No more accidents. No more explosions," Mace said firmly.

Iskat's head fell forward, just a little bit. "No explosions, Master."

Mace gave her one decisive nod and crossed to the door. "Collect your kit, then report to landing pad five. Your team will be waiting for you. They've been fully briefed, and I'll have the mission details transmitted to your datapad shortly. You are third in command. You will do exactly as your leaders instruct. They've been given explicit orders to keep in touch with us regarding your performance. I don't think you need me to tell you that the success of this mission will determine your role in the Jedi Order going forward."

A strange and sudden fear made Iskat catch her breath. For all that she'd told Heezo that she yearned for freedom, she wanted it on her own terms. Being thrown out of the Order—

It was unthinkable.

"Master, I—the Jedi Order is my home—"

"Fear not, Iskat," Yoda said kindly. "Always a place for you there is in the Temple."

"So you're saying this is a test."

Master Windu opened the door. "We're at war. Everything is a test. Good luck, Jedi Akaris."

"Thank you, Masters. Uumay, Klefan. I won't let you down."

With a respectful bow, Iskat walked sedately out of the room and waited until she was alone on the lift to jump up and down and screech. Finally! A mission! Her patience and silence for the last two years had paid off. Tomorrow morning, she wouldn't wake up to meditation with Master Uumay and another day of recitations with the children; she would be on a new and exciting planet. So what if this was a test? She'd passed every test she'd been given.

Well, except for Thule.

In the minds of the Masters, at least.

She had to stop herself from skipping to her chambers, where she put on her best traveling robes and cloak and happily buckled on her utility belt. She considered the yellow lightsaber before carefully stowing it deep in her wardrobe drawer, as Sember once had. Iskat would be watched carefully on this mission and needed to be the perfect Jedi Knight. She would prove that she could be trusted. She took both of her green-bladed lightsabers instead.

At landing pad five, she found clone troopers loading crates onto a shuttle as two familiar figures watched her approach. Her immediate response was excitement, followed by a sinking feeling that suggested things were going to be more complicated than originally anticipated.

"Hello, Tualon," she said cheerfully. "Captain Spider."

"General, it's been a long time," the clone captain greeted her with a brief salute.

"Jedi Akaris," Tualon said before turning away and boarding the ship without another word.

/ 21.

THINGS WERE TENSE AS THE ship took off. Much to her dismay, Tualon still wasn't back to his old, friendly self. He'd told her that he needed to keep his distance, and he had. He was still doing so. She hadn't spoken to him since that moment in the hallway—she'd stopped trying, as it just made her feel even more miserable—and he was out on missions most of the time, anyway. He seemed more somber now that Master Ansho was gone, and Iskat's hearts ached to reach out to him. She knew better than anyone what it was like to lose a master. But the way he'd been avoiding her made it clear that this wasn't a conversation he wanted to share with her, that he had no desire for her commiseration or her pity.

As for Captain Spider, he'd greeted her and then joined his crew in outfitting the ship for their voyage. It was hard to tell someone's mood through a helmet, but Iskat could feel his unease in the Force. He didn't trust her. And why should he? He'd lost fourteen men on her watch after successfully bringing them all home from Geonosis. In his eyes, she was a liability.

Considering the uncomfortable silence, Iskat used her time to scroll through her tablet and read the entire mission brief. They were on their way to an unpopulated moon in the Outer Rim to rescue a slicer known only as Ginntho whom the Separatist Army was attempting to forcibly recruit. The brief didn't say whether this slicer was on the side of the Republic or not, only that they had worked for Count Dooku and had once been a xenoanthropologist. Iskat was annoyed to see that the amount of information she'd been given yet again seemed dangerously minimal. She had the name of the moon, at least—Olgothon 3. She searched for more detail, but there wasn't much available. From what she could tell, this moon was the sort of place that no one cared about.

"There's not much here," she said. "What's our plan?"

The ship was larger than the one they'd taken to Thule, with a communal area behind the cockpit that featured tables and chairs and a few couches. Several clones were relaxing around the room, playing dejarik, reading, or napping, but they didn't seem to be paying attention to either of the Jedi in their midst. Tualon was sitting on the other side of the chamber, as far from Iskat as he could get. When he didn't respond, she stood and walked toward him, standing over him where he sat on the couch.

Perhaps in their personal lives, he could ignore her, but this mission was her chance to prove herself, and she wasn't going to be shy about asking for what she needed to succeed.

When she didn't budge, Tualon sighed as if he had gone as long as he could without giving her attention and had reached the end of his rope. Not that he looked up at her. "We land, gather intel, approach the slicer, and extricate them."

"Yes, I read the brief," she said, unable to hide her frustration. "I was hoping for more details. How do we gather intel? Who approaches the slicer? What if they don't want to be extricated?"

"Did you learn nothing last time, Iskat?"

"I learned that I need more information going into a mission where someone could die!"

He rubbed his temples like she was already giving him a headache. "This is how it works. You go into battle with whatever information they give you, and it's never perfect, and it's often flawed, and you trust in the Force and your training to bring you out the other side. I don't have some secret knowledge that's been purposefully hidden from you. We'll approach the locals, identify the slicer, and select the best way to approach them."

"Do we even know what they look like?"

He held up his datapad. "Again, you know everything I know. Several of my missions have run successfully on less intel. All we can do is keep in close communication and be subtle. Don't let anyone know you're a Jedi. Don't make a scene. Captain Spider will be out of uniform and helping us look while his men monitor the ship and comms."

"So we know pretty much nothing and are just scrambling in the dark."

A snort. "You see pretty well in the dark, from what I remember."

It was the first friendly word she'd heard out of him in years, and something in her chest loosened up for the first time in forever. "I do see well in the dark, sir."

When he finally turned around to face her, she gave him a small and cheeky salute.

Tualon met her gaze briefly and looked away; she'd missed looking into his ember-colored eyes. "Yeah, don't call me that. It's odd, being told I'm in charge of you, that I'm to report on your actions. We grew up as equals."

"And then things changed. You don't have to worry about me. I've been working with Master Uumay, I've kept up my athletic conditioning, and I've spent so much time with small children that I'm completely immune to annoyance."

Tualon didn't laugh at the joke. Instead, he stood, looking into her eyes. "Iskat, I have to know."

Her breath caught. "Know what?"

"Josk. Was there—"

"There was nothing between us, I swear. I could barely tolerate him. He wanted to step in as my mentor, if you can believe it."

He leaned away from her, almost grimacing; she'd guessed very, very wrong.

"No, I—no. I wanted to know if there was any way he could've been saved. What really happened up there? I was so busy climbing I wasn't paying any attention to you two, but something about it seemed off. I just need to know. It's been bothering me all this time."

In that moment, Iskat was very, very happy that she had put a great deal of energy and study into shielding her emotions. She swallowed hard and looked down, careful not to let him see her eyes as she spoke. "We were climbing the canyon wall, the same as you, and I had just noticed the slugs. I don't think Josk sensed them. I tried to warn him, but it was too late. He put his spike through one of them, and then lost a handhold and reached for what seemed to be a regular hole in the rock. A flock of birds flew out and attacked him. They were biting him, and he let go to try to protect his face. But from where I was, since we were both climbing and I was higher up, there was nothing I could do. He pushed away from the wall and just . . . fell. I thought he would catch himself like we were trained to do, or at least slow his own fall, but I guess the venom works fast. The troopers said he was dead before he landed. All I could do was watch."

"But if you'd used the Force—"

"To what, slam him into the cliff face? The bird venom either paralyzed him or killed him. I had to concentrate on not falling myself, or there would've been two dead Jedi." Then she looked up, let him see the pain written in her features. "I think about that moment constantly. All the meditation in the world can't erase that image from my memory. You want to know if I could've saved him? Well, I've asked myself that question every day for two years and come up with the same answer: No. And I feel like a failure because of it."

He reached over and put his hand on her arm. Every nerve in her body came alive at his touch—the first time he'd touched her since the cavern on Thule.

"I'm sorry. I didn't mean to bring up painful memories."

She snorted softly, almost a sob. "So when you asked about that time our friend died in front of me, you were looking for fun stories, or . . . ?"

"I was looking for answers." He withdrew and cocked his head at her. "You're hard to read, you know that?"

I do that on purpose, she thought to herself but didn't say.

"You've avoided me for two years, Tualon. I'm an open book. All you have to do to read me is pay attention."

Iskat had spent those two years at the Temple pretending to fit into a very specific box, and she'd meant to keep up that façade with Tualon, and yet he, out of all the people she'd ever met, shook the box until her brains were scrambled. She couldn't help but be herself around him, which was probably why he was so confused. Against her better judgment, she had a foolish, rebellious urge to show him her true nature in the hope that he would understand her, even though she knew full well that he wouldn't approve of the way she allowed her emotions to move through her, how she was beginning to believe that using them might be a way to enhance her relationship with the Force. He just knew that something about her was wrong. It was like a prey animal's danger sense going off even when it couldn't see the predator hiding in the shadows.

Not that Iskat was a predator.

Just that she was definitely hiding big, possibly dangerous parts of herself from everyone in her life.

Well, except Heezo.

She hated the irony of it. She couldn't be honest with the one person she truly cared about because it might make him go back to ignoring her. She had to put herself back in that little box. Not be caustic in response to sympathy, not be flirty in response to misunderstanding. Maybe if she pretended long enough, she'd become what Tualon wanted her to be—not that it had worked with Sember. Or maybe, if he let her in instead of always pushing her away, she'd learn that inside, away from the Temple, he was a different sort of Jedi, too.

So she went for honest—an acceptable version of it. "I'm just saying . . . it's been hard, feeling like the only one constantly left behind at the Temple. The only Jedi who didn't get sent on missions. I feel like I haven't spoken to anyone our age in a thousand years. So I guess if I'm strange, it's because I've spent all my time with children and an ancient Bimm who calls me a tang tang bird. But if you ever want to know what I'm thinking, all you have to do is ask."

"Okay, then." Tualon cleared his throat. "What are you thinking?"

It came out friendly but guarded, but it was a start.

"I'm thinking I wish we had more information on this mission. On Olgothon 3, and on Ginntho. Especially since a lack of intel made our last mission together go awry."

His smile was sad, like she was a child who didn't quite understand. "Imagine what it's like right now, being one of the few Jedi Masters left in the whole galaxy and being given two sentences from someone in the Senate, handed down through three intermediaries because it's a secret, with instructions on a mission that's highly important to the war effort. And you can't ask questions or dig deeper, you can only look around and choose from who's available—from who's *still alive*—and send them out with less intel than you both know they need. That's what keeps happening—that's what Ansho told me before he died. They're doing their best, but this is war, not a Jedi trial they can control. The longer the war goes on, the more Jedi die, and they have fewer and fewer options."

Iskat swallowed down her thoughts on the war and how, if the people in charge had been willing to do something decisive, they might've already won. Little missions here and there were never going to turn the tide; they would only bleed the Jedi dry. This one slicer wasn't going to change everything.

"I can understand your point," she said instead, bland and careful. "But with all the information in the Jedi Archives, you'd think there would be more details about a moon than 'unpopulated.' Is it an aquatic place? Is it cold? Is it a desert? Was it once occupied, and then something horrible happened? How are we supposed to find one person— who uses a code name and is clearly trying to hide—on an entire moon?"

Tualon stood and walked to the viewport, looking out past the pilot and navigator and into the blazing glory of hyperspace. His gleaming black skin reflected the bluish swirls. "We'll get there, and we'll figure it out. That's our job. It might take a day, or it might take a year. All we know is that it's important enough that they're willing to send Jedi they dearly need elsewhere." Then he gave her a smile—a real smile— showing, to her surprise, that his stark white teeth had been sharpened to points. "And don't worry. I've done this a couple of times. Ansho taught me everything he knew. It's not as hard as it sounds. We get into orbit, we listen in on some frequencies, we identify big cities and small outposts and unsavory backwater bars. We find a likely place and put out word that we need a very special sort of slicer. Suggest that we have the credits to pay them. Throw out the bait, wait for the glabos to bite."

"What's a glabos?"

Tualon sat down at the nearest table and poked at his datapad, turning it toward her to show a slime-covered fish shaped like a ribbon with whiskers and bulging eyes. She could feel him warming up to her. "It's a kind of eel that lives in the cave systems on Ryloth. I had a brief mission there and had to learn how to fish. It was a good way to pass the time while waiting for my target to surface."

That had Iskat's attention. She sat down across from him. "Wait. So you've been to your homeworld? Is that where you changed your teeth?"

He briefly touched his thumb to one of their points like he wasn't quite used to it yet. "Most beings can't fit in undercover on Ryloth, so I was the logical choice. After Ansho died, I was in a dark place, and it helped, having something else to focus on. It was interesting, being immersed in my homeworld's culture. I was the odd one out—most males of my age filed their teeth long ago. It's a rite of passage."

"Did you choose it, or did you have to do it to fit in correctly?" she asked.

"It felt less like a choice and more like the chance to become myself, if that makes any sense. Like it was meant to be." He got a far-off look in his eyes. "I'm definitely not a child anymore."

Iskat was brimming with curiosity; as someone who had no information on her planet or her species, she was fascinated by the concept of Tualon's return to the place of his birth. "Did you like it—your homeworld?"

He shrugged. "It didn't feel like home. Everyone looked like me, but I almost felt like a fraud as I walked among them, like I would never be able to fit in. My commitment is to the Force, not to a job or a family or local politics, and it was hard to connect with the daily rituals of that kind of life. With every sip of Twi'lek liquor, I knew war was ravaging the galaxy beyond. And besides, I prefer the Temple to the way my people live in underground caves on Ryloth." He grinned, showing off his teeth. "I had to pretend to like glabos, but it was slimy and salty. Even our camp rations are better."

"Sorry, sir, but I just checked the crate," one of the clones said, thumping the box he was sitting on. "Nothing but glabos stew for this mission."

"And Gungan shrimp paste," another added. "Buckets of it."

Tualon chuckled. "Then it's all for you, Nic. I'd rather have ration bars."

The other clones laughed along with him, and Iskat began to see what she'd been missing all this time. Not only the excitement of missions and the chance to prove herself and help the galaxy, but camaraderie. Just . . . laughing with someone. Sure, she laughed with Heezo every now and then, and the children made her laugh with their antics, but this was different. This made her feel like she belonged.

She soon learned that the trip was going to be much longer than she'd expected—several days through hyperspace. Their ship had been chosen to accommodate such a journey, and it was a new curiosity, climbing into one of the bunks fit into the wall and sliding her door shut to create a little cocoon. She slept well enough, the ship purring along around her. Tualon was just beneath her, she knew, and that gave the situation a strange intimacy. This boy—well, now man—that she'd admired ardently since their earliest days together was finally talking to her, and he was just a meter away, maybe. If she moved, could he hear it? Likely not. She couldn't hear the clones moving in their own bunks all around. Whoever had built this ship had taken care to offer some privacy, thanks to soundproof materials.

She woke in the darkness that first night cycle and slid her door open to look out into the cabin. There was a slight whirring sound, and she found an R3 astromech droid painted in green and indigo swiveling to focus on her. It beeped softly, and low lights glowed along the floor, showing her where the bathroom was.

"Thanks, but I'm good," she whispered. "Just checking the time."

In response, the droid played a whisper-soft melody, and she chuckled and slid her door shut again. Time to sleep, apparently.

She soon grew accustomed to the rhythm of life on the ship. The ration bars, she learned, were pretty bland, and the protein paste was barely edible. There was a dejarik board in a corner, and the clones often played sabacc. The astromech was called Jatz because it seemed to like music more than most of its kind and would play songs that suited the present mood, or just pleasant background music as everyone relaxed. One of the clones, it turned out, loved novels, and he told Iskat she was free to borrow any of his holobooks, as long as he'd read them first. As time passed and everyone loosened up, she started to learn the names of the clones who had earned them—Spider and Nic she knew, but there were Rocko, Nexu, Doc, Storm, Blue 22, and Whirl. The bibliophile was called Flip, thanks to the electronic sound of him advancing the pages of his holobooks. They'd given CT-0528 the nickname Last Man because he was the only one of her fifteen clones who had survived Thule, which chafed at her pride. The missing clones had been replaced, and it troubled Iskat, that she had no way to know who among their current company was original. She was starting to see the subtle differences in their voices and facial hair and mannerisms. She had thought the clones were all the same, but there were surprising differences.

After breakfast the next morning, Tualon asked Iskat if she wanted to spar, and even though there was nothing she wanted more in the entire galaxy, she was able to contain her excitement and act normal. They had to use tactical batons, since there wasn't enough room for lightsabers, not if the clones wanted to keep their extremities intact. Iskat quickly learned that her two years of intense study at the Jedi Temple had eclipsed whatever Tualon had learned on his missions. The difference in their skill level was shocking, and she wasn't even trying her hardest.

"You've been practicing," Tualon said, a little out of breath and rubbing a bruise on his arm.

"I've had a lot of spare time," she responded with a smile.

Once he'd thawed a little, she and Tualon fell into a routine of training together each day cycle. They began with meditation and calisthenics, then moved to sparring, where Iskat was now the one giving Tualon pointers. Their conversations grew easier, and Iskat felt as if perhaps she couldn't be her whole self around Tualon, but she could be a version of herself. It wasn't exactly dishonest; she was just omitting certain things, and in return, she got to talk with him, smile with him, laugh with him.

He genuinely liked her—or at least, this part of her. Iskat marveled that she'd gone from the echoing chambers of the nearly empty Jedi Temple to a cramped ship with thirty other people and yet felt like she had more freedom here and more room to grow. She began to wish the journey would never end. The excitement of a mission made her feel more alive than instructing the younglings back at the Temple. Teaching was a valuable and necessary task, but Iskat knew that this was what she was meant to be doing, what the Force demanded of her. Her newfound sense of balance and peace was proof of it.

She was meditating at Tualon's side, timing her hearts to beat with his, when Jatz played a merry song of beeps and the ship finally dropped out of hyperspace. Iskat's body felt the change, and she opened her eyes and stood to go look out the viewport for her first glance at Olgothon 3. It was a small, dark sphere, swirled with emerald green and purple. She was very aware of Tualon following her and standing behind her, much closer than he might have just a few days ago.

"There it is," Flip said from the pilot's chair. "Wait, we're getting a comm."

He pressed a button, and the whole ship crackled.

"Who's there?" a deep, masculine voice rumbled.

"This is the *Chalice* out of Chandrila," Flip said.

"State your business."

Flip looked back to Captain Spider, then Tualon.

Tualon stepped forward. "We're just here to fuel up," he said. Iskat had never realized before what a bad liar he was.

"Wrong answer."

The ship's systems exploded with blinking lights and alarms, and Jatz's music switched off as he zoomed to the wall and plugged in, immediately screeching his own concern.

"Sir, we're targeted," Flip said, sounding nervous. "By . . ." He cleared his throat nervously. "A lot of things. Long-range missiles, for example."

"You get one warning." The deep voice chuckled. "If you don't want to be blown to smithereens, turn around and leave Olgothon 3 for good."

/ 22.

IN BETWEEN THE BLINKING LIGHTS, klaxons, and muttering clones, it was hard for Iskat to get a bearing on what was happening. She'd never been in this situation before, and she knew her best bet was just to get out of the way and let more experienced people do their jobs.

Except . . . no one else was really stepping up with anything like confidence.

"Why are you targeting us?" Tualon asked, clearly worried.

"Because you're still here, and because you're lying about your intentions," the voice responded.

"What does that mean?"

A bored sigh. "You're not here to fuel up. There is no fuel here. Even the most basic scan would tell you that. It's a virtually uninhabited moon of a garbage gas planet, and you passed right by Agaris. It's not much, but it's clearly better supplied than this old rock."

"If it's so poorly supplied, why are you there? And threatening people?"

The voice snorted. "You sure do talk a lot for someone who should be turning tail and getting out of range."

Tualon clicked off the mic. "Maybe we try approaching from the other side of the moon?"

Captain Spider nodded. "Fair enough. If anyone's on the other side, they might have more sense."

"Okay, we're leaving," Tualon said into the mic. "Sorry to bother you."

The only answer was the continuing blare of various alarms, but as far as Iskat could tell, no weapons had yet been deployed. Flip turned the ship around, and a few moments later, the cockpit went gloriously silent. Jatz beeped a sigh. Iskat had never been happier to hear absolutely nothing at all. They flew toward the next planet and around the other side of it, as if hiding from the much smaller moon. But they stayed far enough out of orbit that no one on Agaris hailed them.

"Let's wait here for half a day or so," Tualon said, his lekku glistening with nervous sweat. "Hopefully they'll forget us, and then they'll switch shifts, and maybe whoever shows up the next time won't be as unreasonable."

"At least we know not to say we're there for fuel next time," Iskat chimed in.

He shot her an annoyed look. "Why else would anyone stop there?"

"Because they're looking for a place to hide. It's the only obvious reason."

"But then we look suspicious," he argued. "If they wouldn't help us when we supposedly just wanted to buy fuel, why would they be more welcoming if we admitted we were on the run?"

"Because whoever we were talking to must also be hiding. Uninhabited moon, no known resources, it's all the place is good for. He's clearly not a fool."

Tualon left the viewport and returned to the couch in the communal room. "Well, hopefully whoever we encounter on the opposite side of the moon will be easier to fool. We just need to get past their planetary defenses and land."

With the ship floating freely, Iskat felt a new sense of impatience and malaise. She liked the idea of moving toward something, liked the hum of the engines and the calm of soldiers accustomed to the gentle routine of travel time. But now they were so close to their objective and forced to just . . . wait.

Iskat Akaris had never been good at waiting.

She played a round of holochess, barely winning, and making Whirl grunt and kick the table. She tried to read one of Flip's novels but kept getting stuck on the same paragraph. She thought about asking Tualon to spar, but his energy was nervous and annoyed, and she didn't want to get on his bad side. He didn't like it when she beat him on a good day, which she usually did, and just now he'd know if she was going easy on him. No, better not to get in a fight with someone who was already internally conflicted. Now that she'd seen Tualon in charge and uncertain how to proceed, Iskat couldn't help wondering what he would've done differently on Thule if he'd been the one making the decisions.

When it was finally time to bed down, she lay in her bunk, practicing her breathing and thinking about what the next day might bring. Tualon had told her stories of his missions on other planets, but this problem was new to him. Most planets were either so busy or so empty that it was easy to land a ship and get into position from there. But Olgothon 3 was a tiny moon, maybe too empty and lawless, and whoever was on the other side of the comms wanted to keep it that way.

The next morning, Tualon woke Iskat up from a sound sleep, knocking on the sliding door to her bunk.

"This is no time to sleep in," he groused. "Grab a ration bar and come up to the cabin."

Iskat hurriedly brushed her hair and got dressed before joining the rest of the crew. The clones sat around in chairs and on cargo boxes in their full armor, silent and restless. Flip brought the ship around the back of Agaris and approached Olgothon 3 from its dark side. Tualon and Iskat stood in the cockpit with Captain Spider. Tualon's sharpened teeth rasped as he ground them nervously together. As the ship edged closer, the little moon came into focus, its violet waters and dark-green forests swirling prettily.

"Almost there . . ." Tualon whispered.

They were so much closer than they'd gotten the day before, and Iskat bit back her smile as they neared atmosphere.

"Thought you could just sneak on in, huh?" The grumbly voice filled the cabin, and everyone within tensed.

"Sorry, we just need a place to lie low," Tualon said, making his voice a little deeper than usual.

"Nice try, but I know it's the same ship from twenty-one hours ago, and I know that you're the same guy and you're still bad at lying. So here's a truth for you."

Just like yesterday, lights began blinking frantically and alarms sounded. Jatz was already preemptively plugged into the wall via scomp link, whirring and beeping as he tried to solve the problem of how not to get blown up.

"Go away for real this time, or you're going to learn how much I hate liars," the voice barked.

Tualon switched off the mic. "Okay. Ideas."

"We can probably dodge whatever is incoming—" Captain Spider began.

Jatz gave a distressed squeal, suggesting they could not, in fact, dodge whatever was incoming.

"Maybe we could sell this ship and get a new one?" Blue 22 said; he was a bit of a shiphead and probably would've enjoyed nothing more than to stroll around a used shipyard, looking for a good deal.

"No way. I'm not going back to the Jedi High Council with a different ship," Tualon grumbled.

Iskat watched a screen showing little red targeting X's that made her very uncomfortable—surface-to-air missiles, plasma cannons, and ships preparing to launch. "We don't have long," she said thoughtfully.

"Then what do you propose we do?" Tualon shot back.

Iskat stood and looked down at the dark little moon floating peacefully through the sparkling indigo like a jewel in deep water.

"He said he hates liars. So let's tell him the truth."

Tualon snorted. "The truth? This is a stealth mission. We can't tell the whole planet our business."

"I don't think it's a whole planet. I think it's one cranky old guy on a moon. I think it's Ginntho."

"What if he's with the Separatists?"

"Then we line up our hyperdrive and jump before he can hit us. We can do that, right?"

Jatz beeped in the affirmative; proudly, Iskat thought.

"I expect you're coming up with your next tall tale," the grumbly voice said, maybe a little amused. "So you've got one more chance. After that, I start shooting and my ships are airborne. And if you come back within orbit after that, I don't ask again. It's just a bunch of boom boom."

Tualon slammed his fist into the bulkhead. "We have to get down there. We have to get that slicer. And we can't let this backwater bombardier stop us."

"So let's go back to Coruscant and—"

"No!" Tualon roared. "No! We're not going back home empty-handed."

Iskat was silent for a long moment, watching his face cycle from rage to hope to annoyance at a subpar idea and back to rage again. She'd never seen Tualon lose control like that, never seen another Jedi show anything like the anger that was a constant struggle for her. She wondered—had he always been this way? How did he contain it? She'd always thought him an ideal Jedi, but maybe . . . maybe he wasn't as perfect as he seemed.

Which only made her like him more.

She should've held her tongue, but . . . she couldn't.

"It's hard when you don't want to let your mission fail but everything seems impossible, isn't it?"

The glare he gave her was momentarily full of something like hatred, a very un-Jedi-like hatred, but then he looked away, a little broken inside. "Don't, Iskat."

"I have an idea."

"I don't want to hear it. I'm going to see if I can reach Coruscant. We need guidance from the Council."

With Tualon in the back, things were somehow more tense. The red lights flashing, the blaring alarms, the whirs and beeps of a worried R3 droid, the fidgeting clones waiting for someone in charge to do something decisive.

Iskat glanced back and saw Tualon huddled over his comlink, repeating the same insipid phrase again and again, trying to reach Coruscant. She'd admired him for nearly two decades, and this was a side of him she'd never seen before—desperate and failing.

If only he would give her a chance.

If only he would *listen* to her.

But he was like everyone else. He'd seen her worst moments—the column, Geonosis, and Thule—and now he was scared of what she might do.

Maybe that was why she did what she did next—because he'd looked at her with disgust and then refused to hear her.

Maybe she had a self-destructive streak.

Maybe she was just that certain that she was right.

Maybe despite all of her training, she still didn't have self-control.

Or maybe it was because the Force was nudging her in the right direction, because she felt something deep in her soul pushing her gently toward the answer.

Whatever the reason, she checked that Tualon was still in the back of the ship, wasting time on a comlink that couldn't possibly reach that far through the galaxy, and she stepped deeper into the cockpit and switched on the mic.

"We're here to rescue someone called Ginntho," she said.

/ 23.

CAPTAIN SPIDER SLAPPED HER HAND away from the mic as Tualon ran to the front of the ship.

"Tell me the mic wasn't on when you said that," Tualon begged, eyes frantic.

She held herself tall. "Someone had to do something."

"If you've ruined this mission—you might've gotten us all killed—I swear, Iskat—"

As if on cue, all the red lights stopped flashing and the alarms stopped blaring.

"I wasn't aware Ginntho needed rescuing. What do you want with Ginntho?" the voice asked, almost bemused.

Iskat blinked innocently at Tualon. He cursed under his breath and indicated with a sarcastic hand gesture that she should take the mic.

She graciously didn't give him the smug smile she'd been waiting all her life to deploy. "We're on a mission from some friends on Coruscant. Our intel suggests the Separatists are attempting to forcibly recruit Ginntho for some . . . unsavory business."

"And what's your offer?"

She looked at Tualon, confused. "Offer?"

"The Separatists want Ginntho. You want Ginntho, whoever you are. What makes you the better choice?"

Iskat honestly wasn't sure how to answer that. Now it was her turn to gesture at the mic.

Tualon briefly closed his eyes before speaking. "The Separatists want to destroy the Republic, and they don't care who or what gets hurt in the process. We believe in the Republic and in the right of all beings to be represented fairly and have their rights protected. We can get Ginntho to a safe place where they could do some real good, if they wanted to. Or, at the very least, disappear and be free of the aggressive attentions of the Separatists. Especially, we understand, rogue elements of the Banking Clan."

For a long moment, nothing happened. Then the voice said. "Come on down to talk. I'm transmitting coordinates. But remember: I'm not without my defenses."

"We're here to help." Tualon exhaled, visibly relieved.

"We'll see about that."

The comm went silent.

After a few moments, Flip said, "We've received landing clearance and coordinates. Shall I take us down, sir?"

Tualon put a hand on the clone's shoulder. "Please. Everyone, buckle up."

Iskat and Tualon got in their harnesses, and she wanted to crow her triumph but knew that Tualon was exactly the kind of person who would hate that.

"Do you think that's really Ginntho?" she asked. "The voice?"

"It would make sense." Tualon couldn't stop fidgeting, tapping his fingertips in turn nervously. "Otherwise, why would they care if we come into orbit? And why would our answer change anything?"

"Do you think the weapons are real?"

His head jerked around to stare at her. "What do you mean?"

"You saw the moon. It's tiny. No resources. The kind of place you would only go if you were trying to hide out. And if you were there to hide, how and why would you bring a planetary defense system? There's nothing worth defending. Ginntho must be a truly gifted slicer for the Republic to need them so badly; maybe it's just a clever program. Maybe there aren't any weapons at all."

He blinked at her, eyes sharpening. "Is that why you made that ridiculous, dangerous statement against mission orders and nearly got us killed? Because you suspected they were lying about blowing us up?"

She gave a one-shoulder shrug. "Maybe. They kept threatening, but if they really had weapons, wouldn't they have at least let off a warning shot? Something in the Force nudged me in that direction. And it's not like you were winning them over with your answers. Sometimes you have to think outside the box."

"Just because it worked once doesn't mean it's a wise strategy," he reminded her. "I'm supposed to be in charge. We're supposed to be a team. You don't need to be sneaky—"

"You wouldn't listen!"

"Then maybe we're both to blame. I need to listen better, and you need to cooperate more."

A brief flare of anger behind her eyes.

"But I was right."

"Iskat, you were *lucky*."

Funny how I'm always lucky when it's life or death, she thought, but didn't say. It was as if she was tapped into some sense Tualon and the rest of the Jedi didn't have, like she knew things they didn't and had hunches that went against their staunch denials, and yet when she was proven correct, they didn't celebrate her. They just tried to shame her for it.

The ship burned through atmo and landed lightly in a valley of waving green grasses topped with nodding lavender flowers. Huge trees ringed the space, their white and gray trunks snaked with ivy. Nothing but the grasses moved—no animals, no people, no trading outpost like most little moons might offer.

"It's too quiet," Tualon said.

"If it's just Ginntho here, you can't expect a welcome party. At least there aren't any visible plasma cannons."

"She makes a good point, sir," Captain Spider said. "Not that I trust the situation."

The ramp extended, and twenty clone troopers fanned out into the grasses, their blasters at the ready, while eight stayed within as reinforcements. Iskat straightened her robes and took both of her lightsabers in hand.

Jatz rolled to the edge of the ramp and twittered nervously.

"Hello?" Tualon called, which Iskat thought was a little ridiculous.

The voice on the comm had given them exact coordinates, which meant they were precisely where they'd been sent. If the owner of the voice wasn't here, it was purposeful. All the hallooing in the world wasn't going to improve the situation.

A deep *fvoom* noise echoed in Iskat's chest as a plasma shield rose in a large circle to surround both Jedi, their ship, and all the troopers. The clones looked around in concern, aiming their blasters into the grass.

"So Ginntho doesn't want to get shot," Tualon whispered from beside Iskat, where they waited in defensive stances. She lit both of her green lightsabers, and he followed suit.

Something moved toward them in the grasses, swinging jerkily, but the movement wasn't natural. Every blaster pointed toward it. Iskat quickly realized it was the pointed face of a droid. Of course, that didn't mean it was friendly. Or harmless.

Parting the long, green stalks, the droid newcomer appeared just outside the plasma shield, but it was a very strange droid indeed. Painted the dark green of the prairie surrounding them, it had the legs and head of a B1 battle droid, but with two sets of arms. Its torso had been replaced with a glass sphere, behind which sat an Anzellan wearing a knit wool cap. The Anzellan looked cozy inside the glass, with a plush chair and a bank of controls that resembled a ship's computer.

"Hello there," the deep, grumbly voice said from the droid's voicebox. Iskat noted that the Anzellan's mouth moved far too quickly to be speaking Basic, so the droid must've been translating for—her. She was fairly certain the Anzellan was female, for all that the voice was deeply masculine.

"Greetings. Are you Ginntho?" Tualon asked.

"I'd be more interested in answering if there were fewer weapons leveled at me," the voice said as one of the droid arms gestured at the troopers.

Tualon turned off his blade, and Iskat did the same with both of hers. At Captain Spider's gesture, the clone troopers held their blasters at a slightly less aggressive angle.

"That's better. Now, who is asking for Ginntho?"

Tualon made a show of hooking his lightsaber on his belt as he stepped toward the glowing dome. "I am Tualon—"

"You are a Jedi."

"Yes, we both are. We were sent by the Jedi Council on behalf of friends on Coruscant. Ginntho's skills would greatly benefit the Republic. At the very least, we'd like to help them avoid being taken prisoner by the Separatists. We know the Banking Clan is looking for someone with skills of great value. And we've heard that Dooku is holding a grudge for a past betrayal."

"They're all hunting me, you mean. They call me Ginntho, and I'd like to know how you found me?"

"My leaders don't tell me their methods; they only communicate the importance of your value to our cause, and the desperation with which the Separatists are seeking you. We can get you to safety, at which point the Republic would like to negotiate for your services. You will always be free to leave, of course. But if you find this offer agreeable, we should hurry. If we were able to find the moon where you've been hiding . . ."

Ginntho nodded. "It's possible for anyone to find it." For a long moment, the Anzellan considered them, blinking her big eyes contemplatively. "I have known a few Jedi in my time. A bit radical for my taste, but trustworthy, which is more than I can say of the Banking Clan." The droid shrugged with all four arms. "Yes, yes. Let me go pack."

The droid turned around and marched back into the grasses, arms swinging.

"Can we help you to speed the process?" Tualon called.

The droid waved two arms. "No, no. I don't have much. Just wait there, you don't want to go running around this moon. It's hungry."

Tualon and Iskat shared a look of frustration. They were trapped in a plasma dome, waiting for a mysterious stranger to "pack," whatever that meant. It was obvious that the baggage Ginntho brought along would have to fit on the ship, along with everyone already visible, but Iskat definitely hadn't expected to be kept waiting like this. And what did that mean—the moon was hungry?

"Stay ready," Captain Spider called, sounding just as impatient as Iskat felt. The twenty troopers on the ground looked around nervously, unsure from which direction danger might come. The shield included their ship, but they needed to be ready for whatever happened next. The meeting had gone well, supposedly, but there was still a chance this character wasn't Ginntho or wasn't telling the truth. They couldn't relax, but they couldn't leave.

Behind the protective wall of the clones and with the ship at her back, Iskat put away her lightsabers and knelt, putting a hand to the damp ground. She reached out in the Force, feeling the rippling dance of the grass, the steady waving of the trees, the green shoots at the tips of each vine, the possibility in the rich, black soil. She could feel tiny bugs, busy worms, burrowing mammals, and some very aggressive underground turtles. Smiling, she sat and clutched her amulet, reaching further with the Force. This moon, although small, thrummed with life. It was a wild, peaceful place, and—

There.

Something big was moving toward her.

Stalking her.

She could feel its hunger, its feet pounding like drumbeats.

She hurriedly stood back up. "Does anyone else feel that?"

Tualon knelt and put down a hand, frowning. "Something is coming."

Iskat closed her eyes and reached out in the Force. "Step away from the shield!" she cried to the clones. "Weapons up!" The clones, standing between the Jedi and the shield, followed directions perfectly, taking one step back and raising their blasters.

Tualon hurried to her side. "What can you sense?"

"A predator. A big one. It's curious. Unafraid. And hungry."

So that's what Ginntho had meant.

The thumping grew closer, and a powerful odor washed over them, musky and dark and rich. The grasses began to wave on the opposite side of the dome from where Ginntho had disappeared.

"There!" Iskat called, pointing.

The clones spun, weapons up, and Iskat and Tualon ignited their lightsabers.

"Do you think this shield will repel animals?" she asked him.

"No idea, but we're about to find out!"

"Should we fire?" Captain Spider asked.

Before Tualon could answer, Iskat darted forward, swinging her lightsabers as a giant shape galloped out of the grass—and right through the shield. Her upswing caught it in the wide, scaly neck, and it tumbled sideways, muscular legs churning. It was reptilian, rippling with violet and green stripes that looked like dappled shadow and a wide, stout body as tall as her shoulders with a sort of frilled shell on its back. Its long tail thrashed, and its four stubby legs flailed as it tried to stand even as thick, violet blood gushed from its wound. After watching it snarl and struggle for a moment, she slashed its soft belly open, releasing a terrific stench.

"Did you have to do that?" Tualon held the sleeve of his robe over his nose.

"It was that or wait around and ask it whether it was still hungry," she snapped.

Judging by the surprise turning to determination on his face, he also felt the thumping gallop of another beast approaching, and they both turned as one toward the next ripple slicing through the grasses. They didn't speak this time; Tualon did a running leap, slashing at the beast's eyes as he somersaulted over it, while Iskat swung low with both sabers and took off a leg. They both knew better than to aim for the belly again; this creature's digestion was foul.

"How many more of these things do we have to kill?" Tualon asked.

"Hopefully, none."

They turned to find Ginntho in her droid, waddling out of the grasses, tugging along a repulsorsled mounded with crates.

"Thraxsos," the Anzellan muttered. "Useless things. The giant birds that preyed upon them died out, and now they just gallop around, eating everything in sight, including each other. Lost a perfectly good scout droid to a pair of 'em."

Captain Spider directed his troopers to pull the crates onto the ship, and Tualon and Iskat came last, watching the grass for any more approaching thraxsos. Far off across the prairie they could see more ripples and dark green shells headed in their direction, and they hurried onto the ship with their lightsabers ignited as the ramp shut all too slowly. The ship rose, and something thumped against the metal outside, making it wobble.

"They can jump higher than you think," Ginntho said, piloting her droid to the couch.

Iskat and Tualon took seats nearby, and Tualon asked, "So how did you end up here?"

The droid gestured as Ginntho talked, the four arms programmed to move more gracefully than any battle droid they'd faced in combat. "I was on the run from Hutts with a damaged ship and managed to limp here, but there's a reason it's uninhabited. There are no sentient beings, no settlements, no supplies, no parts. No fuel. I set up the fake defense system to scare off anyone who thought about landing because I wanted to continue not being found. Modified the droid's voice to sound scarier and more masculine and got to enjoying it." The Anzellan gestured, and one of the droid arms pointed at the ship's cockpit. "The moment you came into my airspace, I saw the Republic signature. You need better slicers."

"Maybe you can help fix that," Iskat said.

A four-armed shrug. "Perhaps."

"If you knew we were with the Republic, why did you threaten to shoot us down?" Tualon asked.

The Anzellan laughed, a high-pitched sound made strange by the glass bubble in which she sat and the deep voice of her translator module. "Just because I know where your ship is from doesn't mean I know if I can trust you. The first thing you did was lie to me. So the first thing I did was put some pressure on you." The droid hooked a thumb to point at Iskat. "You're lucky the Pkorian here is honest."

Iskat's hearts stuttered.

"What did you just call me?" she asked.

24

GINNTHO'S DECEPTIVELY SLEEPY, LONG-LASHED EYES blinked. "A Pkorian. That's where you're from, isn't it? Pkori?"

The tiny slicer now had Iskat's total attention. Tualon could've been vaporized right beside her and she wouldn't even have noticed.

"I don't know where I'm from. I was given to the Jedi as a baby. There is no record of my home planet or species, and I've never seen anyone else like me."

Ginntho nodded vigorously. "Pkori is a planet in Wild Space." She tapped her whiskery head. "When I was a much younger being, I was a xenoanthropologist. Specialized in studying the cultures of uncontacted planets. They're clannish on Pkori, haven't achieved spaceflight and don't want to, so when a ship shows up, it's a big deal."

"How'd you find it?" Iskat asked. "It's not listed in the Jedi Archives."

"Oh, xenoanthropologists talk." Ginntho laughed, a deep belly laugh. "I asked an old professor about the most unusual cultures she'd visited, and they made the list, so I had to go see them for myself. Fascinating people! Most folk at least want the option of spaceflight, but the Pkorians would probably put a cage around their planet if they could. No ports, no comms, no electricity. Don't speak Basic and don't have a reason to. They only allowed my professor to land because she was Devaronian and they felt some kinship with her, and they only allowed me there because they thought I was a baby. So you've never been home to visit, eh?"

Iskat looked away. "The Jedi Temple is the only home I've ever known."

"Eh, probably not missing much, unless you really love tea and the scent of wet cochukka wool. Quiet, slow place. Not even enough resources to tempt the Commerce Guild. No tech at all. Back then, I was endlessly curious. Now I'd just get bored. It'll be good to be in a modern place again, I suppose."

"How'd you get into slicing?" Tualon asked. "It seems a broad leap, from anthropology to scramble keys."

Ginntho got a faraway look in her eyes. "I've been many things, but I get bored easily. Started with xenoanthropology, did some archaeology and collecting, worked briefly for an Ithorian on Batuu before I got involved with the droid depot there. Eventually moved on to a droid shop with my brother to learn the ropes and rebuild this B1, and naturally started to pick up slicing. It's definitely the most exciting." She looked around the ship. "But it does tend to get one in deep water."

As the ship settled into hyperspace, Iskat asked Ginntho how to spell the planet's name and excused herself to go to her bunk. She pulled out her tablet and searched for Pkori, but there was almost no information whatsoever—just as Ginntho had told her. A strategically useless planet in Wild Space, a fiercely clannish people who resisted technology, and that was it. She pulled up a star map and mentally plotted a course, which was a challenge in itself. If the Jedi were going to deny her access to their records and continually remind her that the past wasn't important, then maybe Iskat would find a way to go back to the planet where both she and Feyra had been born and learn the truth on her own terms. There had to be something important about the lightsaber, and it had to be connected to Feyra. Why else would Master Vey, otherwise a model Jedi, have defied the tenets of the Jedi Code to keep it in her possession, and *hide* it? Why else would she have addressed Feyra with her final words instead of speaking to her actual Padawan?

The journey back to Coruscant was otherwise uneventful. Ginntho was quiet and, although not unfriendly, not an extrovert. Iskat had hoped that her success with getting the slicer on board would win Tualon over, but he was more annoyed with her than ever, and the one time she asked him if he wanted to spar, he just shook his head and left for his bunk.

"Some would call what you did insubordination," Whirl muttered. "The higher-ups tend to frown upon it."

"Someone had to do something," Iskat muttered back.

He lifted an insouciant shoulder. "Glad the job's done. Also glad I'm not in your shoes."

As the ship landed at the Jedi Temple, Tualon finally gave her his attention. "I do the reporting," he told her sternly. "Believe me when I tell you it's best for us both."

She nodded. It was the only option.

As the troopers disembarked, already unloading their crates of equipment and likely preparing for their next mission, Iskat followed Tualon and Ginntho down the ramp. Master Windu and Yoda were waiting.

"I hope your journey was comfortable," Mace said with formality.

"Better than that murder moon," Ginntho admitted. "And better than dealing with Dooku again. Now, Master Jedi, tell me what you're offering for my services."

Yoda chuckled as he led Ginntho away, the battle droid standing out in its garish jungle green against the stately backdrop of the Temple, and Mace looked at Tualon and Iskat in turn.

"Congratulations on a successful mission." He almost smiled, but not quite. "Did you encounter any issues while you were out of comm range?"

Iskat held her tongue and waited to hear what Tualon would say.

"Ginntho was reluctant at first. It appeared as if our ship was under fire by a planetary defense system, but that was merely a test. Once we had established our purpose, she joined us readily. We fought two beasts on the planet surface, but Iskat and I had no problem defending the perimeter. No casualties or injuries to report."

Mace nodded and looked to Iskat. "Is that an accurate assessment?"

Yes, it was. It wasn't the whole truth, not by a long shot . . . but it wasn't a lie, either.

A messy bit of truth can so easily be obfuscated by the word *we*.

"Yes, Master. We"—her eyes flicked to Tualon's—"have high hopes that Ginntho will join our cause."

"Excellent. I'm pleased you two were able to work together to accomplish your goal. Tualon, your leadership continues to progress. And Iskat, this reflects well on the work you've done with Masters Uumay and Klefan. I'm glad to see you back in the field. You two get some rest. We'll have a new assignment for you soon."

Mace left them, and Tualon visibly deflated with relief. He turned to Iskat, his eyes sharp. "That's the story. Don't elaborate further. We did it. Got it?"

She nodded, hating the way that he was both taking credit for her gamble and trying to make her feel shame for defying him. Why did her every triumph get snatched away? Was she doomed to exactly this sort of situation—Tualon, in charge and doubting her, and Iskat, doing what needed to be done when he couldn't and being blamed only when something went wrong? Was this the best she could hope for as a Jedi during this unending war?

She spun on her heel and left for her quarters. Much like when she'd returned from Thule years ago, the Jedi Temple seemed to press all around her, soaring high overhead and reaching deep underground, a heavy sort of cage. She'd enjoyed being in hyperspace, had relished the way the wet, wild ground of Olgothon 3 felt under her palm. When she'd reached into the Force there, she'd felt a fierce burst of deliciously vibrant life, so different from the layers of metal structures and lack of green things on Coruscant. For a big place, the Temple suddenly seemed small and claustrophobic. She longed to be back out in the field, on the way to some new challenge, but she now understood that patience was the only way forward.

Committing herself to finding her calm nonetheless, she bathed and changed into new robes, taking a quick nap to refresh herself after the journey. When she woke up, she went to find fresher food than they'd enjoyed on the shuttle.

Much to her surprise, she saw Master Windu sitting alone at a table, sipping steaming tea from a clay mug as he read through a datapad. For all that the senior Jedi took their turns teaching the younglings, Iskat could remember very few one-on-one interactions with the formidable master, and she found him beyond intimidating. Mace rarely laughed, unlike the jovial Yoda; he had always seemed so stern. Still, she was a Jedi Knight now, and he had complimented her work on the last mission, even if he hadn't known she was the one who'd ultimately won Ginntho's trust.

"Master Windu?" she asked softly as she approached his table.

Mace looked up, his gaze sharpening as he realized who was addressing him. "Iskat."

"I'd like to ask you a question, if I may. If I'm not interrupting."

He swept a hand to the nearest chair, but she couldn't sit; she was too nervous.

"Master, now that I'm a Jedi Knight and approved for missions, might I take a few days to pursue some personal business?"

He leaned back, crossing his arms and tilting his head in a way that felt like a dare. "What kind of personal business?"

Luckily, Iskat had thought this through.

"Before she passed, Master Sember was very excited to visit a trader named Gamodar on Bar'leth. Apparently he had an important artifact for her. I'd like to finish this last piece of business on her behalf. It feels like an appropriate tribute to our work together."

Mace blinked. It felt like he saw through to her soul, and Iskat was in no way comfortable with that. She put up her shields, as she always had, so that he wouldn't be able to look too deep.

"Iskat, it's been years since Sember passed, and we are in the midst of a war. As you know—as you have witnessed—we are losing more and more Jedi every day, and we are a limited population with limited resources. Your skills are needed, desperately." He looked down like he was disappointed in her. "Although your motive is admirable, we do not have time for artifact hunting when lives are on the line."

"But what if—"

Now he sat up and steepled his hands. "Duty comes first, and we must all put aside our scholarly pursuits and work toward a more peaceful time."

She resisted the impulse to let her head hang. "Yes, Master." She almost turned and walked away then, but . . . she couldn't help herself. She had to ask. "One more question, Master. Have you ever known a Jedi who looked like me, possibly named Feyra?"

Mace didn't gasp or betray any sort of emotion, but she felt his attention sharpen as if he'd just discovered a new defect that would need to be monitored.

"Many Jedi have passed through these halls, Iskat. My responsibilities often keep me from meeting them all personally . . . unless they gain my particular attention through constant difficulties. Rather than dwell on the past, you would do well to focus on your present, on the duty before you, and trust in the Force."

It was infuriating, yet again being spoken to like a forgetful child, but Iskat was aware how carefully Mace would be watching her reaction to gauge whether she could still be trusted on missions.

"Yes, Master. You're right. Thank you for reminding me." With a nod of respect, she left, grabbing some fruit to take with her. If she tried to eat in the same room with Mace right now, she was quite certain she'd choke.

The irony of it all was that if they would just tell her the truth, she wouldn't have to keep asking. The curiosity was killing her. It was such a simple question—what happened to a specific Jedi—and yet it was clear the answer was being purposefully hidden. Or possibly erased. If it was merely unimportant, what would be the harm in telling her? To Iskat, their reticence made it seem as if something unsavory had happened. Telling someone not to ask a question never made them stop asking that question. It only made the question bother them more. Was Master Windu so out of touch with the nature of sentient beings that he'd managed to forget about that?

Iskat had considered telling Mace about her dream, but something had stopped her at the last moment. Maybe Mace doubted her decision making and ability to follow orders, but she didn't need him questioning her relationship with the Force and what it showed her. She was competent—maybe even more competent than her peers—and it was exhausting being constantly doubted by those around her.

She wasn't even aware of where her feet were leading her until she was outside in the gardens and entering what she'd come to think of as her private sanctuary. Heezo was there with yet another mouse droid—there were so many!—patiently sorting through its wires while murmuring to it in Mandaba. When he heard Iskat's boots on the stone tiles, he looked up and smiled.

"You've been gone awhile."

"I was on a mission."

"And were you successful?"

She flopped onto the bench. "Yes and no? My superior . . ." How she hated thinking about Tualon that way, especially now. "Nearly doomed the mission, so I stepped in and solved the problem. And I was successful, but now he's taking credit for it while shaming me for taking a risk. It's the worst of both worlds."

Heezo cocked his head. "Doesn't seem like the Jedi way, taking credit for someone else's work."

"Well, he isn't, really. Not in a way I could ever prove, and not that Master Windu would even listen. He keeps saying 'we' did it, which I suppose 'we' did, but it was mostly me. And it sounds like we're going to be sent on more missions together because we did so well. And . . ." She sighed. "I'm not as excited about that as I was before."

"Is that why you're so upset? I can smell it from here."

Her head jerked up. "You can smell it?"

A shrug. "I can smell strong emotions, sure. Most sentient beings pump out pheromones. You're angry. But you're also . . . ashamed?"

Iskat hadn't planned on talking about her recent conversation with Master Windu, but now it all came pouring out. "I found out what planet I'm from, and I asked Master Windu if I could have some time off and planned to go there, but I just got another lecture. Jedi don't ask questions, Jedi don't look to the past. It feels like they're hiding something from me—something big. Like they're covering something up. I feel like . . . I need to know the truth or I'll never rest. For my own peace of mind, and to find peace with my dead master. It was important to her. I can't just let it go. She would've wanted me to figure it out."

"But at least you finally know the name of your homeworld. That's something, right?" Iskat lay on her back on the bench, staring up at the busy skylanes through the dappled leaves. "The name of a planet isn't much. I need to know if Feyra is actually related to me, what she meant to Master Vey, why she left the Jedi, or if she was kicked out or failed the trials." She closed her eyes. "I didn't really like Sember. It's hard to say, but it's true. We just didn't understand each other. But when she died, she left me with so many questions and no one to answer them. Sometimes I feel like I'm . . . rudderless. Drifting."

"Drifting's not so bad. I drifted for a while, until I found what I was meant to do."

"But Jedi are not supposed to drift. We have a calling. We have a mission. I was raised here, but I still don't feel like I fit in. So many different species, so why do I feel like the odd one out? Like everyone can access peace except for me. It's the same Force that flows through us all, and I'm the only one who struggles against the current."

Heezo put the mouse droid down gently, and it rolled in a circle and beeped cheerfully at him as if in thanks. He patted it. "I don't claim to know as much as a Jedi, but I know it's probably better to be yourself and recognize your uniqueness than pretend to be someone you're not. Like trying to wear a jacket that's too small every day of your life. Seems like it would bruise a soul, to feel that way."

"So what then?" she asked, sitting up. "All I can do is . . . keep trying to squeeze into the jacket. I'm a Jedi. I can't just leave."

Heezo shrugged. "You can do magic. You can influence people. You can fight. You can kill." He looked up at her, grinning. "Seems to me like you can do anything you want."

25

AFTER HER CHAT WITH HEEZO in the garden, Iskat's thoughts and feelings ran riot. What if leaving the Jedi was her choice instead of an embarrassing decision by the High Council after too many, as Master Windu put it, difficulties? What could she be, if not a Jedi? Her whole life, she'd tried so hard to be the best Jedi she could be, to run faster and fight with more accuracy and please her master to make up for her many supposed weaknesses, but what had it brought her? All her diligent work had not resulted in any satisfaction. And Heezo was right—it did bruise her soul. It squeezed her hearts like a fist. And she didn't even have the hope Tualon's presence used to bring, not anymore. Now that he'd shown his true colors—and un-Jedi-like colors they were—her feelings for him had cooled.

When it had come down to the decisive moment—Tualon admitting his own fault or borrowing Iskat's success to maintain his standing—he had chosen himself. He wasn't the ideal Jedi she'd always believed him to be.

Now that she was back in the Temple and awaiting further orders, she continued her old habits, rising at dawn each morning to meditate with Master Uumay and practicing lightsaber forms with Master Klefan in the evenings when he wasn't on a mission.

One night at the end of their session, after she'd disarmed Master Klefan in under a minute while sparring with training blades, the elder Jedi took a heaving breath and shook his head. "It would appear the student has outpaced the teacher. Sember would be proud."

"Would she, Master?" Iskat deactivated her blades and went to collect Klefan's fallen ones. "She preferred artifacts to lightsabers. She mainly taught me forms, and we never sparred. I—I always wished she would teach me more about fighting, but she seemed to actively avoid it."

"A lover of peace Sember was. Always happiest with her texts and artifacts," he agreed with a fond smile. "But I'm certain she would be proud of your dedication and tenacity. Her greatest concern was that you had trouble concentrating and could be easily led astray, but it would appear that when you put your mind to something, you have an uncanny ability to absorb and use new information." Iskat held out his training blades, and he took them and looked down at them. "I'm too old to take such a beating. That's enough for one day."

Iskat turned to take her training sabers back to the rack when she felt a small shift in the Force. She spun, blades up, in time to catch Klefan's downswing. Thus began a faster, more aggressive session, with the plump Askajian moving with the grace and power of a much younger being as he jabbed and slashed and even flipped. Iskat grinned and let herself fall into the dance of the duel. Much to her surprise, this time, Klefan managed to disarm her and send her sprawling on the floor.

"Master, you've been holding back!" she said as he held out a hand to help her up.

"Do not forget that the Force is a fathomless well," he reminded her. "Old and squat I may be, but I, too, have my tenacity. Never discount your opponent. They may yet surprise you."

In that last bout, he'd used moves she'd never seen—moves he'd never taught her.

She would add those to her repertoire and ask for more.

It occurred to her that she'd never known Master Klefan to be deceptive, but he'd purposefully lied to her right before attacking her. Not only that, but in two years of training her, he'd withheld the moves he'd used against her. She'd only ever really seen him as a steady and uncreative elder who could regurgitate the Jedi tenets at a moment's notice, but perhaps under that placid façade, there was something more.

For the first time, Iskat wondered how different her life might have been if Klefan had been her master instead of Sember.

Iskat wrapped her fingers around her blue stone amulet, remembering the day Sember had placed its chain over her head. She hadn't taken it off since.

"When you have trouble with self-control, sometimes it helps to have a physical focal point," Sember had said. "This amulet will help you center yourself when all else fails. If you meditate with it, you will find it easier to recall your inner serenity."

At the time, Iskat had seen it as a gift, as something beautiful and special. Now she wondered if perhaps Sember had outsourced a part of her training to the stone, giving Iskat something to connect with and lean into when Sember hadn't really been there for her. She also wondered where the stone had come from, especially now that she knew Sember had kept the lightsaber a secret. Had the pendant perhaps been one of the many artifacts for which her master had haggled on some faraway planet? But no, surely not. Iskat wore it openly, and no other master had ever questioned it.

She had been pouring herself into this stone for years, exactly as Sember had taught her, and yet she didn't feel like she'd truly made the connection her master had hoped for her.

Well, unless she was fighting. Then she felt it.

But not through the stone.

Through violence.

It was all so confusing.

She was learning more from Klefan than she'd ever learned from Sember, and what was more, she was learning that the Force, for her, worked best not through peace, but through ferocity. Something about that didn't sit right.

Each time she took her place to meditate in the garden, Iskat actively sought answers in the Force. For the first time in her life, she *tried*, desperately. Like an injured animal at the riverside, she kept drinking deep, hoping healing and serenity would follow.

They didn't.

She only felt more anxious.

The only conclusion she reached was one that would be considered shocking and unacceptable among the Jedi. She could not find peace through a quiet life of service in the Temple. Her unique connection to the Force blossomed only when she was fighting and killing. As she was living in a time of war, perhaps this was a gift, even if she knew in her bones that if she spoke with any of the wise masters about it, they would be appalled and urge her to seek serenity instead of hoping for chaos. She was looking forward to her next mission. Not to spending time with Tualon, but to being a Jedi. She loved space travel, loved joking around with the troopers, loved meeting new challenges. That first moment, when she set foot on a new planet and connected with its unique, wild signature in the Force—it was bliss. She didn't enjoy hurting innocent creatures, but the fight with the thraxsos had been invigorating. Being in danger felt . . . good. Only when fighting did she truly feel the connection with the Force she so desperately sought. Especially now that she was training with two lightsabers, it was as if all the disparate parts of her body, mind, and hearts came together in perfect harmony.

"Something troubles you," Master Uumay said one morning as they sat silently by the pool.

Iskat opened one eye and considered the old Bimm, who had the calmest energy she'd ever experienced. She couldn't imagine him in battle, couldn't picture him wielding a lightsaber or using the Force to pull down towers of stone upon an enemy.

"Master, have you ever gone to war?" she asked.

He didn't even raise an eyelid. "This is the first war of my lifetime, and I have not been so called. My strengths lie elsewhere, although I would gladly go wherever I was sent."

"Gladly?"

Now his eye opened and rolled over to consider her. "I would not be glad to go, I suppose, but I would be glad for the chance to do my part and serve the Force. We are all made for different tasks, gifted with different talents." A pause. His eye closed. "Have you found your talent, little tang tang bird?"

My talent is killing, she thought but did not say.

Even thinking it felt thrilling—and dangerous.

And good, because acknowledging a long-hidden truth, even if silently, even if secretly, was a balm to the soul.

Instead, she said, "I prefer action to stillness, but I doubt you are surprised by that."

Master Uumay's chuckle was as feathery as his whiskers. "No, that does not surprise me. Your time will come, Iskat Akaris. Still waters don't stay still for long."

As if Master Uumay had seen the future in the ripples of the pool, Iskat was called to the Jedi Council Chamber that afternoon. With Master Gallia now numbering among the dead, only the tall Cerean Master Ki-Adi-Mundi sat in his chair, regarding a datapad. A Kiffar Jedi named Sunghi Silpari waited in the center of the mostly empty circle and gave Iskat a curious look, the young woman's amber eyes echoed by her yellow facial tattoos. They'd been Padawans together, but Sunghi's Padawan braid was gone, suggesting she was now a Jedi Knight herself, although Iskat couldn't recall another ceremony. Sunghi was one of the Padawans who'd avoided Iskat since the column incident; she'd once asked Yoda if he'd ever been frightened of a fellow Jedi, and Iskat had disliked her from that moment on. Tualon appeared in the doorway, and he looked at Iskat with the same distrust she felt for him, and the tension among the three Jedi Knights gathered in the center of the chamber was palpable.

"Tualon, Iskat. I hear your last mission together was a thorough success," Master Mundi said. "You'll be pleased to know that Ginntho has agreed to join our side. Whatever you did or said that helped convince her to support the Republic, well done."

Neither Jedi Knight said anything; they both merely bowed their heads in acknowledgment. Iskat didn't think Ginntho's decision had anything to do with either of them; Ginntho seemed entirely free from the influence of others. She still ached to tell the truth about the part she'd played in that mission, but she wanted to leave Coruscant and make a difference, and she wasn't about to jeopardize her chance to get out into the greater galaxy just for a pat on the back. She held her tongue and swallowed down her growing dissatisfaction.

"Sunghi has just returned from Corellia and will be joining you on your next mission. Many planets in the Outer Rim are under siege. There are rumors it's General Grievous, although we don't have proof. It's clear the Separatists are up to something, and we need to know what. Several groups are being sent out for recon, and we want you on Frong, where they're suffering strafing runs. You'll be with Captain Spider and his crew again." Master Mundi looked down at his datapad as if hoping for better answers there. "If it is Grievous and we can take him into custody, it will strike a staggering blow to the Separatists. Grievous is dangerous, but you are all talented, and we have great faith in you. If it is not Grievous, we need all the intel you can gather. And if you can stop the threat, all the better."

"Will a master be joining us?" Sunghi asked, her eyes quickly flashing to Iskat.

Master Mundi's flicker of annoyance at this question warmed Iskat's soul.

"In a perfect galaxy, we would send masters. But in this one, we're sending the best Jedi we have available, and that is you. Your success will depend on your ability to work together. If you do encounter Grievous, I can only remind you to underestimate him at your peril."

"Yes, Master," Tualon said.

Master Mundi pressed a few buttons on his datapad. "You all have the mission brief. Tualon is lead. Sunghi and Iskat, I know he can count on you for support."

"Of course, Master," Sunghi said, inclining her head. "It is an honor to be sent on such an important mission."

Iskat fought not to roll her eyes. She already had her own datapad out and was scrolling through her brief.

"Is this all the intel we have?" she asked; it was beginning to feel like a constant refrain.

There was almost nothing—some coordinates, a brief mention of the planet's terrain, a list of the areas that had been attacked.

Master Mundi raised a tufted white eyebrow. "This is a war, Iskat. We do what we can with what we've been given. Investigate the damage. Find the source. If it's Grievous, your goal is to capture him alive. Unless you don't feel sufficient for the task?"

Iskat stood up straighter. "I'm sufficient for anything, Master."

"Good. Your team is waiting on landing pad three. Collect any supplies you need and meet Captain Spider there immediately. This mission is extremely time-sensitive." His yellow eyes met Iskat's, and although Iskat didn't know him well, she sensed a weariness and fear there that she would've thought beyond a member of the High Council. "Without Grievous commanding the droid army this war is one step closer to being over."

"We won't let you down," Tualon said. He headed for the door with Sunghi nearly trotting on his heels.

Iskat followed them at a more reasonable pace. On the outside, she was calm and measured . . . but inside, she was stunned.

She was being sent to hunt General Grievous. She'd heard about Grievous from Heezo and from watching the holonet—she was fascinated by the Kaleesh warlord turned cybernetic maniac trained by Count Dooku himself to become the Supreme Martial Commander of the Separatist Army. With four arms, four lightsabers, and an entire army at his back, Grievous had cut swaths of doom through the Republic armies and was seen as unstoppable. He was likely personally responsible for more Jedi deaths in the war than anyone else.

And now, Iskat was being sent to potentially locate and capture him.

She followed Tualon and Sunghi, considering the strengths and weaknesses of these two Jedi Knights she'd grown up with, trained with. Sunghi had never been much of a fighter; she'd preferred research and philosophy to lightsaber training. Unless her recent missions had forced her to expand her skill set and sharpened her physical attributes, it was unlikely she would be able to face down anyone as formidable as Grievous. Tualon, on the other hand, was an accomplished fighter, one with whom she'd trained and fought, and she knew he'd been on dozens of missions and had both seen violence and meted it out.

Still, she hoped she would be the one to find Grievous.

The thought of having the famous general in her sights was more intriguing than it should've been.

It had felt so good, killing the Geonosian soldiers in her dance of death. What would it feel like to capture one of the greatest fighters the galaxy had ever known? To finally prove to the Jedi, once and for all, that her talents didn't need to be contained? As Master Uumay said, everyone had different skills. Perhaps if she had lived in a more peaceful time, Iskat would never have found her destiny.

Maybe it wasn't just fighting. Maybe it was ending Grievous for good.

No. *Capturing.* They were supposed to take him alive.

If they could.

If not?

Well, they needed him out of action, and there were many ways to accomplish that goal.

Without a word, the three Jedi split off to collect their things. Time was of the essence, Master Mundi had said. Iskat hurried to her chamber, where she already had her kit ready. She briefly opened the drawer of her wardrobe and took out Feyra's lightsaber. It was grounding, wrapping her long, red fingers around the carved hilt and igniting the yellow blade. She couldn't help wondering if Sember had done something similar, or if she'd kept it hidden in the back of her drawer, untouched, for years. Iskat would never know. She only knew that one day, she would fight with this lightsaber in one hand and her original green lightsaber in the other, and she would be unstoppable.

A knock sounded on her door.

"Iskat?"

She quickly deactivated the blade and slid the lightsaber into her sleeve. Both of her green sabers were already hanging from her belt. "Yes?"

Tualon opened the door looking annoyed. "Let's go. We have to hurry."

He kept the door from closing, waiting, and she had no choice but to pick up her bag and follow him. She'd have to keep the lightsaber hidden in her bunk on this journey. It would be easy enough to lie and say that she'd built it herself—

Except . . . if the only Jedi on this mission were three young Jedi Knights, then there would be no one present who'd ever seen Feyra's lightsaber before. That meant she could actually use it without an older Jedi Master potentially recognizing it and asking uncomfortable questions. It would just look like another one she'd built to accommodate her unique physiognomy. A yellow kyber crystal was rare nowadays, but it was known that she'd spent years traveling with Sember, collecting artifacts—including a kyber crystal or two.

She smiled to herself. Maybe she would take down Grievous with the mysterious lightsaber. Maybe the Force had led her to it for a reason.

They met Sunghi at the landing pad and boarded the same ship they'd taken to Olgothon 3. Iskat claimed her same berth. It had a pleasant familiarity; not quite home, but something like it. Iskat said hello to the troopers, joked with Flip about the latest holobook she'd borrowed, and complimented Whirl's recent tattoo, a geometric design of triangles behind his ear. She realized that she actually preferred the company of the clones to the Jedi she'd grown up with; after a questionable beginning, these men now knew her as an audacious Jedi Knight who wasn't afraid to make the tough decisions, a valuable warrior who could take down a full-grown thraxso without breaking a sweat. These were men of action, and she had more in common with them than she did with someone like Sunghi, whose connection with the Force was so different from her own that Iskat couldn't begin to understand her.

Although Tualon was chilly at first, five days trapped on a ship hurtling through space was enough to bring him back out of his shell. Sunghi, as expected, was generally in her bunk with a variety of texts she'd brought along. Iskat spent her time playing games, doing calisthenics, and practicing with her lightsabers, and eventually Tualon silently came to join her. They didn't speak as they fell into their old habits, swapping their lightsabers to spar with the tactical batons they had stored on the ship. As their sparring session sped up, Tualon seemed to thaw. With so few Jedi left in the galaxy, perhaps familiarity was more soothing than focusing too hard on the complexities of a childish acquaintanceship turned to an adult relationship forged in the fire of war and tainted with missteps.

"You only smile when you spar. Did you know that?" Tualon said one day, only slightly out of breath.

"And when I'm fighting thraxsos," she added, feeling her grin spread wider.

"You're upset with me, Iskat."

She did not slow as they sparred, didn't pause.

"I am."

She landed a hit on his arm with the baton, and he hissed.

"I'm not going to apologize. I did what I had to do. If I'd told Master Windu the truth, they might've grounded you again. Maybe your ways are unorthodox, but we need people like you."

She stopped and glared at him daringly. "People like me?"

"We need every Jedi we can get." He looked away. "We've lost so many already. It's unthinkable that you might be meditating by a pool when people are dying."

"I couldn't agree more. But you meant something more by 'people like you' . . . "

He stopped, letting his baton drop to his side. "People who take risks. Who go for the throat. Maybe in times of peace, we need Jedi who focus on harmony and serenity—" His eyes shot to the bunks, where Sunghi was probably nose-deep in her datapad. "But now, we need warriors."

Iskat let her baton fall as well. "So you're saying that's why you took responsibility for the success at Olgothon 3?"

The way his eyes skittered sideways—so he did feel some shame around taking credit for her gambit.

"Yes. You did what you had to do at Thule. And then they took you out of the field for far too long, and we lost Zeeth and Ansho and so many more. People I've known all my life, gone in an instant, rejoining the Force from lonely planets scattered around a shattering galaxy. They can't just send you back to teach the children how to memorize pretty words. We need you on the front lines. There's something different about you. When others stop, you'll keep going, no matter what."

On one hand, it sounded like a compliment.

But on the other hand, it also sounded like he thought she was like a battle droid, or a deadly creature. A killing machine.

Rage flared in her chest. Was Tualon even aware of the backhanded compliment? Did he even know what he was saying, or was he just trying to make himself feel better?

"Dropping out of hyperspace," Flip called, and the ship hustled to action, the clone troopers suiting up and preparing their gear. Sunghi appeared from the bunks looking sleepy, and Tualon and Iskat put away their training weapons.

The ship shuddered as it exited hyperspace, and Iskat went up to the cockpit for a first look at Frong. She always loved this part, loved the surprise of it, loved seeing how each planet hung serenely in space, surrounded by the spangled stars. If she'd lived all her life on her home planet—if Ginntho was correct about it—then she never would've seen this kind of view. She would've spent her entire life on the ground, never knowing what happened beyond her own sky.

As they thundered into atmo, the ship got quiet. They passed over a wide swath of charred devastation, a village among the splintered trees still smoking, and Tualon asked Flip to follow the path of the destroyed forest. Judging by the fact that some of the blackened buildings were still smoldering, Iskat could only assume the general or his forces had been here recently. As they descended, they looked for any clues that might indicate who had done this and why. They'd seen no Separatist ships during their approach to the planet. If Grievous was really here, perhaps he was on his own this time, or traveling with a smaller company.

Her mind drifted as she imagined what it would be like to come upon the great General Grievous in some burning forest, to face his four twirling lightsabers and open herself up to the Force with no hesitation, with no boundaries, with no goal but inflicting harm. Master Mundi had made it clear they wanted Grievous taken alive, but a fight was a fight, and not all fights ended with a war criminal offering himself up for surrender.

What would it feel like, her lightsaber slicing through the mix of metal and flesh that was the great general? To stand triumphant over the broken pieces of the monster who had caused so much harm to the innocent people of the galaxy? To return home to the Temple in a moment of ultimate victory and know that she would never be looked down upon again?

Iskat shivered and shook off her vision.

Master Mundi had urged the Jedi Knights to cooperate and to take Grievous alive, and that was what she would strive for. That was the goal. It was unbecoming for a Jedi to dream of something so violent and prideful, and she was horrified that the scene had come to her so readily. She really did need to get more sleep.

At Tualon's command, they landed at the edge of a destroyed forest that had recently seen battle. The trees were black and broken, gently smoking, and the ground was carpeted in ash. Nearby, the remains of a smaller settlement sprouted from the charred ground, its rounded huts resembling teeth in an old man's mouth, brown and rotten. If there were survivors, they didn't reveal themselves. Some of the timbers were still aflame.

"Time is of the essence," Tualon reminded everyone. "This damage looks recent. We won't be making camp. If nothing turns up, we'll turn around and look for a more recent trail from the sky. Whether the enemy is Grievous or someone else, we want to take them by surprise, so we're going to move quickly and quietly."

They crept down the ramp, flanked by clone troopers. Iskat had her two green lightsabers in hand, with the one she thought of as Feyra's hidden under her robes, where it brought her an odd sort of comfort. Her blood sang, her body surging with energy, her senses on high alert. She was hungry for her prey, and the moment her boots touched the ground, she was flooded with rightness.

Grievous had been here recently. She could feel it.

The air was chill, the wind whistling through the broken trees. The charred trunks creaked and cried as they swayed, an occasional branch falling to the ground with a sharp crack to reveal crimson embers within. The sky was stormy gray, the land smelling of smoke and chemicals. Perhaps it wasn't the most vibrant world, especially not after the damage their prey had wrought, but still Iskat felt a thrill to be there, to be part of things, to be moving with the will of the Force toward an unknown destiny.

No creatures moved in the clinging smoke, and as Iskat reached out in the Force, she didn't feel anything dangerous or lively in the area, just sad thumps of starvation and pain. She didn't sense the actual presence of General Grievous yet, but there wasn't much information on his possible use of the Force; she knew that he was mostly cyborg, and that he'd trained with Count Dooku, and that suggested that he might be harder to find than most.

Tualon led them toward the burned village, with Iskat and Sunghi fanned out behind him, lightsabers deactivated so they wouldn't reveal their position. The lack of an enemy signature in the Force might indicate the presence of Separatist droids, or it might mean that Grievous was near, waiting to ambush them. The clone troopers marched behind them, their boots sifting through the ash, alert and with their blasters up. There was no sound but the crackle of burning trees, the ruined landscape crying and snapping and crunching. The wind was the only thing that moved.

With each step, Iskat felt that she was gaining ground on something dangerous, that the very world was holding its breath.

Soon the village was behind them as they followed the path of scorched destruction through the forest. The spires of another ruined city rose on the horizon, and Tualon subtly adjusted their path toward it. They walked on like that for hours, reaching out in the Force for any sign of General Grievous and finding nothing but the death and destruction he'd left in his wake. As the sun began to set, Iskat crept closer to Tualon.

"Maybe it's time to stop and consider our next steps," she whispered, knowing full well he wasn't going to like her suggestion. "Are we going to continue on or call the ship? We can't hit that city by nightfall, and it gets cold here."

Sunghi joined them. "If we fly, we've got a better chance of heading Grievous off before he can destroy another settlement."

"And an army marches on its stomach," Captain Spider added.

Tualon sighed and stopped, looking around. "All good points. If it's even him, he's too far ahead of us. Call the ship, and we'll take a quick break while we wait."

Captain Spider commed the clones left behind on the ship, giving them his coordinates, while Whirl handed out ration bars from his pack. There wasn't a good place to sit, thanks to all the ash, but several of the clones squatted and a few sat on their helmets. Captain Spider held his helmet under his arm as he ate.

"Did the ration bars somehow get worse?" Iskat asked.

"I think they're made out of bilge-bug protein now," Doc joked.

It didn't take long to refuel, and the clones soon had their helmets back on as they waited for the ship to arrive. Sunghi was lost in her datapad, still nibbling her bar, while Tualon and Iskat took advantage of the wide swath of empty ground to practice lightsaber forms beyond the tight bounds of the ship. It felt good to move, a lightsaber in each hand, in tune with Tualon and the new planet that still teemed with life underground, even if Grievous had left his mark above.

And then . . . something changed.

Iskat felt a strange ripple among the clones as they all, to a one, unholstered their blasters.

And pointed them right at Sunghi.

"What?" she asked, looking up.

A blaster bolt slammed into Sunghi's chest, and she fell over, dead.

/ 26.

IN THE NEXT MOMENT, A sharp, shuddering pain racked Iskat's body and mind, stealing her breath and making her hearts stutter.

She felt it—in her very soul—in the Force—

Thousands of lives snuffed out in seconds.

Thousands of Jedi, there and then gone.

It was like feeling her own hearts beating, a comforting background all her life, and then suddenly, surprise and pain and terror, followed by a tragic, empty silence.

What had happened?

Why had—

Who would—

All those Jedi, dead . . .

It beggared belief.

Iskat kept both of her lightsabers up as she turned to face the clones who had just murdered Sunghi. Tualon stood beside her, just as confused.

"Did you feel that?" she asked him as they stared into the barrels of twenty blasters.

"They shot Sunghi," he murmured. "That's all I need to know."

"But it's so much worse, Tualon. They killed . . . all the Jedi. All of them."

The clones were silent, blasters up, as if waiting for some signal.

"Captain Spider, what's the meaning of this?" Tualon barked.

Spider didn't answer. Iskat felt the shift in him, as if the man she'd known for years was gone, replaced by an inexplicably different person altogether.

Perhaps Tualon hadn't felt what Iskat had felt, but he trusted her, and he knew enough to know they were now surrounded by enemies.

Iskat stared into the emotionless faceplates of the clones she'd come to see as friends. Something had changed, something dark and deep and permanent, and she would fight to the death, kill every clone here, if she had to, because she was not going to be shot down in cold blood by these soldiers who'd once fought by her side.

Sunghi's death, the gaping wound in the Force, all these thoughts—

That happened in mere seconds.

And then suddenly Captain Spider and all his men held their blasters at ease, the movement as sharp and precise as if they, like their foes in the Separatist Army, were programmable droids. Spider reached into his kit and pulled out his holoprojector. A cloaked figure appeared, its face and hands hidden.

"Iskat Akaris," a haughty and sinuous voice said.

"Who is this—" she began.

But he cut her off.

"Do you still question the wisdom of the Jedi Council? Do you wish to embrace the talents you have been forced to repress, the passions they deem unseemly and dangerous? Do you wish to see what has been selfishly kept from you, so that you might remain a pawn of lesser beings? Do you wish to be free?"

Iskat could barely breathe as the voice paused.

More seductively, it said, "Do you want to know more about your mother Feyra and how she died because of the Jedi Order?"

"Iskat, what does that mean?" Tualon asked from beside her, desperate and shocked and still reeling from the wave of desolation. "Who is that?"

She was very glad she couldn't see his face in that moment, and that he could not see hers.

She looked at the blasters, at rest now but ready to take her down in a blaze of plasma.

She looked at Sunghi's body, slumped over in the ashes left behind by General Grievous and his army.

She felt the galaxy around her, absent of the Jedi who had raised her and guided her.

She reached inside to the jagged emptiness within, the profound loneliness she'd known all her life, even while surrounded by those who professed to be her family.

She recalled a dream, a vision of a girl just like her who had thrown down her lightsaber and run away into the darkness.

She felt that tug in her soul, the one that had been nudging her, urging her to follow her passions and curiosities despite her Jedi guidance. That part of her that yearned to be free and untethered and unashamed. It beckoned to her, welcomed her.

She made her choice.

"I question everything, and I will always want to know what others would keep from me."

After a pause, the figure said, "Bring her to me."

He sounded, she thought, pleased.

"What about Tualon?" she asked.

"Captain Spider, Order 66 remains unchanged," the voice said. "All Jedi will die."

After a zip of static, the holo clicked off.

Tualon put a hand on her shoulder. "Iskat, whoever that was, they are no friend of yours. Don't give in. You're a Jedi. We must fight, together."

She reached up for his hand—

And removed it from her shoulder.

Perhaps she'd had feelings for Tualon for most of her life, but he had never returned them. Even when she'd let him see who she really was—even when she'd saved the day, twice—even when she'd saved his reputation by taking a risk he wasn't willing to—he hadn't truly seen her.

"I'm sorry, Tualon, but every time I showed you who I was, you urged me to be someone else. Can't you feel it? The Jedi are dead. Everyone we knew is gone. The Jedi Order is ended. And I'm not joining them."

She stepped away from him, and he didn't try to stop her again. Several of the clones peeled away from the circle and took up posts on either side of her, escorting her out of the line of fire. The ship was in view now, settling among the broken trees and sending ashes and black dirt swirling into the air. Iskat walked toward the ramp with her head held high, like royalty ascending a throne. She didn't know what was happening or why, but she wanted what was offered more than anything she'd ever wanted in her life.

She very definitely didn't want to die.

Whatever this was—whatever was happening—it was better than the alternative.

It was better than instant death.

No matter what she'd been taught, Iskat wasn't ready to be one with the Force.

She'd contemplated what it would be like to leave the Jedi, and now . . .

Well, if there was no Jedi Order, then what was a Jedi?

Just some lone zealot, all alone in the galaxy, staring down the barrel of a blaster?

Someone had gone to great trouble to orchestrate this—this massacre.

The pieces clicked into place in her head.

Her team had been one of several sent out to planets in the Outer Rim to investigate incidences of random destruction, to chase the irresistible possibility of capturing General Grievous.

Someone had wanted the Jedi out of the way, far from the Temple, alone in the wilderness with their trusted clones.

They'd been sent out to slaughter.

Perhaps all but Iskat, who'd been offered the one thing she wanted most.

"Iskat!" Tualon called from where the remaining troopers surrounded him, their blasters up and ready.

She paused and turned, taking one last look at the handsome Twi'lek she'd admired since she was a youngling.

"Come along," Captain Spider said, his gloved hand landing on Iskat's arm.

"Iskat, don't do this!" Tualon called. "You didn't want to leave Sember behind on Geonosis. I know she haunts you still. But you'll leave me?"

Iskat shook her head sadly. It was too late to appeal to her guilt, much less her hearts. He'd broken them, again and again, over the years without even knowing it. She'd been foolishly, naïvely infatuated with him all that time. She recognized that now.

And he wasn't even the perfect Jedi she'd thought he was.

He was just another person in charge, coasting on the blood, sweat, and tears of those beneath him.

Just another smiling liar.

But perhaps all the Jedi were.

And, like Sember, Iskat knew that he'd never truly cared for her, not the way she'd cared for him.

Besides, it wasn't like she could save him. She wasn't even saving herself. As competent as they both were, they couldn't face this many clones and live.

"Goodbye, Tualon. You were a true Jedi until the end. Maybe I never was. Maybe I wasn't ever meant to be one at all. But now I'm going to go find out."

She turned and closed herself off from him in the Force, a sharp pinch like a candle's flame going out. She didn't want him to feel the hardness in her hearts, and even if he'd disappointed her, she didn't want to feel him die, another life snuffed out suddenly like all the rest.

As the clones led her back to the ship, past the jagged black tree trunks and through the ash-filled wind, she heard Tualon's lightsaber humming through the air, followed by an eruption of blasterfire. He must've chosen to fight; they'd probably been waiting for her to be out of the picture before finishing him off. The thought hurt her, but it was too late. She'd made her choice.

She walked up the ramp, cinders crunching under her boots, and was escorted to, of all places, the brig. It was just a closet, really, with a bench barely long enough to lie down on. She hadn't even known there was a brig, before that; she'd assumed the narrow door led to storage. The troopers searched her, not ungently, and took all three of her lightsabers, her datapad, and her pack. Much to her own surprise, she didn't fight them. The door slid closed, leaving her with only faint lights around the floor. Numb, closed off, confused, she couldn't hear anything in the ship beyond; the brig was soundproof. She could feel the clones in the Force, sitting silently in their seats. There was something dull and mechanical about them now. Whatever had caused them to kill Sunghi and Tualon—it had changed them.

"Where are you taking me?" she called, but she knew there would be no answer.

The ship took off and jumped into hyperspace, and Iskat had nothing else to do but wait. She realized that she could probably use the Force to bust the door open, but she also knew full well that this wasn't a situation she could fight her way out of. She'd chosen this, whatever it was, and perhaps her current treatment didn't suggest respect or dignity, but she had to have faith that whoever had spared her from certain death would live up to their part of the bargain. The Jedi had never promised answers, only peace. The cloaked figure in the holoprojector had offered both answers and freedom, the two things Iskat Akaris wanted most.

She sat on the bench and closed her eyes. Meditation was supposed to help her better understand the Force and herself, to help her control the emotions that seemed too big and aggressive for her body to contain. But this time, she didn't reach into the Force to calm herself and make herself smaller. She opened herself like a tap that had been dripping for years and was finally allowed to flow freely without any worries that she might be overwhelmed. The Force rushed in and around her like a joyful river, like a happy hound greeting a master kept too long from home. She felt a new sense of fathomless potential, a new fount from which to draw her strength. There were darkly swirling eddies there, shadowy places she'd never delved, and she wasn't ready to fully explore them right now, but she hoped this new opportunity would offer the chance to study them with an open mind. Already, she felt more powerful, more certain.

She didn't let herself think about Tualon, about Masters Uumay and Klefan, about the Jedi High Council, about the younglings she'd grown to know and care for. What was gone was gone. The only path was forward. She had not chosen their fate; she'd only been given the gift of choosing her own.

The troopers regularly slid food and drink through a slot in the door, providing her with enough water and nutritive paste to stay functional. They didn't speak; all their former jocularity was gone. Something huge had changed, something more than just one simple order. She ate and drank as necessary and discovered that the top of the bench lifted up to reveal the sort of facilities one might need in a brig, if one didn't like to do a lot of cleaning. That was the only pleasant surprise.

One day, halfway through her tube of bland gray paste, she let out a huge yawn and realized she couldn't keep her eyes open. As she struggled to stay conscious, the brig door opened. Bright light blinded her as rough hands grabbed her arms. She tumbled forward into oblivion.

When she woke, she was in a cell. Small, rectangular, with high metal walls and one tiny, barred window near the ceiling that let in a wan, milky light. The sound of waves crashing and the scent of saltwater and minerals suggested she was near the sea, and a cold and unforgiving sea it was. She still had no lightsabers, no personal effects, no toiletries. The cell was slightly bigger than the ship's brig had been, but now, instead of that comforting sensation of moving toward a goal, she felt stifled and buried and still.

She began to wonder if the figure on the holo had lied to her, if there was something more at play here. Why would anyone kill all the Jedi but one, and keep her locked up in some sort of prison? Whoever it was, they had to have a plan. Perhaps they were waiting for something to happen. A change in power would require time, after all, and the Jedi were clearly no longer part of the equation.

She thought about screaming, beating her fists against the door, using the well of rage inside her to try to blast open the wall that led to the sea. But Iskat Akaris had been tested before, and she was determined to never be found wanting again. If they wished to find her limits and plumb her depths, they would have to try harder than this. It would take more than another box to break her.

Despite the small window, time lost all meaning. Days here were strangely long, and her sleep suffered further. She spent so much time meditating that she had no idea how long she'd been communing with the Force. She did calisthenics and body-weight exercises and practiced climbing all over her cell. The view outside the small window showed nothing but endless gray water. Meals came at seemingly random times, more nutritive paste shoved under the door. She knew now that they could drug her at any moment, that she was completely in their power. And it wasn't that she trusted them—whoever had masterminded her capture and imprisonment—it was that she understood that she had no choice but to surrender. She'd been doing it all her life.

If she really considered her situation, it was an absolute farce. She'd been offered answers and freedom, and she'd received silence and captivity. For someone who had been offered a second chance, she'd been stripped of all comforts and shoved into a dark hole where her only company was her own thoughts.

The thoughts of Iskat Akaris had not been good company recently.

They were dark, twisted things, her dreams like drowning, and sometimes she felt as if the very air around her was filled with pain, like it had soaked into the walls.

Perhaps it was days or weeks or even months when she again felt the heavy pull of her eyelids as she stared down at the remains of mealy brown paste on her plate.

"Here we go again," she murmured, guiding herself to the floor before she fell fully unconscious.

When she awoke, she immediately realized she was in the brig of a ship again. Perhaps the same ship as before.

A mad sort of laugh burst out of her mouth.

It was just so ridiculous.

She told herself that perhaps this was part of a test, that maybe she was being treated this way on purpose. Before the traditional Jedi trials, which she'd never properly had the opportunity to face, the Padawans were encouraged to spend a period of time fasting and meditating to purify themselves, so she reasoned that perhaps this was something similar. Stripped of her weapons, her supplies, her sanity, she was left only with herself and her worries, fears, and doubts.

Every time her rage rose up, hating the darkness and the confinement, she pushed it back down and clutched her amulet, seeking her newly deepened connection with the Force, that joyous river that had been waiting so long for her to welcome it. She'd put herself in a mental cage for nearly two decades; what were a few more days of physical captivity? She could tell that they were traveling through hyperspace, and it seemed unlikely they would transport her to yet another prison when the first one had been perfectly wretched. Perhaps enough time had passed that whoever was in charge had figured out how to move forward. Maybe she was finally going to get answers. Once she was on the other side of this journey and out of the brig, she could express her dissatisfaction with her treatment to whoever had chosen to spare her life.

When the ship dropped out of hyperspace, Iskat's eyes opened from a deep level of meditation, and she stood, sending out her senses. She knew immediately that they had to be headed toward Coruscant; nowhere else in the galaxy held such massive, teeming amounts of life.

Was she being taken back to the Jedi Temple, which surely had to be empty now?

Was she being taken to the Senate, or to some other governing body?

Or would the ship descend into the lower levels, where the crime bosses ruled and where she'd first explored the possibility of a life without strict control?

She wouldn't know until they wanted her to know.

The ship landed, and after some time, the brig door opened. Iskat was already standing, waiting, her arms by her sides. Captain Spider stood there, his face unreadable behind his helmet. He offered her a blindfold and waited for her to take it and shroud her vision.

"Step out of the brig."

Iskat obliged, and his hand clamped around her upper arm, guiding her across the ship and down the ramp. She couldn't tell by smell or sound where she might be, but the air quality and the noise of the nearby space lanes suggested it was an upper level of Coruscant. It sounded similar to the Jedi Temple, large and empty, but felt entirely unfamiliar. A smooth grate was under her feet, and after she walked through a grand doorway, she could feel a cavernous space bound in metal echoing around her. It felt almost like a warehouse, perhaps in parts unfinished.

As Spider led her forward, the heavy tromp of his troops escorting her in perfect time, Iskat began to feel a powerful presence, dark and pulsing, heavy in the flow of the Force.

They were walking directly toward it.

Toward *him*.

"Welcome, Iskat Akaris," this figure said, his voice crisp and cruel. It was, oddly, not the same voice from the shrouded hologram.

She inclined her head in a nod but did not speak; her words, she felt, were unnecessary.

The blindfold was lifted from her face.

The figure standing before her was a Pau'an. He wore stylized black-and-gray armor with a long cloak the color of dried blood; he seamlessly blended in with the soaring industrial fortress in which they stood. The Pau'an had white skin, burgundy facial tattoos, piercing yellow eyes, and sharpened teeth. He had been a Jedi once, Iskat realized, but he had fallen. He had chosen otherwise.

Just like her.

He held out his hands, presenting all three of her lightsabers, and she took them, feeling like a part of her soul had been returned. She hooked the green ones on her belt but kept the yellow one in hand, unlit. This being—she did not trust him.

After all her time locked in isolation, she wondered if she would ever trust anything or anyone again.

"Are you ready to leave behind everything the Jedi have taught you and finally forge your own path?" he asked with grave finality.

Iskat did not have to give this question a moment's thought.

She'd been waiting her whole life for someone to say those words.

"Yes," she responded. "I am."

Whether it was true or not remained to be seen, but she would not voice that concern.

Much like with the Jedi, she would hold back the questioning part of herself.

Her first interest was in staying alive.

With a sinister smile, the Pau'an reached behind his back, revealing a glowing red lightsaber with a crescent-shaped hilt. Holding her gaze, not blinking, he assumed a dueling position, his yellow eyes reflecting his crimson blade.

"Welcome, then, to the Inquisitorius."

/ 27.

IT WASN'T A WELCOME; IT was a challenge.

Iskat immediately whipped her original green lightsaber off her belt and ignited both blades, one yellow and one green, falling into the position that traditionally answered his own. He began to circle, and she circled with him, her senses going into overdrive as she cataloged his movements (smooth, studied, predatory), his reach (long), the terrain (mostly smooth metal), and what might be available in the area to act as a weapon or an impediment (nothing).

She'd never seen a red lightsaber before, and the color told her all she needed to know about her opponent: He had fallen to the dark side. He didn't hide himself in the Force; he let her feel his might, a heavy and smoldering malevolent energy that, likewise, was reaching out to discover her own weaknesses.

She had none.

She struck first, slashing with one lightsaber and then with the next, very aware that neither of them wielded training sabers. This was clearly a kill-or-be-killed situation. As he easily fought off both her blades with his red one, she began to understand that the Pau'an had skills she lacked—that he was stronger both physically and in his connection with the Force. He was playing with her. A sliver of fear shivered down her spine as he sharply parried every strike with the same ease and care she'd take teaching a youngling. That fear was swiftly eclipsed by anger.

He was testing her, patronizing her.

He thought she was lesser.

He thought she would lose.

She would prove him wrong.

The rage built in her chest, a fire craving something to burn, and she opened herself to the Force, to the depths she'd always known were there but had always taken care to discourage. Thunder filled her veins as her onslaught built to a crescendo. Slash, parry, twirl, roll, jab, hack, slash. This was the dance from Geonosis, the dance of death, the connection to the Force that had filled her with an exultation she'd never known. She broke into a grin as she battled the Pau'an backward, making him stumble once before catching himself and snarling at her.

"Is this the best you have?" he snapped. "I was told you were worthy of our ranks."

Her twin blades twirled around him, green and golden streaks against the dark-gray walls. "I don't even know what the Inquisitorius is, but I assure you I'm worthy."

"There is much—"

With a flick of her fingers, she sent him skidding backward. He caught himself, flung his cape to the ground, and stood tall, his red blade at his side. Iskat didn't relax; she understood that although they were on the same side now, he was still a danger. She held her blades in hand, lit, and waited.

"As I was saying, there is much you don't know. The galaxy changed during your confinement. The Jedi are all but gone."

"How? Why?" She didn't want him to know that she'd felt it happen, but she did want to know the answers. She did not owe him the truth.

The Pau'an bared his teeth and slashed at her, driving her backward. "The Jedi betrayed the Republic, betrayed everything for which the Order once stood. They attempted a coup. Mace Windu himself—traitor, apostate!—tried to assassinate Chancellor Palpatine. He failed."

Iskat fought back, desperately, but his rage made him formidable. "After this ultimate treachery, the cowardly Jedi could no longer be trusted, and so they were eliminated. The clones were given an order— Order 66. The only Jedi who were spared were those who saw through their *lies*." He straightened and pointed his lightsaber at her. "Like you."

"How did you know about me?"

His lightsaber slashed down as if slapping the question away. "It is irrelevant. You are here now."

"What is the truth of my mother?"

A sinister grin. "You'll have to earn that knowledge."

She barely had time to react as he leapt through the air, spinning toward her, the fight continuing in earnest. Her body took over, reacting on instinct, flowing through the Force as if she were swimming with a current, while inside Iskat was reeling. A coup? By the Jedi? Against the Republic they'd defended with their lives? She tried to picture Mace Windu striking down the charismatic and friendly old man she'd met in the Jedi Temple, and she couldn't imagine how Palpatine had survived the Master Jedi's might. To think: After all she'd sacrificed for the Jedi, they'd committed the ultimate betrayal.

And yet . . .

The Pau'an was right. She'd questioned them all along. She'd sensed their lies, swimming under the surface. She'd felt the wrongness in the tenets they required her to memorize, in the hollow dogma they'd regurgitated instead of answering her questions. She'd chafed against the way they fought a war that seemed designed to make them lose. She hadn't trusted Mace Windu, and he'd ultimately proven himself untrustworthy.

No wonder they'd punished curiosity and the courage to question their edicts. Because they had been hiding something, and they didn't want it to be revealed.

All the pieces fell into place, and a thrill of satisfaction rippled through Iskat, adding to her strength and filling her with fierce elation.

She'd been right. All this time, *she'd been right.*

The Jedi had been playing a game. Small measures, small victories, small tactics, never enough to turn the tide. Just enough to make the war drag on endlessly, weakening the Republic forces, distracting the Chancellor, sending their warriors out on useless errands to die insignificant deaths far from the Temple.

All so their leaders could effect a coup.

And another truth followed, one that sounded in her hearts like the tolling funeral bell.

The Jedi had been holding her back for a reason.

They had done their best to keep her ignorant and complacent, to make her feel like *she* was the problem, like *she* was the strange one, like *she* was the one who just couldn't rise to the occasion.

They'd held her back and made her feel lesser . . . *on purpose.*

After all, if she was so busy fixating on her limitations and feeling insecure about meeting their standards, then she wouldn't have time to notice their wrongdoing. She wouldn't have the energy or ability to focus on growing strong. They'd wanted her weak.

And they'd wanted her to think the dark side was something to fear instead of something to be embraced. To be *used.*

Grinning, exulting in this understanding, she changed tactics and used a combo she'd learned from Kelleran, but the Pau'an was ready. He deflected and spun, slashing down with his red lightsaber, but she caught his blade in both of hers. He pressed close, close enough for her to see the wet gleam of his teeth, close enough for her to feel the heat of three blades creeping close to her cheek, his red one slightly crackling. Before, he'd been toying with her, but now that she was filled with emotions, with rage and exhilaration and a ferocious drive to prove herself, he was having to defend himself more aggressively. Growling, she pressed harder, satisfied when he had to stumble back.

"I think not," he said.

He put a boot on her stomach and kicked her away, and they disengaged. Iskat caught herself and twirled her lightsabers and went into a crouch, but he extinguished his blade.

"I think that's enough. You have much to learn, but that's expected. Here among the Inquisitorius, you will whet your skills against those of your brothers and sisters. You will seek the answers that have been kept from you, study the darkest depths of what the Force can do. You will learn that you can only harness your truest strength when you fully embrace your power and don't hold back. Even now, you didn't fully commit, but that Jedi reticence won't last. If you don't rise to my expectations . . . well, you won't survive long enough to worry."

Still, Iskat didn't deactivate her blades. "Who are you?"

He cocked his head, his yellow eyes boring into her soul.

"I'm the Grand Inquisitor, and for the foreseeable future, I'm the one you will want to impress."

He paused as if he expected her to bow or grovel, but instead she threw one of her lightsabers at him, the green blade spinning toward his face. As if expecting this attack, the Grand Inquisitor slashed downward, slicing her lightsaber hilt into two perfect pieces, and that was when Iskat charged.

As if she'd slammed into a wall, her body froze painfully in place, her lightsaber-arm useless. She gritted her teeth and fought against it, barely managing to twitch.

The Grand Inquisitor—he was more powerful than she was.

Exponentially so.

"As I said, you have much to learn," he said crisply, one hand up as he held her with the Force, squeezing like a vise.

With a flick of his fingers, she fell forward, barely managing to catch herself, her muscles trembling. He turned his back on her and walked away.

Iskat stood and kicked away the useless remains of the first lightsaber she'd ever built.

Oh, yes. She would learn.

And then she'd teach this Grand Inquisitor a lesson.

Nothing could stop her now.

PART
THREE

/ 28.

ISKAT WAS AMONG THE FIRST to join the Inquisitorius, and she watched as, one by one, other former Jedi joined the fold. She saw them stalking the halls or limping to the medbay with grievous injuries, but they generally did not interact with her. It was almost as if they didn't see her. From what she observed, she was among the youngest, and also one of the only recruits who hadn't required, as the Grand Inquisitor called it, further coercion.

Perhaps that was why the other Inquisitors already had red-bladed lightsabers and uniforms similar to that of the Grand Inquisitor, why they all went by numbers while she was generally called only Akaris. It was an unfortunate parallel how, even here, where she had chosen her path, she was different.

The other Inquisitors ignored her, but she sensed they had all been broken, somehow, crushed and pulverized and reforged to fit a very specific mold. Iskat was whole, but she had yet to earn her name, her armor, her weapons. There was something the others possessed that she lacked. They told her nothing, silently delighted in their superiority.

She told herself she didn't care, but it chafed.

It was like the Jedi all over again, like everyone else knew a secret she didn't.

But Iskat Akaris was playing a long game.

As time continued to pass, she didn't complain and she didn't ask questions. After her long two years grounded with the Jedi, she knew a test when she saw one. Although she didn't lose time like she had in her seaside cell, there was no calendar, no schedule, no way to measure the world moving on. The other Inquisitors came and went, and Iskat Akaris stayed behind. The Grand Inquisitor would watch her practicing alone with a remote in a training room sometimes, his yellow eyes unblinking, as if looking for something inside her that had not yet surfaced. His probing gaze seemed to scan for any sign of weakness or impatience, and she began to delight in disappointing him.

Whatever this was, this strange tedium, it would not break her, no matter how long it lasted.

If the only things in her life now were self-led training and deepening her newfound connection with the Force while unencumbered with meaningless rhetoric, then she was better off than all the other Jedi she'd grown up with, who were all dead.

And then one day, the Grand Inquisitor appeared while she was doing calisthenics and called Iskat to join him.

"I have a special task for you, Akaris," the Grand Inquisitor said, leading her toward the landing pad. "A mission that requires specific knowledge only you possess."

"I am glad to be of service, Grand Inquisitor," she replied. She had quickly learned that the Grand Inquisitor demanded utmost formality.

"It is known that you accompanied Jedi Master Sember Vey on missions to visit various collectors around the galaxy to obtain Force-related objects. It is this experience I hope to call upon today. You are familiar with a trader named Gamodar on Bar'leth?"

Iskat was now very adept at schooling her face. She had not thought to hear that name again, not after she attempted to use Gamodar and his relics to mask her true intentions from Mace Windu when she wished to visit Pkori. Sember had died regretting never having discovered what unique find Gamodar was holding for her, and Iskat had always been curious what her master had been so eager to collect.

"I have encountered Gamodar twice before in his shop on Bar'leth."

The Grand Inquisitor stopped beside an angular black shuttle and inclined his head toward the ramp. Iskat went within, wishing she had worn something more formal than a simple black tunic, pants, and robe, now sweaty from training. He followed and took the pilot's seat.

"Good. Hopefully you will prove useful as we obtain some relics of our own."

Iskat weighed her options. The Grand Inquisitor did not like questions, but considering they were alone and on a mission particular to her history, it seemed reasonable to avail herself of any information available.

"Is this a common pursuit for the Inquisitorius?" she asked. "Hunting relics?"

His eyes flicked to her as the ship rose into the sky. "Nothing about the Inquisitorius is common, and you will learn more when you have proven yourself. What once belonged only to the Jedi is now ours to claim." The ship shot into the air, and the Grand Inquisitor focused on piloting, his cold mien making it clear that he didn't wish to be disturbed further.

The flight was uneventful, and when they entered the blue skies of its atmosphere, Bar'leth looked the same as it had before. Iskat hadn't been out in the galaxy since the destruction of the Republic, and it was a relief, to see a peaceful planet remaining peaceful. The Grand Inquisitor didn't make any inquiries about Gamodar, but he knew exactly where to find the old Ortolan trader's shop.

He didn't speak to Iskat until he stood by the ramp. "Tell me what you know of this Gamodar."

At first, Iskat felt a trill of horror, knowing full well that the Grand Inquisitor wasn't here to politely haggle and enjoy Gamodar's famous krumpa pastries. This wasn't a general inquiry.

Whatever Iskat told the Grand Inquisitor would be used against the kind old trader, who had a fondness for stray tooka cats and loved to bake.

And yet . . .

Gamodar had artifacts that belonged to the Inquisitorius, and if he was as clever and quick as he'd always seemed, hopefully he would come out of this interaction missing relics but not limbs or his life.

"Gamodar is an elderly Ortolan. He has several pet tooka cats that live in and around his shop and upstairs apartment. He has a stationary IG droid called Lump that acts as a security system—its torso is attached to a counter, and it has blasters to discourage shoplifting. The general shop the public visits is on the ground floor, but all the real treasures are in the cellar."

"Is he armed?"

"Armed? Gamodar?" She thought about it. "I would assume so, but I never saw a weapon on his person or felt any sort of dangerous intentions from him. Lump is always watching."

The Grand Inquisitor nodded. "Does he keep his relics in a safe?"

"He would be foolish not to, but I was never allowed in the basement. I stayed upstairs and played with the tooka while he and Sember came to terms."

"If you wish this Gamodar to remain alive, you will convince him to open his safe. If not, I will destroy him and take what I wish."

She bowed her head. "I understand, Grand Inquisitor."

The ramp came down, and Iskat shielded her eyes from more daylight than she'd seen in ages.

"Impress me, and things will go well. Disappoint me at your peril."

That said, the Grand Inquisitor strode down the ramp, and Iskat followed in his wake.

This was another test, and it would require her to dance along the razor's edge, but she was determined to pass.

"Why, Iskat Akaris! I never thought to see you again!" Gamodar said when she appeared in his open door. The sky-blue Ortolan hadn't changed, and his flipper-like ears were lifted for what passed for an embrace among Ortolans, one that she didn't feel she deserved. After a quick glance at the Grand Inquisitor, she decided she had to fully commit, stepping over a sleeping tooka and accepting Gamodar's embrace.

"So good to see that you weren't one of those awful traitors," Gamodar said. "Sember always seemed so trustworthy, but it just goes to show you. Perhaps we placed too much of our trust with the Jedi . . ." He trailed off and released her, and his little beady eyes blinked at the Grand Inquisitor. "I take it you have a new mentor?" His ears drooped as if he could already tell that this new figure would not wish to partake of tea and pastries.

"I do, and we'd like to acquire whatever relics you'd set aside for Sember. Anything Force related. Before she died, she told me you had a unique find for us."

Gamodar glanced up at Lump, which Iskat was sure the Grand Inquisitor had noticed. For now, the droid's arms remained at rest, but his shiny, silver head was watching the interaction closely.

"I promised Sember I wouldn't let anything fall into the hands of someone who might misuse it," Gamodar began. "But . . . well, I guess that was the Jedi after all, huh?"

Iskat spread her hands. "The Jedi are gone, and we want to make sure the galaxy is truly safe from anyone who might attempt to continue their work."

Gamodar looked her up and down. "Are you part of some official business with the Empire? You don't look like peacekeepers."

"Whether or not peace will be kept shall be determined by your next actions," the Grand Inquisitor said stiffly.

"Gamodar, please." Iskat put a hand on his chest, attempting to influence this being she'd known for so long. "The artifacts, and then we'll be gone, and you can go on enjoying a peaceful life."

For a long moment, Gamodar thought about it, and Iskat squeezed his rubbery blue shoulder. Influence had never been her strong suit, and judging by his haggling powers, Gamodar was strong-willed.

"Very well," he finally said. "I'll be back in a moment."

He trundled down the basement steps, and Iskat and the Grand Inquisitor waited silently. The moment dragged out, and then Iskat heard the rasp of metal and turned smoothly, igniting her lightsaber and throwing it at Lump.

The green lightsaber spun toward the droid, and Lump's arm fell to the floor with a heavy clank made all the louder by the blaster clutched in its brutal fingers.

"Betrayal," the Grand Inquisitor said, raising his lip. "How quotidian."

Iskat's blade returned to her hand, and she sliced it through Lump's head and chest, leaving the droid's eyes dark and its wires sparking.

The Grand Inquisitor watched dispassionately. "Bring me the artifacts or you'll die with him, Iskat Akaris."

Lit blade in hand, she advanced down the stairs. Sember had never allowed her to come this far. It was dark and cool underground, and she followed a short hallway to a heavy metal door.

"Gamodar," she called.

She could feel him on the other side, frightened and angry.

"It doesn't have to be like this. Give us the artifacts and we'll go away."

"Is this what Master Vey wanted for you, Iskat?" Gamodar said, creeping close to the door. "I'm no Jedi, and I know we've been told they were a bad lot, but I can feel the dark side radiating from your companion. It's attempting to take hold in you. Are you even attempting to fight it? Is this what you want?"

She took a deep breath, deactivated her lightsaber, and put her cheek to the door so she could speak softly.

"Much like you right now, I have limited choices. I'm choosing life."

He approached the door. She could feel his sadness, his regret, so close on the other side of the thick metal. He hated knowing Sember was gone, didn't believe she'd been a traitor, felt a deep disquiet with the current state of the galaxy. He was filled with sorrow, for Iskat and for the Jedi.

"There are other choices," he began.

And that's when she put her lightsaber hilt against the door and activated the blade.

A gasp of pain. "No—!"

She did the same with her other lightsaber in a different spot.

Quicker would be better, for both of them.

She felt the tug of his body as he fell and deactivated her blades with a shudder. Quickly wiping away her tears, she pulled a lockpick set from her kit and went to work.

"Old fool," she muttered to the door. "You were never going to change anything. Why couldn't you just cooperate?"

The lock gave way, and she had to use the Force to push the door open, blocked as it was by the Ortolan's heavy body. A tooka sniffed at him, crying, and Iskat rushed into the room, heading directly for the safe. She could feel relics inside, gently pulsing in the Force like a soft, slow heartbeat, and one in particular, deep and dark as a well.

The safe was a massive thing, but few objects in the galaxy could stand against the power of a lightsaber. She soon had it open and was tossing everything that seemed useful into a handwoven basket she found nearby. In addition to the artifacts, statues, and texts, there were jewels and credits and chunks of ore that would carry great value elsewhere in the galaxy. Iskat wasn't sure if the Grand Inquisitor cared for such things, but she assumed wealth was never something to turn down, now that her life of gentle captivity with the Jedi was over.

Carrying the large basket, she ignored the blue shape on the floor and hurried upstairs. Tookas followed her, mewing worriedly, and she wondered who would feed them, now that Gamodar was no more. Upstairs in the silent shop, she held out the beautiful basket, knowing the Grand Inquisitor would only care about the bounty inside—and one object in particular.

"Ah." He reached within and pulled out a triangular red holocron pulsing with dark side power, so different from the softly glowing blue ones she'd encountered before. "Exactly what I was hoping to find." His eyes gleamed as he turned it this way and that, and he didn't put it back in Iskat's basket. He clutched it greedily.

"Bring the rest," he said before giving her a sharp look. "Is that everything?"

"Everything related to the Force and the Jedi, plus some trinkets of obvious value."

A nod, something approaching a smile. "Well, then."

He spun on his heel and strode briskly out into the sun. Iskat gave one final look around the wonderful shop of trinkets that had fascinated her when she was a younger, different being. Lump's torso and face were still and dark now, a tooka on the counter sniffing at a patch of leaking oil. Downstairs, Gamodar was . . .

Well, he'd made the wrong choice and that wasn't her fault.

All he'd had to do was hand her the holocron, and he could've lived.

ISKAT FOLLOWED THE GRAND INQUISITOR to a chamber inside the Inquisitorius Headquarters that she'd never seen before.

She walked into the chamber in plain black robes, carrying her green lightsaber, and when she left the room, her head held high, there was a new crescent-shaped red lightsaber clutched in her hand. Gone were the simple tunic and pants crusted with her sweat. Her new uniform had been perfectly tailored to move with her body while running and fighting, all in shades of gray and black with a high collar and stiff boots fitted with a vibroblade scabbard. The helmet under her arm gave her a terrifying countenance, the same sort of faceless violence she'd once questioned in the clones.

After the ritual, she was formally a member of the Inquisitorius and fully understood her purpose. She'd been brought to the Inquisitorius Headquarters on Coruscant to hunt down the remaining traitorous Jedi, and now that she'd proven her loyalty and her obedience, she could finally begin that task. She was ready. Her old life was as dead as the Jedi Order and she had a new home and a new name, although she wasn't yet ready to use it. She had sworn her allegiance to the Grand

Inquisitor and his masters, and to the task of silencing what was left of the Jedi.

And why not?

Killing was what she'd been born to do.

It was her calling.

All that time, the Jedi had never told her that what she was fighting in herself, what she was tamping down, what she was trying to meditate away—*was the persistent call of the dark side.* And it wasn't some terrible, cruel foreign thing, some cloying lure or trap. It was part and parcel of her, just waiting to be discovered. It was so obvious, when all the lies of the Jedi were wiped away and the evidence was laid out. They'd told her to fear it, to meditate it away, but that was because they wanted to keep her weak. There was a vast field of knowledge, a whole other world the Jedi had actively tried to hide from her, to keep her from tapping into something they couldn't fathom, much less control. All this time, it had been inside her, calling to her, and she had been forced to deny it.

Now she was rushing into its joyous embrace.

She had built two lightsabers with her own hands, but now she would learn to fight with a far more powerful red-bladed lightsaber that could spin like a circle of death.

Yes, as it turned out, the Inquisitorius had many benefits above and beyond the Jedi.

Iskat had options. Now that she'd been granted full status as an Inquisitor, she was encouraged to seek what enticed and pleased her, the materials and clothes and footwear that would hone her lethality. She could furnish her quarters according to her own aesthetics and interests. She was allowed to own things, even encouraged to collect objects that might enhance her education and training. Her blue stone amulet still hung around her neck under her uniform, a reminder of the many anchors the Jedi had used to hold her back. The crystal of her remaining green lightsaber had been part of the transformation of her new red one, but Feyra's yellow saber would rest in a place of honor in her chamber, along with a statue from Gamodar's safe that the Grand Inquisitor had not claimed. Possessing objects, it turned out, could bring a lot of satisfaction.

No wonder the Jedi had discouraged it.

For if a Jedi craved things, they might not be content to sit all day by a pool, meditating on—what? Being lesser, being content with nothing, calming the rage that stoked the fires of growth?

What was the point of spending that much time trying to hide part of your own soul when it was so much easier, so much better, to embrace it?

Struggling with the Jedi way was merely a sane person's response to being fed constant insanity.

Her questioning was over. Now that the Inquisitorius had invited her into their inner sanctum, Iskat had fully opened herself to the dark side and all that it promised.

As she left the chamber and entered the main hall of the metal-plated tower, an old man in a black hooded cloak materialized from the shadows, walking beside her with a crooked cane. Iskat was startled and wary; he had concealed himself in the Force, and she had missed him entirely until the moment he chose to appear. She kept walking.

"There is still doubt in you," the old man said from deep within his black robes, keeping pace.

Dark energy rolled off him like smoke, and for all that he appeared wizened and weak, she knew that beside her strode a being of immense power. She recognized him—from the holo during Order 66, and from before then, when she'd known him as Chancellor Palpatine—but didn't immediately show her hand. She was terrified to her very bones, and he knew it, and it pleased him.

"Not doubt, my lord," she responded. She chose her words carefully, understanding that if she lied, he would know. "I felt different all my life among the Jedi, and I am grateful I was spared their fate. I'm eager to serve the Inquisitorius."

"The Jedi," he mused. "Of course they would ostracize you. They are weak, and they cannot tolerate the strong. Now you have become something else."

Iskat looked down at her hands. She was so accustomed to seeing the brown robes of a Jedi that it was strange, to see her red skin against the stiff black cuffs of her uniform. "I've only ever been one thing, only ever believed myself to be one thing. I've chosen this gladly, but I'm still the same person, and the galaxy has changed around me. I don't know yet what I will become."

He chuckled, a dark sound that echoed. "Yes, yes, in time. It is early yet. You will change, or you will die."

"It is already beginning," she said softly. "My journey with the dark side." She looked up at him. "My lord, are you . . . Sith?"

"Good, good." He grinned, yellow teeth flashing in the shadow of his hood. "Yes, child. I am not the Chancellor you once knew—I am more. I am Darth Sidious, heir to millennia of grand design, dedicated to achieving vengeance for the Sith. The Republic I served is dead." The last two words were a harsh staccato. "Although the great Mace Windu did his best to end me, only one of us remains, and I am stronger now than ever. But you—you have not yet fully accepted your new destiny. I can see how one raised in the Jedi way might have trouble releasing a lifetime of weakness. It is a common thing, to pause at the edge of a cliff. Only some will jump."

"Yes, but where is the cliff?" she asked. "I have no fear of high places."

Quicker than her eye could follow, the old man's red-bladed light-saber was at her throat, so close she could feel its heat, hear its crackle. For all that he had feigned fragility, she could sense him now in the Force, a maelstrom of dark power she could barely fathom.

"Will you jump when it is time, child? Or will you fight?"

"Fight you?" she whispered. "It would not be an equal fight. My lord, if you wanted me dead, I already would be."

Just as quickly as it appeared, the blade vanished, and she took a deep breath and swallowed hard.

"Equality," he growled in disgust. "There is no such thing as equality, there is only dominance or failure. The Jedi believed that all beings are equal, and that if they could control an individual from birth onward, they could brainwash equality and modesty and altruism into every developing mind. Yet the Jedi chose to ignore that any group of children must immediately rank itself from leaders to followers to pariahs." She felt his eyes crawling over her like the barbed little feet of beetles. "But you know that all too well, don't you?"

"I spent my entire life as a pariah," she said curtly.

He nodded and continued walking; she kept pace and kept her distance. "Teachers do not believe themselves to be biased, but there will always be favorites," he continued. "This is a weakness of the Jedi only understood by the child who is always found wanting: Equality is a lie, but revenge? Oh, that is very, very real. That is what we offer you, Iskat Akaris. The chance to become what you were meant to be . . . and to punish those who would destroy you for being different. The chance to fight for your own supremacy. The chance to do what you do best. *To kill.*"

His words seemed to echo back from the stark metal walls.

To kill. To kill. To kill.

"My lord, am I to be Sith?" she asked.

A chuckle. "Oh, no, child. But you will serve the greater cause."

Palpatine stopped and waved a hand at the wall. A hidden door swung open—a door she hadn't seen before. Iskat was curious but not surprised. The building was immense, rivaling the Jedi Temple, and yet it was noticeably empty, and she'd always wondered why. This must be where the full members of the Inquisitorius spent their time. Just like the rest of the facility, the walls were dull-gray metal, as if designed for droids who had no keen eye for beauty or comfort. Iskat wondered if Palpatine met every new Inquisitor to reveal the door, if this was a test or a lesson. Either way, he was watching, waiting. Perhaps she wasn't Sith, but ever since she'd gazed upon Sember's artifact she had felt the call to the dark side, and she was beginning to see that this suited her much better than the Jedi had.

"It began when I encountered a Sith text," she told him. "And then when I stood on the sands of Thule, it was as if the very planet reached out to me. Awakened something in me. The Jedi taught me that killing is bad, and yet . . . I'm so very good at it. I sometimes wonder if I was born this way."

"Yes," Palpatine said eagerly, gesturing her through the door. "Yes, feel it deep within you. See the truth of what the Jedi have done. You were born with a gift, a skill, a purpose. And yet all your life, the Jedi preached oneness while making you intricately, painfully aware of how very different you were. They suggested that difference made you *wrong* somehow, made you lesser, that you should focus all your time and energy on purging that darkness from your soul. The dark side is a part of you, my dear, and it has always been so. That feeling the Jedi forced you to push away was merely an eager and loving hand, reaching out to guide you."

As he spoke, he led her down another long hallway that looked identical to all the other hallways. Iskat committed every detail to memory, knowing full well she'd be expected to find her way on her own, later.

"How do you know all this?" she asked.

"We've been watching you for quite some time," he admitted. "Even before the Great Purge, we knew there were Jedi who were not served by the Order that ruled their lives. I've had spies planted in the Temple, watching for promising adepts who might thrive among our ranks."

"Heezo," she said, understanding immediately.

"Correct."

"I wondered how he always seemed to be in the courtyard when I was there."

"Our Selonian friend once trained to become a Jedi, you know. He did not pass his trials, and they found a place for him in the Temple. But like many who have left the Jedi Order, he still maintains some small connection with the Force. He's exceptionally good at sensing the sort of emotions the Jedi"—it was almost a snarl—"wanted its members to reject."

"Is he here?"

Palpatine led her into a grand and soaring circular chamber ringed by large, round windows with a sunken pit in its center. They stood at the very edge, looking down into what most resembled a gladiatorial arena, complete with the black scorch marks left behind by many lightsabers. Acid-yellow lights lit tunnels leading out of the pit, while Imperial guards loomed between the windows, silent and stoic in their austere crimson robes and masks.

"The droid mechanic is no longer your concern." Palpatine put his hand on her shoulder, the withered fingers as hard and tense as steel. She realized, too late, that he could easily throw her into the pit, and although she had the skills and instincts to catch herself, she still felt the implied threat. "I once told you that I expected great things of you in the future, and I still do. Forget your life among the Jedi and fully step into your future as an Inquisitor. This facility is equipped with the tools a clever warrior might use to advance the skills that some consider un-natural." His head turned suddenly as someone approached them from the hallway.

"Ah. Fifth Brother. I take it you've met?"

Iskat was indeed familiar with the Fifth Brother, and she did not like him. The tall humanoid with his greenish-gray skin, his flat and cruel eyes, glared at Iskat from under his triangular headpiece, clearly un-happy to see that she'd gained access to this restricted area of the facil-ity.

"Yes, Lord Sidious," he said, inclining his head.

"Take Iskat to the library. She is ready." Iskat had hoped that receiving her armor and red lightsaber might make the other Inquisitors more welcoming, but the opposite seemed true. If anything, the Fifth Brother hated her more now. She could feel him in the Force, like a cracked gla-cier, radiating coldness. "As you wish, my lord," he finally said.

Realizing she had been released from an audience, Iskat turned to the old man in his black robes, and for just a second, it was as if he lifted an invisible wall and let her truly sense his power.

Her nostrils flared as her entire body begged her to run, as fast and as far as possible, and never, ever come back.

Then, like a portcullis falling, he was just a man again—or almost.

"Thank you for your wise counsel, my lord," she said.

He inclined his head, amused. "Choose wisely, my dear," he said, al-most kindly. "By now you know there is only one alternative."

The Emperor turned and hobbled down the hall, his black robes soon melding into the shadows.

"Come along," the Fifth Brother said. He gave her a snide look and leapt into the pit far below.

Iskat followed, using the Force to control her fall and land neatly. "How long have you been training down here?"

"It doesn't matter," he said without turning back.

"Then what does matter?"

"If you last long enough, perhaps you will find out."

His tone was as brusque as his pace. Iskat paid close attention to the turns they took through the labyrinthine facility of seemingly infinite gray metal walls, the plates overlapping in a senseless pattern that Iskat found distasteful. The Fifth Brother led her into a lift, and she briefly wondered if getting into a confined space with him was a good idea.

"I won't harm you," he said mockingly. "At least not today. It would be like striking down an infant."

She glared at him, not taking the bait. "Were you a Jedi, once?"

Because she couldn't see it, couldn't imagine this hateful being smiling in brown robes or helping children.

His eyes flashed at her and away, bored. "I am an Inquisitor."

"But what were you before that?"

"Weak."

"How descriptive."

"I'm not here to amuse you, Sister."

Iskat had hoped that she would find like minds here, once she had been fully initiated among the Inquisitors, but if the rest of them were anything like the Fifth Brother, she was going to be disappointed. Perhaps she hadn't truly bonded with anyone among the Jedi, but she didn't feel any kinship with the Fifth Brother. At least she was fairly certain that, unlike the Jedi, he would stab her in the front instead of the back.

Well, honestly, he would probably stab her anywhere he saw a crack in her armor. She doubted honor was one of his defining characteristics.

The lift opened, and they stepped out into yet another round foyer. This facility didn't have the thoughtful, graceful, spiritual elegance of the Jedi Temple; it was equally large but brutal and artless in design, an apt metaphor for the blunt strength of true power compared with the false beauty of haughty lies. The Fifth Brother led her toward a grand doorway, which slid open as they neared to reveal a library. Compared with the Jedi Archives, it was just a simple room, but Iskat had hope that here she might find the answers she'd always sought, whereas Jocasta Nu's archives had only kept her ignorant of the true knowledge within.

"How does it work?" she asked. "Is anything off limits? Is there a librarian?"

The look he gave her was rife with disgust. "Nothing is forbidden. This isn't the Jedi. Among the Inquisitors, you must fight for what you want, and that includes information."

He turned to leave.

"Thanks for the warm welcome," she called, knowing it would annoy him.

He did not stop walking. "No."

She stood there, alone, wondering where to start. Should she research Pkori and Feyra? Or should she seek to gain the skills she would need to survive among the Inquisitors?

She closed her eyes, trusting the Force to guide her, and felt a familiar tug. Her heartbeats sped up as she followed the call to a shelf, where a familiar bundle of skin and sinew sat, pulsing with dark side energy.

Iskat glanced quickly over her shoulder to see if she was being watched; she'd been told nothing here was off limits, but as Emperor Palpatine had reminded her, she hadn't fully released herself from the Jedi strictures that had thus far guided her life.

It didn't matter if she was watched. This was a library, she was an Inquisitor, and she could take what she wished. She reached out, and the moment her long, red fingers scooped up the artifact, she felt a shiver of delight and rightness.

It was the Sith text that she and Master Vey had acquired on Ringo Vinda, their last find together before Sember's death. The Inquisitors must've raided the Jedi Archives—and those secret places she'd discussed with Heezo, the ones where dangerous artifacts had once been hidden deep in the Temple.

Back when she'd first encountered the text, Sember had forbidden her from thinking about it, much less touching it or trying to read it. But now? Now it was in her hands, and there were no pontificating Jedi to reprimand her.

She looked around the room and took the text to a librarian droid that floated in midair like a blackened pupa.

"I need a protocol droid," she told it.

"Wait here," the droid rasped.

After the Fifth Brother and the Grand Inquisitor, Iskat was growing accustomed to the lack of niceties. The Inquisitors were concise with their language and so were their droids. It suited her, saying exactly what was meant and no more, not trying to figure out how to make small talk or properly cushion a request with the correct polite pragmatics.

Soon the library door slid open, revealing an RA-7 protocol droid painted flat black, mouthlike vocabulator glowing the same acid yellow as the lights in the pit.

"I am Six-Aray-Seven," the droid said in a cool, crisp, feminine voice. "What do you require?"

Iskat held out the Sith text that almost seemed to purr in her hands. "I need you to translate this, and then I need information on a planet called Pkori."

/ 30.

UNFORTUNATELY, THE SITH TEXT PROVED ultimately worthless. It was beautiful and ancient, steeped in power, but mostly incomplete, and what little there was consisted of ramblings on how to select an apprentice. No wonder whoever had stolen it from the archives had allowed it to stay in the library; it wasn't useful to life as an Inquisitor and thus wouldn't give anyone an edge. Still, she kept it for herself, placing it in her chamber where it seemed to pulse in time with her hearts and whisper to her as she slept.

This text . . . long ago, when Sember had asked her to sense it, it had woken something in her. When she looked back, she realized that everything had changed that day. She'd begun to question things, to let the dark side in. The text had possessed her, and now she possessed it.

And the effort to read it had not been in vain. Now that she had access to 6-RA-7, and the droid had information on much of the large but secretive headquarters, Iskat understood that although the Grand Inquisitor had promised her access to dark side texts, he had failed to mention that the Inquisitors who'd arrived before her had already cleaned the shelves of the most useful volumes. She began to get the feeling that while the Inquisitors were meant to grow their connection with the dark side, they weren't meant to eclipse their masters in knowledge or power. Of course, that didn't stop her from trying. She just had to do the work herself instead of having it handed to her.

Unfortunately, the droid's databanks were unhelpful regarding Pkori; Ginntho had not exaggerated its lack of technology and presence in the galaxy. The only true discovery had to do with Feyra. The Inquisitorius had liberated the Jedi databanks from the Temple, which meant Iskat now knew the year Feyra had been given to the Jedi . . . and the year she'd washed out at the Jedi trials. Although the common entry she'd found so long ago had been tampered with, there were other ways to access that information—ways that Jocasta and Noxi had kept from her.

Iskat could still recall her dream with perfect clarity, and she could only assume that when Feyra threw down her lightsaber and ran away, it was her moment of ultimate failure at the trials. But where had she gone, and why had Sember kept her lightsaber all those years? As soon as she had the resources, Iskat was determined to visit Pkori and see if Feyra had returned there. If not, perhaps she could find Feyra's family. At the very least, she would finally meet others like her.

But for now, Iskat began a period of learning that she had been yearning for her entire life. She could search whatever she liked in the Jedi Archives with no restrictions, read any information that called to her. She could sit in her room and put one hand on the Sith text and clutch her amulet in the other, probing deep into the dark side and making friends with what she found there. No one told her to meditate on goodness and serenity. No one told her to find her center.

What she had accidentally done with that column as a child?

That was just the beginning.

Tika had only gotten hurt because she was in the way.

Rage had long been Iskat's intimate friend, but she now felt a new sort of rage as she realized the life she might have led if she had not been held back, admonished, put down, swept aside. If she had not always been the outcast. If anyone had taken her hand, encouraged her unique gifts, given her the least bit of personal care, shown her how to truly focus her powers instead of just quiet them—

She would've been unstoppable.

And the Jedi, of course—well, they didn't want her to be unstoppable.

They had done everything possible *to stop her.*

They didn't want her to become anything except pliant. Biddable. Contained.

But now the Jedi were gone.

They couldn't force her into a box she would never fit in. They couldn't pretend that the past had never happened, sweep their many failures under the rug.

And yet . . . information on the dark side was hard to find. The library had been mostly cleaned out of useful things, and any entries in the Jedi Archives were purposefully vague and stood to warn, not instruct.

One day, seeing him in the hallway, she politely fell into step with the Grand Inquisitor. He glanced down at her but did not slow.

"Grand Inquisitor," she began. "I'm learning so much here, but it feels like certain information is . . . missing. I'd like to know more about the dark side. When I left the Jedi, I was promised the answers to my questions—"

"Nothing was promised," he told her, his voice frosty. "Except the chance to discover the truth for yourself. Information does not want to be free. The answers you seek must come from within you. Or perhaps you wish to simply hunt down dark-side objects, as your pathetic Jedi Master once did? That would be an acceptable occupation, so long as you return such information directly to me. But remember: Ultimately, we all serve the Emperor."

"Can I go where I wish, then, as I seek answers to my questions?"

He stopped and smiled, showing his pointed teeth, so like and yet so different from Tualon's, which she'd once admired. "We would expect nothing else. When you are not on a mission you are free to follow your intuition—unless and until you are given a job to do. You will be rewarded for bringing in any rogue Jedi, artifacts, or knowledge of the Force that you find during your own explorations. If you are ready, you will be assigned a shuttle and a company of Purge

Troopers who will follow your every order. The droids at the landing pad will assist you."

Sensing she would get no more out of him, she merely said, "Thank you, Grand Inquisitor."

"I hope you will return from Pkori with new information that will benefit us all, Iskat Akaris, even if you learn only about yourself."

Iskat nodded and walked away, carefully holding herself together instead of showing how chilled she was by his knowledge. The Grand Inquisitor knew where she was from—

Well, of course he did.

She had to assume that whatever she had told Heezo, the Grand Inquisitor and likely the Emperor now knew. It was also possible that the library droids kept records of what was searched.

Iskat was glad to have the freedom to go to Pkori, and yet she didn't feel the time was right. She had not yet received her first assignment, and she worried that if she left, she might miss the chance to prove herself and gain status over the other Inquisitors.

Annoyed and restless, she headed toward the pit, where she heard the sounds of someone battling a training remote. When she looked down from the edge, far below she saw the Seventh Sister, a green-skinned Mirialan, leaping and twirling as she blocked shots from two different remotes with her crescent-handled lightsaber. Iskat stopped to watch her, studying her moves.

None of the Inquisitors had been friendly, but she especially disliked the Seventh Sister; she was needlessly cruel, delighting in the pain of others. There was something broken about her, something unnaturally jagged. They had shattered something inside her, when they turned her away from the Jedi, and what was left felt like a blade that ached for blood.

Iskat leapt to the ground, nearly silent, and the Seventh Sister whirled to face her, lightsaber defensively up.

"The show's not free, even if you've got a uniform now," the Mirialan said, using a swipe of her hand to turn off the remotes.

"I recognize that sequence. You trained with Aayla Secura."

The Mirialan lifted a shoulder. "So what? That life is dead. Now I fight alone."

"Blades don't sharpen themselves."

The Seventh Sister looked Iskat up and down as if deciding whether to buy a piece of jogan fruit at the market. She had tattoos angling down from the corners of her eyes and a line of dots up the middle of her chin. Her dark purple lips twitched, and then she nodded. "Why not? Worst-case scenario, I kill you, and I don't even like you."

Iskat snorted. "Believe me, it's mutual."

"What is your new name, Sister?"

But Iskat wasn't ready to say it out loud, to give up who she was entirely, and she certainly didn't want to hear her new name spoken for the first time by someone she detested.

"I was given my first name. I'll take the second when I choose."

The Seventh Sister snickered. "Sounds like someone hasn't killed any Jedi yet."

I could start with killing you, a little voice whispered in the back of Iskat's head.

Strange thoughts sometimes rose as if testing her, the same sort of impulse she'd felt during that strange moment in the Knighting ceremony when she'd thought about chopping off Charlin's lekku. That little whisper of a voice had a good point, though. Maybe killing the Seventh Sister was a bit much, but showing supremacy over another Inquisitor would definitely garner positive attention here in a way it never had in the Jedi Temple.

"Shall we spar, then?" she asked, pulling her new lightsaber from her back. She kept it in its crescent form, as the Seventh Sister did, her long fingers sure around the wide hilt.

The Seventh Sister grinned and ignited her own red blade. "Thought you'd never ask."

As they circled each other, Iskat felt for her opponent in the Force and was aware of the Mirialan likewise feeling for some sort of weakness. Iskat struck first, and the Seventh Sister easily caught her blade before slashing back, violently.

Iskat swiftly realized the trap she'd fallen into. Having just received her new red blade, she hadn't yet fought with it or even fully explored its build and capabilities.

Oh, well.

That was what duels were for.

She'd watched the others spar, at least—not here in the pit, which seemed to be reserved only for the Inquisitors who had earned their name and uniform, but in the common part of the facility. She knew what her red blade could do, even if she hadn't yet developed sense memory for using it in battle.

They took turns aggressing and defending, exploring one another's reactions. Iskat got the feeling that the Seventh Sister was going easy, toying with her. The Mirialan was older than Iskat was and had clearly been training longer. Iskat would have to get creative if she wanted to win, much less survive.

The next time the Seventh Sister smugly blocked a flurry of slashes, Iskat subtly gestured toward the high, dusty corners of the pit's ceiling, where a cluster of small spiderbats slept. Using the Force, she pulled them down from their roost and sent them flapping toward her opponent, their eight legs waving frantically as they flapped and squeaked. The Seventh Sister fell back for only a moment before slashing at the creatures, and the hot reek of burned flesh bit at Iskat's nose.

"Think you're clever," the Seventh Sister said, slashing the last spiderbat out of her way with a sneer. "I'll show you clever."

With that, the Seventh Sister doubled down, hitting harder and faster. An overhead slash, a backhanded slash, a jab that would've put out Iskat's eye if she'd been one second slower. Iskat went on the defense, until . . .

She remembered.

This was *her* dance.

This was what she was meant to do.

She had to stop thinking so hard and let the Force take over.

She opened up that secret door in her soul and felt a rush of dark, glittering power that flowed through her veins like burning gold. A smile stretched across her face as she stopped thinking, stopped worrying, stopped trying to protect herself and let her body become an instrument to a higher power.

And yet . . . it was different this time.

There was a dark joy in it, a wish for harm, and she was unafraid and unashamed.

She let it in, she welcomed it, she embraced it.

And in return, it flooded her muscles, her bones, her sinews, lighting her up from within like the sun. She was dancing again, flowing, more centered than she'd ever been, more certain.

She wanted to feel her blade cut into flesh, to feel that softness breaking. She wanted to smell blood spilled hot on the metal floor, to feel it splash across her face and catch in her eyelashes. She wanted to stand over the still and broken body of this fellow Inquisitor, this former Jedi, this woman who might've been a friend or a teacher in a former life but who was instead now a rival. Iskat craved destruction like she had never craved anything before, hungered for it like she would be forever empty unless she filled her hearts with murder.

For a moment, the Seventh Sister struggled to catch up, faltering under the balletic onslaught of Iskat's aggression. But then it was as if she, too, drew on the same well, and she fought back with renewed vigor.

"You're going to have to reach deeper if you want to take me down," the Seventh Sister hissed. "I know things you've never even heard of. You may think you drink from the dark side, but you're just a little tooka-cat lapping at a saucer."

Iskat's confidence plummeted as the Seventh Sister all but chased her across the pit. Her boots slipped in the spiderbat blood, and she fell backward, tucking into a roll and landing in a crouch. Seventh Sister's blade was already at her throat—

"Guess you'll never kill a Jedi, after all," Seventh Sister said with a malicious smile.

Iskat ran the calculations, knowing there was no way she could get her lightsaber up before the Seventh Sister made good on her promise. She had to try something new, and that sweet, dark tug in her soul made her fingers curl up—

Iskat's fingers twitched, and the Seventh Sister gasped and dropped her lightsaber, holding her hand protectively to her chest. Her fingers twisted at odd angles, the little bones popping like insects underfoot.

"Maybe I'll settle for killing an ex-Jedi," Iskat hissed back.

She'd never attempted to use the Force on someone's body before, and it took every ounce of concentration she had to focus on the Seventh Sister's fingers and imagine them curled up and crushed like the bodies of the spiderbats littering the ground around them.

"Enough!" The Grand Inquisitor appeared overhead, staring down from the balcony.

Iskat gave one final squeeze, a reminder that she would never be that pliant again.

And she let go.

The Seventh Sister dropped to her knees and looked up with hate in her eyes as she cradled her hand.

"I know things, too," Iskat whispered.

She looked up to see if the Grand Inquisitor was impressed, but he was already gone.

Deactivating her lightsaber, she strode from the room, proud but shaken.

She'd made an enemy today, she knew.

But she'd also made a point.

/ 31.

ISKAT AND THE SEVENTH SISTER avoided each other after that, glaring with grudging respect as they passed in the halls. They did not again attempt to spar; if they did, Iskat had no doubt it would've been to the death. The Seventh Sister's hand was wrapped up in a bacta cast for several days, which was immensely satisfying.

One night, Iskat woke suddenly from a deep sleep to find a red light glowing in her pitch-dark chamber. She pulled her lightsaber out from under her pillow, but something ripped it from her hand. Another red light appeared, then another. As her eyes focused, she could see that there were three flying droids in the room. She reached out a hand, fingers already squeezing to crush one with the Force, but lightning erupted through her body, white-hot and boiling her blood. As she shook, her teeth clenched together, there was another burst of electricity. She fell back in her bed, eyeballs stuck open and unseeing, her entire body in a rictus of pain.

"That's for my hand," she heard the Seventh Sister say. "But this is for me."

Whatever happened next—

Iskat didn't know.

She woke in the medbay, floating in a tank of bacta.

Outside the glass, the Seventh Sister grinned as three black seeker droids with red eyes hovered around her like fluttering spiderbats.

She wiggled her healed fingers in a smug wave. "I suppose I owe you," she purred. She extended a hand, and one of the seeker droids settled on her palm. She gestured toward Iskat in the bacta tank, presenting the droid like a trophy. "Those spiderbats gave me a lovely idea. I hope my little minions gave you sweet dreams."

Iskat's teeth ground together, but she could barely move. Her body was mostly numb, and the Force felt like rainwater in her veins, a weak dribble. Seeing her frustration, the Seventh Sister threw back her head and laughed.

"See you around," she said.

As she sashayed out followed by her droids, jealousy flooded Iskat like black ichor, and she swore she would have her revenge.

It took over a week for Iskat to recover enough to leave the bacta tank and move to a bed. The med droids informed her that the seeker droids had shocked her so hard that one of her hearts had briefly stopped. Somehow, blind and screaming, paralyzed on one side, she had managed to drag herself down the hall to the medbay. No one had come to help her; she had helped herself, and it was the only reason she was still alive.

While she was convalescing, another Inquisitor stumbled into the medbay, slumped around his left arm. It was missing from the elbow down, the wound cauterized and still gently smoking. The droids quickly rushed to help him, urging him onto a bed.

"What happened?" she asked.

He turned toward her and threw his helmet on the ground, revealing piercing blue eyes and grayish skin with scarlike yellow markings. He sneered, as if she was too far beneath him to converse with.

"You'll find out soon enough" was all he said. He did not speak again, and she did not attempt further conversation. After the droids finished their work and he had left, Iskat asked the nearest med droid his name.

"That was the Sixth Brother," the med droid said snippily. "Not that it matters."

Once Iskat was ready to leave the medbay but still weak, she took shelter in her chamber. Perhaps she was stuck in bed, but she wasn't going to take this assault lying down. She was going to find new ways to inflict damage on her enemies—without relying on flying droids like a coward.

Iskat had always chafed against meditation among the Jedi, but she understood now that she'd been trying to shut a door instead of open one. Now, as she closed her eyes and clutched her amulet, she didn't seek her center and attempt to find stillness. She didn't dwell in serenity and peace. She didn't try to let her emotions move through her and pass beyond.

No, this time, she ruminated on what she wanted.

Strength. Power. To be unstoppable. Invincible.

All that time she'd been meditating with the Jedi, there had been this . . . thing.

This little spot inside her that she was supposed to bury deep and ignore.

When she'd come into contact with the Sith text, that thing inside had yawned and stretched and hungered, and she'd worked twice as hard to bury it again.

Now she released it, dived into it, drank from it.

Like dark water, it filled her.

It whispered to her, secrets on the edge of hearing.

Finally, Iskat began to understand that perhaps all the meditation she'd been forced to undergo as a Jedi might be turned against her enemies. Then, her meditation had served to keep the dark side at bay; she knew that now. It was in her—it had always been in her. A secret whisper as if from an old friend, a nudge from the galaxy, a hunch that arose like a cunning snake's head from the darkest of pools. The Jedi had instructed her to use meditation to repel the dark side within her, and they had planned their deception so that a talented master was always nearby to monitor Iskat and ensure that she put up the firmest of doors against the intrusion of what would not stop knocking.

But now she allowed her rage to blossom within her and unfurl, reaching its tendrils through her mind and body like the hungrily seeking mosterna vines in the Temple courtyard. For that was what she held tightly at her core—anger that had become rage. Rage at the Jedi, at the Council, at Sember, at Klefan, at Mace, at Tualon, at her fellow Padawans and then Jedi Knights, at the tenets she had been forced to memorize as if there were anything such as absolute truth. Rage at herself—her old self that had simply accepted whatever punishments and admonishments the Jedi meted out as if they were some all-knowing, all-seeing power worthy of utmost respect, rage that she had never had the courage to trust herself.

The rage that had once simmered now came to a full boil, filling her and roiling through her like lava in her bones.

She could use this—oh, yes, she could use this.

As if responding to her meditation, her body began to heal faster. Soon the med droids visited her to remove the remaining bacta plasters, and Iskat stood, itching for a fight—and a shower. She knew she was still too weak to face the Seventh Sister, but she also knew that she would use this time to further explore that deep well of rage within her and how she might embrace it and learn to channel it into her own storm.

One day, as she stalked the halls of the Inquisitorius Headquarters, restless and ready to fight something, anything, hoping to come across the Seventh Sister, she felt a familiar tug in the Force, the first possible source of warmth she'd encountered since returning to Coruscant.

She put a hand to the wall and found yet another hidden door, which led her into a lower level of the building, through dark corridors she'd never seen before, past mysterious doors, and down a cargo lift. She was smiling as she entered an open chamber filled with tools and droid baths. There sat Heezo, tinkering with one of the med droids she'd recently grown to know quite well.

Heezo grinned when he saw her. "Iskat! So you finally found where you belong."

"Maybe," she allowed. "I haven't been given an assignment yet."

"And what does that take? Something like the Jedi trials? They don't tell me much, and the droids here keep their secrets better hidden than those in the Jedi Temple."

She walked over and sat on a crate across from him, watching his agile fingers twist a spanner in the droid's chest.

"I'm not exactly sure. I became a full member of the Inquisitorius and immediately ended up in a bacta tank, so I'm hoping it will happen soon, now that I'm on the mend."

The Selonian looked up, his warm brown eyes smiling. "But at least now you can choose for yourself, huh? I remember when I washed out of the trials—did I ever tell you that, that I was a Jedi Padawan? I wasn't allowed to tell you anything, you know. After I washed out, I was given the opportunity to work in the Temple—I was good with droids and circuits. I was done training as a Jedi and cultivating my connection to the Force, so I agreed, but in reality, it was no choice. The alternative was returning to a home I couldn't remember, to a place I didn't belong. I stayed at the Temple because it was all I knew, and I was afraid to leave." He held up his hands, his fur puffing out in discontent. "I can't even feel it much anymore. The Force. It's like a broken comm. There's nothing but fuzz. I miss it."

"But you're here now . . ."

He nodded. "Yeah, I still have to go where I'm sent. As long as there are droids to fix, I can be happy. It's nice to see a friendly face, though. The other Inquisitors are a right sour folk. I hope you don't end up that way."

"I don't know how I'll end up." She stood and paced around the chamber, picking her way among the broken droids and crates. "But I do know one thing. I trusted you, Heezo. And you fed my every word directly to your masters."

He cocked his head. "You never told me anything you didn't want to."

"And now? Are you reporting to the Grand Inquisitor?"

He looked around in confusion. "I would assume you're always being watched, wouldn't you? But hey. Whatever happened, look what came of it! You're out from under the thumb of the Jedi. They're not holding you back anymore. You got what you always wanted."

Iskat unhooked her lightsaber from her back and ignited it, considering the red blade. "Did I? Is this truly what I always wanted? I guess we'll find out."

He didn't have time to speak before her lightsaber slashed out in a crimson arc. There was almost no resistance, as if he'd already accepted what was to come. Heezo didn't even try to fight, looking up at Iskat with confusion still written in his gentle brown eyes.

He would not betray her confidence again.

And she would never again trust another soul with her deepest secrets.

She put her lightsaber away and stared at the droid mechanic's corpse.

It was . . . so easy.

She felt no remorse.

Only the sweet exultation of revenge.

/ 32.

WHEN THE MED DROIDS DEEMED her well enough to train again, or nearly so, Iskat braided her hair back and put on her uniform, ready to duel the next Inquisitor she found and hoping it was the Seventh Sister. She was full of energy and a hungry sort of eagerness, as if the dark side was a voracious beast that needed a steady diet of meat to thrive. She stalked to the pit and jumped down, joining the Fifth Brother and Seventh Sister, plus a towering Dowutin who was missing an eye.

"Took you long enough," the Seventh Sister said.

"What do we call you?" asked the burly Dowutin, shaking her tusks.

"Iskat."

"But your new name—"

"Not until I'm ready to claim it."

In response, the Fifth Brother lit up his red lightsaber. "Then come earn it." When she did not immediately aggress, he peevishly said, "Well?"

Iskat unsnapped her cape and let it fall to the floor, then lit her lightsaber, grinning as the red blade hissed to life. "Well, what?"

The Fifth Brother didn't pause even a moment before charging at her.

She parried easily and quickly realized that he was a brute-force sort of fighter, not particularly agile or clever, and that he would've beaten her to death with a stone with the same finesse as he slashed with his lightsaber. Again and again she met his blade, even attempting a few attacks of her own as she grew accustomed to his inelegant but effective fighting style.

Then the Fifth Brother did something terrifying: He smiled.

It almost made her miss the fact that he'd expanded his lightsaber from its crescent form into a circle with two blades.

The difficulty of the duel went up as Iskat was forced to go on the defensive, trying to figure out how to deal with this new variable. She had practiced unfolding her own lightsaber, but it was entirely different, doing so in her chamber and figuring it out in the heat of battle. Instead she did a backflip off the wall, wrenching off a sconce with the Force and sending it toward Fifth Brother's head, where it clipped his helmet and knocked him off balance.

That, at least, earned a cruel chuckle from the Seventh Sister, the sort of sound that suggested it was pleasant to see the Fifth Brother taken down a notch, and that a complete beheading would not have been a bad thing.

Iskat was fighting on a shallow level, though, and it was time to open herself up in the Force, and—

The Force did not meet her joyously.

There was a new presence there, a new darkness.

It was as if the air had been sucked out of the room, a door opening in the vacuum of space and drawing every living thing toward a grand emptiness that promised only death. When Iskat had felt Palpatine in the Force, her body had ached to run. But whatever this endless void was, it threatened to drown her, freezing her in place, making her want to grab on to something solid and hold on for dear life.

The other Inquisitors had gone still, looking up expectantly toward one of the hallways. Heavy footsteps approached, the metallic thunks echoing throughout the silent chamber. Iskat could hear breathing now—deep, robotic, rhythmic.

The Fifth Brother deactivated his lightsaber, the snarl slipping from his face, replaced with—was that fear?

Was there actually something in the galaxy that Fifth Brother *feared*?

"Greetings, Lord Vader," he said, backing away.

Iskat kept her blade on as she turned to find a terrifying figure standing there, flanked by several new Inquisitors who paled by comparison. This man—this monster—was larger than life and practically exhaling the dark side. From his gleaming black helmet to his heavy cape and heavier boots, he seemed a construction of Iskat's worst nightmares, an unholy union of flesh and machine thrumming with—possibly even powered by—an undying rage that somehow spoke to her own.

There was something about him—something familiar.

They'd met before. They'd shared some moment—

"Test your blade," he said, and Iskat immediately knew better than to question him.

She took hold of her lightsaber's hilt, her hand shaking, and sought the switch that would unfold the crescent guard, activate her second blade, and make both blades spin. It was exactly where it should've been, exactly how she would've designed it, and as the blades began to move in a whirling red blur of doom, she was pleased at how perfectly the hilt was designed, how effortless it was to hold.

"Now attack."

Attack *me*, he meant.

Recently initiated, recently recovered from a grievous wound, holding a spinning crimson lightsaber she still hadn't mastered, surrounded by people who were rabid to witness her failure, she considered the figure before her.

Huge, towering, powerful, trained. Filled with rage, flowing with the Force, already a master of the dark side.

She understood immediately that there was no way she could beat him.

She also understood that if she didn't try, he would simply strike her down where she stood.

She'd fought the Grand Inquisitor, the Seventh Sister, and the Fifth Brother, but this, she was quite certain, would be a fight for her life.

And he had ordered her to attack him. Iskat was unstudied with this new blade and understood that the enemy was unbeatable. And yet, for the first time in her life, she realized . . . there were no rules. This was no polite duel with training blades and bows of respect. Perhaps it was a proving ground, perhaps it was an initiation, but it was definitely life or death.

And if she died? Well, then she wasn't worthy to call herself an Inquisitor.

All these thoughts passed in two thumps of her hearts.

Vader stood there, single red blade lit, watching her as she ran calculations, discarding every thought that arose. She needed something more audacious than simply attacking him.

She glanced at the Fifth Brother, lightsaber still in his hands as he watched the intensifying standoff. Reaching out through the Force, Iskat moved the switch on his lightsaber to ignite both blades and set them spinning . . .

And then she threw Fifth Brother directly at Darth Vader.

Because yes, the column had been a mistake, but she'd been honing her telekinesis, and if someone had to rush at her enemy, it should definitely be someone else, preferably someone she didn't like.

Vader was ready and sidestepped the incoming Inquisitor, but Iskat had expected that. She focused instead on the Fifth Brother's glowing blade, sending it upward and toward Vader's helmet as he focused on the incoming body. When Vader's attention was split in two directions, that was when Iskat struck. She ran forward, blades rotating so fast she just saw a shield of glowing red, and threw her lightsaber as she skidded across the floor, whipping out the vibroblade she kept in her boot scabbard.

She had one chance to catch Vader unaware, and she put everything she had into slashing at his groin, where she knew most species had blood vessels and males had a lot to lose.

Right before the blade landed, her hand stilled, caught like a vise in the Force.

"You—" Vader began.

Iskat didn't let him finish. She reached out in the Force and brought her lightsaber sliding back from where it had landed on the floor. The second Vader focused on it, she drove in her knife—

But she'd guessed wrong. The blade thudded against metal, juddering up the bones of her arm.

"Failed," he finished.

Vader's gloved fingers wrapped around Iskat's hand, crushing it, destroying it, bone rubbing against shattered bone, until she dropped the knife. Vader had batted away her lightsaber, and Fifth Brother had moved out of the circle of the fight, taking his lightsaber with him and holding it protectively close. The look he gave Iskat was one of extreme hatred, and she knew she would have to watch her back.

If she lived through this.

Vader pulled her up into the air by her destroyed hand, and all Iskat could do was hang there. His other hand held his lightsaber, and she had to keep her feet away from the blade as she dangled like a foolish child.

"A unique attempt," Vader said. "But not good enough."

His blade rose, the heat of it curling up her back and slicing off her long, braided hair, close enough to leave a red-hot burn on the back of her head. The stench of charred hair and flesh made her nose itch, the blade right by her neck now.

Staring into Vader's faceless helmet, knowing he would either kill her or further maim her, depending on some judgment she couldn't anticipate, Iskat felt more helpless than she had in her entire life. She couldn't physically best him, she couldn't count on help from the other Inquisitors, and she was fairly certain he could use the Force in ways she'd never even dreamed of. The metal limbs powering his body were so much stronger than her own frail flesh and bones, and—

That was it.

She felt inside his helmet with the Force and used it to pull out several wires. She didn't know what each one did, but she knew that they were important. His breathing was not natural. This man—this monster—couldn't live without the help of the machine that caged him.

Vader gave a choking gasp and dropped her—and his weapon. She was ready for it and caught herself as she fell, rolling smoothly to the side and grabbing her lightsaber, landing in a crouch. Vader's black gloves scrabbled at his helmet for a moment before he snatched his lightsaber using the Force and hurried from the room. The gargling, desperate splutters from his helmet told Iskat she'd succeeded.

She stood, proud—

And was thrown into the wall, the breath leaving her body and her skull ringing as it slammed against the metal.

Even hurt, even desperate, even from outside the room, Vader had nearly killed her.

She slid to the ground, and the world wobbled around her.

"Impressive," the Dowutin said. "And you didn't even lose a limb." She winked her remaining eye.

Iskat held up the mangled hand Vader had crushed. "No, but I still need the medbay if I want to keep it."

"The medbay again? So soon?" The Seventh Sister snorted. "I'm starting to think you're clumsy."

The Fifth Brother said nothing, just quietly seethed. The newly arrived Inquisitors were silent, unimpressed or hiding it well. In addition to the Sixth Brother, there was a Terrelian Jango Jumper with three-toed blue feet; a humanoid female with yellow skin, burgundy tattoos, and something like tentacles or maybe lekku; and the long-haired Miraluka who had once been Jedi Prossett Dibbs, whom Iskat remembered from her days as a youngling. Each of them would most likely kill her in a heartbeat if it would advance their position, she was beginning to realize. Iskat wondered if all of the Inquisitors had faced Vader after their initiation, and what it had cost them, besides the Dowutin's eye and the Sixth Brother's arm. She wondered how many Inquisitors had failed this test and lost their lives.

She wondered why she still didn't feel ready to take on her number and join those who had succeeded.

Iskat had always felt different from the other Jedi. But she felt different from the Inquisitorius, too. She was beginning to think that maybe she was the only person of her kind in the entire galaxy.

It was time to finally find out.

ISKAT WONDERED IF SHE SHOULD ask for permission to leave the facility, but then again, the Inquisitorius was not about asking permission. The Grand Inquisitor had told her she might go out on missions of her own, and if he needed her, he knew how to find her. The other Inquisitors were often gone, and when present, haunted the building like disinterested ghosts. While Iskat was impatiently waiting for her crushed hand to heal so she could adequately pilot a ship, she saw her brothers and sisters at a meal or passed them in the halls, but they rarely spoke to her. She learned some of their names, whether through introduction or reputation: The Dowutin was Ninth Sister, the Miraluka once known as Jedi Master Prossett Dibbs was Tenth Brother, the yellow-skinned female was Fourth Sister.

Late at night when training alone, Iskat sometimes heard what sounded like screaming from somewhere deep within the skyscraper she now called home, and when she asked about it, Ninth Sister got a faraway look in her eyes and told her that some Inquisitors had required additional coercion elsewhere to understand their new roles and that nightmares were not uncommon. Iskat was secretly pleased that she had required no such persuasion herself. One night, she saw an unfamiliar figure at the end of a hallway, but it disappeared before she could discern who it might be. She knew there were Inquisitors she had yet to meet, but she hadn't felt the figure in the Force. She half convinced herself it was a ghost. She would meet any new brothers or sisters, eventually, and she no longer had hope that they might be anything other than enemies.

Once her hand again worked perfectly, Iskat gathered her supplies and headed for the landing pad to take her place in the pilot's seat of the *Scythe*, the same shuttle the Grand Inquisitor had piloted for their outing to Bar'leth. Assuming that the people of her home planet didn't speak Basic, she brought 6-RA-7 along.

"I've a particular dislike for pastoral places," the droid said crisply as they walked up the ramp. "Brimming with dirt and sand and other vile substances. I'll need an oil bath the moment we return."

Iskat settled into the pilot's seat and plotted the course to Pkori, which was a complicated trip. It wasn't accessible by well-worn hyperlanes and required several smaller, targeted jumps. Every moment until they took off, she expected someone to run up the landing pad or comm her, demanding answers regarding where she thought she was going or what she thought she was doing.

None came. She was an Inquisitor, not a Jedi, and she owed answers to no one.

Iskat was glad she'd brought along her datapad, for all that she was too nervous to truly study. The trip took days, and at one point she felt a certain nostalgia for her time with Master Vey aboard their ship, but she quickly snuffed out that unwanted emotion. She'd once tamped down her rage to please the Jedi, but now she could ignore her feeble recollection of times that hadn't even been that good to begin with. Sember had held her back, lied to her, encouraged her to be something she wasn't. Their time together may have been comfortable and routine, but it hadn't been warm or worth remembering. Iskat clutched her blue amulet and dived into the black pit of her soul, meditating on the rage there, on the time she'd wasted pandering to a master who'd built their entire relationship on lies and emotional subjugation.

When the ship dropped out of hyperspace after the last jump, she saw Pkori for the first time and marveled at how this mysterious place looked like any other, swirling clouds over shifting patches of green and brown and blue. She scanned the planet and found . . . nothing. No tech, no connections, no power grid. There only appeared to be one large, sprawling settlement on one continent, surrounded by churning gray oceans. She navigated toward what she hoped was a city, and even though she had been told her people had no interest in spaceflight or starships, she was still surprised by the utter silence as she entered the atmosphere.

There was no port, no weigh station, no landing pad. The settlement was densely packed, with no travel lanes wide enough for even a small shuttle. Iskat had to circle a bit before she found a valley just outside of the city where her ship could land safely. Woolly four-legged beasts scattered, bleating, as the ship came to rest, and a shepherd approached the ship cautiously, holding a curved stick out like a weapon.

"Six-Ar, these are primitive people." The droid's big, insectoid head slowly turned to face Iskat. "Be polite. I'll need help finding what I need, and I don't want to insult them."

"You're an Inquisitor," 6-RA-7 said. "You may take what you wish with impunity. If they don't like it, kill them."

"This is a personal mission," Iskat reminded her. "And I'm ordering you not to be rude."

"There are infinite gradations between polite and rude . . ."

"Be polite."

The droid sighed in annoyance. "This is beneath me. I was programmed for translation, strategy, and torture."

"I don't really care."

A droidish snort. "Ah, there's the Inquisitor in you."

Iskat put on a hooded black cloak and walked down the ramp with the droid shuffling along beside her. She was in a tunic and robes, leaving her uniform and helmet behind in the shuttle; she was all too aware how terrifying her costume was meant to be and wanted the people she met to feel at ease. The shepherd shook his stick and shouted at them in a language she didn't speak, full of rough clicks and rolled r's. It sounded like music in her ears and made her feel a fierce and ravenous hunger for home like she'd never known. Sometime in her life, probably even before she could walk, someone had spoken to her in this language, someone who loved her, and her whole body remembered.

"Six-Ar, translate. Exactly, please."

". . . my poor cochukka sheep!" the droid said tiredly. "They'll be off their milk! No one wants sour cheese! This godless monstrosity in the pasture, on my good grass—"

"Forgive me," Iskat said, and 6-RA-7 spoke back to the man in his own language. His head jerked back, his eyes wide with shock. "I did not see a place for ships to land. Where are the records kept in town?"

"You are Pkorian, but you cannot speak the tongue? You associate with this metal construct? You come from the stars?"

"I'm from here, but I was taken away at a very young age."

He smiled and nodded, gesturing eagerly toward town. "Only two have left us and returned. Come, child, the cochukka will keep. There are people who will very much want to see you."

"Who?"

He chuckled. "Your family."

The shepherd whistled, and a boy appeared from where he nestled in a pile of sheep, yawning, to take over his duties. After giving the boy firm instructions, the man led Iskat into town, the dirt path changing to beautiful tiles in shades of blue. As they walked, through 6R, he told Iskat tidbits of gossip—the weather, the health of his cochukka sheep, where to find the best umbikki stew in town. Up close, everything here had a humble beauty that Iskat had never experienced before. Hers had been a world of sleek plasteel, ravaged stone, Jedi elegance, Inquisitorial gray and black. But on this planet, everything appeared to be made by the hands of people who clearly knew and loved what they did. The man chattered about the town, proudly pointing out this temple, that artist, the best cheesemaker; the walk took hours, and he had plenty to say. Iskat could only nod along. She was the only person clad in black, and the people in their brightly colored dresses and robes stopped and openly stared. Everyone was bedecked with jewelry at ears, wrists, throat, and fingers, and the women grew their hair long. The word *Jedi* was whispered in her wake. As they walked, she realized that the scarf in which Feyra's lightsaber had originally been wrapped was the exact color of the cochukka sheep.

The shepherd took her to a grand, hexagonal building of shining ivory and gold and said, "Here we are."

Iskat felt a little breathless, ready to meet what had to be her family, but once inside, she immediately saw that this was not a family home. It was a library, the shelves filled with thick, colorful books. Iskat had seen a couple of old, ragged books while working with Sember but couldn't believe how many volumes filled the shelves, and in such excellent condition. Sember would've been in raptures just to touch one. The shepherd introduced Iskat to the librarian as if presenting two demigods to each other with much bowing, and then departed.

"Do you seek your family, Jedi?" the older woman asked gently. She wore bracelets all the way up both arms, and they made musical sounds as she gestured gracefully.

"I am Iskat Akaris, and I think my mother might be called Feyra."

When 6-RA-7 translated Iskat's words, the woman's mouth dropped open, and she had to blink several times before she could recover her calm.

"Such strange magic," she murmured. "Come along."

Bowing her head, she led Iskat and 6R among labyrinthine shelves that had no obvious method of organization, finally stopping and holding out a hand to indicate that they should give her space. She did a brief ritualized dance and looked up at the ceiling as if praying before pulling out a book and carrying it to a carved wood lectern. When she let the book fall open, the scent of spices and perfumes wafted out. Flowers had been pressed into the filmy pages, and the woman pulled on gloves to search the text.

"Akaris. This is your family tree." She pointed to a tangle of what had to be names, her finger landing on a single line of writing in crimson ink. "Iskat Akaris, given to the Jedi when you were one year old. And this is your mother." She indicated the line just above Iskat's. "Feyra Akaris, also given to the Jedi."

"Is my mother here now?" Iskat asked, unable to keep the excitement from her voice. "Did she return?"

The woman's gloved finger traced a line of script. "Her fate has not been recorded."

"Do you know who my father is?"

"We only track the matrilineal line, the only certain bloodline."

Rage blossomed in Iskat's chest. "So that's all you can tell me? I came here to learn about my past. I need more than this."

The librarian gave her a look of stern reproof. "Do not insult the tree because the makani fruit is sour. Your family compound is not far. Your matriarch lives, and you have many relatives under her protection. She might know more. We record only births and deaths."

"Can you tell me how to find my—matriarch, then? I need answers."

The woman blinked at her. "The Jedi have made you stormy. Of course you must go to your tree. Your matriarch will teach you manners, perhaps."

It was a dig, but Iskat was well schooled in hiding her true feelings. She could've slain this simple librarian with one strike, without even drawing the lightsaber on her back. She could've set fire to the entire library and watched it burn. Let the woman think she was rude; as long as Iskat got what she needed, nothing else mattered. After years of curiosity, years of uncertainty after Sember's last words, she was about to finally learn the truth.

The librarian drew a map for her, and Iskat gave her thanks before heading out into the streets with 6-RA-7 at her side, muttering about dust as they walked. Life on this planet was slow and simple. Old women sat on steps, twisting cochukka wool into familiar yarn as little children chased lizards or tended to gardens growing vertically out of white-washed walls. Women polished beads, hammered metal, braided each other's long hair, laughing in their long, brightly colored dresses. Men passed by, calling out greetings as they led lines of waddling birds or great red oxen with painted horns. No one was training for war or expecting trouble from worlds beyond the stars. Iskat saw no blasters, no droids, no ships. After all that she had seen on Coruscant and beyond, after all the death she'd witnessed, something about it felt insubstantial and silly, as fake and flimsy as a stage play, as useless as the jingling of the bells tied around the woolly necks of the bleating cochukka.

And yet . . . there was beauty here.

As always, she was filled with a sense of wonder at a new world around her, and when she reached out in the Force, she felt vibrant pulses of lush life and an almost innocence. It was so fragile, this place. These people were so open and vulnerable. And no one here had any idea. Iskat was the most dangerous thing on the entire planet.

The map led her to a two-story building, with glimmering stones pressed into the clay bricks in patterned mosaics. These homes didn't seem to have one grand door but were composed of towers and porticoes surrounded by linked gardens and patios with a huge, sprawling tree in the very center, providing shade. Iskat walked a full circle around the compound, looking for a polite way to gain access; these people, once her people, seemed to care deeply about manners, and if she wanted answers, she had to avoid upsetting them. It did not escape her that she could've slaughtered them all, could've obliterated the entire town, and yet . . . something inside her felt a deep, old love. She came here not as an Inquisitor, but as a prodigal daughter.

Around back, a little girl was pumping water out of a well, her hair the same color as Iskat's and trailing down to her waist.

"Greetings," Iskat said through the droid.

The child looked up, her eyes went wide, and she ran into the structure, screaming.

"Might I commend you on your excellent approach," the droid muttered.

Two women appeared from within, one about forty and one elderly but still powerful. She strode confidently up to Iskat, turquoise skirts snapping, and said, "Who are—"

Her mouth dropped open and she blinked several times. Not at the droid—at Iskat. She stepped closer and put a hand to her lips, kissing her fingers and gesturing at the sky.

"I know those eyes," the older woman said, her voice husky with feeling. "I know that scent. You are one of my own. You are kin."

/ 34.

ISKAT STILLED AND INSPECTED THE older woman with a similar curiosity. It was like looking at herself in forty years. Same eyes, same chin, same hair color, although the older woman's long braids were threaded with white.

"It's not her," said the younger woman, and Iskat recognized that she, too, had the same look about her.

"You were hoping I was Feyra," Iskat said, hating the clumsiness of speaking through a haughty droid compared with the musical and expressive tones the women put to their own language. "I was hoping to find her here."

"You are her daughter, then. You are my little Iskat." The eldest woman smiled and stepped forward, arms out, bracelets jingling. "That makes me your matriarch, Beamala. Your mother's mother. Come here and be known."

With only the briefest hesitation, Iskat stepped into a hug that filled her with a riot of emotions. She couldn't remember a time she'd been held like this, cradled, snuggled, touched with such love and warmth. She melted into the older woman's—her grandmother's—embrace. The scent that washed over her was so familiar and filled with love that she wondered if this was what non-Jedi children got to experience every day, unconditional love and affection. This woman didn't know Iskat, didn't know a single thing about what kind of person she was or what she wanted or what she should've been or what she'd done; she simply accepted her for exactly who she was, no questions asked.

A sob broke free, and then Iskat was crying into her grandmother's shoulder.

"Hush now," Beamala crooned, rubbing her back. "It's been too long for us both. We haven't seen you since you were a baby."

They'd—they'd known her. She'd been here before.

For a long moment, Iskat let herself weep as she gave in to years of feeling alone and different, longing for something that wasn't there. The emotions washed through her like waves lapping at sand.

That secret something she'd always been missing—it was this, exactly this. Love, and acceptance. Perhaps even family.

The Jedi thought they provided everything a youngling needed to thrive, but they were wrong. So wrong. Babies needed to be loved and cuddled. Children needed to be seen and known and cherished for exactly who they were. She'd never had that chance. Perhaps a droid or caregiver had held her when she was tiny and fussing, but she had felt no affectionate connection with another being for as long as she could remember, had never felt like she was deserving of love.

Until now.

The other, younger woman—Iskat somehow knew this was her aunt—joined in the hug, and then she felt a little girl's arms wrap around her hips, and several more women came out of the building and joined the embrace. They were all humming deep in their throats, and she could feel each of them individually, their scents similar but unique, like music, their arms warm and jangling with bracelets. No one shied away from her, no one flinched; they enveloped her as one of their own, and she felt an acceptance deep in her hearts, an emptiness that had been begging to be filled.

"I was here when I was a baby?" she asked.

"You were so *busy*," the aunt said into her shoulder blade.

Beamala chuckled. "You were with us here until you could walk."

"Barely a year old, and you were already causing trouble," another one said.

"You would gesture at something you wanted, high on a shelf, and it would float down to your hand," Beamala continued. "That's when we knew you were like your mother, that you were meant for a different life. Feyra told the next visitor from the stars, and a few weeks later, the Jedi came for you." Beamala disengaged, and all the other women released the hug to step back and look at her.

The youngest was maybe five, the same little girl she'd seen by the well. There were two girls about Iskat's own age, her aunt, and a pair of women older than the aunt but younger than Beamala. They all had the same eyes and the same hair color, and they smiled at her with the smile she saw in the mirror every day. She could feel them in the Force, curious and unafraid, familiar and welcoming. They were happy to see her again, genuinely pleased, and this was a new feeling for Iskat.

"We have strong genes, apparently," she said, wiping at her tears.

The women burst out laughing, a raucous and unapologetic noise.

"We do," Beamala agreed. "Now everyone back to your business while I get to know my granddaughter." She beamed and gestured for Iskat to follow her into a garden. Iskat watched the women go, the fond way one girl elbowed the other one and the tender way another took the little girl's hand. It was so easy for them, so natural.

"Next you'll be wanting tea," the aunt said, and for all that it sounded grouchy on the surface, Iskat could sense that she didn't really mind.

"Please." Beamala took a seat under the spreading tree and waved Iskat to the carved wood chair across from her. 6-RA-7 was offered a chair but instead chose to silently stand off to the side. The temperature was warm but not uncomfortable, and Iskat took off her cloak, revealing her black tunic.

"Such dark colors," Beamala chided. "Such thick, stiff fabrics. How does the air reach you? How do you breathe? Let me get you a dress. You must be uncomfortable."

"No thank you." Iskat had never worn anything like that in her life and would feel far too vulnerable. "But I would like to know more, if you'll tell me. About my mother, and about me. Do you know where she is?"

The lines on Beamala's face suggested she spent a lot of time smiling and laughing, but she was clearly no stranger to sadness, and it shone out of her eyes. "Feyra is not with us. We gave her to the Jedi when she was three and she returned to us when she was sixteen. She would not tell us what transpired while she was gone, but she was . . . sad. Restless."

"Always staring up at the sky, like another ship might come to take her back," the aunt said, placing a brightly glazed teapot and two cups on the table, along with a plate of seed-covered sweet cakes. "Like it had been a mistake, to return to us."

"Hush, Ellamak. Let me tell my story," Beamala chided. She flapped a hand, and Ellamak scurried back behind the wall. Iskat could hear her bracelets jangling as she obviously listened in, but she didn't mind the intrusion.

"We were so happy to have her here, but she'd missed out on so much in the thirteen years she was gone. She'd forgotten our ways completely," Beamala continued once they were supposedly alone. "The skills she'd learned among the Jedi did not translate to our life under the tree. She made a mess of spinning, hated carving beads, couldn't cook, said we should get something to do the cleaning. A . . . doid? Dord?"

"Droid. Like this one." Iskat gestured toward 6-RA-7.

"I am not programmed to *clean*," 6-RA-7 huffed.

Beamala nodded. "We don't have them here." She leaned forward and poured steaming, floral-smelling tea into their cups. "Are you a Jedi, too, then?"

"No."

It was the first time Iskat had said so out loud, and it felt like another line crossed.

She was not a Jedi, and perhaps, in her hearts, she had never been one.

"So what happened to her? To Feyra?"

Beamala looked down and played with her bracelets. There were rings on her long fingers, too, the same fingers that had always made Iskat feel so other.

"We tried to help her. To love her. To teach her our ways and help her find her place. But it wasn't enough. She was depressed, and she began acting . . . reckless. Drinking too much galukk, smoking monava weed outside of the rituals. She was gone at strange hours. When she told us she was with child, and gave up her dangerous behavior, we were overjoyed." Beamala reached out to take Iskat's hand in hers. "Children are always a blessing here, the cause of a great celebration." She wrapped Iskat's fingers around the warm ceramic mug, urging her to drink.

Iskat sipped, feeling warmth spread lazily through her.

"Do you know who my father is?"

Beamala waved a hand at the sky. "No. If Feyra knew, she never told us." She paused, staring off into the distance, sorrow lines bracketing her mouth.

"We hoped having a baby might settle her down and give her the purpose she needed, and you did. She was in love with you from the moment you were born. The way she looked at you—like all the stars lived in your eyes. And every day she prayed at the altar that you had not inherited her gifts. But then—"

"Then the jar of seedcakes floated right down into your pudgy little arms," Ellamak said from the other side of the garden wall, prompting a frown from Beamala.

"Yes. Your strangeness began even earlier than Feyra's had. I thought she might try to run away with you—she grew quite secretive, even visited the most powerful hukma to see if her magic could help rid you of what your mother saw as a curse. But she knew you belonged with the Jedi, and she wanted you to find your destiny. She gave you to an old friend who promised to keep you safe, but after the ship left, Feyra wouldn't leave her room and couldn't stop crying, and then one morning, she was gone."

Beamala's head hung, sadness wafting from her like dying flowers.

"She left no message. We never saw her again. We don't even know if perhaps she found a way to leave this place and return to the Jedi. We don't know if she's alive or dead. She left her bracelets behind. Ellamak?"

"I'll bring them."

Iskat's aunt soon brought a carved box containing five bracelets in shiny gold with vibrant thread, the same as all the women wore.

"A woman is given a bracelet each year on her birthday," Beamala explained. "Your mother left us when she was three and was only with us for two years, once she returned. You can have them, if you wish. They are an important symbol of a woman's standing, and when she passes beyond, they are stacked on her gravebranch. She would be proud for you to wear them, I think."

Iskat reached into the box and picked up a bracelet, bright with a rainbow of striped thread. She slipped it onto her wrist and admired the weight of it, then added the other four, enjoying the musical clinking that felt so familiar deep in her bones.

"They suit you," Beamala told her, tears in her eyes. She leaned forward, taking Iskat's hand in her own, their bracelets clattering together. "There is a place for you here, you know. Feyra's old chamber is empty. You can learn our ways, our language. I sometimes wonder if we didn't try hard enough with Feyra, if it was our fault she couldn't find joy here. We would try harder to help you. Perhaps we failed your mother, but we would move mountains to have you with us. Family is everything."

Iskat could feel Beamala in the Force and knew that she was a powerful, confident woman who understood her place in the galaxy and who would fiercely protect all those in her care. If she stayed here, she had no doubt that these women, her kin, would welcome her, flaws and all, and do all that they could to help her find her path. She could speak this musical language, walk freely in a breezy dress, grow her hair long again with no worry that it might be taken from her in a fight.

She could stay here and never fight again.

"I . . . I can't," she said, tears already springing to her eyes.

"Why not? If you are not Jedi, you are free to reclaim your home, are you not? We live lives of peace and plenty, and all would welcome you here."

And they would—Iskat could sense it. She could feel the women around the house, so happy to have her here, so eager to know her better. It was a feeling she'd been waiting for all her life.

But those words—peace and plenty.

What would Iskat *do* in a land of peace and plenty?

She was most herself when she was fighting, when she was killing, when the world fell away and she was carving into the enemy with her lightsabers, graceful as a dancer, brutal as a blade's edge. She lived for the moment when there was nothing but life and death, when she could sense her opponent's next move and counter it before the decision had even been made.

Spinning wool would not give her that same fierce glee.

Making tea and polishing beads would never slake the hunger in her hearts.

She had lived through war, watched her people die, taken lives. She was no longer suited to a quiet, happy, simple life among these innocent, peaceful people with their meaningless, trivial pursuits.

Something in her was broken, and she was a killer, and this planet had no need of killers.

Wait.

No.

She wasn't broken.

She had been born for a different purpose.

She was an Inquisitor. She had a job to do. She had pledged herself to this cause, a cause she believed in and was eager to support with her blade. The traitorous Jedi who had failed her and doomed the Republic deserved to die, and she was eager to bring them to justice.

Not only that, but she was fairly certain that if she simply abandoned her old life and stayed here, the other Inquisitors would be sent to hunt her down as a traitor—and they'd likely take out the entire city, possibly the whole planet, just for fun.

No, Iskat could not stay here. She did not *want* to stay here.

She was restless after just a few hours without some sort of action.

She squeezed Beamala's hand and looked deep into her eyes, hoping the older woman could understand. "I have work to do," she said. "If I tried to stay here, people would get hurt."

"We are not scared of you, beloved. You are kin," Beamala said, almost begging.

Iskat withdrew her hand. "You should be scared of me, Grandmother.

I am dangerous. If I stayed, I would waste away like Feyra, or worse, they would send someone to hunt me. I can't risk them harming you. But perhaps one day, when I have done my duty and lived up to my promises, I can come back to visit."

"You must go where your hearts lead you." Beamala smiled sadly. "And we will always be here to welcome you home again."

Iskat finished her tea and stood, pulling on her cloak.

"Before you go, there is something Feyra left behind that you may want. Ellamak?"

Soon Iskat's aunt returned and held out her hand.

"She cut it off as soon as she came home. We asked her what it meant, but she wouldn't say. Perhaps you will find the meaning in it."

Iskat looked down and gazed at the Padawan braid tied with a scrap of leather. Jedi generally burned their braids. In Iskat's dream, Feyra had thrown down her lightsaber and run away into the darkness. She must've worn the braid home and then cut it off, finally severing her commitment to the Jedi way. Without her training, her connection to the Force would've started to fade. Iskat tried to imagine what it would feel like, returning to this place a failure and discovering that even here, she didn't fit in. The sadness. The rage, at belonging nowhere.

She took the braid, running a finger down its length.

"It's a Jedi thing," she told them.

"What does it mean?"

Iskat tucked the braid into a pocket of her robe.

"That my mother and I have a lot in common," she said.

/ 35.

LEAVING HER FAMILY BEHIND WAS one of the hardest things Iskat had done in her entire life. Turning her back on love and acceptance made her hearts ache, but she understood that it was the only choice. Even though she barely knew these people, she felt the same love for them that they did for her, and the thought of someone hurting them made her want to burn down the world. She had to get off the planet and back to Coruscant before someone noticed her absence and decided to use it to their advantage. She fully understood now that the other Inquisitors would do anything to get ahead, including hurting a rival's loved ones, if they could find them.

Her love for these people . . . it would help make her strong.

She would do her duty as an Inquisitor, all the while secretly holding her family in her hearts. She wouldn't forget them, ignore them, wall them away, as the Jedi once urged her to do. They were a part of her now, as they always should have been.

She had to keep them safe. If someone came to harm them, they would be helpless. She hadn't seen a single weapon the entire time she'd been here. They lived beautiful, colorful lives, but . . . well, they were vulnerable. There was no such thing as true peace. Just because a mining company or land-hungry warlord hadn't found Pkori yet didn't mean the planet would be safe forever. Not unless she made certain it would be.

That was another reason Iskat couldn't stay. If she tried, if she gave in, every day here she would just be waiting for the shadow of a Star Destroyer to appear, blotting out the sun. She would be in a better position to help Pkori as she grew in her powers and ascended the ranks of the Inquisitors. Standing on the planet, there was no way to tell what was happening in the Empire beyond, but as an Inquisitor, she had ways of monitoring such things.

So no, she couldn't stay, but she wouldn't forget.

They sent her away with a woven bag of fruits, seedcakes, and tea sachets. She reluctantly asked Beamala to keep Feyra's bracelets for her; something so beautiful, precious, and specific might be traced back to its culture, if a fellow Inquisitor got curious.

She was satisfied enough with what she'd learned here, even if she'd reached a dead end. Feyra was her mother, the mysterious lightsaber had indeed belonged to her, and the dream had proven true. The only missing piece of the puzzle was Feyra's current whereabouts. If she was still on Pkori, she was keeping herself hidden for a reason, and there was nothing Iskat could do but comb the entire planet for a single person who might yet retain the skills of a Jedi. If she'd found a way off the planet, she could be anywhere in the galaxy.

Iskat had to be satisfied with what she had: the answers to the questions the Jedi had told her to ignore.

As she piloted the *Scythe* into the clear blue sky, bleating cochukka scattered and the shepherd shook his staff, but in farewell, Iskat assumed, not annoyance. The city was so small, seen from the clouds. This place felt too fragile to last, for all that the people had been here for thousands of years. For someone who'd grown up on Coruscant, handmade materials could never feel as safe as plasteel, and loose fabrics could never hold their own against armored leather.

No, this place, this life—they were too soft for Iskat Akaris.

She wouldn't think too hard about what her life might've been if she hadn't exhibited an affinity for the Force. She wouldn't think about all that she'd lost after she was given to the Jedi—family, love, understanding, acceptance. She definitely wouldn't think about the fact that if she hadn't been taken, she might've grown up with her mother, with Feyra, and never suffered a childhood of doubt and loneliness. She would've grown up among these strong, loving women, and perhaps her fate would've been a different, more peaceful one.

The blue sky gave way to the familiar indigo of space, so many stars surrounded by planets, many of those planets teeming with people. The galaxy was so much bigger than her family could even dream. And yet there was room among those stars for places like Coruscant and places like Pkori. There were verdant little moons like Olgothon 3 and desert planets like Geonosis and dark, forbidding places like Thule. Perhaps one day, when the Jedi had been extinguished and every vestige of the Order that had failed her—and her mother—had disappeared, when the Inquisitorius was no longer necessary . . . she would return.

Yes. She would return.

There was a rightness to it. She'd begun her journey here, and when she'd accomplished her goals, and the galaxy was truly at peace, she would end it here, become a matriarch like Beamala, perhaps. She would learn their language and wear their bright dresses, claim her mother's bracelets and earn her own. But she would keep her weapons with her, in case violence ever came calling. Maybe she would even lead these people. Save them from some extraplanetary danger they couldn't possibly fathom.

She smiled as she plotted her first jump back toward Coruscant. She knew her calling, and now she had a destiny.

The trip back to the Inquisitorius Headquarters was uneventful, save for a brief and purposeful stopover, and nothing had changed while she was gone. 6-RA-7 followed her down the ramp and, before leaving for the library, sharply suggested that in the future, her specialized services should be reserved only for assignments of galactic importance and possible assassinations.

As expected, the Grand Inquisitor summoned her almost immediately, and she congratulated herself on her cleverness as she reported to his chambers. She was back in her uniform and carrying a camtono, and he looked her up and down.

"And what did you learn on your . . ." A meaningful pause. "Outing?"

She bowed her head. "I learned that my mother left the Jedi and returned to her home planet. Her whereabouts are unknown."

He tapped his fingers on the armrest of his chair and regarded her with smug superiority. "Foolish of them, to have kept this information from you, knowing full well it would only spark your curiosity. But what is this you've brought—some relic of home?"

Iskat placed the camtono on the ground before him. "I took the liberty of stopping on Takodana, where Sember often met with a trader called Morgest." She disengaged the lock, and the side panels fell open to reveal a lightsaber—one she didn't recognize. "Morgest didn't know to whom it had once belonged, but she readily gave it to me. It was the only artifact she had in her possession. I didn't sense anything else that called out in the Force."

The Grand Inquisitor twitched his fingers, and the lightsaber flew to his hand. He inspected it, turned it this way and that. There was nothing special about it—it could have belonged to any member of the Jedi Order, might be five years old or five hundred. He briefly activated the blue blade and nodded his approval.

"If you must waste time, it is always wise to return with bounty. Dismissed."

Iskat left the camtono where it was and went directly to her chamber, glad that she had not returned from her trip empty-handed. Without the Grand Inquisitor looming behind her and clad in her black tunic and robes instead of her intimidating uniform, it had been easy enough to talk the kindly trader into giving her the saber without any sort of violence. She'd been practicing her influencing abilities, after all.

Life went back to normal, whatever normal was in the Inquisitorius's Coruscant headquarters. Iskat was still eager for her first mission, but until then, she continued to hone her skills. She would spar with whoever she found in the pit. The Ninth Sister was a lively enough partner, but the Eighth Brother clearly wanted an excuse to kill and the Fifth Brother could never, ever be trusted. The Tenth Brother kept his distance, though. Iskat remembered him from her Padawan training, and he didn't seem to want to fight her any more than she wanted to fight him. The Second Sister saw everyone as simple prey, the Fourth Sister always seemed like her mind was elsewhere, and the Seventh Sister loved to fight dirty and was best avoided completely. It was a shame that although they were all finally free of the Jedi's influence, their current situation pitted them against one another instead of allowing them to find solace among those who understood what it meant to see the truth about the Force cult that had brainwashed them as children.

Iskat was on her way to the pit one day, looking for a fresh challenge, when she sensed someone walking toward her in the hallway. The presence seemed familiar, but she could not place it. Her hand immediately went to her new lightsaber, which she could now wield in any of its forms as if it were an extension of her body. That was life among the Inquisitors—she was always ready for a fight, or at least some sort of poisonous barb.

She stopped and waited, the skin on the back of her bare neck prickling as the figure appeared around a corner.

"Tualon?"

/ 36.

"ISKAT?"

He hurried toward her, and she felt her forehead to see if she was feverish, as the med droids had suggested infection was always a possibility, considering how badly Vader had destroyed the bones in her hand and the fact that she almost always had some sort of surface wound from sparring.

But no, it wasn't an infection.

It was *him*.

He looked the same, mostly. Same gleaming black skin, same pointed teeth, same sunset eyes. But he wore the uniform of an Inquisitor, and the same dark, aggressive, fractured aura that seemed to cloak the others.

"You cut your hair," he said before chuckling. "A stupid thing to notice, I suppose, but you always had beautiful hair."

Her hand went to the back of her head, now shaved down. The burn Vader had left there had faded under the med droids' care, but she'd had no choice but to cut off most of the ragged, burned mess of what little hair his lightsaber had left behind. She'd been sad, at first, to lose her waist-length locks, which she'd taken care to keep nice even when she was sleeping on the ground or in a ship for days on end. And yet, once her hair was gone, there was a certain lightness about her, a certain rightness. Now she could be ready to go in mere minutes. Now she didn't have to intricately pin up her braid so her enemies wouldn't use it against her. There was something powerful and feral in losing the weight of that hair she'd carried for so long.

She'd burned the shorn length of it like a Padawan braid, another line crossed.

Still, Tualon had called her old hair beautiful, and it was gone, and despite everything they'd been through, that made her sad.

"How'd you end up here?" she asked. "I thought—"

"Oh. Yes. You thought I was dead because you left me to die." It was as if a wall came down behind his eyes, and even though she'd known him her entire life, he felt like an entirely different person in that moment. "That's right—I remember it now. My memories . . . they did something to my head. But it's all coming back." His orange eyes narrowed, and he bared his teeth. "I'm remembering that I hate you."

She took a step back, trying to understand this new version of Tualon. "They were going to kill us both. I didn't have much of a choice. Did you?"

His hand went to his forehead as his head bowed, his palm massaging the place between his eyes. "Our troopers shot me. I fought back, killed a bunch of them, but they shot me, and I was lying there on the ground under those charcoal trees and—" He shook his head violently, his lekku flying. "I don't know. I don't know. There were promises. I was so angry. With you, and with the Jedi, and I was dying, and—" He looked up, his eyes on fire as he sneered. "Why am I telling you this? You're just the coward who ran away and left me."

The old version of Iskat would've apologized, pled her case, done anything to win him over and release herself from blame. But the new Iskat did not owe this man apologies or answers. He held no sway over her, no allegiance, no love.

"That was then, and this is now," she told him. "Change or die."

His nostrils flared. "Is that a threat?"

"You'll soon learn that everything here is a threat. If you're so eager for a fight, I'll give you one. I'm on my way to the pit. I doubt you'll offer much of a challenge."

She turned her back to him and strode away, and after a moment, he followed. As she led him through the now-familiar halls, her mind caught up with her hearts. This was a new version of Tualon—reconditioned and tortured and broken, only to be remade. The Tualon she'd known had wanted to be an ideal Jedi, and he'd been willing to bend his morals to reach that goal. Toward the end, she'd seen flashes of rebellion in him but none of the open dissatisfaction and disobedience that she'd experienced herself. Had he secretly harbored doubts about the Jedi, as she had? She'd felt rage in him—she'd known he had hidden depths. He must've had some leaning toward the dark side, if they'd offered him the chance to join the Inquisitorius. Was that why she'd always been drawn to him?

Perhaps the screams she'd heard lately . . . had been Tualon's. Was he the shadowy figure she'd seen haunting the warehouse late at night? Maybe somewhere, under all that hate, the old Tualon was still there. She'd seen it, the first moment he'd caught sight of her in the hall—open, friendly, familiar. Perhaps if she could help bleed out the hate, she'd finally have someone among the Inquisitorius she could actually relate to.

Not trust—no, never that. But it would be nice to have someone who didn't want her dead.

The pit was empty, she was glad to see. The other Inquisitors came and went on their missions with no pattern that she could discern, but for now, Iskat was glad that this fight wouldn't have onlookers. Tualon followed her to the edge and looked down, taking it all in.

She tossed him a challenging grin and jumped. He didn't wait for her to land before he'd joined her, plummeting gracefully down into the fighting ring.

"You don't have to hold back here," she told him, remembering that there had been no one there to lead her through those confusing first days. "There are no tenets, no polite bows, no rules. It's less a duel and more a brawl. Have you met the others?"

"No other Inquisitors. I was just given my uniform. I know the Grand Inquisitor, and there were droids, there were others—when they—" He closed his eyes. "I was on the ground, it hurt, and then there was a room, I was strapped in, needles right into my brain, lightning, explosions, and they—I—they—taught me. The truth about the Jedi. What they'd done to us. What they did to the galaxy. Traitors. Assassinations. And then I was taken to the Grand Inquisitor's chambers, and he opened a door, and here I am. I don't know anything about this place except that I hate the Jedi and I'm supposed to . . . do something about that. They gave me a new lightsaber, but I haven't used it yet."

Iskat pulled the lightsaber from her back. "Some things you have to discover for yourself." Keeping it in crescent form, she lit her red blade. "So let's see what you discover."

Tualon pulled his own lightsaber from his back and grinned his old cocky grin. He ignited his blade and ran at her. But she was ready, because he often attacked first to set his opponent off guard. She'd learned that this was also the general style of all Inquisitors, after Vader had schooled them on aggression; maybe she would warn him about that later, and maybe not. As he approached, she gestured off to the side, and a chunk of metal flew off the wall and directly toward him. He leapt over it, and she brought her lightsaber slashing toward him in midair. Their blades met as he landed, and she curled her other hand, pulling the metal plate from the floor and into the backs of his calves. It tripped him up and he fell backward this time, too busy concentrating on her lightsaber to notice the Force-pushed distraction.

The moment he was on his back, she held out a hand.

"You fight dirty," he snarled, furious now.

"So should you."

Instead of taking her hand, he kicked it away and did a kip-up to standing.

Now that they were both on their feet, he circled her like a predator taking the measure of its prey, and she held her lightsaber but kept it in its crescent with one blade, knowing full well he had no chance with a spinning, dual-bladed weapon when he was still this new and damaged. He'd never even lit his weapon before, she realized—

It didn't matter.

He would know if she held back, and considering his current state of mind, it would only make him hate her more.

Despite everything they'd been through, despite everything she was becoming . . . Iskat still didn't want Tualon to hate her.

He attacked, and she parried. The duel was similar to those they'd had countless times in the training rooms of the Jedi Temple, but there was an undercurrent of fury and annoyance that they had once been taught to actively repress. She could almost taste his emotions on the air, a new and intoxicating development. He wasn't holding them tightly anymore; they were shining out of the cracks his transformation had left behind. Frustration at a missed shot, anger at an attack focused on his weak spot, glee at surprising her with a sudden onslaught. As he limbered up and she got to know this new version of him—as he grew to understand himself and his new weapon—a certain dark playfulness fell over the give-and-take of attacks.

He was using his body in new ways, stretching his mind to accommodate a new style of fighting. Iskat did not fully open herself to the dark side and unleash herself upon him; she allowed him to test his newfound powers against her. And yet . . . these were not training sabers. When she caught him on the shoulder, he gave her a look of pure, unrelenting hate and screamed so hard that her whole body shuddered and fell, numb and shaking, to the ground.

She'd never felt anything like it, as if her organs were exploding inside her body.

"What was that?" she asked, looking up at him.

But his hands were at his temples, his eyes closed and his teeth clenched. "Shut up! Shut up shut up shut up! Not the chair—I'll be good, or bad, whatever you want. I can't—it hurts—my head—like worms in my skull!"

She scrabbled away on hands and knees and fetched up against the wall, trying to stay out of his line of sight as he fought whatever clawed at his brain. Pushing herself to sitting, she watched Tualon fighting an even more painful battle within his own mind, as if he saw shadows that weren't there. Whatever the Inquisitors had done to fragment him, and turn him against the Jedi, they had not put the pieces together perfectly.

Or maybe, like a baby bird trying to escape its egg, he had to beat his head against the hard shell again and again until he was free.

Either way, she couldn't help him with this fight, and she had to protect herself. It was almost ironic: She had caused herself damage trying to fit in with the Jedi, and now Tualon was suffering damage as he found his place among the Inquisitorius. Maybe he would spread his wings and fly . . . or maybe he would plummet. Either way, they would soon see what he was truly made of. The other Inquisitors would not be so patient with him, nor would Vader.

That scream, though. Where had he learned such a skill? She'd been briefly incapacitated, and even now, it took more effort than it should've to stand, one hand against the wall. It must have come from the dark side, from the unique way he connected with the Force now. Maybe, like her, he'd had that talent within him all along, lying fallow as the Jedi urged him to cultivate other strengths. If he'd remained among them, maybe he never would've discovered his own depths.

"The fight's not over, is it?" he asked.

The rictus of pain was gone from his face, replaced by a hungry grin, as if nothing unusual had happened at all. Maybe he wasn't even aware anything had happened.

"It's not over until I beat you," she told him.

He had a better grip on himself, and they fought around the pit as if testing its structural integrity. They climbed the walls, somersaulted over each other, and even fought with their fists. Iskat spit blood and grinned fiercely at him, almost proud of what Tualon could do when not constrained by gallantry. She liked this new side of him even more than the Tualon she'd known before. He was cunning, confident, unashamed, passionate. All the things the Jedi had tried to purge from his soul came rushing back. He was almost . . . fun.

And now, Iskat noted with interest, their relationship wouldn't be constrained by the Jedi's rejection of connection.

"I hate you," he told her as they stood, panting, and deactivated their lightsabers. "At least, I think I do. I don't remember all the reasons why. But I remember you abandoned me to die. You didn't look back. You closed yourself in the Force, turned your back, and just walked away. Hid from me like a coward."

"I did what I had to do, and I don't regret it. There was no way you and I could've won against that many troopers. They made sure of it. And I wasn't willing to die for you." She caught his gaze. "Would you have died for me that day?"

"No."

He said it quickly, sharply; like he'd given it a lot of thought.

"Exactly. So how can you blame me?"

A dark chuckle. "There you go, being reasonable about unreasonable things. They . . . they used it. Used you. To turn me. The rage I felt against you kept me alive, even when they'd shot me."

He lifted his tunic. Gray scar tissue marred the smooth black skin of his muscular chest, twisting over his ribs.

"I was on the ground, hoping your ship would explode as it took off and I could watch the sparks like fireworks. I was muttering, *I hope she dies. I hope she dies.* That is a very un-Jedi thought, isn't it? To hope someone dies. And then I woke up in a dark room. In the chair, they told me that if I joined them, I would have my chance to kill you."

She raised one eyebrow, amused. "Is that what today was? You trying to kill me? You weren't trying very hard."

"That's the thing." He stepped closer, looked at her in a way she'd always dreamed he might. "I don't think I want to anymore. I think I might finally understand you. You did something incredible, when we were young, with that column. Incredible . . . and dangerous and forbidden. And because you caused permanent harm, even on accident, they made you regret it every day of your life. Now you finally get to be yourself."

"So can you. That scream—"

"I feel like I've been holding it inside all my life, and that was the first time I let it go."

She nodded. "It feels good, to let go."

He stepped toward her, so close, and the way he was looking at her suggested that for the first time in their lives, he saw her for exactly what she was. And he didn't shy away, didn't flinch. A warmth stirred in her chest, her hearts beating in time, and he allowed her to sense him in the Force, sense his interest and . . .

Well, other things a Jedi wasn't supposed to feel.

"There's just one thing," he said, his voice intimate and husky.

She stepped closer, her lips parting. "Yes?"

He ignited the lightsaber in his hand.

It went straight through her chest, a hot brand.

"We're even now, I think," he said before she lost consciousness.

/ 37.

ISKAT WOKE UP IN THE bacta tank again, and her first thought was that she really was going to kill Tualon if it was the last thing she did. What the Seventh Sister had done almost seemed playful and what Vader had done seemed instructional compared with how . . . *personal* this wound felt. *He'd tried to stab her in the heart.*

He apparently didn't know she had two.

He'd missed.

She didn't know how long she'd been unconscious, but the hole in her chest had healed to a smooth burgundy scar. The med droids soon had her out of the tank and rinsing off in the showers, and then she was back in her room, making sure no one had stolen her belongings and enjoying how much overall healing her body had done while she was being saved from death by a near-fatal wound.

Infuriating, that she'd let her old feelings for him cloud her emotions long enough for him to stab her.

That absolute—

Well.

She'd left him to die, he'd left her to die.

Maybe he was right—now they were even.

Funny, how she'd thought that the old Tualon who followed all the rules might be the one calling the shots when the Inquisitorius had clearly gone to great lengths to bring out a version that was far more diabolical and unpredictable.

He had, at least, given her the chance to live. Not like what she'd done to Heezo. A hole could be patched, but what she'd done to the traitorous Selonian was beyond the current scope of med droids.

As she exchanged her black med gown for her uniform, her comm buzzed.

"Iskat Akaris, report to the Grand Inquisitor's chambers immediately," 6-RA-7 coolly informed her.

She was practically buzzing with excitement as she finished dressing and prepared herself for a formal audience. Finally! After all her time haunting these cavernous halls, honing her skills, waiting for her chance to perform her promised duty, the moment had finally come. Her cape snapped as she marched toward the Grand Inquisitor's chamber. He sat stiffly in his throne, as if its very existence was a chore.

"Are you fully recovered from your injury?" he asked. "The pit was not intended to become a slaughterhouse, and yet between Lord Vader and various quarrels, here we are."

Her hand almost went to the twisted knot of scar tissue between her hearts, but she stopped herself. It was a bad idea, showing any sign of fragility past or present when standing before the Grand Inquisitor.

Or any Inquisitor.

"I am fully recovered, Grand Inquisitor." Because she'd learned that anything else would earn a firm rebuke. He hated long speeches from others almost as much as he hated disrespect.

The less said, the better.

"Good. I trust you are ready for your first mission."

"Yes, Grand Inquisitor."

"News has reached us of two rogue Jedi hiding on Firrhana. You will travel to the Outer Rim, root them out, and destroy them. Do you understand?"

She inclined her head, hiding her glee. "Yes, Grand Inquisitor."

"Look at me, child."

She did, finding his yellow-eyed gaze disturbing.

He leaned forward, fingers digging into the arms of his throne. "This is your first real mission. It is one thing to realize that the Jedi are the enemy, but it is another thing entirely to participate in their necessary eradication. Do not give them a chance to speak, to poison you with their rhetoric, for they will attempt to sway you with their weak persuasion and pathetic mewling. You are a Jedi no longer."

"No, Grand Inquisitor. But—"

He bared his teeth.

"Do you know the names of these Jedi?"

He leaned back and flicked his long fingers. "Names do not matter. They are all traitors. Now go, and do not disappoint me."

"I wouldn't dare."

She nodded and left, grateful to be on the other side of his door. His rooms felt as if they were on some frozen planet devoid of life. As she headed for her own, far less grandiose chamber, her mind was alive with preparations. She'd been waiting for this day, when she would finally put her Inquisitor training to good use. Between her electrocution, her crushed hand, her disloyal stabbing, and, yes, her side trip to Pkori, it felt as if she'd been robbed of time and the opportunity to prove herself. She worried that deep in her soul, the echo of her Jedi training still clung, stubborn as a barnacle, weighing her down. The Jedi had treated her like garbage, first as a fatally flawed pariah and then as a weak-minded, expendable soldier, and she hated them for it.

This mission was her chance to finally purge that last sticky parasite from her body and soul.

In her room, she packed everything she might need for her journey, including Feyra's lightsaber. She didn't know how the other Inquisitors went about their business, what supplies they chose to accomplish their missions. They didn't speak of such things; they only taunted one another and sparred, when they were around at all. Their goal was to eradicate what was left of the Jedi Order, and that meant they were often spread around the galaxy, collecting trophies before coming back to brag about it.

Iskat relished the chance to finally have something to brag about herself.

This time, she took a full complement of Purge Troopers. The *Scythe* was familiar under her hands, the instrument panel now an old friend. As they barreled through hyperspace, she scrolled through her tablet, gleaning all the intel she could on Firrhana. The planet was an old Sith stronghold abandoned after a volcano rendered it nearly uninhabitable centuries ago. She wondered if it would be anything like Thule, a place of barren beauty where she felt an immediate connection. And she wondered why rogue Jedi would choose such a place, given all the options in the galaxy.

Firrhana wasn't terribly far away, and soon the little planet appeared, a malevolent smudge among the stars. It wasn't like Pkori, a peaceful swirl of clouds and land and sea. It was a small, dark thing, mottled green and black, almost like a chunk of rot floating alone in space. As she entered its atmosphere, there was an odd silence. No spaceport, no chatter.

Right up until she got a ping—and coordinates.

Curious but wary, her Purge Troopers at their guns, she approached the designated spot.

Was it possible the Jedi were desperate and signaling everyone who came into the area for help? Did the Jedi even know that the Inquisitorius existed and that they were being hunted? Were they so accustomed to being the galaxy's heroes that they'd forgotten how far they had fallen?

But as she approached, she saw a very familiar ship.

A ship identical to the fighters she'd seen on the landing pads back on Coruscant.

"Whoever is trying to poach my prey has an enemy for life," she snarled.

Her Purge Troopers said nothing. They never did, unless spoken to.

She zipped toward the other ship, which sat unmoving in a grayish-green field. As she approached, she received no further communication, the mystery deepening. Why was there another Inquisitor here? Was she being supervised?

She thought about just blowing it up, but she was fairly certain the Grand Inquisitor would then question her methods. Ambition was encouraged, stabbing a fellow Inquisitor in the back was expected, but destroying valuable ships was probably frowned upon.

The *Scythe* landed with a disturbingly squishy sensation, and she checked that the air was breathable before stepping out into a field of stringy, slimy fungus.

Standing outside the other ship was the last Inquisitor she'd expected to see.

Tualon.

He looked good in his uniform and helmet, but Iskat did not say so.

"Why did you send me these coordinates?" she asked, striding toward him and stopping just out of lightsaber reach.

He pulled his lightsaber off his back and held it but did not ignite it. "To lure you here and kill you, if you presented a problem."

"Only for my prey." She looked around, noting the globular gray fungus clinging to crumbled stone. "Nice place, though. Remind you of anywhere?"

He didn't take the bait. "The past is dead, Iskat. Are you here to interfere with my mission?"

"No. Are you here to kill me again?" she shot back.

His amused grin set her insides on fire; her hatred of him apparently didn't change her physical reaction. "Maybe, if you don't behave. But like I said: We're even now. You stabbed me in the back, I stabbed you in the front. The slate is clean."

She looked him up and down. "Then here we are. Did they give us the same mission? I'm assuming if they wanted us to work together, the Grand Inquisitor would've mentioned it."

He shook his head. "I'm tracking a Jedi." He pointed to a jagged collection of fungus nearby, and Iskat could see the rough shape of a Y-wing already coated in new growth. "That's her ship."

"Who is it?"

"Sorry, but that's proprietary information. Unless you want to tell me the name of your target?"

"Sorry, but that's proprietary information," she mimicked, delighting in annoying him. She didn't know the names of her quarry, and there was no real trust between them, so there was no way to know if they were after the same Jedi or different Jedi who'd chosen the same hiding spot. He knew his Jedi was female, apparently; Iskat knew nothing of her own—only that there were two.

He snapped his lightsaber on his back and sighed. "Then I wish you happy hunting. Stay out of my way or I'll stab you again."

"Stay out of my way or I'll make sure that when my troopers kill you as I walk away, you'll stay down this time."

He pointed at her ramp, where fungus was already creeping up. "Don't stay here too long. Be a shame if Vader killed you for losing a ship."

Giving him a crude gesture she'd learned from their old clone troopers, she went back inside her ship. Her ramp pulled away from the fungus with a sickening sucking sound, and she zipped into the air and away from Tualon.

It was fun, this . . . flirting. Maybe it was laced with innuendo and the very real threat of violence, but it was flirting nonetheless. She should've known he wouldn't be willing to work with her, but it was still disappointing. The other Inquisitors all seemed to have this vicious, distrusting edge that Iskat herself didn't share. She knew Tualon had been tortured—reconditioned—to turn him away from the Jedi and toward the Inquisitorius, but was that perhaps what had also happened to all the others and turned them so cruel, so joyless? Was Iskat the only one who had truly chosen this life without the threat of suffering?

The Grand Inquisitor, she thought, had not required a torture chair. And the Fifth Brother also seemed fully himself. Funny how even here, among those better suited to taking lives than saving them, Iskat still felt like the odd one out.

Now that Tualon had proven secretive, she had to find her Jedi on her own—and before Tualon found them. If he was hunting a different Jedi altogether, that meant that if she got there first, she could claim both his Jedi and her own, if they were clustered together like brainless sheep. But if Tualon got there first, he would take her quarry and leave her empty-handed. Or worse, she might be tempted to kill Tualon and take his trophies back herself. She wasn't returning from this mission empty-handed, no matter how far she had to go or what she had to do.

The sky of Firrhana was thick, dull gray, the air whistling against her ship. Iskat closed her eyes and called on the Force, pressing her senses against the planet's surface like fingertips probing a lock. This was one of her gifts—the ability to perceive things others might not. Tualon had never been sensitive like this, which gave her an advantage. Maybe he'd found the ship. But the ship was clearly empty. She just had to find the Jedi first, and—

There. A swirling vortex of dark side energy.

She jerked on the controls, veering off toward a series of jagged black peaks in a field of blackened lava. As she got closer, she noticed the remains of a temple. It was Sith, surely, and places like that left their claws sunk deep into the land. She could feel it pulsating with old, twisted energy like a wound that hadn't healed right. As the crumbling fortress came into view, a peak just a little higher than those around it, she pushed the ship as hard as it would go and landed on the barren, rocky ground near a grand stone door, its carved figures washed away by time and whittled soft by ash-filled winds.

If she were a Jedi, this was where she'd hide.

The last place anyone would expect a Jedi to be, shrouded by the dark side they'd been taught to oppose and avoid.

She put on her helmet and ran her hands over her various weapons, including the red crescent lightsaber on her back and her mother's yellow lightsaber attached to her belt.

"Be ready," she told her Purge Troopers. "Don't emerge unless I give the signal."

They didn't speak or nod; their stillness was their only affirmation.

As soon as she stood on the ground of Firrhana, she knelt and put a hand to the planet's surface, once again opening herself to the Force. She felt that same old frisson of excitement, to see what would be revealed, and this time she was rewarded by the caress of dark side energy, ancient and deep and eagerly waiting to be woken by someone with potential. The planet seemed barren but wasn't; crablike arthropods burrowed busily through the rock, and leathery reptiles with rudimentary wings for gliding used their black pebbled skin as camouflage among the rocks. Even the stringy fungus was hungry and seeking, supporting a population of tiny, translucent snails with poisonous slime.

The planet had once been bursting with life, but even now, ruined, it had teeth.

And somewhere within this fortress, Iskat could feel the flickers of living beings.

Her Jedi were here—or perhaps Tualon's—but Jedi nonetheless.

Prey.

She approached the grand doors and reached out to knock.

"Who seeks the illustrious Lord Jakadis, greatest bounty hunter of the Outer Rim, bane of the once-mighty Jedi and celebrated collector of Force-relics?" a male protocol droid's cultured voice asked. "And what bounty have you brought to sell? I don't see a prisoner. Do you have Jedi artifacts perhaps? Or are you here to peruse the wares?"

The pieces clicked into place in Iskat's mind.

This fortress wasn't the chosen hiding spot of rogue Jedi on the run—

Her Jedi had likely been brought here against their will. She had to think quickly.

"My master has a Jedi on the ship," she said, keeping her helmet's visor down. "If Jakadis can pay."

"*Lord* Jakadis is always happy to negotiate, especially if the Jedi is high ranking. And does your master possess any artifacts? The Jedi's lightsaber, perhaps? He's especially fond of those."

Iskat unhooked her mother's lightsaber and held it out. "There's your proof. My master will be back with the prisoner shortly."

"We await your return," the protocol droid said with great formality.

Back on the ship, she considered her options.

"You," she said to one of her Purge Troopers.

"Yes, sir," he said in the clone voice she knew so well.

"I'm going to need your armor."

Soon Iskat again stood at the fortress entrance, amazed by her first view through a trooper's helmet. It was surprisingly easy to breathe and see, and there were all sorts of readouts that helped her better understand why the troopers she'd known often preferred their helmets to walking about bareheaded. As for the Purge Trooper by her side, who went by Sixty-Seven, he wore some spare clothes she'd brought along—a loose tunic, pants, and cloak, the hood pulled down low to hide the red tattoo that covered the right half of his face. He wore a pair of binders, and she could sense his annoyance at being restrained, even as part of a deception.

He seemed to have little personality, or perhaps he had chosen to hide it, but he followed orders well, which was why he was on his back on the ground. She'd dragged him here by one leg, unapologetic for the roughness of the terrain. Inquisitors, Iskat had learned, did not apologize, not to one another and not to their underlings. Maybe only to the Grand Inquisitor or Vader or the Emperor, and only when their lives were on the line.

Under her borrowed Purge Trooper armor, Iskat wore a spare black body glove, which briefly brought back memories of Thule. Her red-bladed lightsaber and her mother's lightsaber were both hooked to her belt under the armor's tabard, leaving her hands free to carry the trooper's blaster. Perhaps the armor was overkill, but if this bounty hunter was collecting Jedi, she didn't want to be recognized as a Force user. There was no telling what was on the other side of the door.

"Who is the Jedi?" the droid's voice asked.

"Tualon Yaluna," she said, the helmet's voice modulator rendering her voice gender-neutral. "A Jedi Knight."

There was a long period of silence, and then the door slid open.

"Please follow the lights to the audience chamber," the droid told her. "There, your bounty will be confirmed and evaluated."

With a sigh, Iskat dragged the disguised trooper down the hall, following a helpful line of softly glowing lights along the smooth black floor. She passed a few doors symmetrically arranged along the long tunnel, but it was quite a walk to the correct one. Apparently this Jakadis wanted to lure his visitors deep into his lair, a tactic Iskat understood. She would've done the same.

The lights led her to a door on the right, and when she entered pulling Sixty-Seven, the door slid shut behind her, effectively trapping them in the room. The high-ceilinged chamber was all carved from the same lava rock. It again reminded her of Thule and had that same comfortable thrum that she'd come to associate with ancient dark side relics. There was a large stone altar in the center and a balcony ringing the space, suggesting that important rituals had once taken place here. Reaching out with her senses, she felt an emptiness below and stepped back from what was most likely a trapdoor, settling her trooper where he wouldn't fall and take harm if the trap was sprung.

"Please make yourself comfortable. We will be with you shortly for evaluation and payment," the droid said politely, and then the speakers went silent.

Iskat went into action. With an almost imperceptible gesture, the three cams in the corners of the room went dark, their wiring severed.

"Get up and take the blaster," she told Sixty-Seven, who instantly obeyed. "Whoever comes in here, shoot them and wait for me."

"Yes, sir."

She shed her armor swiftly and returned it to Sixty-Seven, who would likely need it more than she would. Now that she was past the droid and any outer defenses, Iskat needed to be free to move and able to climb. Once Sixty-Seven was armored and ready, she put on the cloak the trooper had worn and climbed up to the balcony, vaulting over the railing and hurrying toward the nearest cavernous entrance that led deeper into the structure.

The doorway led to another hallway, the walls carved with a bas-relief of geometric figures carrying triangular objects and weapons. This was her second time in a Sith edifice, and she felt that same familiar comfort here as she had on Thule. Not the warm, homey belonging she'd felt on Pkori, but a pleasing welcome, as if this place was an aged pet that was happy to call her friend, if not master.

Something was tickling the back of Iskat's mind as she navigated the mazelike hallways and twisting stairwells. There were no more cams or speakers, no disembodied droid voice. Most visitors were probably content to wait in the audience chamber to do their business, or at the very least they didn't object—or couldn't do much about it. She was tracking a ripple in the Force that felt like a Jedi, and the closer she got, the more certain she was that the Jedi she was hunting was someone she knew.

Her path had led her down under the throne room, and she realized that the trapdoor would naturally lead to a containment area. The doors here were smaller and wore ancient locks, and as Iskat approached the first one, a shiver ran up her neck.

She used her mother's lightsaber to sever the lock, then replaced it on her belt before opening the door.

"Who's there?"

The voice was familiar, its mix of authority and fear just as grating as it had been for all those years back on Coruscant.

"Charlin Plaka?"

/ 38.

THE CELL WAS BARELY LIT and primitively outfitted with only a bench and two buckets. The young Twi'lek who sat on the bench, weak and ragged in her shackles, looked up, incredulous.

"Iskat?"

Charlin had always been fastidious about everything from her exercise regimen to her skin care and diet, but now she looked like a hollowed-out version of herself. Her pink skin was pale and smeared with ash and dirt, her eyes were sunken, and her robes stank like she'd rolled around in a puffer pig nest. Iskat could sense her exhaustion and fragility, see the bones pressing against her skin. Too weak to break free. Too weak to do anything.

"You survived? How?" Charlin asked, almost incredulous.

As if it were unthinkable that an outcast like Iskat might still be alive.

Iskat did not allow her lip to curl. "I could ask the same of you."

Filthy and bedraggled as she was, Charlin tossed her lekku in that old, haughty way. "I was with Master Klefan, and we were separated from our troopers. We heard a distress call from the Temple, stole a ship, and escaped. They tried to shoot us down, but as it turns out, I've become an excellent pilot, and we jumped before they could catch us."

"Then how'd you end up here?"

Charlin's nose scrunched up in annoyance. "We had nothing—no supplies, no credits—so Klefan contacted an old friend of his who offered to help us. He sent us to these coordinates and said Jakadis would give us a place to lie low. But when we arrived, we were betrayed. Jakadis is a warlord who collects Jedi and anything to do with the Force. He's obsessed with the dark side. It's everywhere here." She looked around disparagingly. "Can't you feel it? Like a creeping cold."

Iskat held back her smile. "This was once a Sith planet."

Charlin shivered. "It's horrid. I don't even know how long we've been here. A droid brings me food and water, but we don't know what they want with us. I don't even know where Master Klefan is." Her head hung briefly, but then she looked up in confusion.

"But you must be here to rescue us. Who are you with? One of the masters, surely. And where are your robes? And your lightsaber? Is this a disguise? Black is not your color." She stood and held out her arms. "Get the shackles off, and I'll take you to—"

"No."

Charlin looked at Iskat like she'd grown a second head.

"What do you mean, no? I'm higher ranking—"

"I'm fairly certain we became Jedi Knights in the same ceremony."

"Well, someone has to be in charge, and that droid could come back at any time—"

Iskat whipped out her new lightsaber from under her cloak and ignited it.

"Where'd you get a red-bladed lightsaber?" Charlin asked. "And—"

Iskat held her blade under Charlin's chin.

For once, Charlin shut up, and it was immensely satisfying.

"I don't think it's the droid you need to fear," Iskat said, her lips curling up into a smile.

Charlin had always played at being frightened of Iskat, but only in a way that suggested Iskat was untrustworthy and accidentally dangerous. When she openly worried about being grouped with Iskat for training exercises, it was to draw attention to Iskat's incompetence and failures, not to actually ascribe any power to her. Charlin had never taken her seriously, never considered her an equal, much less a friend. Iskat felt it in her hearts, a pulsating hate she'd spent years trying to meditate away but that now rushed in, making her snarl.

Because of this girl, because of Jedi like Charlin, Iskat had always been an outsider.

And because of Jedi like Charlin, the Republic had fallen.

Charlin had bought into every Jedi lie, would've followed Mace Windu to the ends of the galaxy. She was an ideal Jedi, a true Jedi . . . and that meant she deserved to die, just like all the rest.

"What are you playing at?" Charlin asked, real fear rising in her eyes.

"Oh, I'm not playing. I stopped playing the day I pulled down that column. After that, I spent every moment of my life trying to become the perfect Jedi so insecure little insects like you would have no reason to whisper about me. I stopped playing, Charlin—"

Iskat let her red lightsaber almost touch Charlin's throat, making the girl gasp.

"I stopped playing because I had to grow up too fast. Because of you."

Charlin swallowed hard and stepped back. "I don't know what you're talking about."

Iskat chuckled. "Master Klefan," she said mockingly, "what happens if a Jedi can't control their powers? We're supposed to be working on control, but some people"—Iskat rolled her eyes comedically—"seem to be having problems."

"I never said that—"

"Master Yoda, I'd really prefer to work with Onielle. I just feel like our skills are a better match."

"I didn't—"

"Master Vey, Jedi aren't supposed to feel fear, but what if another Jedi makes us feel *uncomfortable*?"

She thumbed her hilt, and the red blade disappeared. Charlin glared at her, as angry as she was frightened. Iskat could feel her in the Force, feel all the emotions the girl had supposedly mastered fighting within. Fear, rage, impudence, confusion.

"You seem *uncomfortable* to me right now, Charlin. I can sense your fear, your rage. Your superiority. All those years devoted to the Order, and just look at you. Pathetic."

Charlin looked away. "Yes, I'm scared. Because I'm helpless and you're supposed to help me, and you're—"

"Holding a grudge?"

Charlin gave a half sob, half laugh. "Acting unhinged."

Iskat put away her lightsaber and looked down at her hand, at the elegance of her long, slender fingers. There was something she'd read about but had never tried. Perhaps she'd played with it when she'd broken the Seventh Sister's hand and pulled the wires in Vader's helmet, but—

She flexed her fingers as Charlin took a step back, glaring like a distrustful tooka.

"Are you sorry?" Iskat asked her.

For a long moment, Charlin said nothing, as if it was possible to ignore a question spoken while alone in a dungeon on a long-dead planet.

"Are you sorry?" Iskat demanded, almost a shout.

"Sorry for what? I don't know what you want from me!"

"I want you to suffer!" Iskat's hands went to fists. "I want you to suffer as I did, because of Jedi like you. I want you to admit you're not the perfect, good-hearted, altruistic Jedi you always pretended to be. You're a bully, and a hypocrite, and a traitor. Or do you truly think you're innocent? I want to know."

"You don't sound like yourself," Charlin said, her voice rough as she cringed away. "You never suffered anything outside of your own head, and I never said I was perfect. But we have to get out of here now. We're both Jedi, Iskat, and there aren't many of us left. We're family."

"You and I were never family, Charlin. We are not the same!"

The last part came out as a shout, and Charlin flinched.

"Okay. Okay. Whatever you say. But you need to get these shackles off me so we can find Master Klefan and escape, and then we can talk about . . . whatever this is. I'm assuming you have a ship?"

Iskat's nails dug into her palms.

"There it is again. You can't even respond to a simple question we both know the answer to. You swipe aside my feelings as if they're silly and refocus on what *you* want. You're not the hero of this story, Charlin."

Charlin sighed, all the fight going out of her drained body. "Okay, Iskat. You're right. It's you. You're the hero." She got down on her knees, held out her bound wrists, and looked up, tears in her eyes. "So please. Save me. I don't want to die here because of some imagined rivalry from when we were younglings. Just get me out of here. I'm begging you."

With a nod, Iskat stepped forward and released the simple shackles on Charlin's wrists. They dropped to the ground, and Charlin stood, rubbing the raw places on her rosy skin.

"Thank you." She looked up and wiped the tears from her cheeks. "Now let's find Master Klefan and get to your ship."

But Iskat wasn't currently open to suggestion. She knew that Charlin was lying to her, had spent years watching the Twi'lek show the one face to the Jedi and another to those she looked down on. Charlin thought she was in charge. Charlin thought she'd won. Charlin *always* thought she would win.

Charlin was wrong.

Iskat focused on Charlin's throat, imagined the tenderness of her windpipe, the slender veins under the flesh. She reached out with one hand and slowly brought her fingers together like she was grasping a goblet. She'd been practicing on drinking glasses and then stones and then spiderbats, and . . .

"Iskat!" Charlin gulped, her freed hands fluttering to her throat. "What—"

Iskat's fingers tightened, and Charlin's body began to lift up off the ground, her toes scrabbling for purchase as she choked on nothing.

"You spent so much time lying about me, making me feel like I was something to be feared. Like I was dangerous. Well, guess what?"

Iskat squeezed suddenly, hard, and Charlin's face turned puce as she dangled limply in the air, legs kicking, fingers fluttering uselessly at her neck.

"*I am dangerous.*"

With one more, violent clench of Iskat's fingers, Charlin's body went utterly limp. Iskat's arm fell to her side, and Charlin fell to the floor with a sickening thump.

Iskat headed for the door, smiling, the dark side washing over her like fondly lapping waves.

"I guess you were right, after all," she said.

/ 39.

SUCH A CURIOUS THING, TO take a life.

First Iskat had slaughtered the Geonosians, but they were faceless soldiers in a war.

That was a fair fight.

Then she'd killed the handful of workers beneath the factory on Thule, but that had been an accident, and she hadn't actually seen any corpses; she'd simply thrown the thermal detonators and run.

That was collateral damage.

And then there was Heezo, but he'd chosen to betray her.

That wasn't fair, that wasn't war.

That was punishment.

But this?

This was personal.

As she looked down at Charlin, Iskat didn't feel remorse or shame or sadness.

Charlin was—past tense—a war criminal. The Jedi had betrayed the Republic, and for that reason they'd been wiped out. The Emperor had already ordered her death. And she'd been foolish enough to get captured. Even if Iskat had graciously ignored all the pain Charlin had inflicted upon her personally, Charlin deserved this death.

No, killing a Jedi was far easier than Iskat had anticipated. Charlin's mistake—the Jedi Order's mistake—was that they'd always underestimated Iskat Akaris. They'd never seen her true potential, never appreciated her unique gifts. They'd tried, in a way, to destroy her.

Well, now she would destroy them, one rogue Jedi at a time.

It felt so good, so right, finding her true purpose.

Iskat turned back and briefly ran her hands over Charlin's body, looking for a trophy, but there was nothing of use. Jakadis must've had her searched before throwing her in this cell. Once Iskat had finished her business here, she would find the bounty hunter's cache of artifacts and lightsabers and claim the plain, highly polished hilt she knew to be Charlin's. It would feel so satisfying, placing that lightsaber in the Grand Inquisitor's hand, officially claiming her first Jedi as an Inquisitor.

And if Charlin had been Tualon's target?

All the better.

The hall outside was silent, and Iskat could feel that all of the other cells were empty—except for one. A few doors down, she found a Jedi she didn't recognize, a Zeltron. The moment the door was open, the woman sat up on her bench, hope shining in her eyes.

"Oh, thank the stars—" she began.

Iskat still had her lightsaber in her hand, and before the woman could finish her sentence, she was dead. As the Grand Inquisitor had mentioned, there was no point in giving her time to weave lies or beg for her life. Considering Charlin had arrived here with Klefan, perhaps this Zeltron had been Tualon's prey. Iskat grinned. Either way, she'd claimed them both. Now she just had to find the woman's lightsaber before he could.

Back out in the hall, she cut off all the locks, looked into each sad, stark room. All empty, even of remains. Jakadis must've been selling the Jedi elsewhere. The lock of one cell had already fallen to the ground, suggesting Master Klefan still had some strength. Standing there, Iskat closed her eyes and reached out in the Force. She felt a slight ripple and followed the familiar tug through the maze of halls and stairwells, deeper underground.

The entire fortress was carved from the inside of a mountain, the ancient, pitted lava rock the kind of black that absorbed all light. Iskat used her red blade to illuminate her path, wishing she had time to stop and inspect the sinister carvings, so similar to the ones on Thule. This place felt comfortable, as Thule had, almost welcoming. She could sense the power of the dark side thrumming in the stone itself, soaked in like warm water in a sponge.

The long hallway she was following ended in a large chamber, and the door was already open. Iskat's hearts sped up as she flicked off her blade and hooked it on her back under her cloak. She knew who was in the chamber, and a red blade would only inspire questions she wasn't yet ready to answer. She cloaked herself in the Force, hiding her feelings as she had so carefully learned to do.

The room was lit with torches and lined with empty shelves. Iskat could almost picture what this place had once been like, these shelves filled with texts and holocrons, their impressions in the Force still echoing down from the past as if their ghosts waited patiently to curl an inviting finger at the next generation of Force-users. Now the shelves were empty. Perhaps Jakadis had sold their contents to the highest bidder. Or perhaps, like the Jedi and the Grand Inquisitor, he'd hidden such treasures somewhere secret, keeping them just for himself.

In the center of the room stood a heavy stone chest, and a Jedi Master Iskat knew very well was doing his best to open it. When she'd last seen Klefan Opus, he'd been sitting beside Master Uumay, plump and wise and offering praise that Iskat had greedily absorbed like rain on parched ground. Now he was suffering the effects of captivity, pathetically weak and significantly slimmer without his epidermal sacs filled. His wrists were still bound by shackles as he scrabbled at the heavily adorned top of the carved chest.

"Need some help, Master?" she asked, and he spun to face her, baring his teeth like a trapped animal close to chewing off its leg.

When he saw her, he sagged with relief. "Iskat! Thank the stars! Come help me with this chest." He chuckled, so happy to see her. "I'm afraid unlocking my cell claimed the last of my strength."

When she didn't move, didn't speak, he cocked his head at her. "But where did you come from? Did Jakadis capture you? Did you escape the cells?"

"No."

She walked over and used the Force to gently push the top off the chest, floating it to the ground with barely a sound. Stashed within were three lightsabers, a couple of statues, a holocron, and a few ancient texts that looked like their bindings might disappear in a puff of dust at any moment. Klefan tried to reach within, but he wasn't quite tall enough, and without any strength in the Force, his lightsaber remained just out of his reach.

"A little help for your old instructor?" he asked.

Iskat reached inside and hefted his lightsaber. It was so rare to hold someone else's blade; it was a very personal weapon. Each Jedi selected their kyber crystal and built their lightsaber according to their own unique inspiration and needs. No two were ever alike. Klefan's weapon felt light in her hand—but then again, she'd grown accustomed to her Inquisitor's blade, with its weightier crescent design.

Klefan held out his shackled wrists, looking at her with complete trust.

The absolute fool.

He still thought her a harmless child, a Jedi through and through.

And why wouldn't he?

She had lived for a kind word, had been obedient to a fault, had offered up her hearts and soul and time to whatever teachings he suggested might help her nurture the altruistic Jedi he knew was hidden within.

Ha. It was no Jedi within; it was the dark side, waiting for her to stop holding back.

Iskat thought about just killing old Klefan Opus right then and there, but . . . well, she liked a good fight. If she was going to murder another Jedi, she wanted to taste a little fear, first. She wanted to enjoy it.

She briefly ignited his blade and severed the shackles easily. They fell to the ground, and Klefan rubbed at his wrists. When he reached for his lightsaber, she let him take it.

"It is good indeed to see you, Iskat Akaris. We thought we'd lost you, child."

That old, familiar rage burned behind her eyes.

This man, who still called her *child*.

This man, who had tried so hard to teach her, to blunt her, to diminish her, to mold her into something she was never meant to be.

Did he not know death when he saw it?

"You thought you'd lost me. And that wouldn't be so bad in your mind, would it?" she snapped. "*Rejoice, for she is one with the Force.* That's what you said when my master died, and it brought me no solace. That was the first crack in the foundation of my Jedi teachings. Because it's a lie."

Klefan looked up, and for the first time, Iskat saw something in him besides tranquillity and willful ignorance. She saw recognition. And cunning.

And she realized that, breaking out of his cell, he had sought his lightsaber before attempting to free the other Jedi. Like a coward.

"A lie? Iskat, I can feel your rage. We've worked so hard together over the years to help you overcome it, but I sense that . . ." A look of horrified wonder came over his face. "You're not even fighting it anymore, are you? You've let it in. You're swimming in it." He shook his head sadly, "Oh, Iskat. Child. Don't fall for the cloying promises of the dark side. That way lies—"

"Understanding? Choice? Freedom? The chance to actually feel my emotions instead of stuffing them down? If you had just listened to me, if you had just *seen* me—"

"Oh, I saw you." His voice was rough now. Ragged. Reproachful. "We all did. We saw the tempest waiting to crash out and destroy everything in its path. I always suspected that when the column fell, it was all because you were angry and wanted to hurt Charlin and Onielle." His eyes had gone hard. "Yes, I always suspected it was intentional. But your aim was off, and instead you deprived Tika of her destiny. We thought we could save you, pull you away from the abyss and teach you a better way."

"Save me?" Iskat hated the desperate hurt in her voice, "I didn't need saving! I was born this way, and you tried to teach me that what I was, was wrong. That I was broken. That I required fixing. And I hated you for it."

"We tried to help you become your best self. You were meant for so much more."

Iskat reached to her belt and pulled out her mother's lightsaber, igniting it. The shock on Klefan's yellow-lit face made it clear that he recognized it immediately.

"Tell me what really happened to my mother," she said, almost a growl.

And even though he was starved to emaciation, too weak even to break another lock, Master Klefan's demeanor changed from her patient old tutor to the soldier she'd seen on Geonosis. This was the Klefan Opus that had surprised her while sparring. This was the Klefan Opus that could lie. His shoulders went back, his feet shuffled into a more defensive stance. He didn't ignite his own lightsaber, but it was ready.

"Are you threatening me, child?" he asked sharply.

Iskat gritted her teeth and deactivated her mother's blade.

Too soon, too soon to strike him down.

"I'm asking for the truth."

Klefan considered her for a long moment before answering.

"Your mother was taken from her planet as a child as soon as she showed signs of Force sensitivity. She was raised in the crèche, just like you, and grew to be a middling Padawan. She did not complete the Jedi trials." He paused as she digested this. "It was the Trial of the Spirit that got her. She lacked focus and concentration, couldn't control her mind. Just like you, Iskat. But we'd been too easy with her, had assumed her species simply matured more slowly. That was our mistake. She left questioning everything, unsure of herself. It was as if her spirit had broken. Although she was offered civilian work in the Jedi Temple, she chose to walk away entirely. She was escorted back to her homeworld and delivered safely to her family."

Iskat's dream flashed in her vision, the pain on her mother's face as her life as a Jedi ended.

"A few years later, her child was identified as Force-sensitive." He inclined his head. "One of Feyra's old friends was sent to collect you."

"Master Vey," Iskat supplied.

Klefan nodded. "Yes. Feyra made Sember promise to help you. Feyra knew you belonged with the Jedi, wanted great things for you, but she didn't want you to fail, as she had. She had trouble readjusting to life among her people. She hoped her dreams would live on through you, that you would become the great Jedi she had longed to be. And so eventually Sember claimed you as her Padawan."

Iskat was reeling. "So that's why I never felt a connection with Master Vey. It wasn't the Force that brought us together—it was a promise. I always felt like a burden, like she didn't even like me, like she didn't want to teach me. But she was keeping her promise to my mother, sacrificing her own true calling to tame me. I . . . I know I barely passed my Initiate Trials. She knew it, too." Hot tears coursed down her cheeks as she finally understood.

"The burden was not yours, Iskat," Klefan said gently. "It was Sember's. She made a choice. Your master believed in you deeply, in your potential and in your ability to become a great Jedi. But she knew firsthand where Feyra had failed, and so she urged you to find calm and focus where others may have pushed you to train. She felt it was her duty to guide you, to help you become something greater; she felt it was the will of the Force."

Iskat shook her head, feelings tumbling through her hearts. "Even this is a betrayal! Sember chose me for all the wrong reasons, and you all allowed her to do so! I never felt any connection with any master, never felt any strong calling. Maybe washing out would've been better. I could've returned to my family, who actually loved me. I could've gone home before it was too late."

"There are no mistakes in the Force, child," Klefan said with more kindness. "You can't cheat your way through the trials. If you passed, even if barely, it was meant to be. Your mother didn't have the strength to become a Jedi. She was like you, but also different."

Iskat looked up. "You keep speaking of her in the past tense . . ."

Klefan reached out to put a hand on her shoulder, and to her own surprise, she allowed it. "Her mind was never the same after she called the Jedi to claim you. She put you in Sember's arms and made her promise that we would keep you safe and help you reach the dreams she had been forced to give up. Sember could tell that she wasn't well, that she was heartsick. Once you were settled in the crèche, she returned to Pkori one more time to help Feyra work through her grief, but there was nothing she could do. Feyra pushed her away, pushed everyone away. And then she went out into the desert of your home planet and . . . took her own life. Sember and I felt it in the Force, when it happened. I'm so sorry you have another burden to bear, but you wanted the truth, and I've kept it from you for too long."

Iskat shook his hand off her shoulder and stepped back, hate flooding her chest. "She was broken, and yet you didn't help her. You abandoned her to die. The Jedi teach that all life is precious!"

"Her destiny in the Force was her own. All is as the Force wills it. Rejoice—"

"No! No, I am done rejoicing in the death of the people I love!"

The world seemed to spin around Iskat as the final piece fell into place.

Her mother truly was gone.

She had taken her own life because she'd lost everything—her future, her lightsaber, her friends, her home, her connection with the Force.

Her daughter.

And all because of the Jedi.

"But Iskat, you must remember that your mother lives on in you," Klefan went on gently as if a seismic change hadn't just shattered Iskat's hearts. "Your mother called the Jedi, put you in Sember's arms, trusted us to guide you on a better path. We strove to make you strong where she was fragile, tranquil where she was tempestuous. You inherited her future. You succeeded where she failed. All her hopes live on in you, and the galaxy needs you. After we rescue Charlin and take care of this Jakadis fellow, we will go into hiding, and—"

"No."

Klefan went still. "No?"

Iskat took a deep breath and stood tall. "Why go into hiding when I have found my rightful purpose? If I am the scion of my mother's hopes, then why would she want me to return to the Jedi Order that failed both of us, and the galaxy? I have chosen to free my hearts and soul from the shackles that have held me down for so long. I refuse to bury the parts of myself that I love best. My mother wasn't weak and fragile, she was just unwilling to allow you to hobble and oppress her. In the end, she wanted to be free of the Jedi, and so she chose her own freedom. I lived too long under those strict edicts, always feeling like a different animal entirely, repressing my true power so that you would find me acceptable and palatable." She snorted. "What a waste of a life."

"Iskat, the dark side has lied to you. You must not give way to your anger—"

"Silence!" Her voice echoed hungrily off the black stone, as if it had waited all too long to feed on such baneful emotions. "I will not take orders from those who have never felt this pain, who have never made any real sacrifice or been sent out to die. You, with your slavish devotion to platitudes—you sat in the Temple meditating while the Jedi ordered us about like holochess pieces! While they let the war drag out, slaughtering millions, murdering their own, just to further weaken the Republic so it would be primed for their attack. You went to Geonosis but stayed out of the arena!"

"We were under orders—"

A snort of derision. "Of course you were. You were just doing what you were told, weren't you? People like you, *cowards* like you—you destroy because you never aggress, you kill with your false hope and impotent strategies. Entire populations died because the Jedi Order chose to wait and see, because you sent your warriors to the planets with the loudest senators instead of the loudest screams, because you wouldn't sacrifice one to save millions. You tell yourselves you're the defenders of the weak, the peacekeepers of all, but you only bring heartbreak and death and betrayal wherever you go." She pointed at him with a long, gloved finger. "If you'd done better by my mother, she'd still be here. Maybe she would've been the master I deserved."

"Iskat, this isn't you. This is the dark side talking, the sinister, cloying energies of this place—"

She curled her fingers, and Klefan whimpered as his throat began to close.

It was easier this time, somehow.

"I will no longer give power to those who would diminish me," she whispered.

She squeezed with her fingers, grinning, feeling the Force begin to constrict around Klefan's throat—

But the Jedi Master extended his own hand, and buffeted her back with a burst of energy, breaking free of her grip.

"I don't want to fight you, child," he said, igniting his lightsaber. "But I will."

/ 40.

ISKAT HAD SPENT MANY HOURS learning lightsaber forms and gently sparring with Jedi Master Klefan Opus. She'd seen him hold his lightsaber at Geonosis, although he hadn't used it against aggressors. She'd seen him patiently teaching the younglings. But other than that one time he'd tested her she'd never seen him actually fight, and she had no idea what to expect, now that it was life or death. He was old and starved, and with his epidermal sacs empty he seemed weak and deflated and awkwardly balanced. And yet . . . he was a Jedi Master. He'd been a Jedi for a long time. Underestimating him would've been a mistake.

For now, she left her red blade on her back and savored the rightness of striking him down with the last lightsaber her mother had touched. Before with Master Klefan, she had always held back to consider things, but this time she immediately aggressed as Vader had taught her, driving him backward with a flurry of slashes and jabs that he parried with an ancient, patient energy. Even under duress, Master Klefan had a tranquillity about him—nothing like the distracted tolerance of Sember Vey, the sternness of Mace Windu, the by-the-book sensibility of Master Gallia, or the playfulness of Yoda—but when he fought, it was as if he were meditating with his blade. When he finally struck back, he had more power than she'd anticipated. Iskat somersaulted backward, giving herself room to maneuver. Perhaps the old man could still fight, but he definitely wasn't built for acrobatics.

"Is this what your mother would want?" he asked as he advanced upon her, lightsaber protectively up. "After all that she sacrificed for you, after the promises she extracted on your behalf, would she want to see you throw it all away and turn to the dark side?"

Iskat knew better than to let him get under her skin. She attacked with the same measured calm; she could wear him down gradually, if need be. "You keep saying there was an anger, an energy in me that you tried to repress. That you saw it in her, too, but failed to control it. What if it was always the dark side, calling to us both? What if we were never meant to be Jedi in the first place?"

"The dark side is seductive," he countered. "It would whisper anything in your ear if it would bring you under its reign. Promise you the stars if it meant securing your heart. It is foolish to assume it would tell you the truth when lies serve it so very well."

"Ah, but the dark side and I get along so much better. I've developed new talents I didn't even know existed because the Jedi hide their knowledge so carefully. If I wasn't meant to have these skills, why do they come to me so naturally? Unlike your meditation, which you forced upon me, and which felt like torture."

"Candy is sweet, vegetables are bitter, but we know which one is better for our health. We know which one will rot our teeth, if left unchecked."

Iskat ducked and spun, forcing the old Jedi to leap or lose his feet at the ankle. He was more nimble than she'd anticipated, but it had cost him. He stumbled when he landed and barely managed to catch himself in time to turn and block her next strike.

"We could start over," he said, beginning to breathe heavily. "We could start anew. The Jedi Order is gone, but perhaps there is a middle ground, where we take the best of the old teachings and explore new paths."

Iskat chuckled. "You would sacrifice your morals to bring me back into the fold? Either that, or you're just lying to buy time. I've seen you lie before. The Jedi are traitors who deserve to die; there will be no chance for redemption. Or are you waiting for Charlin to come save you?"

"She is the brightest student in your cohort."

That little barb struck deeper than Iskat would've preferred.

"If that were true, she would be standing here before you, instead of lying broken where I left her. I guess you were either too weak or too busy saving your own skin to feel her become one with the Force."

Klefan's eyebrows rose. His jowls trembled as realization crashed down.

He was alone here, surrounded by enemies.

But he wasn't giving up. Iskat saw his will coalesce, saw him call on the Force to sustain him. A renewed calmness came over his features, an ease to his body. He focused on her in a way that he never had before, as if seeing her for the first time and determining that she was, in fact, a formidable foe.

He attacked then, using a form she hadn't studied—another one that he hadn't taught her. Iskat hurried to parry and block his lightsaber strikes, off balance as she briefly lost control of the bout. Yes, Master Klefan had always struck her as a patient, indulgent teacher, but he had a lifetime of Jedi training under his belt and had apparently taken care not to teach her certain things—just like a Jedi, to withhold pertinent information in case it could be used against an enemy later.

Still, she had at least one advantage he didn't.

Iskat jumped over his blade, flipping in the air and landing on top of the chest, one foot on either side of the open box containing artifacts of great interest. They called to her like hungry children, but she ignored them. Klefan approached, his intent clear in his eyes, and Iskat pulled her Inquisitor's blade off her back, igniting it as she leapt at him, screaming as she slashed downward with both lightsabers, red and yellow. The red blade caught the old Master on the shoulder, and he fell to his side and struggled to stand, losing his own lightsaber in the process.

Iskat landed lightly, stalking toward him, her hearts thumping in time like a great drum. She felt the furious, singing call of murder in her blood, as if the planet itself rejoiced in this death they both wanted so very much. She stood over her old teacher, blades crossed, his neck in the V formed by the red and yellow beams of deadly energy.

"Iskat, I know there is still good in you—" Klefan began.

The blades slashed violently, and his head slid sideways and landed on the floor.

"Yes, but there is so much more than that," she finished for him.

Iskat deactivated her blades, storing them at back and belt before she reached down to claim Klefan's lightsaber. Then she crossed back to the chest and claimed the other two lightsabers within, slipping them into the hidden pockets of her breeches. As she turned to leave, she looked down at what remained of the once great Jedi Master, and her lips curled into a smile.

"Rejoice. For he is one with the Force."

/ 41.

FOR A LONG MOMENT, ISKAT'S voice echoed against the stone, and then ancient silence descended. This place, this fortress, this temple—it felt pleased with her, as if she had performed some long-forgotten ritual.

Somewhere in the darkness, someone clapped gloved hands.

Iskat pulled and lit her lightsabers again, calling, "Who's there?"

A cloaked figure appeared from the shadows, where she now spotted a hidden door. The newcomer was short and wiry, exuding smug confidence and bristling with weapons. His shiny gold mask, furred cloak, armor, and knee-high boots seemed designed to make him appear bigger and more menacing than he truly was.

Iskat was not impressed.

"Congratulations on your triumph. That was an excellent duel. And an excellent philosophy, if you don't mind my saying so." His voice was cultured, smarmy, almost greasy.

Iskat pointed her red blade at him. "I take it you're Jakadis?"

He executed a courtly bow. "*Lord* Jakadis, in the flesh. I don't normally reveal myself—that's what protocol droids are for, are they not? But I couldn't pass up the chance to speak to you myself. Forget the Jedi and whatever new organization you serve. There are other destinies. Bounty hunters have no gods, no masters. You could live a life free from political or religious influence—free from any influence. You could be truly free, beyond hierarchy. The earning potential is boundless. Together, we could—"

Iskat did not want to know what he thought they could do together, so she set her red lightsaber spinning and threw it at him, adding another decapitated head to the room's stark décor. Perhaps she'd been sent here to kill the Jedi, but she imagined the Grand Inquisitor would be glad to know this puffed-up Jedi poacher was gone as well. The lightsaber returned to her hand like a loyal hound.

She felt no more ripples in the Force, no more living beings larger than the tiny salamanders and snails that lived in the cracks of the fortress, but she was curious about how a pathetic little nothing like Jakadis had managed to sneak up on her. She'd been consumed with Master Klefan, too focused to notice the interloper. Through the hidden door he'd used, she discovered a grand throne room with a tall, carved seat rising up from the center of a black pool. As she walked down the promenade, she felt as if she were part of an ancient ceremony. Long ago, dark side users had walked here, their reflections rippling in the inky water. Someone of great power had sat in this throne; she could feel echoes of their authority soaking the stone like blood. She deactivated her blade and sat on the pitted black seat, her hands on the dragons carved into the arms. For a moment, it was as if she could see hooded acolytes all in black lining the pool with their perfumed censers, chanting in a dead tongue as their queen ascended her throne.

For a moment, Iskat was that queen.

This, this was where she belonged.

Not among the Jedi, not on her homeworld, not as some petty bounty hunter.

She was meant for a different path, and the dark side would be her companion.

A flagon of deep-red wine sat at her left hand, probably abandoned by Jakadis, but his time here had left no impression in the rock. Perhaps he'd thought himself a ruler, but he was nothing but another blood offering to this thirsty stone. Iskat sniffed the wine and sipped it, tasting spiced fruits and age and ash.

This would be her tradition, she decided. Each time she hunted a Jedi and eliminated her prey, she would taste whatever beverage the locals drank, take the moment into her body as a re-creation of this ritual she'd found deep in a long-forgotten Sith fortress. She held up the glass to the empty room.

"To Charlin and Klefan," she said before drinking deeply until the last drop was gone.

The sweet liquid sang through her blood, making her giddy and languid. She hadn't tasted spirits before, but it was as if she could see shadows moving now, as if layers and layers of Force-users walked around her as unseeing ghosts.

Satisfied, she rose and returned to the treasure room. She had no way to carry all the artifacts in the chest for later scrutiny, so she unclipped Jakadis's cloak and used it as a makeshift sack. Without it, he seemed so small and inconsequential. But then again, most beings did, now that she'd stepped fully into her powers.

She found Sixty-Seven waiting in the original welcome room, blaster spinning on her the moment she appeared. He offered no thoughts on where she'd been or how long he'd been waiting. As they strode down the long hall toward the main door, Iskat felt another signature in the Force nearby. She tuned her comlink to the right channel.

"Tualon, where are you?"

"I thought we weren't going to cooperate?"

"We don't have to. I have already found my quarry. And yours."

She drank in the moment of his stunned silence.

"I take it you're not going to give me the lightsaber?"

She smiled to herself. "No. I've had enough of you claiming my glory. But you're welcome to try to take it from me, if you dare." It came out flirty, and for once, she wasn't ashamed.

As for Tualon, he actually considered it. "I don't want to fight you. But perhaps there's another way I could win your favor."

The way he said it made her hearts pound and her body heat up. But even if her hormones were moved, her ambitions remained unswayed.

"I'm only going to say this one time, so hear me well. If you want me, don't let some bounty come between us," she finally said. "I'm not playing games anymore. Either it's real, or it's nothing. I will not be seduced away from my own success."

She waited a long moment as he thought about it.

"You win this one fair and square," he finally said. "I suppose I wouldn't want to try lying to the Grand Inquisitor, anyway. I can prove myself on my own." A brief pause. "And we'll see how you might be seduced." The comlink went silent.

As she and Sixty-Seven walked back to her ship, she watched Tualon's ship take off from just a few klicks away and zip into the sky.

Now, this was a version of Tualon she could respect. Honest with himself and others, ambitious and confident. She looked forward to seeing where the seduction might come in. For all that she'd been drawn to him since they were children, he'd always been neutral toward her, never felt that same tug. But now, freed from the rigidity of the Jedi ways, perhaps he was finally realizing how powerful a partner she might be.

They would make a good team, but not if he thought he was in charge.

No one could rule Iskat Akaris.

/ 42.

BACK ON CORUSCANT, ISKAT CARRIED her cloak of artifacts through the halls of the Inquisitorius Headquarters. She'd already absorbed all the information she'd found in Jakadis's fortress on the flight back, and she'd chosen a few special pieces to keep for herself. These leftover texts and statues might win her some favor, but they wouldn't give any other Inquisitors an advantage once they were added to the library. She understood how it worked now. She would take what she wanted and leave the scraps for everyone else to fight over.

They were waiting for her in the Grand Inquisitor's chambers—the Grand Inquisitor himself and Darth Vader.

"Was your first mission a success?" the Grand Inquisitor asked.

Iskat placed three lightsabers on the pedestal in the center of the chamber.

"You have done well, Iskat Akaris," Darth Vader said.

She looked up into his implacable mask and smiled.

She'd made her choice.

"I am Iskat Akaris no more," she told them. "Call me Thirteenth Sister."

EPILOGUE

YEARS LATER

IT SEEMED LIKE THE USUAL sort of mission. The Thirteenth Sister had been on dozens of trips as an Inquisitor, working alone and with others, and she always succeeded. She was known for her tenacity as well as her predilection for beheadings. She had personally survived being stabbed through the chest, and Tualon—she still couldn't get used to his new name—had been shot multiple times by clone troopers during the Purge, and that meant she wanted to make sure that anyone she killed stayed dead. The Grand Inquisitor finally commanded her to stop bringing bloody heads back to his chamber, as the mouse droids got gunked up with gore and she'd already killed their best droid technician.

Although the Thirteenth Sister would never be truly comfortable around Vader, she'd learned that they had a lot in common, including a lasting hatred of the Jedi and their unforgivable crimes. He was no longer generally a danger to the Inquisitorius; after fighting each new Inquisitor when they received their red blade, anyone left alive was happy to leave with whatever limbs he allowed them to keep, and after that they were merely his deputies. Vader told her where to go, and she went. She had not yet disappointed him and did not want to find out what would happen if she did.

She was pleased the day she was included in one of Vader's personal missions—the hunt for a Jedi who'd been kicked off the Jedi High Council before the Purge and had therefore escaped the fate that befell the majority of his old peers. Eeth Koth had settled on some nowhere desert planet, joined a church, and married like he was just some normal person and not a war criminal. Vader was determined to do what Order 66 had not. That was all the Thirteenth Sister knew. Until Vader told her differently, that was all she needed to know.

Once they'd landed on the planet, Vader told his Inquisitors to follow him and strode down the ramp of his ship. They were in a city like any other, the sort of place where Jedi always seemed to end up hiding—a useless world filled with sand and inelegant buildings worn away by wind and time, a place where people scraped together pathetic little lives and fought over water and were buried in unmarked graves or turned into bricks. Along with Tualon and the Fifth Brother, she stalked along behind her master, glad that her helmet kept her eyes free from the sand that whipped around in the wind.

"Wait here," Vader said just outside a circular courtyard that provided some shade from the pounding heat.

The Inquisitors nodded their assent and watched him use telekinesis to open the door. Just inside, the Thirteenth Sister could feel the presence of someone knowledgeable in the Force—and a fresh new life that held the promise of greatness.

"There's a child," she said.

Tualon strained to see past the gleaming black figure blocking the open door. "Wonder if he'll kill it, too."

"Silence," the Fifth Brother hissed. "He said to wait, not make annoying chatter."

A massive boom from inside the building focused their attention on the door, but they knew better than to disobey Vader's orders. If he told them to wait here, he expected them to wait here, not go running inside to get in the way of the fight that was clearly raging in the small home.

Soon they could hear the clash of lightsabers within. A hole exploded through the wall of the building, and a Zabrak male with a green lightsaber appeared, holding his own against Darth Vader. Tualon eased closer to Thirteenth Sister and gave her a small, secret smile, which she returned. They'd always found an easy rhythm when sparring, all the way back to their days as Jedi Knights. Now that they'd both fully given in to the dark side, it was as if they could tap into the same comm frequency, their minds working in tandem.

They were a formidable pair in any fight, to say nothing of what happened in secret corners of the massive Inquisitorius Headquarters, far from where any of their brothers or sisters might discover their dalliance. Relationships were not forbidden among the Inquisitors, but they knew the others would see their mutual affection as weakness. When everyone was constantly fighting for scraps of power and rank, caring for someone was a vulnerability. Iskat had been promised freedom in the Inquisitorius, but that freedom had its limits.

"Fear. Anger. Resentment. I sense them in you," Vader said as he dueled the Zabrak. "You have let yourself feel, Eeth Koth. It gives you power. More than the Jedi would ever have allowed you."

It was true, and Thirteenth Sister knew that for herself. All those years she'd been commanded by the Jedi to tamp down her feelings, and in doing so she'd been tamping down her power, too. Now that she'd welcomed the dark side, trained among the Inquisitors, and studied holocrons and texts forbidden by the Jedi, she was more formidable than ever. Was Vader going to invite this Eeth Koth to join the Inquisitorius? she wondered. Was there even a need for another Inquisitor when their prey dwindled on a daily basis?

"Perhaps it's the Zabrak in me," Eeth Koth said, fighting valiantly in what should've been a swift tussle ending in Vader's triumph. "Or perhaps now I have something to lose."

"Whatever the cause, it's too late." As if in punctuation, Vader threw the Zabrak to the ground in a puff of red sand.

"Inquisitors—a woman and an infant escaped," Vader said, his flat black helmet lit red by his lightsaber. "Bring me the child."

"And the woman, Lord Vader?" the Fifth Brother asked.

"Irrelevant." Vader returned to his fight, leaving the trio of Inquisitors to do his bidding.

Tualon already had his lightsaber in hand. "Any thoughts on how we approach this? This city's not exactly small. Plenty of places to hide."

"Split up. We'll cover more ground. Stay in contact. Whoever finds them, bring in the others," the Fifth Brother said.

For once, the Thirteenth Sister didn't argue with him. "Agreed, Fifth Brother. They couldn't have gotten far—I mean, the woman just pushed out a baby."

With a nod, they each ran in a different direction.

Once the Thirteenth Sister was a few blocks away from her fellow Inquisitors, she stopped and reached out in the Force—a skill neither of them had honed to the extent she had. She'd always been more sensitive than most, but now, instead of holding her back, it gave her an edge.

"Child of a Jedi . . ." she muttered to herself, hand outstretched. "Let's see if you make any ripples in the Force, little one."

She'd felt it before, outside the home, and she felt it now. "Aha! There you are."

Rather than calling Tualon and the Fifth Brother like she'd agreed, she darted through the city, past crumbling buildings and along a dock over lapping blue water. She could feel the child moving swiftly through the city, knew the mother must be beyond desperate.

There.

Headed for a transport shuttle, the exhausted mother staggered toward the ramp.

"Come, Mira! Quickly! We must be away!" an older Zabrak male called from the ship.

But the Thirteenth Sister ignited her red blade as she moved to block the ramp.

"Or perhaps you could stay awhile," she said.

"No!" the mother begged, sweat dripping down her face. "Please. Please. Woman-to-woman. Don't take her. Don't take my child."

Deep in the Thirteenth Sister's chest, an old memory that wasn't even her own stirred, a child given up by a loving mother, forced into a different life. A baby, passed from one set of arms to another, a ship waiting . . .

"I—"

The woman cradled the baby to her chest, her eyes streaming tears.

"Go. Just go," the Thirteenth Sister said tiredly. She let her lightsaber fall, no longer blocking the ramp.

"Thank you," the woman said, looking deep into her eyes before running onto the ship, barefoot and still in her stained birthing gown.

As the shuttle took off with the mother and child, Tualon and the Fifth Brother ran up to join the Thirteenth Sister.

"You let them go?" Tualon asked, incredulous. "When Vader finds out, he'll . . ." He shook his head. "What have you done?"

The Thirteenth Sister looked at him, her lips twitching with amusement. "Done? Nothing's done . . ."

The shuttle was in the air now, laboriously turning to leave. But the Thirteenth Sister could still see the mother standing there foolishly at the open-air viewport, looking down at her baby with the sort of smile that promised everything would be okay.

"Come to Mama," the Thirteenth Sister said, holding out her long, red fingers and snatching the child from her mother's arms using the Force.

All those years ago, when she'd brought down the column, she'd been so clumsy. But now, after years of practice, the baby floated gently toward her through space, tiny limbs flailing for its mother. She had the Jedi to thank, in part, for that control.

Deep in the Thirteenth Sister's soul, a bottomless well of rage bubbled and churned, a once brilliant fire twisted by the dark side. Perhaps in the past she might've felt sadness for this mother and child, might've recognized the wrongness of separating them. Perhaps once she would've considered what her own mother had felt, giving her up, would've seen a reflection of Feyra's pain in Mira's eyes.

But now she was an Inquisitor. Even if they hadn't broken her like they had Tualon and some of the others, she'd . . . changed. The Sith holocrons in her chamber whispered to her in her sleep, and dark energy seeped out of the altars she kept near her bed like swamp gas creeping into every crevice. She could feel it, almost like a vapor suffusing the very air, and she willingly breathed in deeply. The dark side had always been part of her, and she welcomed its ongoing enrichment, knowing it would only make her stronger.

She had grown to love cruelty, and she knew only that the child belonged in Vader's hands or dead, that it belonged anywhere but in the hands of a treasonous Jedi and his Jedi-loving wife.

"No!" the mother cried, reaching vainly through the viewport as the ship disappeared into the sky.

The child landed in the Thirteenth Sister's outstretched hands. "See?" she told Tualon.

"Never should've doubted you," he said fondly. "But why?"

"Because she appealed to me, woman-to-woman." The Thirteenth Sister looked into the child's pinched, screaming face. "Now she'll never trust another woman again. Or, most likely, anyone. I took her baby, and I took her soul."

And it felt good.

It felt *right*.

It felt like payback for what she'd suffered as a child.

If this Eeth Koth and his wife couldn't protect their baby, then did they truly deserve the chance to raise it? Ever since the Purge, Koth had simply been a walking corpse. Time had caught up to him, that was all. And Vader had claimed this child for reasons of his own.

The Thirteenth Sister carried the child in one hand as she led her brothers back to where Vader would be waiting. Her cape snapped in the hot air as the child squalled and squirmed. It felt disgusting to her, like a grub, but she was as gentle as she knew how to be.

The Inquisitors found Vader still dueling Eeth Koth—or playing with him. The man had been nearly beaten to rags, while Vader looked as he always did, timeless and inevitable in gleaming plasteel and leather.

"I will save my family," Koth said, desperate, his lightsaber shaking in his exhausted grasp.

"Do you think so?" Vader asked, gesturing with his lightsaber as he watched the Thirteenth Sister approach.

"Mission accomplished, boss," she said, holding up the child.

Koth couldn't help focusing on the infant in her hand, and that was his mistake. Vader ran him through with his red blade, and not in some harmless place that might be mended in a medbay. Koth fell to the ground, leaving his child fatherless. Not that it mattered; the child would soon have a new home. Vader took the baby, its pinched face reflected in his visor as it screamed.

"Quiet," he commanded.

The child instantly fell silent and did not cry again.

Back on Coruscant, the Thirteenth Sister watched as Vader handed the child over to a pair of nanny droids under the watchful eye of the Grand Inquisitor.

"Ah, Lord Vader. Welcome back. It seems your mission was successful on at least one level."

But Vader's response did not sit well with her.

"I was successful on every level, Grand Inquisitor. Eeth Koth is dead. Your Inquisitors performed their roles well."

The praise was unusual and welcome, but Vader had claimed the victory as his own. Perhaps he'd lauded the Inquisitors, but he knew full well that the Thirteenth Sister was the one who had found the child before the ship could take off. Tualon and the Fifth Brother had failed. If not for her advanced senses, they might've missed the ship's launch entirely and lost their quarry. And yet he'd reduced her work to a single sentence giving equal praise to her brothers.

Dissatisfaction writhed through her like eels. She had never been so foolish as to assume that the Inquisitorius would be perfect, but she was sick of doing all the work only so that her superiors could pat themselves on the back. The infighting and backbiting were ferocious, and if not for her deepening relationship with Tualon, she would've felt even more alone than she had among the Jedi.

When she'd stood there, surrounded by troopers with blasters, forced to choose death or something else, the Grand Inquisitor had promised her freedom.

This is no freedom.

She was just as tethered, just as held back. She could only go where she was ordered to go. That brief independence in her first few weeks here that had allowed her to go to Pkori? That window had closed almost immediately, once the Inquisitorius had been up and running at full strength. Now life had been reduced to missions and time in the medbay. She couldn't say no. She could only bow her head and say, "Yes, Grand Inquisitor," and hurry to her ship. Saying no—or even thinking about saying no—meant Vader might invite someone into the sparring ring, and then they might lose an eye or an arm.

At least she still had Tualon. At least she still had something like trust.

After their successful mission, all the present Inquisitors gathered in the common room in some grim echo of a party. No one trusted anyone, no one particularly *liked* anyone, and yet the Grand Inquisitor wanted them all together like some twisted approximation of a family.

Sitting down at a table with Tualon, she pulled a plain bottle from her bag and put two glasses down. Tualon watched her pouring the amber liquid but did not smile. He generally, wisely, only smiled for her in secret, when they were alone.

"To one less Jedi in the galaxy," he said, holding up his drink.

"To one less Jedi," she repeated.

They drank, and the rough liquor burned a trail down the Thirteenth Sister's throat.

"Eeugh, what is this stuff?" he asked her, spluttering.

"It's called dust juice. Disgusting but potent," she told him. "We said we'd drink something local from everywhere we kill a Jedi. Believe it or not, this is the best that horrible planet had to offer."

It had originally been her own personal tradition, of course, begun in the Sith throne room Jakadis had foolishly attempted to claim as his own. That wine had been a fine vintage, deep and red and warm as blood. But this stuff left a horrid taste in her mouth . . . much like the way Vader had stolen her thunder.

Tualon leaned forward. "I hope the next Jedi's hiding out on Corellia or Alderaan. Those planets know their way around a libation. I mean . . . dust juice? Brutal."

The Thirteenth Sister poured them each another glass, hoping to blunt her rage before someone else noticed it. None of the other Inquisitors asked to partake of the bottle; several of them had made it clear they regarded this little ritual as childish.

"You know, it won't be too long until there won't *be* a next Jedi," she said. She'd been thinking about it a lot lately, actually—the future. With so many Inquisitors and Darth Vader constantly at work . . .

Well, perhaps it was time for the next stage of her plan.

She'd promised herself that when the galaxy was safe, she'd return to Pkori and, for the first time ever, live life on her own terms. Maybe it was time. Maybe Tualon would join her.

"Yeah, we've gotten too good at our jobs," he agreed.

"What do you suppose he'll do when they're all gone?"

"Who do you mean?"

She looked at Tualon, and the world swam a little. The dust juice may have tasted like the water rinsed off a filthy bantha, but it was strong.

"You know. Him," she said, eyes sliding toward Darth Vader.

Tualon took up his glass, and she briefly wondered if she should stop him from drinking it. When he drank, he lost inhibitions, and that meant that he spoke a little too loud, made himself a little too vulnerable. It was fine, even welcome when they were alone—he'd told her several shocking secrets about his former life among the Jedi—but just now, surrounded by people who would love a reason to attack one of their own, the Thirteenth Sister wanted to keep him safe. For herself.

"Oh, right," he said, and an indiscreet smile crept onto his face. "I don't know. I'm sure he'll keep himself busy. A guy like that . . ."

The Thirteenth Sister felt a cold shadow fall over their table, but Tualon was oblivious.

"He'll always find someone to kill," he finished, throwing back his glass as Vader loomed over them and ignited his lightsaber.

For a long moment, there was no movement, no sound but the hum of Vader's lightsaber.

"Lord Vader . . . is this a test?" the Grand Inquisitor asked cautiously. "More training?"

The Thirteenth Sister could feel Vader in the Force, and was sure it was a test, but she couldn't communicate that to Tualon, and the absolute fool was too drunk to realize that he was projecting his feelings too much, that his concern for the Thirteenth Sister was pulsing along with her hearts—

Vader sensed it, too.

Was it a test?

"No," he said.

His red blade arced down toward the Thirteenth Sister, but Tualon pulled his own lightsaber in time and caught Vader's strike.

"Interesting," Vader said, as if they were having a general conversation around a cup of caf.

"Run!" Tualon shouted, and the Thirteenth Sister made her choice. She ran.

When she was just out of sight, she heard Vader say, "I sensed a connection between the two of you. An attachment. A weakness you believe is strength. The death of Eeth Koth should have served as a lesson to you about such things." The Thirteenth Sister heard her lover's body slam against the wall.

"Apparently it did not," Vader finished.

"Why, what did she do?" Tualon asked as he stood, still worried for her.

"That does not matter. Concern yourself with only one thing." A menancing pause. "Now you've done it, too."

Tualon was already up and running, and the Thirteenth Sister slightly slowed until he ran by her side, her lightsaber ready in her hand. Vader wasn't directly behind them, but then again, running wasn't one of his many skills. Knowing Tualon was still a little muddled with dust juice, the Thirteenth Sister took the lead, heading outside toward the busy skylanes of Coruscant.

"You're sure you have no idea why Vader attacked us?" Tualon asked her.

Oh, she had an idea.

Vader had felt it.

Not just her . . . yes, fine, call it *love* for Tualon.

Her affection and tenderness and weakness.

But also . . . her general dissatisfaction.

Her anger.

Her rebellion.

Underneath the hard exterior of the Thirteenth Sister, Iskat Akaris still desperately longed to be truly free.

To take orders from no one, to fear no one, to go where she willed and do as she wished.

She wanted to go to Pkori again, finally see the beauty of Corellia, and pretend she was just some silly fool in love.

It was getting to be boring, just being someone else's soldier.

But she wasn't about to tell another Inquisitor that.

She'd told someone her true feelings once and look where that had gotten both of them. She was here, and Heezo was dead.

"Are you insane? I know better than to cross him," she said—which was also true. "Look, Vader doesn't need a reason to kill people. He just kills them." It wasn't enough, though. She'd had feelings for this man for so long, feelings that had changed and morphed and grown over the years. And he finally cared for her, too, and he'd done this foolish, foolish thing. For her. "I just can't believe you got in his way for me, I mean."

He flashed a sharp grin. "I've told you how I feel. I guess now I've proven it."

And he had. He'd told her, late one night, after several glasses of Toniray White, that he loved her, and she'd purred in the back of her throat and stroked his lekku and said, "I've been waiting my whole life for you to say that." But she didn't return the sentiment. After Heezo, she couldn't trust anyone with feelings that real.

"I guess you have," she said now, hearts fluttering even as she ran at top speed down a catwalk. "Still, it was stupid. He'll be coming for us." They'd reached the end of the catwalk, and she leapt over the edge, igniting her lightsaber. "We'll have to kill him. No other way."

"I know, and then we run." He was in the air beside her, falling gracefully, a once perfect Jedi now a perfect Inquisitor, a fully confident killing machine. And then he said the most beautiful thing she'd ever heard. "Not easy, but think about this. If we pull it off . . ." He turned to look at her, backlit by the Coruscant sunset. "We're free."

As she hurtled through the air, she picked her target, a simple speeder, pointing it out to Tualon.

Tualon, whom she was supposed to call her *brother*. But this wasn't a family. These weren't her siblings. The others monsters.

She didn't even like them, and she was sick of pretending they were equals.

If Vader wanted her dead, then she didn't have to pretend to be an Inquisitor, whatever it was. She could kill him first and escape. Follow her hearts and intuition around the galaxy.

And if she really felt a need, she could kill Jedi on her own without being ordered around all the time and attacked out of nowhere.

She and Tualon landed gently on their target, and the speeder driver turned around to stare at them in utter disbelief.

"Keep driving," she snapped, and he did, because what else was he going to do?

A pulsating quiver in the Force pulled her attention back to the traffic lanes, where Vader rode on his own speeder, driven by shock troopers.

"Keep him steady," she told Tualon.

Using the Force, she yanked an engine off a passing speeder and threw it at Vader with all her might. It missed him but tanked his speeder, sending it down in a fiery heap. The Dark Lord of the Sith lightly leapt off his plummeting ride and landed on a second speeder.

"Now!" Iskat told Tualon, and they threw their spinning lightsabers directly at him, shearing his speeder into three useless chunks. Vader didn't leap this time—he fell.

And then managed to land on a new speeder, as if he'd done this a dozen times.

"We need something bigger," Tualon said as they caught their returning lightsabers. He turned to Iskat, grinning. "Throw a speeder at him, darling."

So Iskat returned his grin and unleashed the burning power inside her, flinging a speeder at Darth Vader at a velocity that should've crushed him—

But didn't, because he returned the favor, throwing the speeder right back.

It was in that moment that Iskat realized that sparring with Vader . . . wasn't sparring.

That even if the Inquisitors who fought him had walked away with missing limbs, Vader had still been gentle, almost kind.

When completely unleashed, his powers were absolutely diabolical.

Up until that moment, she had thought herself his equal. But he was unstoppable, a killing machine with Force powers beyond her wildest dreams and nightmares.

And now he was leaping from speeder to speeder, directly toward them.

"Vader's still coming!" Tualon said worriedly, flinging his lightsaber at their enemy.

"Just . . . fight the fear. Focus. We'll do this together. That speeder. Right at him, as fast as we can. Ready . . ."

Because their only hope was to work together. She wasn't enough on her own.

She needed Tualon.

She had always needed Tualon.

Ironic that just as she realized this, she was in the fight of her life.

They threw a speeder at him, and he batted it aside like it was a toy. They threw another and finally caught him. Vader fell to someone's deck, landing heavily. But this time, he didn't leap up. He lay there, badly damaged. Sensing their chance to take down their master, she and Tualon leapt to join him.

"I don't believe it. We actually beat him!" Tualon said.

"Not yet. He's still alive."

And she was going to do her best to change that.

They were going to kill him.

If Vader was dead, she and Tualon could escape. They were Inquisitors, which meant they knew how Inquisitors worked, how they tracked their prey. It was a big galaxy, and they knew how to disappear. They could close themselves off in the Force, find some quiet place to settle together. They could go back to Pkori and hide.

Or they could return to headquarters and claim supremacy. After all, anyone who killed Darth Vader had surely proven themselves beyond all others. Perhaps leading the Inquisitors would be more exciting than taking orders.

She was done, she realized, with taking orders.

Iskat had always wanted to master the Force, to be the best Jedi and then the best Inquisitor, but now she understood that her connection with the Force was what kept her under the control of others. If she hadn't been so special, no one would've cared.

Forget the Inquisitors. Forget the Jedi.

Perhaps her next great adventure would be learning how to live without the Force.

"Darth Vader, after all this time, after all our work together, I really only know one thing about you," she said, lightsaber poised to strike him down. "You deserve this."

But as she struck, her arm was caught in the viselike grip of the Force. Vader was hurt, his body a rictus of pain, but he was . . . using that pain. Channeling it. His fingers shook as he held her and Tualon in the crushing grip of the Force, raising their bodies up off the ground.

Iskat reached deep inside herself, calling on that well of strength deep within she'd always depended on. She'd held it back for so long, then used the dark side she found there to fully blossom. But now that deep well proved to be only a shallow pool compared with the endless sea that was Darth Vader. Tualon was likewise trapped, and Iskat wanted to reach out and hold his hand, touch his face, stroke his lekku. There was so much she wanted to say to him that she'd held within herself, so much she refused to say now in front of Vader.

So she gave Tualon a smile—a real, honest smile, full of love—and settled for two words she thought she'd never have to say.

"I'm sorry."

The look he gave her was full of tenderness. Funny, how he'd been a tough Jedi and a kind Inquisitor, at least when it came to her.

"It's all right. I don't think either one of us expected to die in bed," he said gently. "Not after the choices we've made. And at least now we'll be free—"

Vader used the Force to switch on their blades.

It was the second time Tualon had put a lightsaber blade through her . . .

And the first time she'd put one through him.

Because Vader had forced their hands.

And this time, no medbay could fix it.

They faced each other, and she was looking in his face as it happened. Their eyes locked, hers bright blue and his the orange of embers. They wore soft smiles, the sort they'd only ever shared behind closed doors. Her blade through his chest, his blade through one of her hearts. There was a rightness to it, a completed circle.

And he was right.

Iskat Akaris was finally free.

CREDITS

Even if *Star Wars* books are written in space, they are not written in a vacuum. The author would like to thank:

RANDOM HOUSE WORLDS

EDITORIAL

Lydia Estrada
Alex Davis
Tom Hoeler
Gabriella Muñoz
Elizabeth Schaefer

COPYEDITING AND PRODUCTION

Cindy Berman
Nancy Delia
Barbara Greenberg
Susan Gutentag
Laura Jorstad
Erich Schoeneweiss

ART AND DESIGN

Scott Biel
Elizabeth A. D. Eno
Ella Laytham

MARKETING AND PUBLICITY

Lauren Ealy
Maya Fenter

Ashleigh Heaton
Lisa Keller
David Moench
Eliana Seochand

LUCASFILM

Jennifer Heddle
Jennifer Pooley
Michael Siglain
The Lucasfilm Story Group

SPECIAL THANKS

Charles Soule
Anthony Jones
VooDoo Val
Matt Griffin
Craig, Rhys, and Rex Dawson
Holly Frey
Kevin Hearne
Chuck Wendig
Mike Chen
Stacia Decker
The kids of OSCAR #832

ABOUT THE AUTHOR

DELILAH S. DAWSON is the author of the *New York Times* bestseller *Star Wars: Phasma*, as well as *Star Wars: Galaxy's Edge: Black Spire*, *The Violence*, *Camp Scare*, *Mine*, *Disney Mirrorverse: Pure of Heart*, the Minecraft: Mob Squad series, the Hit series, the Blud series, the creator-owned comics *Ladycastle*, *Sparrowhawk*, and *Star Pig*, and the Shadow series (written as Lila Bowen). With Kevin Hearne, she co-writes The Tales of Pell. She lives in Georgia with her family.

delilahsdawson.com
Instagram: @DelilahSDawson

Read on for an excerpt from

SHADOW OF THE SITH

BY ADAM CHRISTOPHER

CHAPTER 4

"LUKE? UNCLE?"

Luke Skywalker opened his eyes and looked up from where he was sitting cross-legged in the middle of the stone-flagged floor. The teenager who had called him was standing half in, half out of Luke's hut, the look on his face both expectant and clearly embarrassed that he had accidentally interrupted Luke's meditation.

Luke sighed but didn't move from his position. The fact was, he was glad of the disturbance. His meditation had been . . . difficult.

Again.

"Ben, I've told you before."

Ben Solo ran a hand through his mop of black hair. "I . . . ah, yes, I'm sorry . . . *Master* Skywalker."

"The ways of the Jedi are many," said Luke, "and they include discipline and control."

"Of course, Master."

"And that includes knocking before entering," added Luke, with a smile that was soft and friendly.

Ben smiled back, but the expression was fleeting. He shuffled a little and looked around the stone hut. The small building was no different from any other in the temple grounds, but Luke knew the look on Ben's face.

Luke told himself to go easy, but not just because his Padawan was his nephew. Far from it—family ties had little to do with the teachings of the Jedi Order that Luke had worked hard to reestablish. Detachment and distance were required for the pure focus the Jedi constantly strove to achieve, and for Luke, there was a simple satisfaction in adhering to those tenets.

But Ben was trying his best, and Luke knew it wasn't easy for him, being out here in the forests of Ossus. The land was picturesque, the temple calm and ordered, the life of the Padawans one of training, with little time for leisure and, even when their schedules allowed, few facilities for it.

Ossus was *exactly* the kind of place a sixteen-year-old like Ben Solo would find crushingly dull, the studious life perhaps nice in theory but boring in practice.

But Ben was trying. More than that, he was good—even now, as Ben just stood in the doorway, leaning one shoulder casually against the frame as he ran his hand through his hair yet again, Luke could feel the power in him. It was a beautiful flower, growing inside his Padawan, waiting to blossom into something wonderful. Sometimes Luke thought Ben would one day be as powerful as he was.

The Skywalker legacy ran deep.

Luke raised an eyebrow, then laughed, the growing silence in the hut clearly making Ben even more uncomfortable. That wasn't something Luke had expected in his nephew—he was a fine boy, but there was an edge to him, a slow anxiety that simmered just below the surface. Luke put it down to an eagerness to please him, as the temple's Jedi Master. But it was also reflective of an internal struggle, Jedi versus family, nephew versus uncle, Padawan versus Master. Luke knew it couldn't be easy for Ben, no matter how hard he tried to hide it.

And sometimes he tried to hide it too well.

"So what is it, Ben? You want me for something?"

At this, Ben snapped into focus, even composing himself enough to give his Master a small bow.

"Sorry, Master. You have a visitor."

"A visitor? I wasn't expecting anyone."

"I didn't think I had to ask your permission to see an old friend."

Ben turned at the new voice as another man entered the hut.

Luke pushed himself to his feet to greet the new arrival.

"Of course not," said Luke. The Jedi and the visitor clasped their hands around each other's forearms. "It's good to see you, Lor."

Lor San Tekka released Luke's arm and stepped back to give the Jedi Master a more formal bow. Then he stood and clapped a hand on Luke's shoulder.

"I never take an audience with a Jedi Master for granted," said Lor. He turned to Ben. "Young Ben Solo, you look well. How goes the training?"

Ben gave the older man a stiff bow. "Greetings, sir," he said. "And . . . uh . . ."

Luke laughed. "He's doing fine. In fact, I couldn't hope for a better student."

"I am very glad to hear that," said Lor, before turning back to Luke. "I have some information you might be interested in, Luke, if—"

Now it was Luke's turn to lay a hand on his friend's shoulder. "I'm always interested." He glanced at his Padawan. "And you should be studying, Ben. Lor and I have a lot to discuss."

Ben looked at the pair of them and bowed again, but Luke noticed the frown on his face. "At once, Master." Then he stood tall and, giving a look to Lor, left the hut.

Luke wandered to the doorway and watched his nephew stalk away down the grassy slope. Over by the other cluster of temple buildings, an orange-skinned Twi'lek woman, Enyo, was leading a class of younglings through a series of exercises with training blades.

Luke turned and headed back inside, guiding his friend by the arm. "Actually, I'm glad you're here," he said, stopping in the center of the stone hut.

"They're still happening, aren't they?" asked Lor, facing Luke's back.

Luke nodded, then turned around. "And they're getting worse."

"Worse? Or stronger?" Lor cocked his head. "There's a difference, Luke. You just need to listen to the Force, it will guide you."

Luke's lips twitched in amusement—but the expression was mirrored by Lor San Tekka. He raised a hand.

"I know, I know, an adherent of the Church of the Force dares to instruct a Jedi Master." Lor gave a quiet chuckle. "Maybe I'll learn one day, but I'm an old man with old habits." He folded his arms. "Do you know where your vision takes you?"

Luke fixed his gaze on the old man. "That's where I want your help."

Lor frowned. "I am always happy to guide, Master Skywalker, but only for one willing to follow." He spread his hands. "The Force itself remains a mystery to me. I'm not sure what you think I can do."

Luke stroked his beard. "I want to try something." Luke folded himself down into a cross-legged position again in the middle of the room.

Lor stayed right where he was. "Luke, are you sure this is a good idea?"

Luke glanced up. "I need to find out what these visions mean. If I meditate, try to describe what I'm seeing as I see it—"

"Luke, I'm serious." Lor lowered himself to his knees in front of his friend. "I'm not a Jedi. You know that. There must be someone else in the temple who can assist. Ben, perhaps?"

But Luke shook his head. "You're the only person who knows about the visions, and I want to keep it that way."

Lor lifted his hands, his jaw working as he tried to work up some kind of protest, but in the end he just sighed.

"Very well," he said. "I will stand vigil. Tell me what you see and perhaps the Force will guide me as it guides you."

Luke nodded. "Thank you." He lifted his chin, and closed his eyes, and—

In another world, he opened them, and looked around, and saw—

Nothing. Darkness. A . . . void, empty of anything, a space without limits or dimensions, a place that didn't even exist outside of the confines of his own mind.

And yet a *place* nonetheless.

Luke took a step forward, not really feeling anything beneath his feet, because there was nothing there. His footfalls made no sound, and took him no distance. He looked around, straining to see, even while knowing there was nothing to see, no light, no energy, no anything.

The suddenness of this vision startled him. He had been visiting this place in his meditations for weeks now, but the strange dark world usually took a while to appear, Luke's consciousness drifting away from reality as he focused his mind and body on the meditation. And then, as though falling from a great height, he succumbed to a dark gravity he couldn't escape, and he was there.

Over the years, his meditations had gotten deeper and deeper, as he delved into the recesses of his mind, not just to unlock the potential he knew was there, just out of reach, but to try to commune with the galaxy around him. The Force, he knew, was a living thing, in the crudest terms an energy field that bound the universe together. The Force was not a power, not something to be wielded, or used, or manipulated. Rather, it was something that allowed others to share in it—a thing vast and alive and yet not sentient.

In that respect, his friend Lor San Tekka was right. Adherents to the Church of the Force were not Force-sensitive, but that didn't mean they didn't understand it, or those who could tap into the field that underlined the very fabric of being.

But this time, it was different. He had closed his eyes and suddenly he was *here*. Luke knew that without his own iron grip on his emotions, he would be afraid now, and rightly so. But instead he turned that feeling that even now grew inside him into something else, using it as fuel for his senses, heightening his awareness of his surroundings.

And the void, he realized, was somehow . . . *aware* of him, of this visitor, this intruder from elsewhere.

Luke concentrated.

Yes, he felt it now. It had come and gone before, in previous visions, but whether the presence of Lor San Tekka really was doing something or not, it didn't matter, because it was stronger now.

A presence.

The void was not empty.

He concentrated.

It was dark, but it was different from the black awfulness he had felt in the Emperor's presence, even in the presence of his own father, so many years ago. That was something he could understand. He knew where it came from, knew how the light could be corrupted and twisted, turned to darkness, that darkness wrenched and abused into a tool of power that had no place in the light of the Force.

This void was not a part of that, but it was still alive, and Luke was not alone.

Then the void changed, becoming a reality, not an abstract.

Luke was somewhere ancient, somewhere distant.

Somewhere . . . hidden.

Black ground. Black sky. Both flat, cold, like metal. Lightning flashes, electrical discharges that snapped from sky to ground in great pillars of energy, illuminating gray dust that formed low, suffocating clouds, like the sky itself was pressing down on the ground, the world between it squeezed until it cracked.

Desolation. That was the word for it. The landscape, the place, was blasted, by eons of time, the air dry and charged with a dangerous electricity that danced over a ground of black basalt that was already immeasurably ancient.

And then, he—

"Well?"

Luke opened his eyes. He was sitting on the floor. Lor San Tekka was kneeling in front of him, hands pressed down on his knees. It didn't look comfortable.

Luke pursed his lips, surprised that his vision had gone just as fast as it had arrived.

"Tell me what you saw, Luke," said Lor. "Describe it to me."

Luke stared into the middle distance as he brought the memories back to the front of his mind. He described the void, and the blackened landscape—and the dark presence he sensed.

Lor listened carefully, then he stood and began a slow pace of the hut, stretching out his legs, his knees clicking loudly, each accompanied by a wince.

Luke watched him. "Does any of that mean anything to you?"

Lor stopped pacing and pursed his lips. "We've been to a lot of places, Luke. We've seen a lot of things."

Luke nodded. That was quite true—the two had spent a lot of time in each other's company since the death of the Emperor and the fall of the Empire. Luke was driven by a desire to reestablish the Jedi Order from, essentially, absolutely nothing. It was to Lor that he had come, eager for the old explorer's help in hunting down relics and artifacts that had a connection with the Force. Together they followed the star compass Luke had uncovered from Pilio, mapping out the network of Jedi temples that were scattered across the galaxy—perhaps half of them not even remembered after the Empire's purge of the Order four decades before.

Their voyages had been largely fruitful, too. Luke had amassed quite a collection of antiquities at his own fledgling Jedi temple—books, tomes, papers, and data cards; ritual items, sigils and symbols of power; technology, including lightsabers, the star compass, and more. All of which Luke and Lor had studied, the older man's deep knowledge of the Jedi Order a boon to Luke, who was eager not only to learn but also to *understand* as he tried to rebuild the Jedi.

"I sense a *but* coming," said Luke.

Lor began to pace again. "It could be a real place, or it may just be what it is—a vision, a representation of the darkness that must always exist where there is light."

"But why now? I've never had visions like this before."

"The influence of some artifact, perhaps? We have collected and studied many products of the dark arts, Luke."

The suggestion was plausible, but it didn't feel right to Luke. Truth was, his focus had drifted over the last few weeks, his daily rituals and training with the younglings—a strict, unwavering routine—suddenly became disrupted. Luke had handed basic responsibilities to his senior pupils—Ben included—while he holed himself up in his quarters, trying to understand the visions. But he hadn't handled any Sith relics in a long time. He knew full well the danger such artifacts could pose.

"I'm sorry," said Luke, unfolding himself from his position and standing up. He brushed down his cream-colored robes and ran his cybernetic hand through his mop of ash-brown hair. "I don't know what I thought this would achieve." He paused, shaking his head. "But this . . . place, whatever it is. I'm seeing it for a reason, Lor. I can feel it."

"Oh," said Lor, clapping a hand on his friend's shoulder. "Of that, Luke, I have no doubt. No doubt at all. I just wish I could help you in some way. Research, fieldwork—the search!—there, I feel like I can be of use. But standing vigil over a Jedi who is looking into his own mind?" He clicked his tongue. "I'm a little out of my depth."

Luke laughed softly, relaxing again in the company of his old friend. "Perhaps you're right," he said. "But why did you come to Ossus, anyway? You said you'd found some information?"

"Well," began Lor, "it's going to sound a little . . . anticlimactic, shall we say, after all that."

"Go on," said Luke. "I'm interested."

Lor nodded. "You ever heard of a planet called Yoturba?"

Luke frowned. "I don't think so."

"Mid Rim, nothing remarkable," said Lor, "but the Lerct Historical Institute is running an archaeological dig out there."

Luke felt his eyebrows going up as his interest was piqued. "Have they found something?"

"No," said Lor. "Not yet, anyway. But they have uncovered a large settlement. I couldn't find any record of the Jedi having a temple on Yoturba, but the period is correct. I thought we should take a look. If, of course, you can spare the time from your own temple."

Luke stroked his beard in thought, then he nodded.

"Of course," he said. "We should go. I could use some time to think, anyway."

He stepped past Lor and walked out of the hut. Standing at the top of the small hill on which it stood, he looked out and saw Ben had taken the place of Enyo in leading the training session.

Luke lifted his hand, catching Ben's attention. The young man nodded in acknowledgment and began to bring the training session to an end.

"He's going to make a fine Jedi one day, Luke," said Lor, joining his friend at the door. "And learning the responsibilities of the temple while his Master is away will do him a world of good."

Luke nodded, then patting his friend on the shoulder, turned, and headed back inside to prepare himself for the expedition ahead.

CHAPTER 5

THE JUNKYARD, SOMEWHERE
NEAR THE INNER RIM
NOW

IF THE MOON HAD A name, he didn't know what it was. Nor did he much care, about the moon, about anything.

Not anymore.

As far as he knew, he was alone, although he hadn't bothered to explore much beyond the confines of the junkyard in which he had made his home. The moon, like so many others in this sector, was the size of a planet—standard mass, standard gravity, standard atmosphere—and while it was cold it was livable, and that was all that mattered.

And he called it . . . actually, he didn't call it anything. He didn't need to. He knew the coordinates, yes—he did *occasionally* venture beyond the moon's gravity well, but never far. He was happy right where he was. There was nothing out there for him.

So the moon was simply the moon and the junkyard was just that, a junkyard. Hardly poetic, but then he'd never had a taste for literature.

Whose junkyard, again, he didn't know, and he didn't care, and he had made no attempt to learn in all the time he had been here. Oh, it was old, that much was obvious. The debris here sat in strata like a geologic landscape, layer upon layer upon layer of metallic and ceramic refuse, the decayed remnants of starships from long-forgotten civilizations, empires, republics. On the surface, the material had been ground down by the pervasive wind—wind that howled and moaned, and at night seemed to *sing* among the ruins, like it was a life-form all of its own—into a kind of rough, silver sand. From this top layer protruded larger fragments, some more intact than others, some even recognizable, despite their age and antique design. Thruster pods, their innards long since collapsed, formed great tubes, some of which stretched for hundreds of meters across the junkyard dunes, looking like casings from some giant, metal-eating worms that lived perpetually below the surface. There were other parts, too, all skeletal, all ancient—superstructures and frameworks, cockpits and engine housings, and if he dug below the surface, kilometers and kilometers of plastoid cabling, some of it in shockingly bright colors, reds and yellows and blues, the tough substance infinitely less susceptible to centuries of rot and decay than the rest of whatever ship it was that'd had these wires and conduits as its nervous and circulatory system.

He didn't know where any of it came from, and he didn't care, because he wasn't here for salvage. There was absolutely nothing of use in this former dumping ground, abandoned in ages past, and that was precisely why he had picked it, because that meant there was no reason for anyone else to come here, either. Perhaps, one day, the junkyard moon would be the target for element hunters, equipped with the tools and knowledge to extract pure, raw minerals, metals, metalloids. Or maybe that had already happened and this was what was left.

It didn't matter. The only thing that did was that he was alone, and nobody came to visit the moon, and—perhaps most important of all—nobody even knew he was here.

The only thing that mattered was that the name of Ochi of Bestoon would be slowly forgotten.

Good. Because his current mission required the help of no one, and if he was going to find what he was looking for, he needed to be alone and undisturbed.

"Master!"

Well . . . while his existence was solitary, he was not, strictly speaking, *alone*.

"Master!" came the high-pitched, quavering voice of his droid again. "M-m-m-master."

Ochi paused and gave a sigh, the sound amplified and echoed through his respirator. Yes, the atmosphere was breathable, but he suspected that inhaling the silver sand wasn't the best thing to be doing over the long term, and he certainly hadn't come here to die. Far from it, in fact.

Ochi pulled back the hood of his cloak and knelt down by his droid, a small unit that consisted of two main pieces—a single wheel with a rubberized tread and a flat-nosed, cone-shaped head—connected by an articulated arm, with three long green slots that formed the droid's optical array. As Ochi crouched beside it, the droid rolled a little in the silver sand, the three short antennas on the back of its head quivering, as though it were afraid of being so close to its owner.

"What is it, Dee-Oh?"

"I-I-I-"

"Spit it out," said Ochi, "or I'll leave you outside again tonight. See how your lubricant likes the cold again, eh?"

At this, D-O rolled to the top of the silver dune the pair were trekking up, then stopped. There, its head shook, like it was trying to get Ochi to take a look over the crest, beyond which lay their encampment.

Ochi followed the droid up the slope—the machine was nothing more than a low-intelligence data storage and retrieval unit, but Ochi had been impressed by the sensitivity of its sensors in the past. If D-O dared get Ochi's attention, there was usually a good reason for it.

Usually. Because right now, as he scanned the encampment, careful to keep his head low, Ochi couldn't see anything he wasn't expecting to see.

He sighed again, stood tall, and turned on the droid. From his belt he slipped a short piece of dull-black pipework, one of the few useful bits of scrap he'd picked up when he'd first arrived. He wasn't sure what it was made of—it was black and polished, more like stone than metal, but it had a slight kink in it—nor did he know what it had been made for, originally.

But whatever it was, it did everything he needed now.

Ochi swung the pipe, clipping the back of D-O's head, sending the droid sliding forward and knocking its nose into the sand. As the machine burbled in fear, Ochi put his boot on the back of the droid's head and held it down. D-O's wheel spun uselessly, kicking up a silver plume as it tried to free itself.

"Maybe one day you'll learn not to waste my time, *droid*," said Ochi, whispering the last word like it was an insult. Then he lifted his foot and gave the back of D-O's wheel a kick. The droid rolled down the slope a little and managed to pull its head from the sand before coming to a sliding stop. It shook its head, trying to dislodge sand from its workings.

"Sorry, master. S-s-s-sorry, master. Sorry."

"Shut up," said Ochi. "What was it that you couldn't just spit out and say?"

The droid twitched, and it turned its cone-shaped head up to look at its master.

"Movement. Master. Movement. Movement."

Ochi looked down at D-O, then turned and walked back up the slope. He looked down at his encampment for anything unusual, out of place.

In his time on the moon, he'd made himself quite comfortable. In the center of the flat area sat his ship, the *Bestoon Legacy*. The main ramp was open, but Ochi had built a temporary extension onto it with maintenance scaffold pipework and a heavy plastoid tarp, expanding his available space while keeping the sand out of the ship itself. Behind the tarp screens he had dragged equipment crates and other bits of the *Legacy*'s interior fittings to make himself a proper work space.

But Ochi couldn't see or hear anything out of the ordinary. One corner of the tarp flapped as the wind picked up, the moonsong growing louder as dusk approached. He'd have to fix that corner, he thought, before taking a step down the slope, his boots sinking heel-first into the dune. Behind him, D-O shivered and made a squawking sound, like its vocabulator was finally about to short out completely. Ochi paused and glanced down at the droid.

As much as he hated it, despising the stupid machine as the only company he had on this wrecked moon, he *did* trust it.

If D-O had detected movement, then there was movement.

Ochi dropped down onto one knee and, reaching under his cloak, extracted a battered set of quadnocs. Flicking the cloak clear of his shoulders, he pulled his hood down and put the quadnocs up to the goggles of his respirator. As he adjusted the device, his vision filled with a scratchy but enhanced view of the area below, his ship, the workshop, and the debris around it crawling with data and tracking lines as the quadnocs ran an analysis, presenting the user with a mess of data that Ochi supposed would be useful, if he'd ever figured out how to interpret it properly.

He scanned carefully, slowly, left to right. The wind continued to pick up, spinning the silver sand into eddies, the air humming through it. The quadnocs locked onto the shifting particles, giving Ochi range, degrees of movement, any number of reference points that were of no use at all.

And that was the problem. The metallic sand played havoc with sensor readings. It was another reason why nobody came to this moon, why any ship flying on even a low pass was unlikely to spot his ship, parked out in a clearing in the junkyard. D-O had learned how to adapt and filter this interference, but now, as Ochi felt the quadnocs growing warm through his gloves while the device tried to process what it was pointed at, he wondered if even his little droid was reaching the end of its usefulness.

He lowered the quadnocs and looked ahead. A dust devil had spun up near his ship, the miniature twister rising up, dragging the glittering silver sand into it, before dissipating just as quickly as it had formed. Then the wind shifted again, blowing Ochi's cloak across his mask before he pushed it away, and then, for a moment, everything was still.

There was nothing down there.

"Time to adjust your sensor array," Ochi muttered to his droid, as he stood and headed down the dune. "Or I'll adjust it for you."

Behind him, D-O shivered again, muttering to itself, then it followed its master at a safe distance.

The inside of Ochi's makeshift work space was cluttered but, despite the loose side of tarp, mercifully free of sand. Once inside, with D-O shooting in behind him, he secured the entrance flap, then went to the corner to fix the loose tie. Satisfied with his work, he stood, unclipped his cloak at the throat, and tossed it over an equipment crate before brushing any lingering sand off himself and making his way up the ramp and into the *Bestoon Legacy.*

The craft's interior was spacious but crammed with more of the plastoid crates, stacks of them piled up against the walls, more dragged out into the open, their sealed tops popped to reveal their contents. Several crates were also arranged as a table, another as a stool. On top of the table, the contents of several more now empty crates were spread out.

There were books, and charts, and even papers, most of them ancient and brown, written on the processed pulp of trees or the finely prepared hides of animals—rarities of some considerable value simply as objects, regardless of the information inscribed or printed on them. There were some newer documents, their synthetic sheets bright and shiny compared with their ancient counterparts. Balanced on a stack of two crates all on its own was one large tome, its spine broken long ago, the pages stained and crooked and mostly separating from the binding. On top of the open page was a large-format datapad with a stylus.

Ochi walked to the table while D-O scooted off into a corner, where it had made a nest out of discarded papers, a cozy, almost hidden spot next to its recharge port.

Ochi looked down at his work—his *research*—for one minute, two minutes, three minutes, then hissed in annoyance. His only routine was a daily five-kilometer trek around the junkyard, and it was supposed to clear his head, allowing his subconscious to work out problems and puzzles while he just focused on putting one foot in front of another.

Today his subconscious hadn't done much at all. It was tired, like its conscious counterpart. Ochi had been studying the books for a long time.

Probably far too long.

He sat heavily on a crate and took off his gloves, then his respirator, dropping both into an open crate full of more ancient documents that sat at his side. He rubbed his bald scalp, the yellowish skin tight with burn scars, the lights on the cybernetic implant that wrapped around the back of his skull and covered both ears winking softly. He leaned over the table, the two circular, black, cybernetic eyes embedded in his smooth face focusing on the text he had not yet been able to translate. He reached for his datapad, a pale tongue running over his lipless mouth, as he got back to work.

He would crack the text, and he would find that place, that blasted planet that was both cursed and blessed.

Exegol.

He was close. He knew it. He could *feel* it.

At least that's what he told himself, like he could just wish it to be true. Because Ochi of Bestoon had been looking for Exegol for a long, long time, and however hopeless a part of him knew his task was, he refused to give up.

He'd been there once. He was going to get there again.

But Exegol wasn't just in an unknown region of space; the ancient planet was deliberately *hidden,* screened off from the rest of the galaxy, whether by design or by some by-product of an arcane ritual, Ochi didn't know. But . . . he'd made it before, he could make it again. He'd crossed the Red Honeycomb Zone, that murderous expanse of crimson chaos that shielded the planet of the Sith. He'd reached it. Exegol. He'd *been there.* He knew what secrets the dark planet kept. Secrets that would be his. The things he'd seen, the things he'd learned, on his short visit all those years ago. Secrets the Emperor had whispered in his ear, secrets Darth Vader had hinted at.

And Ochi knew that was just the start of it, a merest fraction of the power that lay slumbering below the cracked black surface of that dead planet.

Power? Ochi laughed. Oh yes, he'd wanted power, once. Power, and riches. But he had never wanted to use those spoils to rule—because, look, ruling a galaxy? What was the point? He supposed if you did rule a galaxy, you'd have . . . what, staff? Servants? Minions? Drones, who did all the actual work while you sat back on your ebonite throne and reaped the rewards?

No. That wasn't for him. Maybe it hadn't been then, either, but it certainly wasn't what he wanted now. Power came in many forms, and the kind he wanted now was entirely different in scope.

What Ochi of Bestoon wanted was the power to live, to heal, to become . . . himself, again.

Ochi had lost track of time, but it had been years now since he had crossed the nightmare gulfs of the Red Honeycomb Zone with Darth Vader himself, Ochi an unwilling companion to the Dark Lord of the Sith as he investigated the Emperor's secret works. There, on a planet hidden from the galaxy, they discovered the vast fleet the cultists and their enslaved workers were slowly building—Star Destroyers, hundreds of them, each a thousand times more powerful than those commanded by the Imperial Navy. The ships were equipped with huge cannons, their power matching that of the Death Star's own planet-destroying armament, the energy channeled and concentrated by shards of kyber crystal, those pieces cleaved from a huge mountain of the stuff amassed at the heart of the cultists' fortress-temple.

It was this kyber mountain that had scarred Ochi. As he watched the crystals being ripped from their formations, they had screamed out in pain, releasing a burst of energy that seared the skin from his skull and burned his eyes from their sockets. And still, the Sith Eternal tortured the crystal hoard even as they divided it, imbuing the kyber—so they believed—with even greater power for the fleet's mighty weapons.

Ochi remembered the pain. He remembered the darkness. And he remembered the voice of Emperor Palpatine, deep and melodic and almost soothing, as the Sith Eternal repaired him, replaced his eyes, gave him the cybernetic head unit to compensate for the damaged parts of his brain.

But to be repaired was not the same as being healed. After the accident, Ochi wasn't the same, not just because of his injuries but because of something else, deep inside him, that had changed.

He had seen the light of Exegol, and it was beautiful. Powerful—the power to destroy, but the power to heal. To renew. To make whole again.

True enough, he had survived. He had left Exegol, returned to the service of one master or another—Vader once more, Lady Qi'ra and the Crimson Dawn, others—all the while the voice of the Emperor echoing in the dark corners of his mind as the memory of the hidden planet of the Sith shone ever brighter.

It did so now, brighter and hotter than ever, a burning red light like the heart of a screaming, tortured kyber crystal. Ochi was older now, and yet he felt like he was only just getting started, getting things together, embarking on his real purpose, the real reason he'd been placed in this Sithforsaken existence in the first place. What he needed was time. What he needed was life.

What he *needed* was to be himself again. To be whole again.

Healed, not just repaired.

And Exegol was the answer. The Sith Eternal could grant him those wishes, and if they refused, he would take their power and do it himself.

Only problem was, he couldn't get there.

Nobody could. The Red Honeycomb Zone was vast and unnavigable, a nebulous hellspace nobody would dare cross without the correct navigational tool, shielding Exegol as though the planet didn't even exist.

What Ochi needed was a Sith wayfinder.

He didn't know how they worked, and that didn't matter. He'd seen Vader's in action—you just . . . well, you just plugged it into your navicomputer, and the wayfinder handled the rest.

Ochi flipped back a few digital pages in his datapad and cast a cybernetic eye over the diagrams he'd managed to cobble together. A wayfinder was a strange thing, more a piece of art than an advanced technological device; a sculpture in iron and glass, trapping a magical fire within. He didn't quite know who or what the Sith actually were—the Emperor was scary as anything but he paid well and Vader was . . .

Well, Vader was a weirdo was what he was, but Ochi had seen what he'd been capable of, had glimpsed the power he seemed to have at his beck and call, a dark reflection of the Force that the Jedi whom Ochi had hunted back in his glory days of the Clone Wars had wielded.

Ochi didn't much understand or care then, and he still didn't now. But a wayfinder? Now, that was something real, a tool to be used.

Of course there were complications. There were only two of them, because . . . of course there were only two of them. Something the Sith had come up with, an ancient rite or belief or whatever they thought, because the Sith were the Sith. So fine, two wayfinders. Vader had one, Ochi assumed the Emperor had the other.

Problem was, Vader was dead and so was Palpatine. Did that mean the wayfinders were destroyed?

Or were they just lost?

Ochi believed the latter to be the case.

Or at least . . . that's what he told himself. And all he had to do now was find one—a small, pyramidal relic you could hold in one hand, somewhere out there in a galaxy that was very, very big.

Ochi was nothing if not determined. He'd spent too long on this chase to give up now. Years of research, and he wasn't done.

Because he'd found clues. The Sith wayfinders were written about in the ancient texts he had amassed as part of his relic collection. Sith Lords, Masters, and apprentices rose and fell in a cycle over time that was almost mathematical, and those who served them came and went as well. The Sith wayfinders, the keys to Exegol? No, they would not be lost or destroyed so easily. There was a way to find them, and Ochi was close.

The book was old, the pages brittle and burned at the edges, like the tome had been snatched from a burning starship just in the nick of time. Some pages were more badly damaged than others, which made the painstaking task of translation even more difficult. That was why he had D-O. The data storage and retrieval droid had belonged to some scholar Ochi had killed on Primus Cabru when he raided the library there, and the damn thing had actually begged for its electronic life after it had seen its master die. Ochi had seen its utility—D-O was programmed not just with hundreds of languages, but with complex algorithms that enabled fast textual analysis and comparison with other materials stored in its surprisingly large databank. Exactly what Ochi needed.

Ochi put the datapad down and looked around, wondering where the stupid droid was. He felt his anger flare, and he stood, reaching for the black metal rod.

"Dee-Oh? Dee-Oh! Droid! Come here, I need you." Ochi's cracked voice echoed around the interior of the *Bestoon Legacy*. He stood from the makeshift seat, puzzled at the droid's lack of reply.

Truth was, he had come to hate that droid. It was small and stupid, programmed with a personality that seemed rodentlike, barely even sentient. It was timid, and weak, and constantly afraid. Sometimes, as he lay in his bunk at night, listening to the singing sands, wishing he had a drink or two or three or four, Ochi thought he should wipe its central processor and start over from scratch.

An empty threat, and he knew it. Because, as irritating as it was, the droid now contained the sum total of his research, and thanks to its analysis algorithms had even come up with a potential, although only partial, navigational chart for Exegol. Ochi would still need a wayfinder, but at the back of his mind he always knew he had the option to just blast his way through the Red Honeycomb Zone and take his chances. It was likely suicide, but then again, you should always die doing what you loved, right?

This was why Ochi hated D-O. The droid's data was both essential and useless, a constant reminder of Ochi's own failures, his research painstaking yet thoroughly incomplete and, as a result, unusable.

"Droid!"

There was a noise, a fluttering, like a stack of old, precious papers had been knocked from its precarious balance on the edge of one of the crates. Outside, the wind sang through the silver sands, a mournful wail.

Ochi's cybernetic eyes flipped through to infrared as he tried to detect the heat signature of the droid. Shaking his head, he turned—

—And fell back onto the decking in surprise as he came face-to-face with an intruder.

"What the—?"

The intruder was tall and thin, clad entirely in a long black cloak, with a long, narrow hood. From his position on the floor, Ochi could see, under the edge of the hood, the face of the intruder. It was a face he had seen before.

Or rather, *hadn't* seen. The intruder's head was entirely wrapped in tight black bandages, thick swaths of them, around and around, with no visible holes for eyes, or nose, or mouth.

"You!" Ochi scrambled backward on the decking, then stopped as his backward-reaching hand connected with something behind him. He felt around, his fingers sliding on the silver sand that dusted the boot of the person standing behind him.

Turning on the floor, he looked up at another robed figure, identical to the first. And then, from behind this second intruder, stepped two more.

"How did you get in here?" Ochi asked, as he looked at the circle of cultists of the Sith Eternal who had somehow materialized in his ship. His heart thundered in his chest as he felt—

What, exactly? Fear? Surely not. Ochi was afraid of no one (he told himself). But . . . yes, it was fear. Fear that he'd been caught, that the Cult of the Sith Eternal had been watching him, had seen what he was reading, what he was studying, had worked out what he was trying to do, and had come out of the red nebula in person to stop him.

So yes, he was afraid.

"Get up."

Ochi jerked his head around at the voice, but it wasn't the first cultist who had spoken. They had been joined by yet another new arrival. This person—a woman—was also dressed in black, but not in the robes of a cultist. Instead she wore a long, close-fitting outfit, part tunic, part cloak, that flared out to form a tattered, scalloped edge that swept around her boots, the whole thing looking old and worn. Her hands partially bare, the thumb looped through the ends of her sleeves revealed the woman's blue skin. In one of her hands, she held a cylinder of black metal about thirty centimeters long. She wore a mask of burnished bronze, which was framed by a cascade of long, dirty deep-blue hair.

It was the mask that Ochi couldn't tear his gaze from. It frightened him, more so than the sudden presence of the cultists. It made him . . . feel things, in ways he didn't understand, in ways he couldn't describe, like merely *looking* at the mask triggered something deep inside his mind, some primal urge to scream and run and to never stop running.

The mask looked old. The surface was dull and scratched, pitted with divots. The eyes were two catlike angles of black glass that glinted in the light of the flight deck even as the rest of the mask seemed to absorb light. There was no nose, and the mouth was indicated by a line of black rivets, forming a downturned grimace. The mask was strange, somehow industrial and protective but also a work of art, a carefully sculpted thing from a culture long extinct. It was beautiful, and it was terrible.

"Get up," said the woman again. Even her voice made Ochi involuntarily flinch. It was definitely female, albeit processed through the strange mask, giving it a grating, metallic edge. But there was something else in the voice, too—it was like there was someone else speaking at the same time, matching the woman's words exactly, but this voice was male and it was somehow distant, a relic of somewhere or sometime else, echoing perhaps not in Ochi's cybernetically enhanced ears but somewhere inside his mind.

Ochi pushed himself to his feet. He looked around, not able to see D-O, suddenly wanting the stupid droid by his side, the feeling entirely irrational but still comforting. Then he drew himself up to his full height, which was not quite to the eyeline of the black mask. He took a breath and sighed. If this was it, then . . . this was it. He was outnumbered. He just hoped it would be quick.

"Okay, get it over with," he said. "I'm not going to beg or plead or grovel. I'm tired and I'm old but for what it's worth, I'm not sorry. Not now, not ever. You can't blame me for trying."

The cultists were still and silent in the circle that surrounded him. Ochi turned on his heel, casting his gaze over the group. They were all the same, black hooded robes, their features hidden behind the tight weave of black bandages.

Except the one who had spoken.

He turned back to the leader and looked her up and down. Now that the shock of their arrival had passed—now that he was resigned to his fate—Ochi found his fear evaporating. He no longer had anything to lose.

Ochi nodded at the woman. "I haven't seen you before. What are you, some kind of a priestess or something?" He waved his hand. "No, I don't care." He turned to the book on the crate. "I guess you want these back, too. Fine, take them, I'm not going to need them anymore, am I?"

The woman didn't speak, and the cultists didn't move. Ochi idly leafed through the book, then, glancing around the group, turned to face their leader again.

"Well?"

"Exegol."

Ochi's cybernetic optics adjusted themselves. "What about it?"

"You seek Exegol."

Ochi glanced around again. "Yes. You know I do. That's why you're here, isn't it?"

"We can show you the way," said the woman in the black mask. "We can give you the path through Red Space. We can give you what you seek."

Ochi licked his lipless mouth again. "What?" he asked, after a pause of several seconds. "You're just going to, what, take me there? Why would you do that? The path to Exegol is a secret—your secret."

"A secret indeed," said the metallic, grating voice of the woman in the mask. "A secret we can share with you." She tilted her head ever so slightly to one side, as though Ochi was an interesting specimen to be studied. "Once you have earned it."

Ochi stared at the woman—and then, despite himself, burst out laughing. He doubled over, taking great whoops of air as he lost control. He could feel the skin around his cybernetic eyes stretch, his whole face beginning to ache as the scar tissue was pulled tight.

"Exegol!" he managed, between gasps of breath, his arms folded across his middle as he laughed again. "You're just going to *take* me to Exegol? A personal escort to a hidden planet?" He paused. "Oh, wait, wait, no, not an escort. You said you'll give me the secret. Right, the secret. Don't tell me, a wayfinder! You're just going to hand one over. Is that it? After all these years, all my work, you finally decided I was, what, worthy enough?" He drew himself up to his full height and was almost ready to spit on the tattered edge of the woman's black cloak when her arm shot up, bringing the metal cylinder up in front of Ochi's scarred face. He gasped and stumbled backward.

That cylinder. He knew what it was. Vader's wasn't identical, but he knew exactly what it was and what was about to happen.

This was it.

Afraid again, Ochi did the only thing he could. He turned to run and—

Darkness. *Nothingness.* He found himself looking into a void so complete, so absolute, so pure, it was like looking into the heart of a black hole.

He turned around. The darkness was all around him, enveloping him. He could see nothing. The cabin of the *Bestoon Legacy* had vanished, along with the cultists and their leader, replaced with this pure void.

His cybernetic head implant took a moment to process what was going on, then gave him a simple systems report.

His eyes had been turned off.

Yelling in rage, Ochi spun around again, his arms outstretched. He took a step forward then reached down to feel, but somehow there was nothing around him, not the crates, not the decking, not the intruders. He stopped where he was and felt his face, his fingertips running around the hard rims of the electronic optics embedded in his eye sockets.

"What have you done?" he asked the darkness. "I can't see. What have you done!"

And then he felt it, a presence, a form looming over his shoulder, so close he could almost feel the breath against his skin. He flinched, ducking down as though to avoid someone approaching him from behind, but as soon as he moved, it was there again, at his shoulder, leaning in, invisible, intangible, but a presence nonetheless. It felt huge and cold and . . .

It felt wrong.

OCHI OF BESTOON.

That voice. By all the gods, that *voice*. A deep bass rumble, the enunciation so clipped, so perfect, so deliberate. Slow and low, a voice Ochi knew well but had never imagined he would hear again.

"No," he whispered. "No, it's not possible."

The voice chuckled, softly, the sound just enough to turn Ochi's insides to ice water.

ALL THINGS ARE POSSIBLE, OCHI OF BESTOON.

It was the voice of Emperor Palpatine. The *dead* Emperor Palpatine.

YOU HAVE BEEN CHOSEN.

The voice was now echoing from all around the darkness. Ochi looked up, shaking his head, and then he fell to his knees, his head bowed.

What nightmare was this?

I HAVE A TASK FOR YOU TO PERFORM.

The Emperor's voice now moved, left to right, right to left, above, below, around.

YOU WERE ONCE A HUNTER. SO YOU SHALL HUNT AGAIN.

Ochi stammered, unable to find his own voice.

YOU WILL FIND THE GIRL. YOU WILL BRING HER TO ME.

Every word the dead Emperor spoke was a threat, every syllable dagger-sharp and dripping with poison.

Ochi wished the cultists had come to kill him after all. He shook his head.

"I don't understand," he said. "I don't understand."

MY DISCIPLES WILL TEACH YOU. COMPLETE THIS TASK, AND YOU SHALL HAVE YOUR REWARD. YOU SHALL HAVE THE PATH TO EXE-GOL.

And then the voice changed to one tinged with sadness, regret, the voice of a frail old man, a soul long lost. If anything, this just made Ochi even more afraid.

YOU HAVE FAILED ME BEFORE. DO NOT FAIL ME AGAIN, OCHI OF BESTOON.

Before Ochi could respond, there was a searing roar, sounding in the infinite darkness like a mighty electrical storm unleashing its fury. The darkness around him flared with a brilliant red light, and instantly he could smell ozone and could feel a sharp tang on the back of his tongue. As his optics adjusted to the glare, he found himself looking directly at the point of a long blade of red energy, buzzing like a trapped and angry insect, the core brilliant, almost white, surrounded by a perfect halo of deepest scarlet.

Ochi fell backward and knocked into his worktop, sending the crates toppling over, taking the ancient Sith text with them. He hit the deck and looked up, his eyes now operational again, and found himself look-ing up at the woman's black mask as she held her lightsaber a scant few centimeters from his face.

"You have your task," said the woman, and suddenly the blade wasn't there, the lightsaber deactivated.

Ochi let out a breath and looked around. The cultists remained as still as statues, and now the woman in the black mask was sliding her lightsaber back onto her belt.

"I . . . I do," said Ochi. He pushed himself up again, using a toppled crate behind him for support. As he stood, the crate shifted and he fell again onto his knees, catching the edge of a kneecap on the decking. Pain shot up his leg. He winced, then moved to rise again, slower this time.

"But I don't understand," said Ochi, through gritted teeth. "He told me to find the girl. What girl? I don't know what he was talking about." He paused. "How is he even alive? The Emperor is dead. Everybody knows that."

"You are a hunter, Ochi of Bestoon," said the woman, ignoring his question. "Once you were the greatest in the galaxy." She cocked her head again, the mask exaggerating the movement. "Or so you claimed. I hope our Lord was not mistaken in choosing you for reactivation."

"Reactivation? Is that what you want to call it?"

The woman did not answer.

Ochi shook his head. "I still don't understand. The Emperor said you would . . . teach me something?"

At this, the woman in the mask nodded and one of the robed cultists stepped forward. From beneath their long robe they produced a dagger. They held it out in front of them, by the handle, the blade pointed at Ochi.

Ochi looked down at it. Like the Sith wayfinders, like the weird mask the leader of the cultists was wearing, the dagger looked like the product of another age entirely. The weapon was a dull silver, and while the blade was straight, it was lobed, shaped with two bulbous sections separated by a short, squarish serrated portion. The edges of the weapon were bright, like they were freshly machined. The blade itself was plain, the hilt a short, thick curve of metal.

Ochi looked up at the cultist's bandage-wrapped face.

"What is this?"

The cultist did not speak, but they held the dagger forward.

Ochi looked at the masked woman. "Is this for me?"

The black mask inclined in acknowledgment. "Take the blade."

Ochi shrugged and reached for the weapon, expecting the cultist to hand it over by the handle. Instead, they moved the weapon again so the blade remained pointing at Ochi.

"Take the blade," said the woman.

"Yes, but, I don't understand—"

"You will. Take the blade."

Ochi found himself cowering under the commanding order. He reached forward, both hands carefully taking hold of the blade, mindful to keep the cutting edges clear of his palms.

That was when the cultist pulled the knife back and up, toward themselves. Ochi cried out, first in surprise, then in pain as he realized what the cultist had done. He collapsed onto his knees, cradling his cut hands, curling them into fists to try to stop the blood that was now beginning to ooze out between his closed fingers.

"What did you do that for?" he yelled up at the woman in the mask. "You've nearly crippled me."

"Your wounds will heal," said the woman, "and this blade will tell."

She gestured to the cultist. Ochi turned to watch, his injured hands still pressed tightly against his chest.

The cultist held the dagger out, tilting the blade down so it caught the light.

As Ochi watched, the blade began to glow, softly at first, but then with a light that deepened to a red—the same red as the woman's lightsaber. The light spiraled then began to coalesce, almost like particles of dust spinning around the blade. The light was sucked in toward the blade, and then a pulse traveled along the blade, Ochi's blood vanishing, like it was absorbed by the metal itself as the light slowly moved along it, leaving in its wake lines of densely packed symbols, intricate and delicate, the light engraving them in the surface from hilt to tip. When the light reached the point, it flashed and was gone, leaving the dagger's blade smoking slightly in the air.

Ochi dipped his head, the agony of his injured hands refusing to abate. He closed the irises of his cybernetic eyes, this time thankful for the peaceful darkness, and shook his head.

"What must I do?" he asked, finally.

"Find the girl," said the woman. "Bring her to Exegol. There the Sith Eternal will guide the galaxy to its destiny and you shall find that which you seek."

Ochi shook his head. "Even if I find this girl, how do I get to Exegol? I need to know. You need to tell me. Show me the path. Give me the coordinates, or a beacon, or something. Give me a wayfinder."

"When the time is right," said the woman, "the blade will tell. Keep it with you, always. The blade is your key."

Ochi opened his eyes.

He was alone.

He stood, letting his hands fall to his sides, the blood continuing to drip onto the decking. As he looked around, he heard a hissing sound and detected the faint rise of steam.

He looked down. The blood from his hands was dripping down onto the dagger, which lay on the decking. As each drop hit the blade, it hissed, like the dagger was white-hot, the blood vanishing as it evaporated.

No, it wasn't evaporating. The blade was absorbing it.

He bent down and grimaced against the pain as he opened his hand and picked the weapon up, by the handle this time, which was pleasantly cool against his burning hands. The blade was clean, the engraving on it looking as old as the weapon itself, like it was part of the original design. He recognized the script. He'd only seen scraps of it in his texts, and he'd never been able to translate it, but he knew what language it was.

Ur-Kittât. The old tongue of the Sith, forbidden since the days of the Old Republic, inscribed in the unique runic alphabet that Ochi had also seen engraved on the walls of the Sith Citadel on Exegol.

As he held the dagger, Ochi felt . . . something. Not a presence as such, but something smaller, if just as malevolent. The feeling was, he realized, coming from the dagger itself, like the relic was somehow . . . alive.

Alive, and hungry. For blood. For death.

For killing.

Find the girl. Bring her to Exegol.

The blade will tell.

Ochi laughed. *Now* he understood.

Because the Emperor had done it. He'd used the secrets of Exegol and had overcome death itself. That was all Ochi needed, proof enough that Exegol was the answer to all his prayers.

Palpatine was back, and Ochi of Bestoon had work to do.

ABOUT THE TYPE

This book was set in Minion, a 1990 Adobe Originals typeface by Robert Slimbach (b. 1956). Minion is inspired by classical, old-style typefaces of the late Renaissance, a period of elegant, beautiful, and highly readable type designs. Created primarily for text setting, Minion combines the aesthetic and functional qualities that make text type highly readable with the versatility of digital technology.

A long time ago in a galaxy far, far away. . . .

STAR WARS™

Join up! Subscribe to our newsletter at ReadStarWars.com or find us on social.

 @DelReyStarWars

 @DelReyStarWars

 StarWarsBooks